The Never-Ending Tales of Dara's Bar

The Never-Ending Tales of
Dara's Bar

"Where story-tellers tell"

A portmanteau entertainment

Brian Thomas

In the film world, an anthology film – which is also known as an omnibus film, package film, or portmanteau film – consists of several different short films tied together by a single theme, premise, or brief interlocking event, sometimes each with a different director. See page 247-248.

Stories are strange. Nothing is stranger than stories.
David Rain, *The Heat of the Sun*

There is no greater agony than bearing an untold story inside you.
Maya Angelou, *I Know Why the Caged Bird Sings*

It's like everyone tells a story about themselves inside their own head.
Always. All the time. That story makes you what you are. We build
ourselves out of that story.
Patrick Rothfuss, *The Name of the Wind*

We are, as a species, addicted to story. Even when the body goes to sleep,
the mind stays up all night, telling itself stories.
Jonathan Gottschall, *The Storytelling Animal*

We are all aliens to ourselves, and if we have any sense of who we are,
it is only because we live inside the eyes of others.
Paul Auster, *Winter Journal*

"Strawberry fields... nothing is real..."
Lennon-McCartney, *Strawberry Fields Forever*

Stories within stories within stories within stories.
And life goes on, regardless

Dara's Bar is dedicated to all those who want to write
but "don't have the time" to work on the book
they would like to create.
Don't be as hesitant as Will…

You know how **Thunderbirds** *begins?*
Five...
Four...
Three...
Two...
ONE....

And here we are…

Scenario

Unless you know it is there, *Dara's Bar* is easy to miss.

The place is set to the right of a narrow and shadowy alleyway accessed by a flight of a dozen granite steps, raised high above the sloping side street of a busy rural market town. **And here it is**… Almost looks as if it's deliberately hiding away, as if it doesn't want to draw attention to itself.

Is that too many *it*s? Maybe it is. So here's another. Its entrance is set flat against the northern red brick wall and marked with a projecting red-and-yellow neon globe incongruously advertising *DARRAS BAR*, spelled D.A.R.R.A.S and perhaps the work of an inattentive sign writer. Most people walk straight past this concealed watering hole at the top of the steps without giving it a second look, often passing by without breaking stride.

Some perhaps catch a glimpse of the steep and daunting stairway from the corner of an eye, maybe giving a brief, distracted glance up into the depths of the courtyard, at the empty windows on the first and second floor of the farthest building and its disappearing ground floor alley, its own secrets lost in the gloom. They barely register the slanting sunbeam throwing half the area into bright sunshine, bleaching the ragged stone blocks comprising the southern wall and throwing the north wall into darkness where only the glowing circular bar sign cuts through the gloom.

But still it is there, *Dara's Bar*, hiding itself away from the high street rush and tumble and its urgent pedestrian flow: a specialist place; a place that seems to be waiting for the right person to grip the metal handrail and make that briefly taxing climb, to open that garish purple door and check out the murky space within and its life-changing secrets.

It is a place for story-tellers; a safe place, a place where those story-tellers *tell*.

It's a place where those who have found the creative well dry might want to pause, dip and bathe. Inside it is warm and welcoming and just as you might imagine it…

Arrival

I didn't know how I ended up in Dara's Bar.

I had been walking the streets thinking about starting a new writing project and just came across the roughly-painted purple door as if it was a kind of destination of destiny. There was a red and yellow neon sign hanging overhead, shaped like a dinner plate and buzzing electrically like a busy bees' hive. I reckoned a drink was what was needed to lubricate the creative brain cells that had been locked in unresponsiveness for so long that they felt concreted to the inside of my skull.

So I just walked in without any further debate about whether I actually needed alcohol, whether teatime was the best time to take alcohol, whether I would become woozy and unable to function afterwards, and with no concerns about whom I was likely to meet and where it would all lead. Even as a feckless neophyte, I liked to tell myself I valued meeting people; I even liked finding myself in new, unexpected and potentially inspirational situations, and I especially liked the carved wooden sign over the entrance that read *WHERE STORYTELLERS TELL*, which was just the ticket for me – or should had been, once. So I just placed my writer's hand on the metal plaque casually screwed to the keyhole side of the door and inviting a *PUSH*. I pushed, the chunky door gave easily and I wandered in.

The first thing that struck me was how dark it was inside, as if there had been a power cut or I had abruptly parachuted into an electricity-free seventeenth century tavern, and my eyes took a bit of adjusting to the gloom. But then I realised how bright the setting sun had been outside, shafting down and reflecting from the stone walls of the narrow alley where I had spotted the bar sign poking out from the shadowed right hand corner at the top of a steep stone staircase. There was a soft but heavy clunk as the door closed behind me and I realised the room was much brighter that I had imagined, much of it shining from an array of neon bulbs spotlighting the parade of bottles and optics, all reflected in the glass

13

panels behind the bar area and making them look more numerous.

A line of softly-glowing lamps was sunk into the canopy over the long bar on the left hand wall and in the middle of it, between two separate rows of triple beer pumps poking upwards like a brace of chubby cricket stumps, was mine host. Thinking back, I can scarcely remember how he looked. All I could say now was that he was male, attentive, courteous and welcoming. He had the look of one of those TV personalities whose calm, friendly nature puts you at ease straight away. In fact, he was a dead-ringer for – oh, what's his name? That comedian. Never mind. When you think that I spent most of the next God-knows-how-many hours sitting next to him, a pint either in hand or resting on the decorated fibreboard coaster beside me – the glass being constantly refilled by my convivial companion, its dimples reflecting the sparkling glow of the optics – it was strange that I had so little memory of his face. Yet, I suppose, not so odd, considering what happened later.

Anyway, even before I had the chance to properly take in the setting: the corner bookshelves, the dusky landscape paintings, the small crowd of patrons resting in easy chairs and lost in a smoky haze – yes, they were *smoking*; cigarettes, cigars, even a pipe… Even before adjusting myself to my sudden new surroundings I had opened my mouth and spouted, a little too loudly, "Your sign says DARRAS BAR. Are you Darra?"

The barman nodded. "Dara's my name, it's true," he replied, pronouncing the name correctly with an extended letter A instead of double-Rs.

"There should be an apostrophe before the S on your sign," I said.

"Should there, now?"

"Right. And maybe one R in Dara. Sign writers are terrible these days. Can't spell and never know where or when to put an apostrophe."

I found myself spouting all this nonsense, while my brain screamed: *What are you doing, Will? You've just walked into a place filled with people you don't know and you're rattling on like a stallholder trying to force-sell some cheap bed linen in a shoddy street market. 'Come on ladies, only a fiver...' What will they think? For God's sake, shut up!*

"You don't say," was the neutral response.

"I've even seen words like *cats* with an apostrophe: *cat's*." I made a downward air punctuation flick with an index finger, ignoring my complaining brain. "As in *Come and see our cat's* – cat, apostrophe S. Ridiculous. They shouldn't get paid."

"Right."

14

I knew I was talking too much, a nervous complaint I'd had since I was little, especially in the first flush of unfamiliar company. Finicky too. God, I could be finicky. Always straightening up picture frames if they appeared to hang at an angle, even if they were only a couple of centimetres adrift; always wanting the kitchen coffee mugs to hang on the same hooks just so I didn't have to look in their direction if I was stretching out for a particular handle. Stuff like that. I instinctively reached out and straightened the nearest coaster, placing it in line with the edge of the bar.

The barman, Dara, nodded patiently. "Uh-huh. What would you like to drink?"

I pointed at a pump handle.

"How's the *Authors Ale*?"

"Smooth and nutty – just like some authors," Dara added with a gentle smile.

"Pint," I said, finally managing a concise sentence, even if it was only one syllable, and Dara began pouring.

"The name's Will," I offered. Dara nodded. "Will Buckwater."

"Uh-huh. Nice to meet you."

"Thanks."

"So, what brings you into my humble establishment?"

I looked to see if Dara was being facetious, but his expression was comfortably benign as he finished pouring and passed over the lamp-lit amber sleever. He bore an accent lightly, but I couldn't tell which nationality.

"Saw the sign from the street. Fancied a pint," I responded, taking a sip.

"Ah."

There was a natural gap in the conversation, though mostly because I had stopped blathering and started supping; also I began to take in the room.

It was much bigger than I had at first thought, but was still small enough to seem cosy and spacious at the same time, more *un-cramped* than especially big. It was large enough to accommodate a modest wagon train of arm chairs and sofas, all in comfortably worn brown leather with matching cushions. There was a big fireplace with some glowing embers, as if it was much later in the day, and a couple of big book cases at the back and opposite the bar, each crammed with a selection of hardbacks in various sizes and colours. It looked much like my bolt-hole at home, only larger and without a writing desk, and packed with more furniture and more people. I even spied a piano. So, not much like my home office after all, which was generally disused these days and was, in any case, a box room – full of boxes of stuff I never seemed to get around to emptying.

15

And no fireplace.

The simmering logs in the fire crackled and there was a quiet hum of conversation, way below the level of my noisy introductions, and I began to feel more at ease.

"So, what do you do?"

"Sorry?"

The barman repeated his question as he began distractedly running a paisley tea towel around a soapy glass mug.

I told him. Clerical stuff. And he nodded. There was another pause.

"I also write," I added before I could stop myself.

"Anything I might know?" Dara asked.

"I doubt it," I said, apparently looking pretty dejected, to which Dara responded sympathetically: "You never know."

I shrugged. "When I said I write, I meant I *wrote*."

"Ah, you stopped. Voluntarily?"

"Involuntarily," I said. "Lost the knack. The interest…"

"Really? How was that?"

"A long story – and a boring one."

"We have nothing but stories here. And the time to tell them. Please proceed."

Dara put down the cloth and the glass and leaned on the oak panelled bar. He was partly obscured by the six pump handles, some plain black, others with colourful decorations.

"Not really," I said, not ready to unzip my emotional baggage for a stranger, especially after my audacious entrance a few moments earlier.

"Tell you what," Dara said. "Everyone here is a writer, a storyteller. That's why they come here. This is the place where storytellers tell – that's why it says that on the sign outside. Not a bunch of drunken oafs rambling on about dreary episodes from their lacklustre lives, but real spellbinders; people who can catch your interest in just a few words. At least, that's what they tell me!"

He smiled another warm and encouraging smile that washed over me this time, making me feel less wrapped up in my own self-pity.

"Why not listen to each storyteller tell their tale?" Dara added.

"How's that going to help me?" I sounded a bit jaundiced and ungrateful, but Dara took it in his stride.

"Well, you're here, you have a pint and nothing much else to do but listen. Firstly, imagine it's you up there," he replied, waving his hand vaguely around the space, as if to encompass a busy proscenium packed with expectant punters. "Think about a story that you were going to write but never got around to."

"I couldn't do that."

"What, you couldn't think of a story? Aren't you supposed to be a *writer*!"

"No, I mean I couldn't get up and read it aloud to an audience."

"Come on, it's easy," Dara pressed, his hands moving illustratively.

"Look, remember this about an audience: if they already know you, then they already know that you'll entertain them, otherwise they wouldn't be here to hear you. And if they don't know you – as in this case – well, anticipation should do the trick. A new face, ooh! Perhaps someone has told them you're good; that's why they're there. Perhaps you're an unknown quantity: exciting! People like their minds to be transported elsewhere, so all you have to do is get off your haunches and do what you're good at. They're open pages those punters, if you'll excuse the poor analogy, all waiting to be written on. And even if you have an 'off' night they'll be on-side encouraging you because no-one wants to turn out for the evening to be entertained and go home feeling disappointed. Who likes to go to the chippie and walk along the promenade afterwards with their open bag of goodies going 'Well, these chips aren't very good'?"

"If you're bad, you're bad. You can't suddenly change the chips."

Dara smiled. "We change the chips we're given all the time – that's if we have the will to do it, Will. Anyway, forget all that, relax on your stool, sup your ale and listen."

So I supped my ale and listened.

After all, life has its consequences, doesn't it?

The first storyteller of (it turned out) an enthusiastic queue, eased himself from a dark brown arm chair with a gentle parp of pants cloth on leather. Lightly wielding a green ring binder and nodding to acknowledge the small crowd of what must have been familiar regulars, he stepped into the beam of a mini spotlight suspended several feet above his head that was soft enough not to unbalance the calming murkiness of the room but bright enough to illuminate the pages directly below.

The first thing I noticed about him was how much he resembled my father, an engineer in the RAF and therefore a man unburdened with the customary service moustache of the fly-boys. The reader had the same

17

ruddy complexion, a similar stumpy nose, seemed about the same age as dad when he was in the service, and similarly held his head to one side as he looked around the assembly, though tilted to the left rather than the right side that my dad had favoured, as if he had a slight crick in the neck.

My father had been relocated all over the country to air force bases after the war, mainly in southern and west country villages or in base accommodation, dragging his long-suffering wife, my mum, along with him before retiring through an unspectacular injury. A trumpeter in a services jazz band he had continued his musical career with several local groups after settling in his Somerset home until he lost his "lip" and couldn't toot with appropriate conviction any more, or without drenching his shirt front in spit. I was born not long after my dad was demobbed and my younger sister came along a bit later, and rather unexpectedly after a drunken weekend my parents spent in a popular seaside resort.

It felt a little like a curtain had been wound back to accommodate an orator, the stage was set and the featured artist was on the blocks. Oops, mixed metaphor. Never mind, press on. Reader one opened his lime binder, cleared his throat and began. He announced the curious title with a slight flourish as if introducing himself to a minor royal and Dara said "please commence your tale."

There followed an unexpected opening gambit.

The Long, Long Night of the Bunny Ruse

1 Bunny Run

If there was one thing Dan Shutter hated most it was chasing the damn rabbits.

Still, he had to remind himself, it was only for the rewards.

Even so, it was hell on his rapidly aging bones.

For a start, at 55 he was not as fit as he used to be and not up to all the darting along side streets, across slippery flagstones, grassy parkland and down dingy alleys, mostly in the dark; and his quarry were always quicker than he was. He was too young and too much in debt to retire and too old to scamper.

Secondly, he had been a professional photographer for 30 of those 50-plus years and kept asking himself how it had come down to this. How? It was a job, of course. And if he ever caught one of these pesky rabbits and it turned out to be the right one, well, there was a fortune to be made if it played ball – cooperated, that is – and there were all those assurances that it would play the pecuniary equivalent of a full round of squash if apprehended. He'd just have to make sure it did what it was told, if that ever happened.

Still, there were times in the rain when the joke, now puerile at best, wore very thin indeed and he'd come close to packing it in.

He'd started his working life as an apprentice cabinet maker, specialising in bookcases, and he was very good at it. It wasn't well paid, but money wasn't everything and clomping about at night, often drenched in a downpour, far from his bed and with only a one in twelve chance of hitting the cony jackpot was enough to make Shutter walk away with no regrets. Almost. That one in twelve chance might just come his way, and then he would be the one laughing! Whatever, he was still sick of chasing the damn rabbits. Or, to be more precise, he was sick of chasing the damn humans in their damn rabbit costumes. Especially at night.

Fortunately, or perhaps unfortunately considering his delicate personal circumstances, this was his last chance.

He wheezed as he skipped across a deserted lamp-lit highway, in and out of the cars parked silently on each side, keeping his head low and his disappearing prey in sight, making sure he didn't make undue noise or turn an ankle in one of the shadowed roadside drain covers.

Mind you, this time it was different. This time it wasn't even official. This time is was just a hunch, following an instinct rather than a formal assignment, using his nose for the first time in a long while, this time wheeling a pushbike with a squeaky wheel. He would rather have left the bicycle behind, but the venue where the assignment was focussed was just down the road from his home, so he'd taken the bike for a spin instead of the car; traffic was light at that time of night and pedalling to the assignment would give him a bit of extra exercise which, God knows, he could do with.

The other thing that was different, of course, was that on this occasion there were two of them to follow, not one: two six foot tall grey rabbits with fluffy puffball tails and long, erect Bugs Bunny ears providing the extra height. Just like the rest of them, only this time in tandem. That had never happened before and Shutter was determined to find out why. They had emerged from concert venue Chesterton Hall a little furtively, from a side door none of the other paparazzi had spotted earlier. The only reason Shutter had seen the exit was because his bike had been chained up in the small customer car park at the rear of the building and when he rushed back to fetch it, bunnies bursting from the foyer and a handful of snappers off in pursuit, he found a flat tyre to patch and inflate. It took him ages, the job made more difficult because he was furious at being left behind.

A long while later, long enough for him to be out of the running tonight, he was clipping the pump back into its prongs when the strange twins appeared. He ducked down behind a Daimler when the little-used theatre door opened. Instinct. He had not expected to see the bunny twosome and, as they began sneaking down the concealed alley that snaked away from the back of the venue, peering around furtively in their comic cowls like real conies crossing a country road at dawn, he made up his mind to follow. He was back in the game.

But back up. The reason he was here in the first place, clumping about in the early hours when he should have been in bed, was down to Bunny Delf the singer – the new, top-of-the-charts, bona fide, flavour of the moment, one hundred per cent solid gold *ENTERTAINER*. The young man who had smashed his way to the number-one-selling retail and download artist slot on the back of one hit single and a clutch of well-chosen television appearances; the lad whose name was on everyone's lips, the lad whose creative antics were being featured in every newspaper and magazine, the lad whose publicity photographs had sold around the world, the lad whose carefully constructed publicity blogs had been published and republished and rewritten time and time again, the lad about which editors were screaming for more material.

And also the lad who had unilaterally decided he would give no further interviews. The lad who had unilaterally decided not to allow the media to photograph him again, creating a new mystique.

So pictures and stories about Bunny Delf were at a premium, worth a fortune to the lucky hack or snapper, and that was why the singer was followed wherever he went: gig venues like the Chesterton Hall, hotels, night clubs, airports, train stations, anywhere. All the time his loyal entourage kept Bunny's face out of the public glare. Media contact at live concerts was limited to an official PR team comprising one Press aide and one photographer, but as Delf performed wearing a mask, similar to the Phantom of the Opera but more flattering, any shots were largely identical. But they were still of great commercial value, being the only ones available. It irked his record company only briefly; for as long as sales kept rising and the increasing mystery surrounding their client deepened his current facial obscurity was just a minor inconvenience.

Why had he done it? the public asked. *Had his appearance changed? Had he been disfigured? Was it an accident? Sudden natural or medical deformity? Plastic surgery? What did he look like now? What was the scam? Was it even really him?*

Shutter's bicycle clattered and squeaked noisily as he emerged from the back alleyway and joined a pebble-dashed courtyard on the other side of the street. The bunny duo slipped around a distant corner and he hoped his pursuit hadn't been rumbled. There was a certain air of inscrutability, of secrecy, about this particular chase that he was yet to fathom and he didn't want faulty transport to blow the gaff.

He recalled that when pressure to see Delf unmasked hit fever pitch and punters began sneaking mobile phones and miniature digital cameras into clubs and parties in the hope of netting a candid and highly lucrative snap of their idol cavorting without his disguise, the singer decided to act. He hand-picked twelve loyal aides and commissioned a select costumier to run

21

up thirteen rabbit suits as a means of frustrating both the following Press corps and hordes of the more unruly and demanding fans.

The trick was this: before a concert, club, party or hotel appearance, "Bunny's Dozen" (i.e. Bunny and his twelve aides, the raucous pop-joke equivalent of a baker's dozen) would arrive en masse; afterwards they would disperse in all directions, no-one knowing which was the Bunny head man himself, so they were forced to split up to follow them all on the off-chance of nabbing the right one. In order to make this game more palatable to a voracious Press, the record company issued an undertaking that the first media person to successfully track the right rabbit, i.e. Delf himself, would be guaranteed a brand new on-the-spot interview and unmasked photo shoot.

To prevent representatives attacking individual rabbits and pulling off their disguises, editors were warned that any such behaviour would result in all advertising from the company and its associates being permanently withdrawn and their publishing/media chain being forever barred from any future official reportage of the Great Delf Legend, a ban that extended to many of their even more popular acts, of which they had an extensive roster.

This otherwise fragile position was backed up by the fact that Delf, as the secretive son of a revered ex-journo, gave a chunk of his huge fortune to the widows and orphans' fund of reporters and paps killed or injured in the line of duty, so even non-Union snappers tended to respect him, and the Mavericks who tried to scupper the deal, no matter how frustrating it was, were scrupulously discouraged by their self-policing colleagues. Besides, at the end of the day it was all a bit of fun, a sparring match, a contest between media rivals, and the publicity camp gave a reluctant but collective nod and decided to concur.

Shutter thought the whole enterprise was stupid, fraught with difficulties and unknown dangers and bound to fail. Still, he had one trump card to play in the game: he thought he already knew Delf's true identity, something carefully obscured by his puppet masters.

A few years back Shutter had depped on a photo assignment for another pap to shoot a local gospel choir that was gaining a big following thanks to its handsome young vocalist, one Jonny Salvation.

Yea, right!

Jonny took stage in front of a four-piece band and a small choir of pretty girls each Sunday in a large local church just south of the city centre and Shutter was immediately struck by the purity of his teenage voice and the comfortable way he performed. Not long after he took the shots and got the names Shutter heard that Jonny had been signed by Smoke Records, a notorious pop-only label, and had disappeared from sight – and certainly from the church that had engendered his career.

At the time Shutter had planned to turn pukka journalist, only briefly, to write a story about Jonny's potential rise to fame, his historical society pieces for the weekly rag giving him confidence to try something meatier. But the idea had been scotched by the artist's new manager, anxious that his protégé protect his career by having no links with religious music, "poisonous" (as he put it) to a successful chart career. ("*Well, look at Cliff!*" Shutter did and thought Mr Richard had a much better record of chart success than Jonny would ever be able to generate, which ultimately proved to be the case). After this, Jonny Salvation vanished from public view, so he might well be masquerading now as Bunny Delf. Same label.

If this was the case, then Shutter would recognise him right away as Johnny – now under another new manager and only, what, about eight years older – was, short of having major facial disfigurement, an exceptionally striking lad with a small beauty spot on his right cheek and a Kirk Douglas dimple in his chin.

God, Shutter needed this job to work out. It was offering a substantial cash "reward" plus the additional lucrative national and international syndication fees for use of his pix and words. He was desperate. His credit cards were maxed out, he couldn't pay his rent, his wife had had enough, especially when he lost their house, and was on the verge of leaving him; his beloved son had moved out of the area and hadn't talked to his father in years. The gambling hadn't helped; he just loved the horses. It was the task in hand or oblivion.

2 Bunny Warrens

As he rounded the corner he came to a cobbled square and saw bunny and bunny disappear down a distant side street with a furtive series of glances left and right. Shutter was hot in pursuit, literally, perspiring heavily despite the cool night air and the onset of drizzle. But his bunnies must have been roasting in their all-body suits including face muzzles with their diamond shaped textile noses and long nylon whiskers. Mind you, he supposed they had youth and excitement on their side and a lot fewer belly pounds to cart about. The narrow thoroughfare, only wide enough for two wheels, was just past a local pub that stretched along the pavement to Shutter's left, its windows dark now but with a dipped spot lamp still illuminating the sign board for *The Crow*.

The Crow, Shutter recalled, was originally called *The Crown*. But after a stray Guy Fawkes rocket had obliterated the N one chilly November night, the newly-appointed landlord took the change as some sort of heavenly counsel and, once it had been agreed with the brewery, he had the regal ring on the swinging sign repainted with the profile of a great black Corvus, its huge beak seemingly pecking at the Victorian brickwork, its piercing left eye gazing down on the street below with inappropriate menace.

It was at this point, while he was still several yards away from the pub, leaning on his bike taking a welcome breather, watching the bunny duo disappear from sight once more and mulling over the decorative new symbol and the cluster of empty picnic tables below it, that Shutter saw two men roll out of a side door, a discreet exit for after-hours drinkers. One immediately lunged forwards to grab at the stem of an extinguished antique street lamp for balance, managed to catch it and instantly slid down the smooth, painted shaft into a stooped ape-like pose, squatting on one hand and two knees, holding on for dear life with his free hand as his mental balance veered between swaying and spinning; the other lurched next to his mate, still upright but on jelly legs, and grabbed the pole. It was the upright inebriate who spotted the loitering photographer in the light from the pub doorway just before it clunked shut and he instantly reacted.

"Hey, granddad, is that a camera?" he slobbered loudly, showering his partner-in-ale at his feet with spit.

Too close to avoid the two drunks, Shutter veered to one side and nearly slipped on the glassy mizzle-moistened tarmac. He had no time for this. Bunnies were a-running.

He remembered that a colleague from the Press pit at a significant metal concert back in the eighties had been set upon by a gang of fans on his way out of the auditorium who wanted to steal his camera to get his pictures of their favourite performers in the act. When he resisted they took him around to an alley and beat him into a coma before stealing the wrong camera, the second of two he was carrying – the one that only contained pictures of his grandmother's cats. The man had never worked again and Shutter was going to make damn sure nothing like that ever happened to him. Which is why he carried a taser stun gun in his backpack.

"Hey, wadda-bout a pikki?" the second drunk called while his colleague finally slid completely to the ground to adopt a foetal position. "Jussa two o-vus…"

24

With that, the shaven-headed youth equipped with a gold ring in one ear and a vacant expression, lurched forward with surprising if unsteady swiftness and flung his arms around his prey. Shutter was crushed, but fortunately only by the frail squeeze of a man not entirely at one with his wavering mobility. He dropped his bike, shook himself free and the youth toppled back a few inches and glared into Shutter's face.

"We just wanna liddle pikki," he slurred, frowning. "Come on, jussa liddle pikki…"

There hadn't been time for Shutter to unpack the stun gum. He was keen not to be pummelled by a brace of alcoholics, albeit mostly legless, but reckoned the one on the ground was out for the count and the one actually on his feet was too unsteady, like a rag doll, to be any real threat. It was time for subterfuge.

"OK, mate," he said. "Back up to the street lamp, get your mate on his feet, and strike a pose.

The bald-headed drunk gave a toothy smile and quite literally tottered backwards to collect his embryonic friend. He tripped on the edge of the pavement but amazingly remained upright; then he dragged his slumped chum, complaining loudly, to his feet. Seconds later the pair of them were leaning on either side of the lamp post and grinning like wall-eyed monkfish.

Shutter reached for his flash gun case, hanging loosely to one side on a cord around his neck along with his old but trusted Nikon 501, solid enough to be a weapon on its own, and whipped the stubby device from its leather case. He always kept his Canon Speedlite 600EX II-RT well charged – it was his most modern and expensive bit of gear, after all; his last major expense – and he had used it to extricate himself from several dodgy moments in the past.

"Right, lads – smile!" he shouted, closed his eyes and let off a flash.

It was blinding, as if a lightning bolt had suddenly struck the ground, especially in the feeble, flickering defused orange light of the overhead crow lamp. Drunk one, previously secured to the pavement, let out a terrified squeal and returned there with a thud, tucking himself into an even tighter and wetter ball, whilst drunk two shrieked as if electrocuted and crashed to the paving slabs to join his bogus unborn vertebrate.

"Goodnight, lads!" Shutter replied, picking up his bike and dodging any potential flailing arms likely to grab his ankles and detain him further.

The pavement drunk screamed: "I'm fucking blind!" whilst his slightly more capable compatriot made an optimistic appeal in Shutter's wake as he hurried away: "Thanks, mate. Send us a copy…"

This mission is cursed, Shutter muttered to himself. *Just like my bloody life…*

He aimed quickly for the alley where he had last seen the bunnies. It ran between two rows of four-storey Edwardian houses and Shutter hurried down the narrow conduit, his knees beginning to ache and his bicycle rattling along beside him like an irritated toddler. Though he knew his home patch very well, he rarely visited this part of the city and had forgotten that a swift right hand dog leg led him straight into the tiny and little-used Reisenden Square, frankly more of an alcove than a grandiose plaza. It was at this point that the determined lens man nearly signed out for good as the sharp turn made him lose his footing on the shining, drizzly paving surrounding the Reisenden monument and he toppled to the right, cracking his forehead on the corner of a marble slab as he hit the ground.

It was a miracle that he remained conscious, but as he lifted his head with an accompanying groan of pain a gash opened up over one eye and blood began pouring down his right cheek. He swore bitterly and pulled a large cleaning cloth from a side pocket that he used to wipe down his gear and dabbed the wound. Then he tied the duster around his head, making him look like a fugitive from the French Revolution and in the back of his mind he could hear the little memorialised squirt, who had taken many a pratfall in his life, laughing hysterically from the afterlife.

He had forgotten all about Reisenden, a globetrotting Franco-English clown from the 1930s, much like the acclaimed Italian-Brit Charlie Cairoli but less acclaimed. He also didn't know why he'd overlooked this hazard. After all, he'd photographed a distant relative of Reisenden next to the monument on some anniversary or other a few years back for a feature he'd written for the local weekly newspaper under his historical society hat and he'd thought then how dangerous the thing was, with its greasy flagstones and granite surrounds – especially for anyone coming upon it unexpectedly around the corner, in the wet and dark and at speed.

As he sat there on the ground, damp seeping into the seat of his pants, dizzy and dabbing at his freshly-wrapped wound, he remembered that Reisenden – German for traveller – was born Richard Brodeur, son of high wire artiste Ecclete Brodeur, errant daughter of a family of noted Paris embalmers and wife to Auguste clown Rene Brodeur (*Le Grand Farceur*, the Big Joker, master of slapstick), part of the popular troupe *Les Booboos* in a travelling circus. They performed all over the world, from the Cirque Mendrano in Montmarte to the Blackpool Tower Circus, and Ricky Brodeur had been born in Shutter's home town whilst his parents were on a brief English sabbatical.

Ricky naturally followed in parental footsteps and began performing early, adopting the alias Little Dickie due to his diminutive stature. He took to the sawdust at Circus Krone in Munich, ironically at the same performance attended by Adolf Hitler and featuring the famous Cairoli who Hitler presented with a watch, which Cairoli later threw away. The adolescent Ricky (Dickie) also won praise from Hitler that day, dubbing the lad a *süßester kleiner Landstreicher* (sweetest little tramp) – but only once the Fuhrer had established that Dickie was a real boy, as initially he had thought the lad was a dwarf and was about to have him arrested when the pfennig dropped. Instead, he presented the tiny vagabond with a small floral chamber pot fired in the kilns of Burgkirchen which the ten year old later lost in a bitter cribbage dispute with the circus juggler.

The ambitious 'Reisenden' dogged the senior footsteps of the much more popular Cairoli (pseudonym 'Carletto') for years, playing in many of the same cities in various guises, and was also a master of the oboe, clarinet and music hall song, his vocals delivered in a bracing counter tenor shriek even long after his voice had broken. But Brodeur had exhausted himself by the time he hit his sixties and died after walking off the end of the North Pier at Blackpool after an especially exhausting performance, fatally crashing through an angler's row boat moored below. He had already been awarded the freedom of his home town as one of only three notable sons of the borough, and the city council subsequently funded the monument in his memory: the very monument that had just cruelly punctured Shutter's forehead.

The photographer was livid. Not only had he been delayed by two drunks but now he was both cut and bleeding and reliving an old newspaper article he detested in the first place. To add insult to injury, he was in danger of losing his lucrative quarry too. He leapt dizzily to his feet, his forehead pulsating like a battered drum skin, grabbed his bike and launched himself into the roadway that ran past the north end of the square and snaked around the block to the rear of *The Crow*. It was at this moment, as he stepped off the kerb, that his run of bad fortune lost him his tatty third hand Pashley-Morgan.

He didn't actually lose it. He could see where it was: crushed under the wheels of a large white van that had swerved unexpectedly around the corner to his left, snagged the handlebars, and nearly floored Shutter as well, mashing his bicycle into a twisted flat-pack version of itself. The driver shouted tersely at Shutter, the words lost in the echo of a fractured exhaust reverberating off a parade of Edwardian frontages, but while the vehicle slowed it did not stop. With an angry howl, Shutter picked up the remains of his only transport, its frame bent, its wheel crushed, and tossed it behind a grit bin, where it would quietly begin rusting until removed by some refuse collectors four weeks later.

He'd lost them. He'd lost the bloody money-maker bunnies!

Only he hadn't. Not yet.

There was still a chance.

A light flicked on in one of the third floor bedrooms and a head poked out of a half-open window.

"Hey, you down there! What's all the racket about?"

"Nothing, mate. Don't concern yourself," Shutter called back, sourly.

"Don't you know what time it is? I've got to get up in the morning!"

"Then you'd better get back to bed!" Shutter barked, adding "Tosser!" before swiftly lurching across the road and out of sight.

"Drunkard!" came the diminishing response and the window banged shut, triggering several other bedside lamps to blossom.

Shutter growled to himself like an old, defeated dog. Drunks, clowns, manic van drivers... How many more obstacles? When the circumstances of life keep throwing you sideways with cruel distractions it means that you're not destined to reach your goal. What was the point? He slowed to ambling pace.

Then he rallied. Still, without the flat tyre at the outset... It wasn't all grim. At least he was in the chase. The *only* one.

And, apart from the stroppy residents, there was one thing about this part of town that was working in his favour. His suspicions about two bunnies in tandem, appearing long after the competition entrants had scuttled away from the venue, suggested that this was something else: a tryst between the two of them; maybe a secret tryst between Bunny himself and, what – a groupie? He perked up. Now *that* would make a picture worth a few bob! And if that was true and the nervous lovers were heading anywhere, they had to be heading towards a hotel. And the only hotel nearby was the Marsden, the one part of these unfamiliar streets that rang a bell.

Shutter had a friend at the Marsden Hotel. A friend who had promised to look out for any members of the Delf retinue booking rooms or, indeed, any impromptu guests dressed in rabbit costumes. Shutter had optimistically organised this a couple of weeks earlier when he heard the young singer was performing in town because the Marsden Hotel was within an acceptable trotting distance of the concert hall. This was his final chance to catch up with the little squirt and earn some non-taxable, cash-in-hand dough – if his friend was on duty and alert, that is.

As if on cue, his mobile rang. He rummaged in a pocket and pulled it out. The screen lit up. There was a one-word text message: COTTONTAIL. The code word he had agreed with his Marsden contact.

28

The bunny has landed!

Shutter's heart leapt – and immediately sank again within a breath.

Something was very wrong here. His Marsden contact had already told him earlier that day that none of the Delf team had booked into the place – so who were this errant duo? Did they have nothing to do with the contest at all? Were they merely two unconnected people who just happened to be wearing custom-made rabbit costumes and leaving the very venue where Delf was performing? No, that was equally ridiculous. Fans? No, the fans knew nothing about the challenge – as far as he knew, anyway. Whatever, something wasn't kosher.

Of course, the next thing was to check the identity of the bunnies, and if he ended up gate-crashing a pair of innocent party goers who were coincidentally togged out in Delf bunny garb, well, he could explain himself by saying he'd been caught in a hoax. So he finally eased his pace, let himself calm down, relax, begin strolling. No-one else was on the case and the potentially amorous duo were unlikely to be going anywhere other than their hotel room for quite some time. His crossed his fingers that things would work out, and that he would make some money and restore his life. Then he reached up to dab at his head wound, still stinging, through the yellow cloth; he winced, shrugged and strode off into a rapidly descending and dreary mist imbued with new impetus.

There was still a chance, albeit slim.

Before the railways came to town, the Marsden Hotel had been an important staging inn for stage and mail coaches, providing a resting point for both passengers and horses. As well as supplying food, drink and a bed, the inn was equipped with a large and well-appointed stable block – long since demolished and replaced with extra rooms – along with a team of hostlers to accommodate, refresh and replace tired teams. Its disputed and probably erroneous claim to fame was that it had been one of the first such stations to report raids on the South West coast by squadrons of the French navy during the Nine Years War in 1690.

It was originally *The Bull and Rosette*, when the city had its own cattle market, but was later renamed after English surgeon William Marsden (1796-1867) whose sage advice had helped local businessmen set up a free hospital in the borough, Marsden having had some success with a noted dispensary in Holborn, London, that later became the Royal Free Hospital. The determined Yorkshireman had argued that poverty and sickness were "only passports" and the city's overseers agreed. Though he was close to an important local Alderman, hence his passing involvement in the scheme, Marsden never visited the city he had influenced nor stayed at its hotel, eventually passing away at a similar establishment in Surrey.

The main entrance to the Marsden comprised a sturdy portico supported by two concrete pillars, its flat roof decorated at each corner with a large floral display in a circular tub. There were bay windows projecting on either side of the columns revealing the interior of the public bar on the left and the restaurant on the right, both illuminated now by low, defused lighting as each had been closed for at least an hour. Shutter pushed open the glass-panelled entrance doors which automatically clumped shut behind him and spotted his contact hovering nervously behind the reception desk to the left of a wide ascending staircase enveloped in a plum carpet.

The stocky receptionist looked like a Dickensian villain with his shaved head and earrings – how Shutter imagined escaped convict Abel Magwitch from *Great Expectations* might have appeared. In reality, he was really a kind and gentle soul and took his duties very seriously.

"I won't get in trouble for this, will I?" he asked.

Shutter brushed his concerns aside with a small wave.

"Absolutely not," he said. "I know people. It'll all work out fine."

"Why do you have a cleaning cloth round your head?"

Shutter cautiously touched the yellow duster, applied after his unscheduled brush with the Reisenden memorial. He gingerly slipped it off and, though it was blood-stained, he found the wound underneath had stopped bleeding and a crust sprinkled with golden threads was forming over the gash. He scowled as the far end of the sticky scab peeled away painfully, stuck to the cloth, though fortunately the cut remained dry.

"Looks painful," his contact said, catching his friend's wince.

"Nothing," Shutter replied, adding "bloody clown" to a raised eyebrow of perplexity.

He looked around and realised how hungry he was. "Restaurant's closed, then?"

His contact, Bill Kowalczyk (from *kowal*, Polish for "blacksmith," which he wasn't), nodded.

"New chef likes to get home to his new wife. He's Italian," he said.

"Bloody hell, Luigi's not back again?!" Shutter replied, astonished. "Not after that… *incident?*"

Luigi (not his real name) was a chef at the hotel in the nineteen-eighties, noted for both his fine cuisine and his unpredictable belligerence. Not long after his arrival he set up a lucrative deal with a local smallholding to provide all the vegetables for his kitchens. But the only way for his supplier to unload was to use a narrow back street with yellow lines on either side – hence a local traffic warden kept ticketing the delivery van. This had such a demoralising effect that the owner of the farmstead told the chef that he might not be able to continue serving the hotel because of the pending fines and he might need to find another source for his greens. Luigi was furious at the prospect of losing such a convenient, reliable and inexpensive supplier.

The following week, the chef caught the warden in the act, and thereby the irresistible force of a pumped-up *capocuoco* met the immovable object of a dogmatic civil enforcement officer. The chef challenged the warden, mid-ticket, and the warden replied "Mind your own business, Luigi" (where the incorrect name originated). This naturally ignited the misnamed chef's fuse, to which the confidently racist warden, one Ken Grawler (his real name), barked "Listen, Luigi, we whipped your lot in the war when you all ran away like a bunch of panicky rabbits, so why don't *you* run along now," adding "And if you don't like it here, why don't you go back to your own country?"

At this point, according to a report of the court hearing featured in the local evening paper, Luigi (actually Giuseppe) stalked back into the hotel to re-emerge with a meat cleaver. He screamed at Grawler, ripped the ticket from his supplier's windscreen and hurled himself towards the startled warden. Grawler saw the look in the chef's eyes a fraction before his armed leap and knew he'd met his match. This was one enemy combatant who wouldn't be retreating to his own lines and the warden did the only expedient thing: he legged it.

He was chased by his cleaver-wielding assailant for much of the High Street – startled shoppers parting like reeds before the prow of the *African Queen* – before making a wise but reckless dive over the parapet of a small stone bridge that spanned a local river. Grawler narrowly missed a wild swipe of the cleaver an inch or so from his haunches as he made his panicked plunge, fortunately hitting the water fairly painlessly on a receding high tide and swimming away urgently with the current to the echo of a string of Neopolitan profanities. Giuseppe was bound over to keep the peace by local magistrates and fined £150 for brandishing an offensive weapon with intent to endanger. But Grawler was also chastised for instigating the overreaction by both baiting the chef and ignoring the fact that his smallholder was entitled to some grace to lawfully unload his produce.

"No, it's not him, thank God!" Kowalczyk replied, disrupting the memory. "The new chap is lovely, with a much nicer disposition. Anyway, you want to know where they are?"

Back to the bloody bunnies.

"Room 42, third floor."

Kowalczyk produced the key he had been squeezing in a damp palm below the counter. "Can't let you have this. I'll have to let you in. And, please, no trouble."

3 Bunny Punch

Kowalczyk released the door lock with surprising tenderness, the key hardly making a click and, as he stood back to give Shutter access to the room, the door similarly opened without a sound. It was unlikely that the occupants would have heard an unlatching anyway as there were raised voices coming from the interior. Kowalczyk and Shutter exchanged anxious glances, and then the latter eased the door wide and stepped inside, his camera in one hand at the ready, flash unit attached.

There was a short corridor with doors to bathroom and toilet units on the left side. At the end, about eight feet ahead, Shutter could see the foot of a big double bed and the figure of a bunny poised there, straddling a pair of equally bunny-wise legs. The upright bunny was naked to the waist, exposing firm young breasts, a glistening almond skin and a dark afro. Oh, and a pink tail. That's what the photographer had earlier registered in the back of his mind that was incongruous, the out-of-place *pink* tail, but the significance of his fleeting glance in the low outdoors light had not sunk in at the time. A female bunny! This didn't follow the established script at all and suggested some premeditated alternative.

As he moved closer and more of the bed came into view, Shutter noticed that the horizontal occupant, also half-naked in his bunny costume, seemed to be restrained and struggling, his arms disappearing out of view; he also became aware that a heated argument was taking place, mainly one-sided, with the girl shouting abusively at what seemed to be her captor.

Then Shutter spotted the knife.

The girl, stunningly beautiful and the most arousing creature he had ever seen, was brandishing a large carving knife over her head, swinging it down and up again in short but treacherously threatening gestures. *Oh, my God*, he thought. *This is about to become a crime scene.* He asked himself: should he rush forward and stop whatever was transpiring, or should he take the risk and take the photograph he was here to capture? It might not be Delf, but it was still a story. Even so, could he ignore the danger of the situation?

That issue was resolved for him as he gingerly stepped forward to get a

32

better view when he landed abruptly and heavily on a loose floorboard that immediately gave a loud and anguished creak. The girl swung round, a final fatal down-swing suspended in mid-thrust, and she stared at him, panic in the glare of her heavily-mascaraed eyes. Instinctively Shutter unplugged the Speedlite whose burst had felled the drunks at *The Crow*, unhitched his Nikon and hurled the heavy camera at the pretty assailant. Before she could properly react, the object hit her in the side of the head; she gave a cry, dropped the knife into the duvet folds and tumbled off the far side of the bed to the floor with a leaden thud.

Shutter rushed into the bedroom, checked that the girl was safely unconscious and swung round to look at the other occupant of the mattress.

Painfully secured with nylon zip ties on each wrist to the struts of the brass headboard was the now mask-free singer Jonny Salvation: Bunny Delf. He looked both terrified and embarrassed and his eyes were watering unhappy tears. But his features were perfect: the same beauty spot on his right cheek and the famous actor's dimple in his chin. Not a scar or any other blemish in sight; a skin so white and smooth it could have belonged to a face cream model. So the disguise had been a commercial affectation after all. Smart kid. Lots of big headlines, big queries; lots of keeping his presence, if not his actual countenance, in the public eye – though nothing Prince hadn't done before, and with greater aplomb.

Without a second thought, Shutter reclaimed his camera, checked it was undamaged, re-affixed his flash unit and took a string of pictures. Delf was too astonished – and relieved – to object. Then Shutter calmly placed his gear on a corner dressing table, removed the wrist straps, transferred them to the comatose girl on the floor, and stood back with his hands on his hips.

"Thank God," Delf gasped.

The singer shuffled down to sit on the end of the bed and began rubbing his wrists where the ties had bruised the flesh, his almost fatal bunny disguise now languishing across the duvet behind him. The muscle relaxant he had been subjected to earlier was beginning to leave his system, though he was still unsteady, a little dizzy, his eyes drowsy and vision momentarily blurred.

"Thank *Dan Shutter*," his liberator corrected him. "And now, Mr Delf, you really do owe me that interview and photo session!"

Once free of his rabbit disguise, showered and dressed, filled with coffee and resting his eyes behind Ray-bans, Bunny Delf flopped on to the edge of the bed and sang like a Berkeley Square nightingale while Shutter recorded every word on a pocket tape recorder.

He said the girl, still groggy, slightly dented and secured in the bathroom, had approached him after the gig and skilfully seduced him back to the Marsden, where she had booked a room under her own name that afternoon. She'd convinced Delf to abandon the silly chase-the-bunny scenario, though to retain its spirit with their flight to a hotel. And to keep her and the singer's identities a secret from any passing pleb or journo, she had obtained a similar costume (stuffed into an unassociated Prangsta bag) so that they could sneak away for a night of frantic passion – except, in her case, a night of casual homicide assisted by a large shot of crushed cyclobenzaprine tablets in her quarry's wine.

This beautiful but treacherous young woman – one Avril Bruecher – was a former member of the gospel choir that used to back Delf in his former incarnation, Jonny Salvation. Over the months she formed a deep crush on him and begged him to take her with him to Smoke Records to join his new troupe of backing singers. He agreed, but within weeks had dumped her as his girlfriend for another pretty warbler and when Avril screamed at him for his deception, along with what she saw as a criminal shortfall in payments for her vocal services, the previously-adorable Jonny had her fired from the label.

Not only had his first single hit the charts but the record company failed to promote Avril's work and wouldn't let her out of her backing vocals contract to go solo. The whole sorry episode destroyed her career – she was now a waitress in the Marsden Hotel restaurant – which led to her decision to destroy Jonny's future as well.

She got wind of the bunny ruse through a friend in the industry, had a costume made and blagged her way backstage at Delf's Chesterton Hall gig, gaining access mainly through her striking looks and an empty promise of sexual favours to the principal security guard, where she planned to skilfully entrap her former lover Jonny and hopefully end his undeserving rise to fame as the reborn Bunny.

In the intervening months between her singing job and the Chesterton ploy, Avril had radically changed her appearance, had work performed on her nose and her hair, spent many hours in the tanning salon and lost a stone or two with some serious static biking. Delf, as usual full of himself, did not recognise her, as she'd planned.

Her subterfuge had worked flawlessly – at least until a hungry shutterbug burst into their hotel room unannounced and delivered the knockout blow.

With the girl out of the way, Shutter secured his interview and mug shots from the still agitated Delf, though the unrepentant Avril Breucher continued to protest at the top of her ample songster's lungs in the background, her voice echoing studio-like from the bathroom tiles.

4 Bunny Tail

The story, along with snaps of both the star and the unjustly-treated songbird, brought the lens man seemingly endless column inches, especially the part of the story about the less-than-doe-eyed vengeful bunny. It also engendered a revival of Shutter's status within the industry, a grand thank you from both Delf and his indebted management team, a new fashion wardrobe, and a healthy wodge of cash that annulled his financial difficulties and saw the return of both his wife and, grudgingly, his irascible son. He even bought a house again – but this time, outright.

Within a year he had retired on his earnings, stopped gambling, lost three encumbering stone in weight and moved to a quiet rural location a long way from the smoke where he revisited his love of cabinet making. He intended to keep his head down, way down, way down deep in his boots, seeped in comforting obscurity. No more did he want to be languishing in second rate hotels in order to chase blokes in rabbit costumes around city streets late at night in all weathers – a practise that had wisely ceased since the knife-wielding fiasco, at least with Delf and his record company. One might have thought that Shutter wanted to be as far away as possible when the prospective bunny perforator, the livid Avril Bruecher, finally got out of jail. But all is not entirely what it seems in the pop music industry.

For Avril was not jailed, or even arrested. She was therefore not charged with any offence and escaped with a clean slate. Delf's manager and the head of Smoke Records took control. They intended to turn the whole incident to their advantage – and they did so with astounding success. On the night in question Delf had telephoned his manager for help. He babbled on about the horrors of the evening accompanied by the self-explanatory background noise of Avril banging on the bathroom door with her head as her wrists were still restrained by the second-hand ties. The manager, one Jake Solitaire – a burly fellow with a sharp Northern tongue, a loud suit, distinctive gold signet ring and a huge, pungent cigar – raced to the hotel and immediately went into a parley with his singer and the photographer. Shutter could have the story, the snaps, everything, he said. But on one condition: that history should be re-written with the label taking command of the situation and milking it for its outstanding publicity value.

Avril was brought back into the bedroom, further concussed from the head banging, and told that her intentions had changed; that she had only wanted to frighten her beloved Bunny because of the "shameful" way she had been treated, which had not been his fault. It was that version of events, or she would go to jail. She nodded miserably, knowing there was no escape from a plot of her own doing; then the cuffs were removed and

35

she slumped on to the end of the bed, Delf leaping aside nervously; she bowed her head, and began sniffing back tears and rubbing both her wrists and her forehead, her initial plans defeated.

During the conversation that followed – watched spookily by two detachable rabbit heads placed together on a side chair, ears drooping but still erect enough to appear to be listening – the presence of a knife and her plans to dissect her target with it became lost forever in the revised scenario. Still under contract to Smoke Records, Avril was told she would return to the label and a post as Delf's main backing singer; her salary would be hiked, she would be paid her disputed dues and could even front a few songs as featured singer. However, Delf made it clear that Avril would not be his girlfriend again, EVER, which elicited a small whimper from the still-smitten but less-homicidal former gospel girl.

Even then Solitaire, who was one of the most intimidating men Shutter had ever seen, nearly blew the deal (and also a cloud of choking fumes from a double corona in her face) when he told Avril: "Listen, chickie, you had it easy. You may feel you were done wrong, but at least you weren't raped by a rapper." But the subsequent indignant flare-up was short, a fairly sussed Avril spotting quickly that her bread was about to be buttered on both sides financially, and once she agreed the stated terms, she signed the bottom of a document "to be drawn up later" and flopped back on the bed, hugging her rumpled bunny costume about her like a comfort blanket.

Shutter was paid handsomely by the company to keep his mouth shut and for saving their protégé's life, on top of his generous fee for winning the bunny ruse and the fortune to be made from selling his new version of the tale to the news media. He was also hired to re-shoot a fully clothed, family-friendly re-enactment of the now-fictionalised incident in the actual hotel room where it had never quite transpired, Avril now armed, not with a knife, but with a small and fairly safe plaster ornament of a mallard (leading to one tabloid headline of *Duck, Bunny!*).

This all provided extra publicity for the Marsden, whose management also received a profitable kick-back. A grinning Bill Kowalczyk was extensively interviewed by the tabloids, who lapped up the story, with his lucrative (and mostly ludicrous) revised version of events. *"And I wondered what was going on when these two huge rabbits lolloped into reception. But one of them, the girl, I could tell by her voice, had a room key, so I knew they weren't real and just assumed they'd come from a fancy dress party. It wasn't Easter, or anything, mind..."*

As for Avril, well, she become a featured singer with the label and secured two minor chart hits. There was a colourful appearance on the *Graham Norton Show* where she sang a truncated version of her latest hit

My Love Has Gone and wore so many feathers in her paisley bucket hat that one of the other guests collapsed in an eye-weeping bout of hay fever. She enjoyed a brief liaison with an unmarried backbench MP and BAME advocate, produced two children by a session bass player, who she married when she became pregnant, and then mostly disappeared from public view. She kept singing, playing night club dates and wedding receptions with her own quartet, which included her husband; she also kept a small shrine to her dear Bunny in an alcove of their country cottage, and continued to waitress at the Marsden for the lunchtime crowd where she was occasionally recognised and asked to autograph a table napkin.

Bunny Delf went on to acquire two new girlfriends (who just happened to be twin sisters), a burgeoning cocaine addiction and the kind of megalomania usually reserved for reclusive millionaires who have lost touch with reality. Tragically, he was killed in a coach crash eight years later in Italy on the eve of his largest chart success and a short period of international mourning followed including the release of two Greatest Hits compilations and a separate album of outtakes and demos.

Rumour had it that the coach driver, who plunged his vehicle over a steep coastal cliff en route to a gig in Naples, had swerved to avoid hitting a large, white rabbit squatting in the middle of the road. A witness told his local newspaper that he remembered the rabbit specifically because it was so unusual, with its *coda rosa*.

Its pink tail.

Remembering the Easter Bunny

"It's a story of perseverance," said Dara as storyteller one returned to his seat to an appreciative laugh and a ripple of enthusiastic applause. "It's Dan Shutter's last chance to resolve this ridiculous Bunny business, one way or another, hopefully in his favour, before he gives up and resumes his life."

He went on: "Remember, Will, you should never give up. But it's Shutter's choice here. He thinks the whole proposal is stupid, like so much of our daily drag, and he's sick of it. Still, circumstances offer him a final opportunity. It wasn't planned. His bicycle's broken, he's wet and cold, he's running into all kinds of dangerous or painful diversions, yet he keeps going. Then the stroke of luck, the phone call, and the final denouement, where he nets the prize in an unexpected way and his shabby world comes out of the gutter.

"Sometimes all you have to do is keep going, even if there's a proverbial Force Ten blowing in your face. Often there's only a cross to bear because you've allowed yourself to be nailed to it."

Having dispensed with his sage advice and a brace of clashing metaphors, Dara leaned over, still wiping a pint mug, gave me a piercing look and said in a low voice: "The story's also about hiding identity. When people hide behind masks – perhaps like you – they can never be sure who or what is lurking under that façade. And there's a fear that dropping that mask of assurance, or insurance, may leave them vulnerable to whoever or whatever is veiled by the masks of others."

I bristled slightly and said I knew about masks, that I wasn't stupid, and that I never wore a mask. I was ME, all the time. The ultimate WIZZYWIG: *What you see is what you get.* It was all the others who couldn't see the authentic self. Perhaps I'd been too honest over the years, every thought or emotion I'd ever had lighting up like neon signs across my forehead. Maybe a mask was just what I needed: a huge, thick one, like the previously-mentioned phantom of the opera, but without the associated disfigurement... and the dreadful sub-operatic hollering.

Dara shrugged.

Then I said that the only real-life Man in a Rabbit Costume story I knew was one told to me by my Uncle Donald. He had known this guy, a milkman apparently, who made extra money for his family by entertaining at children's parties.

"This was long before you had to be screened by the security services before you could even look at a child; the days when parents were attentive enough to know which uncles were 'a bit funny' and kept them well out of unsupervised reach of their kids," I said.

"Anyway, this chap used to dress as the Easter Bunny, come that time of the year, and one time he got a booking to go to this big house and bounce around with the kids for about an hour, pocket twenty quid and beat it. Well, the weather was dreadful, howling and pumping it down, and he fell behind in getting to the venue for the celebrations. Because he was 'five minutes late' the hostess, a plummy-sounding lady with large jewellery and the demeanour of an especially ripe Conservative women's committee chairman, told him that he'd been replaced at the eleventh hour by a clown, who conveniently lived nearby, and he could say goodbye to his fee."

I did the annoying air-quotes again, and a silly voice when repeating a bit of character speech.

"So he sloped back to his car and found it wouldn't start. Slumped into the driver's seat, rain still pelting down outside, smelling of old sweat, damp cotton and Polyester, he asked himself why he did this; why did he humiliate himself for a few extra quid every now and tomorrow? It was a Saturday and the garage was closed in the afternoon and he wasn't a member of an auto recovery service so he had to walk home. To make things worse he'd left his change of clothes at home, so he'd have to walk two miles dressed as Tufty Fluffytail. He thought about hanging around and asking Jakko The Clown for a lift, but the mighty Jakko only lived around the corner and he'd only driven to the gig because of the weather, so he'd be unwilling to spend his fee driving way across town for the man he'd replaced. Anyway, he was a spiky little council rat-catcher who took great satisfaction in other people's misfortune – probably because his job, which saw him slopping about in sewers, underground river beds and other unsavoury places, was both filthy and demoralising – so he was sure to say no, and with considerable attitude.

"So, bunny walked home, the full two miles; no taxi because there were no pockets in the suit for a wallet or loose change; he'd stored his key fob in one of the ears. He arrived soaked to the skin only to find his costume had shrunk a size smaller and he had to cut it off with kitchen scissors. By the next morning he had retired from the entertainment business."

Dara laughed heartily and it was my turn to shrug.

"Now that would make a good tale to tell!" he said. "Oh, By the way, Tufty Fluffytail was a squirrel."

"Whatever," I replied and made dismissive gestures. "The guy still stank of bogus animal costumes."

But my mind was elsewhere.

Funny, but I had always wanted to dress up in a full size rabbit costume, like the pap story, with huge Bugs Bunny ears sticking up like antenna; not for a children's party, but to bring a sense of the ridiculous to my staid little office at work, where everyone sat around unapproachably grim-faced and the only peeps you ever got out of them were to discuss a case history – but very low key and quietly, hushed, almost reverently, as if they were in a Victorian library or museum with a supervisor looking down on them from a high chair. The alternative proof they were still living was offering up an aggravated grunt if a pen rolled off a desk on to the floor. In the lunch break they would shuffle off to the canteen and talk about the office tennis club.

We had all these paper files on local residents claiming various sorts of benefits from the state, their details still secured in thick cardboard folders despite the recent arrival of some pretty basic computers. I know most of us took a peek in the files from time to time, to check out someone we knew, just to see if they had some dark and unwholesome secret that we could store away in our own non-cardboard mental storage slots and smirk about. We couldn't use any of the information, of course; that would have meant dismissal and possible legal action, as we all had to sign the Official Secrets Act, so breaking that was a serious no-no. But we could still allow ourselves a childishly secretive smile whenever we met the person in question.

Then I remembered who the bunny storyteller so resembled; the resemblance I had spotted immediately: my father.

Being an engineer, he was good at everything. He did all the work in and around the house; we never needed to call in a tradesman. He did all the electrical, plumbing and carpentry jobs, built kitchen cupboards and my bookshelves, laid carpets and lino, did all the mechanical work on the family car and would have put it through the MOT too if he'd had the authorized certification. He painted the house, cleaned the guttering and washed the windows. And I reckon he could also have built a Spitfire in the back garden if he'd had the right number of parts and enough room for the wings. He hated the fact that I was completely hopeless, inept and

41

blessed with ten thumbs when it came to practical handyman tasks. He often told me: "You're no son of mine – my son would have had the washer off that tap in ten seconds without spilling a drop of water in the sink," and so on. He saw me as a directionless, unambitious commercial pen-pusher and if I thought I was going to be a storyteller of any note – well, I wasn't. He was a bastard.

Sorry.

A stirring in the room brought me back to the time and place as another reader rose to speak. This second storyteller looked a bit like the aforementioned Uncle Donald, what with the balding pate and a pallid skin that suggested he had spent most of his life in a dark, dank cellar. Contrarily, my uncle had spent most of his life out of doors, though only within the boundaries of a tatty house clearance van. Despite working all year in all weathers, he had failed to attract any enhancement of skin tone – or, indeed, any improvement to his employment status. I'd seen little of him since I was a kid and that suited me fine as he was a typical white van man, terse and uncommunicative and with a reputation for both driving aggressively and too close to other motorists' bumpers; also for blocking up the small, residential village cul-de-sac where he lived with a succession of bulky, rusted old trucks that could have belonged to anyone, and probably did.

I assumed my uncle's al fresco life made him an active kind of chap, though for all the infrequent times he was around I never saw him actually carrying anything; he was either relaxed in his cab with a newspaper, a sandwich and a Thermos Flask or leaning against the bonnet puffing on a fag, which reminded me of a story he once told me about his childhood, which he always related proudly. On the day he left school for the final time his headmaster told him that he would "never amount to anything. You'll just spend your life hanging around on street corners." And that was pretty much what Uncle Donald had done ever since, apparently to his great satisfaction.

He had teamed up socially with an equally lethargic former school chum and the only thing that ever motivated the pair of them was an evening supping watered-down bitter in a sparsely-frequented pub under an old railway arch in a scattered hamlet a few miles out of town. His chum Geoff was a machinist in a small manufacturing plant on a modest and unfashionable industrial estate on the debris-scattered and overgrown site of a former power station, recently demolished; he was married with two small daughters and kept pigeons. Uncle D never took the plunge himself – either with a wife or a pigeon – and had a pretty ambivalent view of women: on the one hand he liked their looks, but only if they were what he personally determined as pretty, and on the other he was constantly criticising and demeaning them as if they were a mentally-deficient sub-human species. This was probably the result of his having to look after an elderly, disabled, incontinent and demanding aunt for two decades before she finally died and left him nothing for his troubles but a poorly executed self-portrait – both in oils and a tatty frame – and a wardrobe stuffed with pre-war dresses all smelling of camphor.

Speaker two, the Uncle D clone, cleared his throat, a loose bundle of papers rustling in his slightly unsteady hands, a parade of coloured pens clipped conspicuously to the top pocket of his tweed jacket, and began. He seemed confident.

Booth's Grand Finale

He thought he would never hear that awful name again.

But suddenly it had come back into his life, rattling around in his head like the clapper on a bell that had long since lost its resonant ring, reducing the impact to a dull thud. It was making his forehead tacky with perspiration and triggering his heart to start thumping much too fast for a 60-year-old, even one who has looked after himself.

Shaun "Axe" Bell.

A name with a long and grubby history.

As a retired cop, Dexter Booth had every right to assume that his departure from his job, the force and the city where he had worked for three decades in order to hibernate in a small, isolated rural community more than 200 miles to the west would have thrown a pretty effective security blanket around his future, making it unassailable.

Apparently not.

He shivered. How had Bell – the dreaded "Axe" – found him? Four and a half years of isolation should have ensured his dealings with that rangy animal were closed, filed and forgotten. Then again, news of Chief Inspector Dexter Booth's departure from CID had probably made the rounds of the various penal institutions that Axe had frequented, so it wouldn't have taken a genius to track down the man who had hounded him for three years, until a colleague finally made the decisive arrest and secured the conviction, just hours after Booth's retirement.

Of course, he knew what Axe was looking for now, now that he was free. Or rather *who*. And this time, after all the inveterate inmates Booth had dealt with during three decades of policing, it was not about him, not about the departed CI. It was about *her*.

Booth knew he should never have taken the girl. It was wrong, even if he had done it for the right reasons, and for some other reasons less clear or ethical. He should have handed her over to the right people. He had never broken the law before and, in fact, had done his best to uphold it for the thirty-two flawless years he had been its custodian.

It was not kidnapping, it was not abduction: it was a spontaneous, knee-jerk act, a sudden impulse brought on by human kindness and decency: at least that's what he told himself at the time. It had been a caring action, the right thing to do and the girl had always been free to walk away whenever she was ready. Yes, it had been the correct move with hindsight – even if it was more about filling a hole in his own life and in his own heart than rescuing a young woman in distress. And that decision might now lead to things much worse, less morally defensible, if Axe tried to harm her in any way.

Booth stared coldly into the hall mirror. His silver hair made him look older than his natural years, but at least he appeared distinguished, like an ageing professor, orchestral conductor or senior surgeon. Though pale-skinned, he was mostly free of telltale wrinkles, both through exercise and a bunch of quality face creams. He still had the small scar on his forehead that Axe had managed to inflict with the edge of a cell chair in a stupidly unguarded moment, upsetting the even continuity of the policeman's features.

"Shaun 'Axe' Bell," he growled to himself. "You're not having my daughter!"

Booth had first encountered Shaun Bell and his closest lieutenant Norman Palk, who later adopted the fitting nick-name "Chancer," when they were hot-headed 12-year-olds appearing on burglary and theft charges at the local juvenile court. Booth was giving a fresh-faced trainee bobby his first glimpse of the local justice system for the under-aged. His closest friend in the service, Sgt Geoff Clayton, now an Inspector, had long been subjected to the boys' unchecked lawlessness when they were children running riot on a local housing estate, each an offspring from notorious criminal families. But for Booth it was the first time he had seen such abject wickedness in two young lads and envisaged a grim path ahead for them both.

At the hearing the chairman concurred with Booth's unspoken evaluation and berated the duo for their "shameful" acts – taking money, records, cassettes, jewellery and a leather jacket from an isolated rural property while the occupants were at the village pub and, after setting an outhouse on fire, scarpering on stolen bicycles. He warned them that a stunted future awaited the duo if their current "day of reckoning" was not heeded and remanded Bell to an assessment centre for eight months and his partner in crime, the titular 'Chancer,' to a two-year supervision order. Booth was certain that evaluation reports from an exasperated Sgt Clayton had influenced the sentence. But even when elderly chairman Stafford Rawlings highlighted the boys' "lack of parental control" – often being out thieving at one and two in the morning – both stood stoically before him, bearing a hint of insolence in their defiant expressions. Neither parent appeared at the hearing to support their tainted offspring, despite a court-appointed defence solicitor's earlier appeal for them to do so.

It was hardly surprising in Bell's case: his mother was an alcoholic, banned from several local watering holes due to her unruly behaviour including launching a trainee chemist through an open window when he (innocently) looked at her "all peculiar," and was at home comatose. His father, one of the long-term unemployed since leaving school, was missing without trace following a suspicious burglary that bore his hallmarks.

Compelled by frustrated social services managers to find a "real job" before he ended up permanently at Her Majesty's Pleasure, Bell Snr took over a butcher's shop when the owner retired. Backed by a government grant and help from the local council and chamber of trade he quickly proceeded to run the business into the ground. It was here that his equally indolent son discovered a love for sharp cutting instruments, though the place was eventually closed due to serious public health infractions and Bell Snr returned to his previous non-occupation of 'hanging around,' soon to be augmented by a little light-fingered maintenance of his personal finances.

Booth remembered that Daddy Bell had pleaded guilty at Magistrates' Court to twenty-two cases of breaching hygiene regulations and two specimen charges of selling meat unfit for human consumption during his spell as a butcher. Walls, floors and ceilings of all four of the food rooms were described as "dirty" – pretty much an understatement as most of his paraphernalia and equipment was caked with gunge. The roster included a blood-grimed sink, a rusty band saw, a "filthy" screen between the main shop, its chill/freezer area and loading zone, and "inadequate cleaning provision," including a broken sink. All rooms "showed indications of infestation by rats, mice and insects" and in one corner, according to district council prosecutor Graham Rawson, health inspectors found "a rancid pile of meat, including bones, fat, pigs' heads and intestines that rose more than two feet from the floor, was four feet wide and eight feet in length" – and the tarpaulin screen divider passed over this reeking sludge every time the adjoining rooms were accessed. Booth remembered being physically sick after the hearing as both he and Clayton had bought their sausages from the grubby Bell Snr because his shop was conveniently located just across the road from the central police station.

As for the story that Bell Jnr had used an axe to disable a fellow drug dealer, well, that had little truth to it, other than the fact that loathsome Shaun was a violent and dangerous thug who could easily have pulled such an unsavoury stunt. In reality, Bell had actually detained and restrained his economic rival, a rather brutish-looking supermarket shelf-stacker called Harry Cheed, himself on the cusp of being lengthily incarcerated for a string of misdemeanours, and had indeed threatened to cut off his fingers should he continue to disrupt Bell's profits from his 'happy pills' (many and various) and 'happy dust' (cocaine).

Cheed had heard that Bell had a reputation for extreme violence – a rumour perpetuated by Bell himself, but supported by accounts of the number of beatings he had carried out on anyone who crossed his path unfavourably – and struck a deal. If he (Bell) promised to lay off him, he (Cheed) would stop dealing immediately and would also come up with some story, "within seven days," that would enhance his captor's reputation.

"I can make you *legendary*!" Cheed promised, rather foolishly, as he claimed a week's grace from a serious face-mashing. Then he sat about worrying about how he was going to talk himself out of his unrealistic and outrageous commitment.

Fortunately, at least for Cheed, fate intervened and the slimy shelf-stacker was able to realize his boastful promise within just three days when he accidentally sliced off the top of two of his fingers attempting to repair the chain of his classic but battered motorbike, an early sixties Manx Norton, in the kitchen of his cousin's council house. He was rushed to hospital, told doctors what had really happened, the severed distal falanges of both fingers were reattached and he was released with a noticeably bandaged left hand – the one he had not moved out of the way quickly enough.

Within days and within his deadline, Cheed had let it be known that Bell had 'axed' him. And so the myth was born, along with the nick-name. Until, that is, Dexter's chum Geoff had learned the truth from a former surgeon, now attached to the medical facilities of a local prison for his pre-retirement years, who had been on call the day Cheed had been admitted to his practice, blubbering and bleeding and cursing the whole Norton empire.

Anyway, to get back to the day when it all went both south and (I guess) north too for Chief Inspector Dexter Booth: a decline and ascension simultaneously overnight on the occasion of his retirement from the force.

There was a farewell party at the Station with all of Booth's colleagues, past and present. Even the Deputy Chief Constable attended briefly to croon a few supportive words before hastily departing to join his boss at a thorny meeting with city businessmen about proposed policing arrangements for a forthcoming arts festival planned for the spacious grounds of the city centre cathedral that needed some sensitive handling and the presence of Uniformed Top Brass.

It was the night of November 5 and the cheers and happy toasts were accompanied by loud bangs and fans of coloured lights illuminating onyx skies over the city's houses. To add to the CI's cheery send-off there was even a small bonfire topped with a roasting Guy on a patch of green next to the station car park. After an hour or so, Booth was ready to go home. He had still to finish stripping the last of his belongings from the house he had now sold, in light of his move to his quiet rural village 200 miles away over the next two to three days. There was a lot to do.

At this point, his boss, Supt Carol Graveney, who had been wearing a secret smile all evening, pulled him aside and asked him if he would like to undertake "one last assignment – purely off the books." Carol has been an imaginative and supportive boss over the years and Booth agreed immediately, though puzzled.

"You can only be the equivalent of a civilian advisor now," she told him. "You're no longer a serving police officer. You were officially stood down from noon today."

Then she told him what she had in mind – as a "final, special gift" to thank Booth for his outstanding service over three decades. Booth had permission to accompany his friend Inspector Geoff Clayton and his team – in his own car, of course, and with no professional involvement – on an important drugs and vice raid at midnight on the headquarters of none other than local thug Shaun 'Axe' Bell. And Booth hugged her.

An hour later, Booth was at the wheel of his Ford Mondeo tucked in behind a force convoy of cars and vans, surreptitiously making their way through a maze of narrow and unfamiliar backstreets, on their way to Bell's covert address. The air was foggy with the smoke of expended fireworks adding an eerie flavour to the clandestine enterprise. It was less than five minutes before the bulk of the fleet pulled up silently at the back of the huge but silent building with Booth parking well back and to one side; three patrol cars made their way to the front, equally stealthily, via the main highway. The rear-aspect conglomeration of flats and ground floor shops looked sinister in the half-light and the decaying mist of the Fawkes spectacular as the block dominated the far end of an empty market service yard. The back of the building was lit with one small lamp, extending from over a doorway; a couple of security lights on the opposite side from the rear of the eastern market square shops sent their accompanying shadows spookily flickering towards the place they were about to breach.

The centre of Axe Bell's illicit rented empire comprised four floors rising from a small concrete yard where the bottom windows were boarded up; a black fire escape wound from the yard to the top floor to meet a flat roof. There were three exits either side of the rear yard and the back of the building, comprising three separate but upper-floor-connected units, was divorced from the service yard it overlooked by a high wooden fence marked with wide, secured exits at each end.

There were three entrances at the brighter front face of the building from a trio of unconnected business premises – an empty butcher's shop (not Bell Senior's) with FOR RENT signs in its windows, an estate agency and a charity shop – all facing a pedestrianised shopping street; a narrow alley on the agency corner led down to the market service yard where Booth had parked his car. This commercial frontage had a sense of pre-Regency days about it, with the tight brickwork and tall, multi-paned windows of its first and second floors, a shorter roof space with half-size windows, and the bow windows of its street-level shops. This historic illusion was shattered by the severe plaster work around those otherwise picturesque ground floor windows, the garish modern shop signs, a cluster of TV and satellite aerials on the roof and the jagged strips of pigeon spikes on the window ledges. The back of the place was more a higgledy-piggledy confusion of plaster, concrete, Perspex and hardboard as if the area had become generally neglected but casually patched from time to time over the decades.

On the brief walkie-talkie signal "*Go!*" from Inspector Clayton, the area suddenly erupted as more than a dozen officers, some armed, stormed the building. They smashed open the doors of the two shops with back staircase links to the rest of the building – the former butcher's and the charity shop – and also the rear fence entrances and back doors; several scampered up the fire escape and began smashing through windows. Numerous cries of "*Police!*" echoed around the service yard where Booth sat in his car gripping the steering wheel firmly, attempting to discourage himself from joining the raid. He was about to give in to his craving to be back on duty when he saw a movement on the nearside of the alley that accessed the shopping street. A previously hidden door flew open and a figure in a black hoodie tumbled out and raced into the service yard behind the Mondeo. As he flashed past, the retired CI caught a glimpse of a face. It was Norman Palk.

"*Chancer!*" Booth growled.

He was too late to take pursuit himself – the lad was wiry and fast – and there was no way of summoning help without his own HT (handheld transceiver), surrendered with the rest of his service equipment at the end of his final shift. Even so, he could still prevent further escapes by blocking the entrance to the alley with his own car which he gunned into life and steered cautiously into place. In fact, he could do even better by blocking that obscured exit, he reasoned; that hidden door that Chancer had left ajar in his haste. Booth stepped out and marched to the door just as a splintering crash echoed behind him – the sound of one of Axe's henchmen attempting an unsuccessful dive to freedom through the unforgiving panes of a back window.

Booth swung the alleyway door open and found himself at the entrance to a narrow corridor, lit faintly by a light from a second doorway on the right hand side halfway along the murky passage. He gingerly approached the light, poised to deflect any sudden attack from another scampering Axeman. From the depths of the property he could hear bangs, thumps, angry shouts and the occasional bark of a German shepherd as the police team rounded up their reluctant suspects. The door was also ajar and Booth gently pushed it open with two fingers, keeping cautiously clear of the entrance. The tiny box room was gloomily illuminated by a single stubby candle on an upturned crate. But what caught the CI's eye was the figure resting in a single wooden chair in the centre of the room. It was a girl, dressed in jeans, red boots and a tee shirt, turned away from him, her head slumped on her chest. Apparently unconscious, she was zip-tied by the wrists to the arm rests. Booth gave a growl of anger and hurried to the chair. He slipped a pen knife from his overcoat and sliced through the ties. The girl remained head-down and deathly silent; her freed arms dropped to her sides but she stayed rooted to the seat.

"My God, what have they done to you, lass?" Booth growled and reached forward to check the girl for injuries and a pulse. He lifted her face into the light of the flickering candle and her honey blond hair tumbled aside. What he saw chilled his blood.

"*Rose?!*" he gasped.

He tottered backwards, almost lost his footing and stared incredulously as the girl's head lolled back on to her chest. Without another thought, he lifted her into his arms, carried her back to his vehicle, gently laid her in the back seat and covered her motionless but low-breathing body under a large blanket. He turned to seek out his friend Geoff to report his find but stopped immediately and stared at the back of the overhanging building.

"No," he said to himself. "This one's for me."

51

He got back in his car and drove away. He'd speak to Geoff in the morning.

Maybe.

The raid proved more successful than even the eager Geoff Clayton had imagined. Not only did his team impound more than £150,000 worth of drugs, from amphetamines to cocaine and heroin, but they also caught their importer Sean Bell in the midst of savagely beating a half-naked young woman restrained by leather straps, adding 'sadist' to his growing criminal CV. Axe had time to leap out of an open window and down the fire escape, somehow managing to lob lighted fireworks at police before he was finally felled by a taser and bundled handcuffed and kicking into the impenetrable cage of a paddy wagon. As a final indignity, he was later found to be dosed to the gills with White Lightning, a designer version of common or garden bath salts* and a bit of a wanky embarrassment for a self-confessed hard man.

Intelligence that brought about the triumphant haul came from a young police cadet who had secretly infiltrated Bell's small but effective gang, loosely referred to as the Axe Handles, and passed on a tip that a major drugs shipment was due on the fourth. Also subsequently, this particular cadet was given a serious dressing-down by his father – none other than raid co-ordinator Geoff Clayton – for carrying out an unsanctioned, and highly dangerous undercover exploit. Quietly, the 17-year-old was also generously praised by his dad for his courage – and for being the one police representative, not even a proper copper, to trigger the downfall of a nasty little local crook his father had been anxious to net for some years.

Booth thought at the time of Bell's downfall that the little thug would be incarcerated for a very long time. But here he was, nearly five years down the line, getting that call announcing the release of the Axe from prison. It came from his friend Geoff, of course, who just said: "He's out. You'd better keep her out of sight."

It was clear that Axe had a long memory and had never forgotten the girl who had been spirited away from him on the night of the raid, and how it had taken him years and too many cigarettes and unwanted favours to track down where she had gone – and who had taken her.

---

*Page Footnote: Bath salts contain stimulants called cathinones, similar to amphetamines and known to both create a euphoric state and promote an increase in violence – a bad deal for someone with the natural disposition of a vicious thug.

"How the hell did he find me?" Booth asked Geoff.

"Contacts. You know the prison network as well as me," Geoff replied. "I'm not sure that he has your address, but he apparently knows the town and the college where she's studying. You should keep a lookout, Dex. Maybe get some professional help."

"You know I can't involve the law…"

"I know. But after all this time…"

Geoff Clayton, his dearest friend, was the only other person who knew the truth about 'Rose,' and had been instrumental in keeping that information secret ever since the raid. Booth had sought out his help as soon as it became clear that his new and damaged house guest was planning to stay with him and that a host of complex consequences needed expert massaging.

He returned from the raid that night five years back and slowly and stealthily helped walk the unsteady and still partly-drugged girl he had rescued from Bell's seedy headquarters into his quiet, high-hedged rural terraced house. She was barely able to communicate, but Booth told her she was safe, that nothing bad was going to happen to her, but she needed to recuperate. He warmed her some milk and led her up to a small bedroom on the first floor. He laid out sleeping togs, made for a teenage girl about her size, and left her to undress and sleep. Then he went downstairs, poured himself a large whiskey and flopped into an arm chair, exhausted.

Rose, he sighed. How could this be? Was life playing a cruel trick on him? Or was it somehow putting him in the right place at the right time to save a soul he had not been able to save once before?

The first thing she said when she tottered into the kitchen at 11am the next morning, sleepy-eyed and still dressed in her borrowed night togs, once owned by Booth's daughter Rose, was "Where am I? And who are you?"

Booth told her, seated at the kitchen table with a newspaper and a mug of very strong coffee. He had been unsure how his guest would react to what he had done. The first thing he learned was that the girl was called Ellie. Overnight he had come to terms with the fact that she was not his long-lost daughter Rose. She was a few years too young – though, Christ, she looked so much like her with her blonde hair, high cheeks, blue eyes and dumpy little nose. Just like her mother. Rose's mother… No wonder he had been so expertly fooled by first impressions in the muted light of a candle. He explained where he had found her and the circumstances. She looked concerned but steely and he wondered how Bell had ever got the drop on this determined teenager.

"He got what he deserved," Ellie replied, accepting a coffee but turning down an offer of toast. "The bastard! He killed my mum and God know what he was planning to do with me…"

"He killed your mother?"

"Not in any way you can convict him," Ellie replied, cradling her coffee mug between her hands as if to warm the shivers brought on by thoughts of what might have happened if Booth had not rescued her. There was a hint of the West Country in her voice.

"Mum was an addict. Bought her stuff from Bell. Said she could handle it, but she couldn't. Lost her job at the council. When they heard about that at school they began pushing me around, calling me "druggy babe" and being really horrible. Then mum overdosed and left me stranded. Dropped dead in the street. Made school even worse, especially as Dad did a runner when I was three and there was no-one else."

"What happened?"

"Bell offered to look after me. I was really dumb. Went with him, he drugged me and then you found me. He had a school friend of mine too. Took us together. Did you find her?"

She described her friend and Booth told her a girl answering the verbal portrait was in hospital but would make a full recovery, at least physically; they had reached her in time, though he didn't add "before Bell was able to beat her to death," which is how Geoff had put it.

Ellie nodded, as if she understood anyway.

"He said my dead mum owed him money. I said she didn't and he said 'Oh yes she did, she died and I lost a very lucrative income, so I'm taking it out in kind – like *goods and services* – on you and your friend.' Fawn wasn't really my friend, I'd just met up with her at the mall, recognised her from school, and that's where Bell and that little creep Chancer picked us up and promised us – what was it? – a safe haven." She snorted derisively. "Some *safe*! I was stupid, but there were people asking what happened to my mum, I was always around because the school holidays had just started, and then my missing shit of a father turned up and took charge and I… I ran away."

"No-one tried to find you?"

"You did."

The long and short of it was this: after several hours of soul-searching on both sides Ellie asked if she could stay with Booth, "just 'til I get my life together." His friend Geoff dealt with any fallout, any paperwork and obscuring any trace of one Ellie Marsh. She was just "a kid who slipped

54

through the cracks." It wasn't the first time, thought Booth bitterly. Ellie's father expressed little interest in the whereabouts of his estranged daughter and any pecuniary offerings remaining from his ex-wife's estate went to him, the main reason for his unscheduled reappearance. After that he disappeared again. Booth and Ellie moved from the area together and because of her likeness to Rose Booth, Geoff also created a new identity for Ellie as Booth's former daughter. Ellie/Rose felt she had found a truly safe haven and Booth felt like he had his beloved daughter back. She rather liked the new name, as long as it didn't make her look too much like "a girly-girl. I have a brain," she added, and Booth nodded with a smile. She did, indeed.

Her attentive and secure custodians found her a place at a nearby community college and she began studying animal care and management, fired with a new motivation and aiming for a bachelor's degree in applied animal science. She took to it immediately, "like a pig in shit" Geoff quipped in one of his overseeing calls. All was suddenly bright and beautiful. At least until the fatal phone call that put the former CI on red alert.

He thought about taking Rose out of college and hiding her somewhere else; he didn't know where or how and didn't want to impose further on his relationship with Geoff who, after all, was still a serving police officer, recently appointed a CI in Booth's place. But something had to be done, and quickly. Yet again, fate found a way of intervening.

This time it was the turn of Sean 'Axe' Bell to be hog-tied to a hard chair and treated to the kind of harsh restraint he liked delivering to defenceless schoolgirls. His wrists were zip-tied to the arm rests, his ankles similarly attached to the chair legs and his neck roped to the chair back, restricting any sudden head movements. Booth had not forgotten the prison injury Bell had inflicted on him, and nor had Bell, who had received a six-month addition to his sentence for the attack.

"*You can't fucking do this*," he barked at Booth. "I'm a free man now. I've got *rights!*"

He could shout as loud as he liked, Booth thought. He would not be heard, being detained in an isolated barn deep in the countryside, surrounded by fields and woodland and offered to Booth on a 'no questions asked' basis by a recently-acquired farmer friend attached to Ellie/Rose's college course.

"And what about the rights of the girl you killed?" Booth barked back.

He was stalking around the chair brandishing a sickle with as much

55

menace as he could muster, which was pretty easy considering the circumstances.

Bell had appeared in Booth's new manor driving an unremarkable old rattletrap, a green 7cwt former butcher's van with a windowless back, white cab roof and rusty wheel arches. His intention had been to abduct Ellie/Rose and extract his pound of flesh. But he had been spotted stalking the pretty student outside the college by her farming tutor who frustrated Bell's plans by accompanying his target after college hours to the spot where Booth was waiting in his Mondeo to collect her. This tentative rigmarole went on for forty-eight hours until Bell was finally ambushed. Her farmer protector left the pretty student apparently stranded by a bus stop just down the road from the college, with no sign of her ride home, like a goat staked out for a hungry tiger. Not his plan, not Booth's, but hers. It wasn't long before the scruffy van pulled up beside her. Bell just had time to sling open the driver's door, point a pistol at her and snap "Get in!" before he was blinded by the flicker of a focussing red dot and the twin contacts of a Taser X2 hit him in the forehead. Booth had fired the immobilising weapon from the hedge behind Ellie/Rose and Bell collapsed immediately, hanging from his seat belt like a broken marionette.

"What girl? I never killed no girl," he barked back at Booth in the secluded barn, shuddering in an attempt to free any of his restrained limbs.

His sharp grey eyes, straggly black hair and hooked nose gave the lad a feral appearance and it was hard to see why he always had such an elevated reputation with the ladies – though, to be fair, these were often very young, inexperienced and under-educated girls; older women saw him for exactly what he was, a brute and a coward, and the younger ones soon became wise to his games, if they survived them. Booth wondered what his daughter Rose had seen in him. Perhaps it had just been her age and rebelliousness: her dad was a copper and her new boyfriend was *dangerous*, a *crim*, took *risks*. What happened might never have happened at all if she hadn't been staying with her dad for a few days at the moment her mother had died. Booth still blamed himself for everything.

When he was a Sergeant, Booth met a young community PC and they had a clandestine but passionate affair that led to her becoming pregnant. They agreed to keep the affair quiet to protect their respective careers and Joy, the PC, moved away to another county to live with her widowed mother. She had her baby (a girl, Rosemary) and then returned to the Force. Only Geoff knew the true story. Joy kept in touch with Booth, writing to him regularly with an update on Rosemary's progress and her own small advancements.

One Christmas, when Rose was fourteen she asked to visit her father for a couple of weeks and while she was away she met up with Alex Bell and his crew with a bunch of other kids in a town centre coffee bar. She found him exciting in her own immature way, at least until Booth found out who she was seeing.

He barred his daughter from continuing the liaison and they had a major row. The bad air only dissipated when Rose had a call to say that Joy had been rushed to hospital after a fall and was in a critical condition. She packed a bag immediately and set off to be by her mum's bedside. Booth paid for the taxi and they made tearful farewells to each other, Booth promising to follow "in a few days." But he never saw Joy again as she died in hospital that night. He later learned from Joy's mother that a rupturing brain aneurysm had triggered the fall that led to her fatal head injuries. As sudden tragedies often dictate, he never saw Rose again either; she died at the same time as her mum in an unprecedented road crash.

His chum Geoff, then a senior traffic cop, attended the incident where her taxi had been hit broadside by a careering bread van, sending it smashing through a barrier and over a steep drop into a railway siding. The cab driver and his passenger Rosemary, in that mercy dash to her mum's bedside, were killed instantly. As if that was not painful enough, Booth later heard that the van had been veered off its course by the happenstance sideswipe from another vehicle that was escaping a high-speed police chase. The rogue car hit the off-side of the bread van and then streaked in front of it, cutting across its bonnet and causing it to swerve into the opposite carriageway and straight into the taxi. But the worst thing Booth learned was that the car had likely been driven by Sean 'Axe' Bell who had somehow managed to escape his pursuers and later claimed the car, clearly his, had been stolen while he was "down the pub" with his mate, Chancer. Despite the lack of convincing evidence, Booth had no doubts that Bell had been behind that fatal wheel.

In answer to his fevered question, Booth told Bell: "Who did you kill? A taxi driver and a beautiful young girl just starting out on her life's journey. She was called Rosemary, Rose – and you went out with her for a short time."

Bell allowed himself a salacious smirk. "Hey, I go out with a lot of chicks. Guess I'm blessed."

"Not so blessed now."

"I remember that accident," Bell said, ignoring the comment and looking like he was actually bothering to think. "Yea, wasn't me. Someone nicked me car. Tragedy. But these things happen when coppers decide to run down innocent citizens."

"Oh, it was you alright. Everyone knew. And you were never innocent."

Bell shrugged, though with difficulty in his restraints. "Couldn't be proved. Anyway, as I said, I was somewhere else."

"In the pub with your equally honest chum Chancer."

"Right!" Bell nodded affirmatively. The rope chafed his neck, but he still managed a second smile. His confidence seemed to be growing. He recognised Booth as an honest man and he somehow knew he was safe, despite the biting set of ties.

"So what'ya gonna do, copper? Kill me? I don't think so. You'll just let me free and I'll go back about my business…"

"Thieving, drugs, violence? Some business, son."

"Nah, that's in the past. Got an honest job now." Another grin.

"You're about as honest as a crooked smile, Alex." Booth was not good with aphorisms.

"Or a crooked copper? Nah. Told you, I'm done. Start in the county highways depot next Monday."

"Then what are you doing here?"

"Holiday."

"Very funny…"

"So you can just let me go, I'll pop off and get me Kiss-Me-Quick hat and a cornet and we'll say no more about it. I'll drift off into the wind."

"What, and wonder when you're going to turn up again, unannounced, and take another pot at my daughter?"

"Just something to keep you on your toes, man. It's good for coppers."

In truth, Bell had created a dilemma for the retired Chief Inspector. There was, indeed, little he could do. Not only had he illegally abducted a teenage girl – no matter how honourably – and had given her a false name into the dubious bargain, but now he had now assaulted and incarcerated a legally innocent man without due cause (even the gun was insufficient cause as it was found to be made from Isoprene). Here was a man just out of prison who in the eyes of the law had served his time and was no longer guilty of anything other than an insolent manner, a bad haircut and a rubber gun. If only that were true: the unspoken threat was still there. But facts were facts: empty threats made under duress and packing a toy weapon were insufficient for more than a stiff warning and a possible fine.

Booth untied his quarry, took him out of the barn and led him back to his van, parked in a neighbouring field next to a small lane. He gave the grinning thug directions back to a main road around three miles away, warned him never to look for Ellie/Rose again and bid him a cold "Now fuck off!"

He hung his head as he told Ellie/Rose what he had done, but she took it all in good part.

"What else could you do?" she reasoned. "You're a good man, and I owe you my life… dad."

Booth glowed at the rare and unexpected appellation, but was still concerned.

"I think you've given him a big enough scare," Rose told him. "He may be full of bollocks… Sorry, bluster. But at the heart of it – not that he has one – he's just a scared little boy let down by his shitty parents."

"But what if he comes back?"

Rose looked around the kitchen where they stood.

"I'll just clock him one with that frying pan," she said, and for the first time in ages Booth laughed.

It was several weeks before Booth heard the news update.

His chum Geoff, fresh from organising another successful collar, phoned in exuberant mood to say that there would be no more shenanigans from Sean 'Axe' Bell. The lad had, as expected, gone back to his old ways and his old headquarters and not to the county highways yard as claimed. He had been keeping a lower profile and the police had yet to catch him in the act again when something extraordinary happened.

"He was out in his van one day, that pootling little rust bucket he drove down to your neck of the woods," Geoff told Booth. "Don't know quite what happened, but it seems he got tipped by another driver – a speeder; we never caught him. This was one night when he was taking the motorway to…"

He noisily shuffled some papers down the phone. "…Bristol, I think. Speeder disappeared and Bell spun off the carriageway and down this deep embankment into an abandoned concrete pig unit about fifty feet below. Hit it with one hell of a bang apparently, according to the boys from traffic. Pancaked the front of the van and the front of himself. Went through the windscreen as he wasn't wearing his belt. It wasn't pretty. So Bell has tolled his final toll. Bet you're relieved."

"I am," Booth said, taken aback. "And his buddy Chancer?"

"Small fry. Still in the wind."

"Ironic accident, considering what happened to Rose," Booth said. "A bit coincidental."

"Karma," said Geoff.

There was a long pause.

"You wouldn't have been anywhere in the area of that pig unit at the time, would you, Geoff?"

There was another long pause.

"Might have been," said Geoff.

Life's an Education, Education's a Life

"I've got real sympathy for Ellie's situation at school and afterwards," I said as Dara continued polishing.

"You were bullied, I take it," he said.

"Oh, yes. One lad was a bloody nuisance. He'd start pushing me around, hitting me on the arms, in the back, pulling at my blazer, even ripped the school badge off the breast pocket once, and when I tried to walk off he'd follow me, fists clenched and always shouting the same thing: '*I haven't finished with you yet!*'

"Well, that was until the day I'd had a big row at home with my folks and wasn't in the mood to be hassled further. I'd had enough of Mr Bully and thumped him for a change, right in the chest, in the middle of the cloakroom. It wasn't a hard thump, but it took him by surprise and he lost his balance and fell over. He lay there for a moment, red-faced, looking back up at me, startled and swearing, and then he got up and stamped off, and I never had a problem with him again. I wouldn't say he became a mate but, well, he kept a respectful distance and we'd nod at each other occasionally when passing."

For a moment I was back at my old secondary school, could see some of the faces, even sense the rubbery scent of gym shoes and feet and the antiseptic whiff of a dirty caretaker's mop sloshing around the floor tiles of its uniformly beige-painted corridors. And then the incident that remained with me all my life emerged, as if drifting from the cover of an autumn cloud: in my mind, one of those great injustices that had never resolved itself.

It was the last day of term, the end of the scholastic year and the end of me and my fellow pupils' education. We were fifteen and ready for the working world, ready to make money to buy our own things and maybe get a cheap car or a motorbike when we were old enough so we could pick up girls: finding new girls, interesting ones, ones willing to go the extra mile as most of our class females were pretty stand-offish and dating older lads who were already working.

As you can guess, discipline was very loose on that last day; the teachers had retreated to the staff room to share some bubbly and a few anecdotes and the classes were milling with exuberant teenagers keen to be away from their four-year detention centre but still anxious to have those last couple of hours with their school mates, some of whom they might never see again. It resembled a Wild West saloon in our block, though without the bar brawls and gunfire. The leader of a pack of lads from our group was engineering the corralling of girl classmates in our dedicated classroom, cutting off all exits and trying to whip up skirts and pull down knickers to a lot of whooping, frantic retaliatory face slapping and general mayhem. Up to that point, as far as I remembered, boys' sexual proclivities had been limited to loitering in the stairwells and trying to get a glimpse up girls' legs towards the secret zone.

At some point their leader Roy, that was his name, a stocky and determined lad with floppy brown hair and a cold stare, spotted one of the better-looking class lovelies trotting into our first floor block from the outside hallway. Suddenly aware of what was going on, she headed for the class on the other side of ours with increased speed and a determined expression, trying not to look to the right where her friends were valiantly fighting off the probationary rapists. Her route took her down a narrow gap between the desks and the outer windows and I was near her exit door, inadvertently blocking her route. I had no intention of joining in the raucous debauchery to my left and was as surprised as pretty, pig-tailed Melanie – that was the girl's name – to find myself a potential threat. Roy saw what was happening out of the corner of an eye and swung round, his attention distracted from a struggling redhead with freckles who was about to kick him in the groin.

"Hey, Willie! Stop her!" he cried, a look of red-cheeked lust on his mean little face.

I had just a moment to decide, but it was a no-brainer for me. Not only did I hate brutish Roy and what he was orchestrating but I also went buttery-kneed whenever I saw Melanie's best friend Melba, the green-eyed girl who I had idolised for several terms even though she thought I was a jerk. So I felt a need to be the hero, the white knight, the jerk who proved that even a jerk can be chivalrous. So, just before the now-hurtling Melanie barrelled into my chest I stepped aside, with the hint of an understanding nod. She said nothing, barely looked at me, and kept going, disappearing into the fabric of the room behind me and out of harm's way.

At this point a tumbling Roy pulled to a halt in front of me looking furious.

"You *cunt!*" he snapped.

And then he spat in my face. He had a fist pressed into the palm of his other hand as if he had been planning to hit me; then he stalked back to where the action was still taking place muttering something about seeing me later for some nameless retribution that fortunately never came.

And the worst thing about it – well, you can always wipe off a bit of gash spit – was that Melanie never thanked me; never even acknowledged what I had done: the honourable thing. And her friend Melba, with whom I was desperate to gain a couple of Brownie points, still gave me the blank look when I saw her for the very last time an hour or so later, on that final day of school, just a few months before I chanced on a newspaper article saying she had joined the Army with a picture of her looking stern in her new uniform. At least she had gone for a career – and a respectable one at that – and not the expected stay-at-home option for girl school leavers at that time comprising an unreliable husband, 2.4 children, a council house and a part-time job in a laundry.

I don't know what it was about Melba that attracted me. I was only twelve when I first met her, after all. Whether it was her tinkling laugh or her bright smile, or even her budding pre-teenage breasts, I remember these were all alien to me as they were reserved for other people – so as far as an intimate relationship with Will Buckwater was concerned, I knew I was the one who was toast. Now she was striding out towards her awaiting father's car, the unmolested Melanie by her side, looking like assured little madams on the path towards their splendid but ultimately separate futures, of which Melanie's was going to be the least ambitious: husband, kids, job on the Co-op checkouts. I had done what I thought was the right thing, and I had been slighted by everyone. I was glad to be out of the place. At least, as a small consolation, I realised it wasn't me but Roy and my father who were the real cunts.

Why was it so important to have thanks for doing the right thing? Well, it was not so much thanks, though that would have been nice, but some recognition, at the very least, that what I did was kind; something that deserved more than just a cheek splashed with saliva from a shithead. The school business was a family thing, though. My father claimed he'd had a bad time, though I doubted that somehow, and my mother was bullied, and that I can believe. Sister Brenda didn't fare much better than me, though she was quieter and kept her head down, so the bullies tended to leave her alone. At least no-one spat in her face. Still, I guess most people have some grim memories of their own scholastic hell.

Me? I couldn't get out of school fast enough when the release bell clattered for the end of the day. I'd rush home to gobble down my tea and watch sci-fi puppet shows like *Supercar*, *Fireball XL5*, *Stingray* and my favourite, *Thunderbirds*, about a family of heroes on a secret island in the Pacific Ocean who selflessly rescued folks in trouble in their futuristic rocket ships. Creators Gerry and Sylvia Anderson swept me away from the trials of my young life with thrilling stories of fantastic selfless deeds and I even pathetically fancied dark-haired oriental beauty Tin-Tin Kyrano, innocent niece of arch villain The Hood. All the derring-do from these magical marionettes set me scribbling my own fanciful nonsense under the covers when I should have been getting the right amount of zees for the scholastic day ahead.

I wrote a science fiction story for my father when I was ten and the man at first said he didn't have time to read it and when he had finally huffed his way through it three days later he threw it at me with the dismissive "Would never happen!" Sometimes I would show the result of my torch-lit jottings to a couple of select classmates, but they were always tight-lipped and non-committal; not unfriendly, but not encouraging either. They would laugh occasionally, though not always at the funny bits and I eventually gave up trying to impress them – entertain them, even – and retired into Will's internal world where I could be whatever I wanted to be without someone else's permission to exist.

I remember my time at a local boys' primary school, where everything seemed geared to physical fitness when a lot of allegedly healthy leaping about and stretching was ruthlessly encouraged in the large tarmac playground at the back of the 19th-century building. They had this regime where part of a workout on the half acre space involved a back stretching exercise on wooden mats. You had to lie on this block of slatted maple boards, put your hands on your kidneys and lift your legs back over your head so the tip of your plimsolls would touch the ground behind. My friend Jim, who was a bit on the heavy side, could never do this and one of the more sadistic gym masters would then come across, chide him for being chubby, and force his legs down to the ground, causing Jim's own knees to crush his belly and chest so he couldn't breathe. It terrified him and when he ran out of excuses for skipping PE to avoid this continual confrontation his body benevolently developed in-growing toenails which let him off any participation in sporty procedures – a condition that mysteriously cleared up once he had left the suffocating shroud of the education system.

"I've always been a bit introverted – not able to talk to people," I said, unlike my earlier bar entrance claims. "I can listen all right, but it's the talking for talking's sake that I could never do. Left me isolated – oh, back as far as when I was at school."

"You seem to be able to talk to me," Dara said.

I shrugged and held up my pint mug. Sparks glistened off its glass dimples from the bright little spotlights over the optics.

"Must be the beer," I said. Dara didn't reply.

"The kids at my primary school never seemed to be interested in anything that interested me," I said. "They preferred to link arms over shoulders until they were in this great wheeling aeroplane propeller of bodies, shouting '*Cowboys and Indians! Cowboys and Indians!*' to attract others until they had enough for the game, and then the line would break apart and the kids would rush off in all directions, firing imaginary guns and arrows and making dramatic '*Keh! Keh*' of '*Foosh!*' noises. The Indians always lost, like in the Westerns we saw on TV, and once out of the game they either sloped off looking sullen after their swift dispatch or they'd immediately switch sides by joining a rival group chanting '*US Cavalry! US Cavalry!*' Which was another opportunity for the mock redskins to get punished. If I'd played they would've made sure Mr Outsider ended up an Indian... It would be a Native American now, but the PC brigade wouldn't allow such a game anymore..."

"So how do you manage to write, with all this non-communication?"

"You don't need to talk to people to write about them; you just have to listen, observe. I can't think of a mute author at the moment to buoy up the point, but Beethoven was deaf and being unable to hear his own music didn't stop him composing incredible stuff."

I took a long swig and pushed the empty glass towards Dara for a re-fill.

"Same again?"

I nodded and he poured and returned.

"What I would really have liked to have been was a piano player: jazz piano player. Just sitting there creating notes as part of a trio or a quartet without having to exchange pleasantries about the weather or sympathising about someone's gammy leg – someone you've never met in a story told by someone you hardly know. But my folks didn't have a piano nor the kind of spare money to either buy one or pay for me to have lessons."

Of course, my father was fit as a fiddle and, as I said, thought I was a wimp. He'd done all this forces training, even though most of his active service had been with a spanner, and he always wanted me and my younger sister out in the fresh air. Out of the house, more like, as he hated kids, even (or maybe *especially*) his own. He was particularly nasty to my sister, but he never laid a hand on either of us; his approach was psychological, more about getting under the skin: telling me I was useless and basically just frightening Brenda, who was incredibly gullible back then, which is probably why she made such a bad choice when picking a husband.

Father would ask her if she wanted to do something, like go out with him to the tobacconist's in town or to the museum for an afternoon stalking the stuffed animals. He knew she liked going out with her dad, but he'd always catch her on the hop with these offers, when she was involved in some other pressing issue in her mind, like a difficult teacher, a knotty bit of homework or an over-attentive boy. She'd procrastinate while she gathered her thoughts and knowing she'd always come with him anyway, dad would go: "Is it DO or DON'T? It's a simple answer, my dear. Do, Don't? Give me your answer!"

"*DO!*" she'd bark back, rattled.

"Then you must be Daisy!" he'd reply with a grin, and he'd guffaw at his pun about the old Victorian song *Daisy Bell* that she'd never heard and embarrassingly continue to call her Daisy for the rest of the day.

"*Daisy, Daisy, give me your answer DOOOOO!*" he would warble occasionally, and publicly, and Brenda would do her best to retract her head into her shoulder blades like a mortified tortoise.

But that was nothing. The worst thing was the mice.

My father was obsessed with these off-colour cartoonists, a lot of them American that he found through illicit Forces channels. I guess you'd call them sick as their humour was both unpleasant and excessively graphic: hardly *Peanuts*, more a cross between, maybe, the post-war Robert Crumb and his hip sixties shtick, the satirical Jules Feiffer and the gross-out Charles Rodrigues whose tales of dead friends and a pair of clashing Siamese twins always made father hoot. He was especially taken by this guy called Zash Cavern, who was probably the worst of the nasties. He'd started out in the late forties as one of the founders of *Stab Comics* – though the publication had to change its name after a series of unconnected knife incidents in schools and switched its title to the no-less-offensive *Scab Comics*.

None of its readers noticed the rebranding, apparently. Anyway, he loved this maniac Cavern who specialised in what I can best call 'splatter' cartoons and was so trendy, amongst a certain sort, that he got to collect the most popular (most appalling) of his illustrations in his own paperback called *Skating on Thin Mice*. I kid you not!

Brenda used to have nightmares about the title alone. Father loved the book and used to leave it around the house for others to dip into and guffaw at. Uncle Donald was one of them, of course. Mum thought it was pretty crude stuff, but she never contradicted dad. Every time Brenda was the tiniest bit naughty father would wave a finger at her and say "You're skating on thin mice, my dear!"

66

She knew the reference and hated it. She used to complain "Skating on *fat* mice would be bad enough, dad, but thin ones don't have a chance!" and father would laugh. Then she saw the drawings and didn't sleep for three nights.

Well, within a couple of years of my getting my feet under the government services desk both my parents died. They were only in their fifties. I wouldn't say we were estranged by then, but they were rarely home in their last year or so. They were both in well-paid jobs, which meant daily life was comfortable, if a little emotionally frosty. They tolerated each other and me, never spoke to Brenda (unless it was to do with segmented rodents), and only came alive when travelling abroad, so all their spare money and time went into that, from long weekends to extended breaks in exotic places. They ended up having some sort of fatal disaster on a cable car in Switzerland – upsetting for me at first (and bloody tragic for them), but as they had never really been around for me and Bren I can't say I truly missed them.

A fastidiously organised pair, they left me the house in their wills (the only good thing my dad ever did for me, so I guess he came through at the end). But there was little capital left due to the continents-hopping which meant that whilst I had a roof over my head I also had all the associated costs of its upkeep – and the funerals. I was additionally charged with looking after Brenda. She was still at school, just, and would continue to live in the family home until she abandoned me to get married, which wasn't long in coming. We got on OK but she just wanted to flee that awful house. Until then I became chief cook and bottle washer for the pair of us. This is when those parts of my education that I had managed to endure – that's school, followed by an intensive commercial course at a local Tech and a lot of home study – led to my rising fairly quickly in my government office job to a level where my pay at least matched my outgoings on domestic bills with a little left for indulgencies. And when Brenda left I had a spare room I could lease out to make some extra pennies.

I offered to submit articles for the house journal, with the aim of getting the necessary commercial experience and setting myself off on the path of writing for money. I didn't expect to make much at first, but it was the initial stage of opening a window of opportunity. It never happened, though. My line boss was wedded to breathlessly tedious subjects and I just couldn't bring myself to drop to his level. As for fiction, well, I might just have suggested a weekly column on dough-making for all the interest that proposal generated. I went back to scribbling bits at home, but they never came to anything either, so I just stopped wasting my spare time and passed it in front of the TV, or nestled in other people's books – cheap ones from charity shops...

"You drifted off there for a moment," Dara said, breaking into my thoughts and returning me to the present and its pressing scenario. He nodded towards the performance area and a figure hovering in the spotlight.

Storyteller three was an oddball character.

He was quite tall and balding with the noble features of a true statesman but the unlikely garb of tweed jacket and trousers, suede shoes and a pink check shirt with red and yellow bow tie in bright polka-dots.

He reminded me of a clown – another clown entering the arena – and also of my old science teacher at secondary school, though this was only in stature. That teacher, Mr Elias Babbington, had a little more hair, and it was jet black and receding on each side so that it brushed back from a sharp point in the centre of his forehead. That particular feature, along with the flowing black robes Babbington insisted on wearing despite the fire risk associated with flapping them about in front of lighted bunson burners and small boys armed with matches, gave him the appearance of a night apparition, a stalwart of those Hammer horror films we shouldn't have been old enough to see: which is why the kids called him *Dracula*.

As Number Three took the floor he assembled a fold-up music stand, placed his manuscript on the rectangular rack and pulled over an old piano stool from a battered, unused John Spencer & Co upright wheeled into a corner. He sat with a grunt and a puff of dust from the chequered fabric seat, indicating how little the piano was used.

There was one other unusual thing about him: as he slumped down he folded himself into the stooped shape of a much older person, his face changing to accommodate a personality that was not his own (*another mask?*) and when he spoke, well, he sounded just like an elderly woman – a "vociferous lady in her late sixties," as he put it, peering out from familiar green eyes at the surrounding pack and adding a parchment croak to his voice. Now fully occupying the frame of an old lady, he read out the title of his story in character to some gentle laughter and began his narration, accompanied by some artificial arthritic grimaces, as if he was conversing with some invisible party in an adjoining chair.

Big Slip-Up at the Chattery Shop

Come on, we can sit out here in the back room, away from the melee. Give us some privacy. Things to talk about, hum? I can watch the shop through the hatch, roll back the sliding glass pane if anyone wants me, and Nina will deal with the last few customers. You take the armchair in the corner there – that's it! Chuck the toy kangaroo over behind the door; he belongs to our driver, calls it *Roo*, likes to have it on the passenger seat of the van when he goes out delivering or picking up donations. Tidy myself up. Slip off the tabard and fluff up my dress. Better. Comfy now. Right! Can't believe I'm a celebrity. Local paper. Ooh, such fun! Put your little tape recorder on the table there. That's it.

So, what is it they say? "Charity shall cover the multitude of sins." That's my life for certain, ha ha. Others have called it "That most excellent gift." Whatever they say, it's served me well for the best part of my working life. And now I'm leaving *I'm* the one getting the excellent gifts: "*In recognition of your long and devoted service*" it says on the card.

I can't believe I've been here nearly three decades. But I always wanted to help people and when they advertised the deputy manager's post all those years ago it seemed just the thing. Lots of changes since then. Now I'm running the show with my own deputy and six volunteers. Well, at least I was. Now I'm off, retiring. What a thing. And what a location! Don't you love it? Bang in the centre of the High Street, with the old fountain across the square with the oak tree next to it, framed like a picture in our bow window. It's like coming on holiday every time I come to work. I'm going to miss it.

I started the year we bailed out the Falklands. Bill, my late husband, was beginning to get sick then and we needed the *extra*, so I rallied round and went to the Sits Vacs. Streets were all covered with flags and bunting the week I arrived – to welcome our boys back home. The manager back then did a special display of toy soldiers in the window, arranged on a map of Argentina from an old atlas. Couldn't do that sort of thing now: too un-PC. Can't even advertise Christmas now, in case we offend the Muslims. The ones I know say they don't care: it's *our* tradition, like Guy Fawkes. Anyway…

The location's brought in loads of folk, buying or browsing and bringing us bags of things. They like to pop in for a chat, so we ended up calling the place *The Chattery Shop*, not a charity shop, ha ha. Or a *thrift* shop, as they call them in America, apparently. Ages ago, that was: the naming. Don't know who thought of it. I know we're part of a big charity organisation, but they let each of their shops name themselves, as long as it's underneath their own logo and brand colours – so we called ourselves that. Good, eh?

They've all been very kind to me now I'm finally on my way: the chocolates, flowers and the champagne. That was from Nina, bless her. Would you like a glass? No? I must stop, it's my third already, but I do like a little tipple. Only since Bill died, mind, a few years back. He was a railwayman for 20 years, like his father. Then he was with the Post Office for a while, in the sorting office, before the angina got him.

I've lived in the town all my life, and my parents before that. I went to the local primary, then the big Secondary and started at the laundry in 1963. That was the year President Kennedy was shot. They had a big black and white TV at work in the canteen and we all stood round watching it, couldn't believe it. You remember that man Jack Ruby? He looked exactly like Nina's great uncle Ken, only without the hat. Anyway, I met Bill a year later, when I was still a teenager, at a railwaymen's Christmas dance and we started going out.

We were married in '66 at St Winifred's and the organist, bless her, played our song, *I Love You Because*. Bill was a great Jim Reeves fan all his life, had loads of his records. I brought most of them to the shop when he died, did a display, sold them on, all a bit painful. He couldn't have children, bless him, but my sister has a couple, grown up, one with babies, so that made up for it. Allowed me to be a granny, at least.

You've noticed the re-fit. Shop's all bright and sparkly now, new fittings and so on. For the new manager. Actually, it's my deputy Nina, so I hear,

70

moving up one. Good luck to her. If her time here is as happy as mine...
etcetera etcetera. Ha ha.

They've been happy times, mostly. The worst time was what I called The
Big Change, back along, when head office decided to make us – finger
quotes – "more commercially viable by encouraging greater footfall in a
competitive market environment." Whoopsie-do! Putting the prices up to
pay for another bunch of pencil-pushers, I said. I'd been running the shop
myself for a while then, full-blown manageress. Anyway, in came all these
new regional bods who wanted to change everything – and not for the
better either.

One of the first was a young man about 22 who was awfully curt with
customers, re-jigging displays while people were actually looking at them,
getting in the way. *Darren*. He was a thin lad with spidery fingers and
multi-coloured jumpers and a real pain. Interfering, acting all superior to
me and the clients. Quite rude to our van driver, telling him he should
bring donated stuff round the back, out in the yard and up the staircase –
hell of a steep drag for him – instead of traipsing through the front of the
shop with loads of plastic sacks. Anyway, Darren left suddenly, something
to do with stomach pains, and good riddance.

And another glass. This is nice stuff. Well, in as much as I know
anything about champagne. All I know is the bubbles get up your nose and
make you sneeze. Choo! Hubby Bill was a milk stout man and I always
liked a splash of brandy and Babycham when we went out to the club.

So! After dippy Darren we had brash Glenda, or Mrs X as I used to call
her because that was how she should've been certified: unsuitable for
children – or adults, come to that. In she comes with a flourish and *do this,
do that*. And she was from *Basingstoke*! What did she know about our little
rural town? Didn't help that Bill had only passed away about a month
before and I was a bit fragile, using work to soften the blow, though I don't
want to sound all soppy about it. Anyhow, she told me how to do the books
properly; told me to take care to separate the donated goods from the
bought-in stuff, that's the things head office has to pay for, buys in bulk
and vans around to its branches. The bought-in stuff is why all our prices
went through the roof and all the grannies and the benefits people began
complaining. She didn't care: all sounding brass and putting the i – i.e. *her*
– into Charity in a big way.

She wanted to change the opening hours from 9.30 to 8.30. I said no one
wants to go poking around charity shops at half eight in the morning, not
even those on their way to work; that was her idea. Besides, the volunteers
don't want to start that early and that would leave me on my own to mind
the shop, take in donations, rotate the stock, stick the rubbish you can't sell
into black bags out back for the bin men. Anyway, I mentioned Health and

Safety and she backed off.

Sorry, I got into a bit of a rant there, didn't I? Must be the champagne. It's just that running a small shop has its difficulties these days and, yes, I know charity begins at home, but I couldn't stand the woman. You can edit that bit off the tape, can't you? Recorders are so small these days, aren't they? Not like the blooming great Grundig reel-to-reel Bill's brother had. Used to tape the cricket on the radio.

Are you sure you wouldn't like a glass? No? Fair enough. I'll just have one more... Mmm. Now, where was I? Oh, yes, Mrs X.

She made me change the window displays to show off more bought-in stuff like cheap and tacky china figurines made in a mock-English style in Shanghai or somewhere. About as appealing as whooping cough and pricey considering they weren't proper porcelain. And when December came she demanded I take down the Nativity I'd put together with the volunteers because it might upset "people of other faiths." Really! "Bad for business," she said. "Might have a brick – and those windows cost an arm and a leg to replace." You know. She criticised me for spending too much time talking to the customers instead of pushing new lines, and wanted to replace most of the volunteers for being "a bit past it." Cheeky mare.

Anyway, she died, head office stopped bothering us and I got back my full managerial status. We had the police around briefly, but that soon settled down. See, Mrs X, *Glenda*, liked to arrive at the branch late in the day and snoop around on her own. We've got this yard out back, one floor down from the shop, where we store all the rubbish bags that are going to the tip. There's a metal fire escape that goes down to the yard, all the way from the third floor rooms below the roof, and she goes out there one evening, on her own as usual, nosing around the upper offices. It'd been drizzling apparently and she slips on the wet steps, goes over the rail and hits the concrete below, lights out. Ironically, she missed all the black bags full of chucked-out fabrics that might've broken her fall. Some to-do, I can tell you.

So. Me. Again, ha ha. The future? Not much to tell there. I'm going to spend more time with mum now. I moved in with her after Bill died. She's in her nineties and a bit woolly to be honest and needs quite a bit of TLC, but she can get around OK, without a stick. Sometimes she thinks our garden belongs to next-door and the postman's got a parrot in his van, things like that, but she's no real trouble. Bit incontinent but not enough to flood the house, ha ha.

Well, maybe one more glass...

Oops, look at the time! Need to close up soon, but we can stay on a few more minutes if you like. Today's my last day – but you know that. Reason you're here. Never thought I'd say that, last day, but it has to come to us all. Cheers.

The shop's always so quiet after closing, except for that one strip light in the back over the bookshelves, hums away like a little bee. I don't like killing things. If there's a spider or a fly or a bug I always get it on a piece of paper or in a jar and tip it out the window. Nina says she always scrunches the snails on the driveway outside her place when she's walking home. I couldn't do that, I'd feel awful, make me sick.

You know, before the late Glenda arrived we used to serve coffees and teas here for any customers who wanted them, but she stopped all that. Wouldn't let us ask "black or white?" We had to say "with milk or without?" Political correctness gone bonkers. Even Mrs Chinnery, she was born in Nigeria, thought that was daft.

Course, truth be known, that's how we got rid of Darren – you know, the thin one. He got to be such a nuisance, upsetting me and the volunteers with his nit-picking and his horrible kitschy jumpers, that I started slipping small doses of Epsom Salts into his coffee three times a day. Eventually put paid to that cocky little so-and-so. Took his leave rather *quickly*, ha ha.

Mmm, this is so nice. Not too fizzy.

You can never tell how people are going to be, can you? Whether they're going to get on with you or not. Especially those people you have to work with.

The regional boss I had before grotty Glenda, well, she was a poppet, really good to me. It was through her that I stayed in the job for so long. We got on like fiery houses.

I used to keep things back for her; special things; things that were probably a bit grand for our little shop-in-the-sticks. Jewellery, watches, the occasional piece of Spode. "Oh, that'll be just right for head office," she would say. Of course, I knew that the nearest they would get to head office would be her living room, because I often saw her wearing a pair of earrings or a brooch, or maybe a Tissot or a Skagen and I recognised them from some distressed deceased's relative's clear-out that had come in a few weeks before in a shoe box. I didn't mind because, I mean, she wasn't that well paid and it all helped to keep her in good stead – and me in a job, too, which was a big plus, especially with Bill's medical expenses.

I remember we had this dead chap's stamp collection in once. I'd been off for a few days with flu and came back to find that dopey Darren had priced them all individually and put the box out on the counter. I only realised what it was when I saw a customer rummaging through them and picking out a penny black marked at two quid. I don't think it was an ultra-rare one, not printed upside down or something, but that wasn't the point. So I took her money, let her leave and quickly squirreled the box out back.

73

For head office. Each individual stamp was in one of these little paper pockets – really nice collection, good condition. I reckon they fetched quite a bit, the lot together.

Do we get much trouble? How do you mean? Oh, from the customers. Occasional drunk, they're easy to get rid of mostly. The odd smelly one, unwashed; they're always the ones who want to hang around and chat the most, stinking the place out. A bit of minor pilfering now and then. Nicking from a charity shop! That's some kind of cheap, isn't it? I mean, look at our prices! No, that's just wicked; stealing from a charity.

Oops, the bottle's nearly empty. Just enough for one more, then I must chase you off and lock up, give Nina the keys.

Did you see the nice farewell flowers they gave me, and the painting? Of course you did. I'm so lucky. Most excellent, as they say. Like they say about charity, don't they? That most excellent gift. I said that before, didn't I? Mmm.

And there – down in one and it's all gone! Nice champagne; most excellent! Right, pause to compose my thoughts. Ooh, the room's getting a bit swimmy and I'm starting to giggle. Can't have that!

Anyway. Let me lean a bit closer. That's better. More *intimate* – for passing on state secrets. Ooh, you've got a nice face, close-up. You married? Course you are: quite a catch! For the right lady.

So, I was telling you about Mrs X. Well, I gave Mrs X a gift, a leaving present. Actually, I *was* the leaving present, really.

I was here when our late, unlamented Glenda came in the night she died, all spiky and nosy and wanting to see the ledgers and saying things like I was unhelpful, overweight and a bit whiffy. She was on about the books, suggesting impropriety with money, which was such a wicked, slanderous thing to say, and not true, not me, not with my girls, they're honest and hard working. She started on about the quality of the stock and the unattractive way we were displaying some of it. Then she was on about the store room being cluttered and began stamping up the stairs to the upper offices.

Well, I was going home – I'd had enough and it had been a long day, busy. Then she yells at me to come up and see the "disgusting mess" in the yard below.

Well, I trudged up, three flights of stairs to the top floor. I just wanted to be out of there and I'm not my best on stairs, better downwards. But when I get to the top floor she's on the fire escape, Glenda, right at the top, leaning over pointing at the black bags in the back yard. I went out and looked down, to see what all the fuss was about. A cat or a dog, maybe a rat, had nibbled open a couple of the bags and there was a bit of a mess –

nothing that couldn't have been tidied up with a brush before we re-opened.

Then she turns round and she's complaining about the state of the back windows, as if that was my concern. I'm a shop assistant not a bloomin' painter and decorator. Anyway, then she backs up against the railing and is leaning backwards to look up at the roof, rambling on about loose slates and pigeons, when her foot slips. She jerks backwards, goes to grab for the rail, and something snapped inside: I'd had enough. I just batted her hand aside and gave her a gentle shove. She went back over the railing like an Olympic diver, legs in the air, then a smack as she hit the concrete yard. She looked surprised as she went. Little squeak, no scream, big thump. I could see she wasn't going to get up, so I left her there, locked up and went home. Nobody knew. Police found her in a routine night patrol.

I went straight back down after she fell, quicker this time, spring in my step, and called head office: left a message saying that I was leaving for the day, given the time, and that Glenda was in the shop with her own set of keys so I was locking up behind her and she'd leave and secure the shop when she was finished. Then I went across to the newsagents over the road and I could see Bernie the owner was still inside, tidying up, so I knocked on the window and he came over and let me in.

I told him Mrs X was still in the shop and poking around and we laughed about it, then he made us a cuppa and while we were drinking it I had the brainwave to say "Did you hear that?" Like I'd heard a noise. Faint one, but still there, you know. On the telly they call it 'establishing an alibi.' Well, he said, no, he hadn't heard anything, so I said it must have been my imagination and we finished our tea and I took the bus home. It all came up at the inquest and they reckoned Glenda must have slipped on the fire escape and fallen not long after I left the shop, due to the closeness of the time of death. Nobody suspected me, especially considering the amount of cash found in her handbag!

Head Office asked me to leave, you know, which is a shame. Lots more changes since. Well, I'm getting my pension and I'm a bit forgetful these days, putting things in the wrong place, confusing people, saying the wrong things sometimes and not realising it. Just like my mum, I suppose. Bill would probably have said he loved me because of it. Nina's a lot younger – a bit more what head office is looking for these days, to attract the younger shoppers with more *disposable income.* Don't really know what the future holds for me now…

Whoops, nearly had the bottle over there. Still, it's empty…

And here's Nina to lock up; looking very determined, tee-hee. You're off too, are you? Well, it was nice to meet you. It's very good of you to come down and interview an old girl about her retirement. Don't forget your little tape recorder. Your photographer came at lunchtime and took some nice pictures – one in the main shop, one in the stock room, one with all the girls and the flowers and things, one snap of all of us lined up on the fire escape steps with champagne glasses raised...

I hope I haven't said too much out of place, I'm not used to the Third Degree. No, seriously, you've been very charming. If I've spouted off, it's all that booze, makes me chatty as an old hen. The chattery shop chatterbox, eh? Cluck cluck, tee-hee. So use some *judicious editing*. When do you think the article might appear? I'll have to order a few copies for the family, friends – and myself! Sometime next week? Oh, the next edition! That's quick. Could be front page? Gosh, you'll make me feel all important. I'll get a swelled head.

I wouldn't have thought I was that interesting; it's just a job. Not exciting. Just doing a bit of charity in a difficult world. They say it's a gift...

***

"That enough?" reporter Dave Phelps asked his wife Nina as they moved away from the pickled Alice Carter, manageress, retired.

"More than enough!" Nina replied with a mixture of shock, delight and bitterness. "It's taken me two years, but I knew I'd get there."

She also knew that the reputation of her late mother Glenda – Alice's despised Mrs X – would be vindicated at last. Alice had no idea of the family connection when she employed Nina.

With the murder confession already on tape it would not be long before the not-so-sweet Alice Carter explained to the authorities how, after the fatal shove, she had stuffed Glenda's handbag full of enough cash from the previous week's takings to implicate her former boss in the thieving that her own shop manager Alice had been carrying out for years – a fiver, tenner or a twenty at a time. The retirement interview ploy had worked a treat and justice would finally be served.

Nina squeezed her husband's hand, then politely ushered the tottering Alice out of the shop and locked the door behind her for the last time. She did not offer Alice a lift home.

Seeking Charity

For the final few lines of his story, post-monologue, our remarkable chameleon became himself again. His own self restored, his story told, he stood, pushed the stool back to the piano, bowed to the ripple of audience applause and sank back into the comfy arm chair he had left earlier, his previous obscurity in the background murk regained.

I'm no stranger to charity shops myself, and many of them are just like the one in that story, though without the casual death plunge. I buy all my books within their disinfectant-scented walls; never get anything new from a dedicated bookshop as literally everything can turn up on charity shelves at any time, cover prices ranging from pence to a few pounds – and I'm in no hurry to read the latest blockbuster anyway. They create new worlds for me, these cut-price tales; worlds a lot kinder or more interesting and exciting than the one I barely exist inside where no-one cares, my writing is unappreciated or openly disparaged and people hide in their own defensive cocoons. Old weirdy Will…

I get ideas, writing ideas; they expand my consciousness, take me into ideological playgrounds I never knew existed – from fictional tales of delicately-structured and poignant relationships to less-fictional exposes of a dangerous New World Order intent on brainwashing and moulding the population to its greedy will. I don't know how much I believe about any of this stuff, from tender human emotions to their darker side, but I keep an open mind. Sadly, most of the minds I encounter are as closed as a… well, just closed; rejecting any alternatives to the comfortably-bland ideology they've permanently locked themselves into. *"As long as my favourite soap opera is still on, I'm happy…"* I hear that all the time. Keep the herd happy with bread and circuses…

I was starting to tell Dara some of this stuff when a large, hairy guy appeared from the shadows and stepped centre stage. He was thick-set and tattooed on each arm but his sharp blue eyes belayed any biker appearance, suggesting a sensitive soul behind the spreading facial mat. With his leathers and a crucifix at the neck he could have been a bass player in a heavy metal band and that reminded me of my own teenage days singing in a modest little combo playing covers of other people's hits in a string of smoky pubs and clubs. The engagement didn't last long: I was so nervous and unsuited for the front-man responsibilities that it initially only lasted for one gig. Still, at least I was there.

I turned to Dara to say something else but he just tipped his head to stall the interruption and took my glass for a refill before storyteller four began his tale.

(*See page 87*)

PRO$ROCK PIZZA$

Quick Menu
(See main menu for full details)

The Genesis Pizza
Supper's ready with this one! Five meats, four peppers
and three cheeses to Phil you up!

The Yes Pizza
You'll awaken to this spicy seafood pantry again and
again – close to the edge of what's possible from a kitchen!

Emerson, Lake and Pepperoni Pizza
You'll need infinite space for this hot meaty monster; lots of chilli
plus your choice of toppings. It'll be touch and go if you can finish this one!

The Van Der Graaf Generator
Your time starts now with this killer of a pizza. A medley of meats
including the darkness of black pudding. Best enjoyed with a glass of la Rossa!

The King Crimson
Sex sleep eat drink dream – all great. But remember to tackle this one-time
21st century pizza main first. No cat food or larks' tongues – just
a great veggie pizza that'll keep your eyes wide open!

The Gentle Giant
Proclamation: on reflection this might be the best ham and pineapple pizza you've
ever tasted, and we're so sincere about that. Great choice for a reunion!

The Portnoy Special
A muscular, triple bass drum dream of a pizza with a dozen special
transatlantic toppings. Twelve steps... to heaven!

The Iron Maiden
The number of this beast is definitely #1. Holy smoke, an
aces high rocker of a pizza you couldn't imagine in your wildest dreams!

Extras and sweets
Marillionaire's Slice: Chef's dessert of the day, topped with sugar mice
The Pinky Floyd: A chilli, beetroot and raspberry dip to leave you comfortably numb
All of a Rush: The side orders, including potato skins, potato wedges,
cheese balls and garlic mushrooms to put you in the limelight and satisfy
both hemispheres
Tangerine Dream citrus sorbet: A 220 volt smash – a dessert dream
Soft Machine ice creams: Ten out-bloody-rageous flavours

The Genesis Pizza

Should you go back? he asked himself as the song came to an end. He tugged off the heavy but comfortable over-ear headphones and strands of his shoulder-length hair caught for an awkward moment in the adjustable headband. *Fuck,* he said to himself next as he picked the blond threads away from the slider, *I'm losing enough hair already at my age without pulling it out like this. Sloppy.*

Chance, a song by the eighties progressive rock band *Kleptomania Hyperprism* that had been playing on his Tascam HS-20 two-channel stereo recorder was still a great number, he thought: punchy, hooky, melodic and with solid lyrics and a great riff or two. It was one of his best compositions and one the band – *his* band – had performed with gusto, from a time when it was fairly successfully treading the boards of local pubs and concert halls. Without a doubt, it was a *Klep* song that would stand up brilliantly in the Noughties, even after that twenty year gap – especially with the enthusiastic contemporary revival of all things Prog – and its old 'live' cassette recording from a local gig was still impressive enough to put a spell on its composer/drummer.

As for that voice! My God, she could sing, even for her age. Then there were those two guitars – lyrical at one moment, harsh and antagonistic at the next – and the swirling keyboards, providing both an orchestral wash and an upfront spluttering of feverish Hammond, a.k.a Keith Emerson in full flow: *wow!* The stabbing bass, reminiscent of the late great Chris Squire, and his own drumming, band leader Phillip Redcar, 'Phil of the

81

Skins,' influenced by everyone outstanding at the kit from Buddy Rich to Vinnie Colaiuta via Neil Peart, to a whole host of others. His timing was pretty sharp too, from his teenage revelations listening to bands like Gentle Giant, Egg, and maestros like Chick Corea and Frank Zappa. Finally – last, but far from least – his song writing, encompassing everything outstanding from Genesis to Leonard Cohen. It would be tragic if Kleptomania Hyperprism didn't have a present-day revival. Even with that name! That had been Gordon's idea. Gordon!

Phil had called the four guys with the proposal, of course, having kept in touch with them over the years as they went about their elsewhere tasks. They all still played, though not in any major public fashion; maybe the occasional pub gig or wedding reception, working with other players, and privately noodling away at home. It would be a challenge to assemble them once more and a further test to actually get them back on stage together with no deps.

The historic roster comprised those twin guitars: a raucous, bald and overweight sales manager called Gordon Breen and his total opposite, a Laurel to his Hardy, the thin and bespectacled retired theology professor Don Welker; they were joined by recalcitrant bass player Bill Loadstone, lank-haired and permanently stuffed into faded denim, a former postman now partly disabled following a career-ending attack by a pair of guard dogs while he was delivering a package of wedding napkins to a small industrial shed. Finally, there was keyboardist and company director Terry Cowell, again the converse of bassist Bill, being ultra fit, neatly groomed, outfitted in expensive leather jackets and the owner of a successful haulage business. All old men now, but hopefully all still possessed with that singular spark that had made *Kleptomania Hyperprism* something special.

But Phil's trump card, if she showed up, was the gorgeous Sara Trieste, the ebullient former lead singer who had entranced all of them, even though she was just 15 when she joined the band, and had especially hypnotised Gordon who had carried a candle for the dark-haired beauty ever since. Mind you, even Gordon acknowledged that he would probably never be able to get within ten feet of her now, under her professional sobriquet Sahara, the owner of a string of beauty salons favoured by a bevy of illustrious celebrities.

Unless she joined the group again, of course…

Phil told his motley posse that the timing was perfect, with each former member now living back in their home town, a busy but modest city with a cathedral, a recording studio and a thriving music scene. The mellifluous Big Big Train had played there once, to great acclaim and a packed auditorium, and there were rumours that Swedish growlers Opeth might add the place to their tour schedule in the coming year. Even so, his former band mates hadn't seemed that keen on reforming – not even when he promised to do his best to encourage their gorgeous former lead singer to join the party. Well, except for Gordon, who was clearly up for it, whatever kind of it might transpire.

Still, he managed to set up a meeting to thrash out the idea in convivial and appropriate surroundings. Everything was set, his new songs were ready, his papers were in order, his demo recordings of the new songs had been duplicated on disks, his fingers were crossed and he was filled with anticipation. And Phil the grand drummer, writer and organiser still managed to be late…

The painted sign made the large, segmented gastronomic disk with its mix of chopped meats and peppers look mouth-wateringly appealing as it rocked slowly to and fro on the evening breeze.   Stripped proudly across its centre was the flashing red neon script that gave the name of the eating house, *PROGROK PIZZAS*, with a fancy treble clef taking the place of the G and the parallel lines of a dollar sign scoring the **S** like a crossed cheque.

PRO♪ROK PIZZA$

Two elderly men approached the sign, collars raised against an early September chill, lumbering slightly with a rhythmic side-to-side motion, though neither was especially stocky. The first, quite athletic-looking, paused for a cursory peer through the plate glass windows at the brightly-lit interior, his hands cupped either side of his brow; the other, slim and bespectacled, peered up at the glowing sign, said "Looks like the place" and they both went inside, eager to get out of the cold. A wave of comforting warm air hit them as a bell over the crimson door pinged to announce their arrival.

The restaurant was empty, save for one blond waitress in her early twenties, scuttling around behind a rudimentary bar at the far end of the narrow room, and two generously-padded old men who could have been her joint grandfathers. They were deep in conversation over a fluorescent pink menu in a nearby niche but looked up when the bell sounded. A string of strident greetings followed. As the newcomers joined their more punctual friends at the corner table near the front of the café hands were grasped, backs patted, drinks ordered and menus surveyed, gestures tempered by the guarded camaraderie of people who have not seen each other for some while.

"It's been a long time," said the man who had peered through the window, a swarthy and muscular fellow who looked like he worked out regularly. He wore a black leather jacket, tee shirt and jeans and had short, spiky onyx hair and a drooping black moustache. His name was Terry Cowell and he played keyboards in *Kleptomania Hyperprism*. Or used to.

The biggest of the quartet, spread generously over the edges of his padded red leather seat, appeared never to have lifted a weight in his life, except for his own generous tonnage. He nodded his acknowledgement, his huge clean-shaven head marked with the tattoo of a Celtic rune. They called him Gordon Breen, and Gordon played guitar in *Kleptomania Hyperprism*. Or used to.

"Sure has, Terry," he said. "How's the haulage business?"

"Turned more than 500K last year," Terry replied, giving his biceps a distracted stretch. "Nice little earner. How's the sales game, Gordie?"

"Pretty profitable. Stuck in the office now," Gordon replied, his thick fingers gripping the edge of a menu, his eyes straying to the tasty fare on offer. "Top management, like you."

"No problem with the tattoo?"

"Been with the firm too long. They never noticed it under the beanie back when I was out travelling."

"And what about Bill?" keyboardist Terry asked, addressing the other seated early arrival as he slipped off his leather jacket, draped it across the back of one of the table's four vacant chairs and flopped down with a relaxing sigh. "Still sorting letters?"

Bill Loadstone shuffled uncomfortably in his chair. His green eyes looked a mite furtive, his grey hair hanging lank to his shoulders; his denim jacket was peppered with stickers and buttons advertising band names, mostly those led by the bass, his chosen instrument.

"Retired," he said, with an air of bitterness. "Got set on by a pair of attack dogs when I was trying to deliver a parcel. On disability now. I can still walk, but it's painful." He glanced down at his lap and added: "At least the tackle still works. Just…"

Terry noted the adjustable aluminium walking stick with the grey PVC handle and grey rubber ferrule leant against a corner alcove; he gave a fleetingly sympathetic nod and turned to the fourth customer, Don Welker, who he'd met outside, the thinnest of the quartet with fluffy auburn hair, reddish cheeks and a dumpy nose tipped with round, metal-rimmed spectacles: the retired theology professor, complete with check woollen sweater, and the other guitarist.

"And you, Don. Still convening with The Almighty?"

"I don't teach anymore," Don replied, a hint of the melodious air of a country vicar in his tone. "Otherwise, I am in fine fettle and rather puzzled by our, otherwise most pleasant, meeting this evening."

"Oh, that's Phil!" Gordon snorted. "His idea. Get us all together again after, what, twenty years?"

"So, where is he?" said Terry.

"Late, as usual," Bill added. "Always the last at a gig."

"Which is crazy for a drummer, with all that kit to set up," said Gordon, easing his bulk into a more comfortable position on the insubstantial café chair. "Pretty poor for our esteemed leader."

The bell pinged as the red door opened again and, as if on cue, a wiry individual in a parka, hood up, fussed into the room sounding flustered. He had bright blue eyes, blond shoulder-length hair and a flimsy soul patch under his bottom lip. He was carrying a buff cardboard folder. Phil had arrived: Phil the drummer, writer and general organiser and the reason they were all here tonight.

The quartet let out a teasing cheer at the advent of their missing administrator and Gordon added: "Be late for his own funeral."

"Sorry, guys. Had an emergency at the care home. How's it going?" Phil rolled up to the table, slapped down the folder and patted his four compatriots on the back. Limping Bill the hound-harassed ex-postman winced but did not complain.

They exchanged brief reminiscences: Gordon was permanently office-based locally after several years of travelling the length of the country marketing eco-friendly cooking ranges; his estranged second wife was director of an arts centre and his only son was married and living in Canada. Transport boss Terry's family had also moved on, including his wife, leaving him alone in a suburban bungalow where he spent little time anyway, except when he was rearranging classical tunes on his domestic piano; his band gear was in storage. The dog-damaged Bill, though retired as a postie, was working part-time in the city's sorting office, running a small internet business with his wife and seeing his daughter through medical school; he played bass occasionally in his local for a trad jazz group. Don was still married to his childhood sweetheart after 30 years and the couple had a young son. Though retired, Don was still very much involved in campus life at the city's University where he gave occasional guitar lessons; he was currently writing a book on the origins of Christianity.

Phil surveyed his former cronies with a smile. Here they were at last, together at one table after two decades, drawn from all over the county to this little cafe in a quiet city centre side street. He knew *Progrok Pizzas*, a cafe dedicated to the best of British and European progressive rock bands from five decades, was the best possible venue for the gathering of all six members of the band Phil had formed, moulded, managed, written all the songs for, recorded and marketed for three years until their acrimonious split in eighty-whatever; the band, through numerous cajoling phone messages and emails, he was now planning to reform. At least, *hoping…*

His colleagues had been transfixed by the hundreds of colour and monochrome photographs and posters of celebrated musicians covering the walls and ceiling around them – Bowie, Springsteen, the Beatles, Dylan, Elvis, Lemmy, Gabriel, The Who… Now they were equally taken with the menus and their exotically-titled fare from the disquietingly Day-Glo pink menu. At a nod from Phil, waitress Jilly wiggled over in an appealing way to take the order, pen and pad raised expectantly.

Ample Gordon surprisingly plumped for the mega-sized King Crimson Pizza, described thus: *Sex sleep eat drink dream – all great. But remember to tackle this one-time 21st century pizza first. No cat food or larks' tongues – just a great veggie pizza that'll keep your eyes wide open!*

Athletic Terry chose the Emerson, Lake and Pepperoni Pizza promoted with the line *You'll need infinite space for this hot meaty monster; lots of chilli, plus your choice of toppings. It'll be touch and go if you can finish this one!*

With an ironic smile, battered bassist Bill picked the Gentle Giant Pizza, with the strap line *Proclamation: On reflection this might be the best ham and pineapple pizza you've ever tasted, and we're so sincere about that. Great choice for a reunion!*

For Anglican plucker Don it was the Van Der Graaf Generator Pizza. *Your time starts now with this killer of a pizza. A medley of meats including the darkness of black pudding. Best enjoyed with a glass of la Rossa!*

Drummer Phil took the Yes Pizza. *You'll awaken to this spicy seafood pantry again and again – close to the edge of what's possible from a kitchen!*

Jilly noted their drinks order, gave one of her delightful wiggles and sauntered back to the bar and out of sight into the kitchen at the rear.

As she disappeared, the familiar synthesizer introduction of a much-vaunted prog classic suddenly boomed from the café speakers and Terry gave a cry of delight as ELP's *Tarkus* swelled up into the previously peaceful background. "Now that's perfection!" he said, flexing his pianist fingers across the table in time with the disk.

"Hang on," Gordon said after a couple of minutes, screwing up his ruddy cheeks. "That's not ELP!"

"No, it's Jordan Rudess," the *Klep* keyboards player replied. "From his solo album *The Road Home*. Made after he joined Dream Theater. It's…"

"It's awful," Gordon interrupted angrily, going redder. "It's gotta be Emerson or nothing! How could you offend Keith's memory with an imitation?! What's this guitar solo? What's this naff vocal?"

"Hey, that's Steven Wilson singing…"

"Oh, don't set me off about Steven bloody Wilson…"

"Hey, Keith thought the track was alright!" Bill responded, suddenly remembering how much he and Gordon had argued back in Klep's halcyon days. "He said that Jordan's reading – what was it? – '*spits cordite, making Tesla Coils run for cover.*' Great line. So I'm happy with that, Keith was happy with that, and you should be happy too, Gordon. Don't be a prog snob, mate. Listen to all those jazz runs. It's brilliant – and Jordan's salute to one of his heroes!"

"I still reckon Keith was secretly pissed, not flattered," Gordon muttered.

"Well, I think it's okay too," Terry began.

He was interrupted by a voice booming from the kitchen door and a huge figure emerged from behind the bar.

"Who's complaining about my choice of music?" it asked.

"Les!" Phil cried. "Or is it still *Ogre*?"

"And what's happened to the mask?" Don added.

Enter Les Parchment, owner and prime chef of *Progrock Pizzas*, a bearded colossus with the look of hairy vintage wrestler Giant Haystacks. Before buying the café and transforming it into a shrine to his favourite rock music, Les had been the mainstay of legendary local three piece rock-blues unit *Ogre*, a name that he was often partial to using himself, as a nom de plume, when he ran a local guitar shop in the seventies. He was also remembered as *The Masked Guitarist* – a role immortalised in a cartoon poster drawn by his bass player and hanging in a frame over the bar – from a time when he wore a multi-coloured wrestling mask on stage, along with a yellow sweat shirt, short blue cape and shorts and crimson lace-up boots. Ogre was best known for its Hendrix, Groundhogs and Rory Gallagher covers.

Les reached down below the bar and reduced the volume of *Tarkus*, but he didn't turn it off. Then he strode across and shook the hands of his guests – even the critical Gordon who had the decency to blush, though that might just have been his weight, which he carried less gracefully than the taller and wider Les. They exchanged pleasantries for a moment and then Les made his excuses – "Better cook your food!" – and returned to the kitchen. Jilly poured and delivered the drinks on a tray and then returned to the bar while the revitalised band members supped and chattered, finally getting down to business.

Naturally, Gordon was first.

"We'll have to have roadies if we're going to do this," he demanded. "We can't lug all that gear about ourselves anymore."

"I did most of the lifting," the ultra-fit Terry reminded him. "You always needed help with your amp, anyway."

Wounded postie Bill added his two penny's worth with his grumble: "I can't manhandle Terry's Hammond these days, even with his help. And I can't sing the chorus to *Rounded* any more. Can't hit the high notes."

"And no-one's going to remember that Yes song it segued into," Gordon added.

"*Time and a Word…*" Phil prompted his portly guitarist.

"Whatever. And that bloody chorus: *Now I think that I'm rounded, Though I've never been grounded, With these lyrics I've been POUNDED, And I'm left feeling ASTOUNDED…*"

"It didn't go like that…"

"And, let's face it, Terry was never a Wakeman."

"It was Tony Kaye on that Yes song – and I think his style suited Terry perfectly," Phil replied while Terry took the thyme to nod sagely. "Anyway, I've re-arranged that song, without the Yes piece. Thought it might be a bit elderly for today's punters."

"Sara sang *Time and a Word* so sweetly," Don said clerically, under his breath.

Terry jumped in: "*Rounded*. Wasn't that the song about Gordon?" And he rubbed his belly suggestively. There was a brief chuckle before he added his own gripe. "I'm not wearing costumes again, like when we went all Glam-Prog. Or any of that damn face paint. Gave me skin problems."

"Not this time," Phil explained. "Tastes move on."

"Haven't we all," Bill murmured unpromisingly, absently stroking his damaged leg.

Theologist Don steepled his hands below his chin and mused: "I'm not against giving the old guitar a public airing again, even if it will be a bit louder than my contributions to the occasional church concert. But it doesn't really fit in with my Christian studies. Besides, you're an atheist, Phil."

"I'm an *agnostic*, Don," Phil said. "I may not be a Neal Morse, following a more religious path, but I certainly don't write black metal material. It's all pretty acceptable to the parish pious."

"Well, except for the fact that it's very loud. I don't think we could rehearse in the church hall."

"We never did. Anyway, I've found us a place, through Les, and it's a good size, a pretty dead room acoustically and really cheap."

"And it isn't as if we need the fame at our time of life," Don added. "We didn't even need it then, with our real jobs taking up so much of our lives."

They all remembered how they entered a talent competition a while after they had formed the band and won the first prize, a day in a local recording studio, plus a guaranteed airplay of their song on the local radio station sponsoring the contest. This was after singer Sara left and keys player Terry took the vocal chair. After one of the two tracks they laid down was aired, one fan rang in to say Gordon's guitar solo put him in the Rock God territory, along with Clapton and Page (though this was possibly facetiousness). Gordon, who was being interviewed at the time, live, was asked what he thought about being a God to which Gordon replied: "Oh, I can't answer that. I'm too busy feeding the 5,000. That's the number of watts pumped out from my amp." It was meant to be funny, but wasn't especially, and the band's popularity took a decided dip for a few weeks.

"Not my finest moment," Gordon said. "But I still think it was funny!"

"Remember when we were booked at that pub *The Lute Player's Elbow*?" Terry asked.

"*The Lute*," Phil corrected him.

"That's it! And we got there and the place was locked up and all the lights were off. Tried to ring the place from a phone box over the road: nothing. Then one of the neighbours came over and said the brewery had shut the place down overnight because the landlord had absconded with most of their proceeds, as well as their top waitress, and was being pursued in Spain."

"They gave us the elbow, all right," said Don.

"And we didn't get any loot," Phil sighed.

"Don't think they ever found him," said Gordon.

"What about that fight at *The Golden Pasture*?" Bill said. "When that twat with a Mohawk threw a pint mug at the stage and it hit the lighting rig on top of Gordon's stack, toppling it…"

"Right on my head," Gordon growled.

"You went out like a light – well, with the lights," said Terry, smirking.

"I was out for about five minutes and had this bloody great bump," Gordon replied, rubbing his head nostalgically.

"It's OK, it's gone now," grinned Don.

"And what about your Uni mate, Crichton?" Phil asked Gordon. "That idiot with the pyrotechnics."

"Hey, they looked pretty impressive…"

"When they worked. What about that time at Yeddington House when Crichton let off this massive explosion that blew Terry off the stage, set fire to the seating area carpet and filled the place with all that acrid black smoke."

"Well, at least it was the final chord of the last number…" Gordon said piteously.

"We just had time to clear out before the fire brigade arrived," said Terry. "Met them in the car park. I remember you told them it was some chemistry students buggering around."

"And you all black-faced from the smoke and looking like Al Jolson," Bill told Terry.

"The Uni was investigating that for weeks," Terry replied. "Just as well no-one actually saw Crichton plant the thing."

"Even though it was at the front of the stage," said Don.

"The audience were pretty stoned," Phil added. "We were lucky there. Didn't even get a bill for cleaning the carpet."

Then there was the first gig at a student ball where the band's then road manager (who didn't last long) provided all the additional stage gear – lighting rig, huge p.a. system, mikes, etcetera – but neglected to include the stage box, the crucial piece of equipment that linked it all together; and they had to rush around an hour before their debut looking for a replacement box from another band supplier as the original contractor had gone to Swindon for the weekend. Then there was the time that Bill had arrived for a gig and found his daughter and her friends had removed his bass from its case and replaced it with cans of fruit, which led to another wild dash in the night.

Finally, to Phil's relief, they got down to the practical issues of reforming: what gigs would be available, would they make money this time, would they actually record and release some of their songs to back up the return – and would it be a tour or just a series of scattered gigs on weekends and bank holidays? It began to get complicated. There was another pregnant pause in proceedings and then Gordon raised his hand, as if he was back in school.

"One thing," he said. And he put his finger on the elephant not currently in the room (except for him). "All this planning, all this recollecting, is academic unless we can get Sara."

There was a further mutual silence, accompanied by the closing bars of a muted musical ministering from Jordan Rudass.

"Do you think she'll turn up?" he added, hopefully.

"Still keen?" Don asked.

Before Gordon could reply Phil piped up: "I doubt it. I finally tracked her down on the net and sent her a bunch of emails with date and place and reason for. She sent one reply saying it was great to hear from me after all this time, gushed about the five of us and her business clients, but no commitment for tonight."

He remembered the poster they designed to promote those early gigs: a fantastic head-to-waist colour photograph of Sara dressed in a low-cut purple evening gown (approved by her parents), gripping the mike salaciously, her matching purple lipstick glistening in a spotlight, her mouth wide open in a sensual bluesy cry, her black tinted eyelids closed with apparent yearning, the image accompanied with the strap line: *She'll steal your soul and bathe it in spectral colours. KLEPTOMANIA HYPERPRISM.* This was a pretty loose tag that only came about after Gordon spotted the second word whilst rifling though Phil's record collection and insisted they "call the band that!"

"Hyperprism?" Phil responded. "We can't. That's an Edgard Varese piece from the 1920s."

"So it's out of copyright…"

"I don't think so…"

"So we'll steal it anyway. We'll say we couldn't help ourselves. A touch of, um, kleptomania set in."

And so a name was born. It sounded right somehow. It didn't have to make sense.

Still, back to Sara. Could the band go on without her?

"Do you really think we can reform?" limping Bill asked. "I mean, aren't we getting a bit past all this leaping about. We're all post-fifty and haven't played together in twenty years."

"We never did do much leaping," Terry said. "Certainly not from the organ, anyway. We're not likely to that now, either, with your leg injuries and Gordon's weight."

Bill nodded, pathetically.

"Hey, I'm comfortable, OK?" Gordon responded, lightly patting his favourite body part after his genitals.

"I've got a bunch of new songs," said Phil, tapping the folder beside him. "Lyric sheets, a couple of demo CDs. And you've all got copies of the set we used to play." No, it was Sara who used to do all the moving, he thought.

"Still got the attic studio, then?" Terry said and Phil nodded. He was about to say more about his set-up when Don interrupted.

"Hey, look at us," he said. "We're a bunch of old men. The only thing that would sell us to a crowd nowadays is having a bright young thing like Sara upfront and shining."

"There's nothing wrong with the music," Phil interjected, defensively, though in his heart he wanted to agree.

"Didn't mean to suggest it, Phil," Don replied. "It's great. And I know there are a lot of old fogies having a second and even a third wind on the Prog front now, just like ancient jazz and blues players. But is it all going to be a bit too much for us? I mean, with respect, look at Gordon's, um, immensity and Bill's disabilities."

Terry jumped in: "Anyway, as we don't have Sara I can't take over all the vocals from the keys again – and you certainly can't sing them from the drums, Phil. Not all of them, at any rate."

The debate went on acrimoniously for several minutes over copious amounts of drink until Jilly arrived with the pizzas and they all tucked in, assured that their formidable lead singer was a no-show, and turned to other matters, further amusing recollections and anecdotes, and the mood finally lightened.

"My son came in from school one day – he was only five – and, out of the blue, came out with 'Daddy, what's buggery?' I didn't know what to say," Don related.

"So, what *did* you say?" Terry asked. "Must've been tough for you, what with the whole Christian thing."

"Well, I said it was a difficult word that he should avoid and that I would explain it to him when the time was right. Then I just distracted him with some other business and he forgot about it, thankfully."

"You should have told him it was a cartoon rabbit," Phil threw in without a beat.

"What, *Buggery Bunny*?" Terry replied, cracking up.

"Catch phrase: *Who's up, Doc?*" Phil added, and the table erupted.

Don still managed to look embarrassed and, as with his young son, he changed the subject, attempting to introduce a bit of culture.

"All these thinkers here," he spread his arms. "Together in a café. It reminds me of Paris in the 1930s."

"You were *there*?!"

"Be quiet for a moment, Gordon! You know, when Jean-Paul Sartre and Simone de Beauvoir first heard about phenomenology in that coffee bar that led to Sartre's big opus, existentialism."

There was a moment's puzzled silence at the abrupt change of course from the genial God botherer.

92

Gordon spoke up first. "Jean who?" he said, looking both pasty and perplexed, a small portion of baked broccoli dangling from his lip.

"Philosophers," Don replied. "They're not a Gallic folk duo, Gordie. I'm trying to say they had this sudden illumination over the way they thought about things, about life. And here we are, after all this time, looking for…"

"I heard Sartre could sing jazz tunes and was one for the ladies," Phil said. "Just like Gordon."

"I don't like jazz," Gordon said, guiltily. There was a pause. "Except for Weather Report. And, OK, I still like the ladies…"

"Right back to Sara, and before," Bill said quietly, with the disappointed sigh of Eeore the donkey.

"Don't start on about Sara," Gordon retorted, a delicious image of their former lead singer flashing before his puffy eyeballs. "That was a long time ago. And she's clearly not going to turn up!"

"I was just saying that maybe we could get a breakthrough tonight in what we want to achieve, like Sartre and Beauvoir," Don said, attempting to point his friends towards Christian positivity using a philosophical imperative.

"Like Gordon, Sartre attracted the ladies, just like Phil said, even though he was an ugly mother," Bill added, adjusting the lie of his walking stick and showing a surprising knowledge of French philosophy. "Sartre, not Phil," he clarified. "Two of a kind."

"Up yours, Postman Pat," Gordon snorted, but with a self-satisfied smirk. Yes, he always had done well with the lassies, especially when he was a little less lumbering.

"Sartre also did Donald Duck impersonations," Phil added sharply, tapping the folder beside him to a glare from Don. "Can we get on?"

But they didn't, putting the big decision off for as long as they could, tucking into their beers and food.

Gordon was shovelling in his massive King Crimson, his colleagues astounded that a man so huge had gone for a vegetarian option, which he explained away as his attempt to eat more healthily, a claim rather diluted by the dustbin lid size of his meal. Still, wiping a drooling of mozzarella from his chin, he decided it was time to add his tale to the sudden dip in dialogue.

"We had this milkman in the village, back-along, and he was known to stay longer at some houses than others," Gordon said. "Places with pretty widows or where the husband was away a lot of the time. You'd see his cart parked outside for ages, and then he'd come out looking a bit ruffled, red-faced and tucking his shirt in."

"We get the picture," said Terry. "Giving more than a pint-a-day service."

"Don't know if he could manage a pint," Gordon said, with a coarse grin. "But he was definitely providing a servicing. Anyway, there was this redhead called Sheila that he was partial to, lived on a big plot near the top of the village. And, on the day I'm getting to, her husband was away in the clouds on his hang glider. He had this stiff-winged thing with a motor and was always pootering around the village. Only this day his wife thought he was in town on business.

"Anyway, hubby comes buzzing over the village and he's got this huge pair of binoculars with him. I think he was a bit of a perv too and liked to spy on women sunning themselves in their back gardens. So they said – nothing proved. Rumour afterwards was that he'd twigged that his misses was having it off with the milkman, but again nothing proven.

"So, Mr Rotors was flitting over the property when he saw Mr Milko trotting out of *his* house, about 50ft below, and looking a bit, what's the word? Furtive! So, hubby's trying to get a close-up of the house to see if he can spot his wife looking half-dressed or whatever when he loses his grip on the binoculars. That's what he told the police. So these bloody great German field glasses go spinning away from him, he nearly loses it and just misses crashing into some trees, but the 'noculars come down and hit Milko square on his cap just as he's getting into his cab. Kills him outright.

"Well, hubby gets away with it – doesn't even get to court – as the fuzz said that even if hubby had known about the affair there's no way he could've aimed a pair of 'noculars from so far away so's they'd hit anyone on the noggin and the matter was dropped. Milko had no family anyway and hubby and wife got divorced not long after. Makes you think, don't it? You never know what's gonna fall on you from a great height…"

With further 'on cue' timing, the outside door suddenly flew open and hit the far wall with a heavy bump, its plastic OPEN sign shivering on its chain like a frightened flat fish. There was a sudden inrush of cold air, a scattering of desiccated autumn leaves and the muffled sound of traffic growling up the distant high street. The gobbling gourmets stopped gobbling mid-gobble, Bill's walker crashed to the floor and five jaws proverbially dropped as a deep and silky feminine voice purred "*Hello, boys!*"

Framed by the doorway, leaning impudently on the handle with her head on one side and lit with a quizzical smile, was a very tall, slim and stunning woman. She was dressed completely in black: black knee high boots, black leather trousers, black leather belt with silver studs and buckle, black tee shirt with a claw-like Magma insignia in gold across her ample bosoms, a black choker around her neck with a pearl stud in the centre, a long black duster coat and a black corrugated beanie from which spilled a wild cascade of jet black hair flowing down over her shoulders.

Sara Trieste had arrived – making an entrance again, the way she always did on stage all those years ago.

Gordon croaked: "Christ, it's Floor Jansen!"

"Sara!" Phil cried, his chair toppling back as he leapt to his feet. "We thought you weren't coming."

"Well, I'm here now, Phil and it's great to see you guys. I can see that you've started without me, but I need the loo!"

With that she sailed towards Jilly, ordering her pizza and a mineral water on the hoof, and disappeared into the Ladies. Phil closed the entrance door with his foot and picked up his chair.

"She came!" Gordon breathed, overwhelmed.

Apart from her jaw-dropping looks, Sara Trieste had acquired a sweet, husky and seductive voice of warm molasses and her long-time admirer felt a sudden stirring in his loins that he had not experienced for several years.

"She looks amazing," said Don admiringly. "So glamorous – and strong."

"She's strong all right," Gordon agreed. "Certainly if the past is anything to go by. She was a star discus and javelin athlete at school, apparently. Strong arms. She could beat me off any time I got too frisky."

"Lucky you!" said Phil with a vulgar smirk.

"No, I mean she could push me off, fend me off. Not the other! I never got anywhere with her in the rumpy-pumpy department, unfortunately. You know that! Not for want of trying. God, she's still as amazing as when she was... underage."

"Not jail bait any more, that's for sure," Terry sighed and returned to his Emerson, Lake and Pepperoni.

When she returned, Sara swept into the empty seat next to ringmaster Phil in a cloud of exotic perfume and five old men sighed with gratitude, even the theologian.

So far their meet-up had been like one of their songs, Phil thought: a twiddly little keyboard intro (their tentative first greetings, full of mystery about what was to come); a slow but strident theme (full of confidence for a grand denouement somewhere down the line, each player setting out his individual stall): a sudden aggressive riff (taking the subject of their gathering by the proverbial horns and running with it wildly as if pursued by Pamplona bulls); the big vocal narrative (what's planned and how to achieve it); more riffing (a repeat of themes already established); and the rising promise of a grand finale yet to emerge – all of it undertaken at unwarranted length. Now here was the mood-shifting climax: the arrival of the femme fatale. Everything changes, he thought, and everything remains the same.

"It's great to see you again," Gordon said, for once ignoring the remains of his meal. "I was sorry when you left."

"You asked me to leave, remember?" she replied, her eyes twinkling with mischief.

"That's only because I fancied you like mad and you were sleeping with *him*," chubby Gordon replied, pointing at scholastic Don.

God, did I actually say that? he asked himself. *Well, too late now – and it was true.*

"That's what he let you think – and me," Sara replied. "Sorry, Gordon, but you never used to look after yourself – um, you never changed your rehearsal clothes and, frankly, you tended to whiff a bit, especially when you wore that Neoprene suit to a gig for a gag – and you're still a bit disorderly now."

Gordon ruffled. "I don't smell. I'm just a bit... matured. Sort-of antique fragrant. Comes with being a bit generous round the middle."

"Bloody generous, mate," said Bill.

"Aged like an old cheese," Terry added, smiling. "But with great lasting power."

"Anyway," Sara continued, before another battle broke out. "We just went around together. For a start, I was too young to drive, and for other things too. I was only fifteen, for God's sake. So Don took me to and from the rehearsals and the gigs – and saying he was my boyfriend, and all that suggested, was a good way of keeping you off my case."

Gordon snorted and took a bite of his Crimson.

"Don't be upset, I was fond of you, I was fond of *all* of you. It's just that I wanted to *sing* not *shag*." She paused. "All that came later." She paused again. "Though not that much later. And not with Don, bless him." She gently squeezed that theological arm on her other side and Don peered at her over his fragile specs, offering a sweet little smile with a hint of historic longing.

That done she grabbed the back of her chair, spun it round and dropped back into it, spreading her legs either side of the seat with her arms across the back like a determined saloon girl.

"So," she said. "Are we going back on the road?"

96

No-one knew what to say; then they suddenly exploded as one in an elated melee of assent and tumbling greetings.

"I never thought you'd come," Phil said, gripping her nearest shoulder lightly with affection and happily tapping his portfolio with the other.

"Wouldn't miss it for the world," Sara said.

Her ruby lips pouted slightly as she spoke and, for a moment, Phil could see a glimpse of that pretty teenager who had taken their band by storm two decades earlier. At first he had made it quite clear that there would be no female vocalist, to avoid anything divisive among five hormonal men. But then he was totally charmed by her audition – arranged by infatuated Gordon, of course, who had seen her warbling in a folk duo – a performance that led to a succession of triumphant part-time gigs.

"Where have you been and what are you doing now?" Don asked her.

"You look stunning."

"Thank you, Don. The years have been kind to you too," Sara said – or Zara as she had always preferred to be called back then. Terry used to joke that she liked a Z at the start of her name because she was like a female Zorro, always favouring black jumpers and slacks. She also reminded him of beauteous Avenger Emma Peel. Nowadays, Sara was known as Sahara and ran a string of top drawer beauty salons, popular with a number of prominent actresses, girl bands, solo artists and other celebrities.

She was beginning to explain how the business had come about when Jilly suddenly appeared as if from a magician's hat with her meal. SaraZaraSahara had chosen the Genesis pizza, slim and extra-crispy. *Supper's ready with this one! Five meats, four peppers and three cheeses to Phil you up!*

"Now that's a corker too," Gordon said, wishing he'd made the same choice.

"Plenty of nourishment for a growing girl," Sara said.

"Hey, if you get any taller you won't get out the door," Terry chimed in. "It's amazing how you've grown – transformed! How tall are you?"

"Six-one."

"*Jesus…*"

"No, I don't think He was that tall," Don murmured, and he would know.

A hovering Jilly asked Sara if she could get anyone anything else, noting that the guys had nearly finished both their pizzas and their drinks while Sara had started neither. As she drew level with the table the door behind her crashed open again and the pretty waitress gave a sharp shriek as she was grabbed from behind by a youth in a hoodie who back-kicked the door shut and aimed a pistol at the diners.

"*Nobody move!*" he barked.

Behind the hood the interloper was sallow-skinned and sunken-eyed, as if he was either very ill, very drugged or very hungry. Perhaps all of the above. Tufts of blond hair rippled over the top lip and cleft chin of his undernourished face like the tentative early stages of some kind of beard or an indication of low self-care. He was slightly taller than the waitress, was holding her tightly and his gaze was close to murderous.

"What the fuck…" Gordon began

"Shut it, fatty!" came the reply.

As for Jilly, at the sound of the cracked and menacing voice she gasped: "*Norman?*"

"Not Norm, you know that," he growled, easing his hood back with his gun hand.

"*Chancer…*"

"Better! Yea, it's me, babe – now let's go quietly down to the till and let's empty it – and the rest of you stay nice and quiet in your seats and no-one will get hurt. You could put your wallets on the table to save time."

They were all looking at the gun and wondering where the hell the lad had got it from. It appeared to be real enough. Terry, who was a bit of an expert on firearms, whispered to Phil: "Looks like a Browning M1900. Yank gun, probably came in from Belgium. Can do us damage…"

"And keep your lips buttoned," Chancer added, glaring at them and pulling both a trembling Jilly towards the bar and generating every possible fifties gangster movie cliché he could muster. "*Wallets!*"

The music had long since changed to Transatlantic's *The Whirlwind* which, at seventy-eight minutes, provided little opportunity for Les the Ogre to hear any café commotion from his isolated position in the kitchen, occupied with fulfilling telephone orders.

"Why aren't you with Alex?" Jilly asked, now terrified of the boy she had once dated at school since she heard of his criminal activities with a dangerous criminal known as 'Axe.'

"He's banged up," Chancer replied. "Now shut up and empty the till."

The group of musical pensioners (and one hottie) watched the show, each wanting to act but not knowing how to intervene – how to protect both Jilly and Sara – and Gordon just wanted to get under the table and hide. Nobody had produced their wallets.

It was at this inopportune moment that Bill got a sudden severe bout of cramp in his injured leg. Unable to stop himself, he leapt to his feet and banged his chair back with a pained cry of "*Oh, shit!*" Chancer, who had taken his eyes off the shop's clientele for a brief moment while he ogled the till, swung back and took a shot at the frightened postman. There was a huge bang and Bill gave another shriek, this time hit a glancing blow in his already-tender thigh. He fell back into his chair and buckled.

Phil was on his feet immediately, glared at Chancer and barked *"That's enough!"*

Jilly squirmed, at one hopeless and scared, at another embarrassed and angry. Then she stiffened and, with sudden resolve, grabbed her former boyfriend's gun arm and pushed it towards the floor. He only had the chance to bark *"Bitch!"* before Sara grabbed her untouched Genesis Pizza and lobbed it across the café on a perfect trajectory with Olympic force.

The Genesis Pizza hit the little thug in the forehead. He screamed, bits of hot meat, cheese and peppers cascading into his eyes and under the lip of his hood. Sara bounded forward and gave him a karate chop to the shoulder, Jilly leaped aside and Les appeared from the kitchens in a white pinny and clutching a pizza peel, dangling at his thigh like a large fly swatter, with a startled "What the fuck's going on?"

He saw his shocked waitress, the swaying youth and the dangling gun and without further ado punched the intruder in the face, his knuckles ploughing into warm pizza topping in the process. Chancer pirouetted to the ground and Gordon, in a remarkably energetic burst for one of his size, lurched across the room and fell on the felled felon's chest. Chancer gave a winded wheeze and passed out. A cheer went up.

"Looks like your pizza choice has brought us to the Promised Land," clerical Don said to Sara.

"I told you she was a prizewinning discus thrower at school," Gordon said from the floor. "And it looks like she's mastered kung-fu as well."

"That was some throw," Phil said, joining the tableau and putting his arm around Sara. "You're still amazing."

"So," she replied with a wide smile. "I repeat: when do we go back on the road? I'm really looking forward to singing *Rounded* again, especially with that lovely Yes tune."

Bill was patched up by a bright and breezy paramedic in a yellow and green ambulance and the hapless Chancer was picked up and cuffed by two grim-faced patrol officers in their yellow and blue BMW. The former told Bill "It's just a flesh wound, mate. Quick clean and a plaster," and one of the PCs told Gordon "Not this little pest again. His mate's in jail, you know, and I reckon pizza face is about to join him." His partner added: "But not at the same one. Not having them conspiring anymore." Chancer just whined: "Get me a towel!"

As for the historic six-piece *Kleptomania Hyperprism* – their name sensibly but unimaginatively paraphrased to *Klepto* – performed a series of triumphant shows in the city and across the country, fronted by the dynamic Sahara and at one stage providing support for hot new band Windchime and a revitalised but equally-mature Focus. The tour, supported by a major agency, was an unexpectedly harmonious affair: the band members didn't fall out; they recorded an album with the backing of the same radio station that had broadcast their original contest winner; they even won a coveted award for best newcomers from a national rock magazine; and they sang *Rounded* better than they'd ever sung it before. A happy ending made both in heaven and popular romantic fiction. Everything was going extraordinarily well and the men had each put their jobs on hold to accommodate a potential brighter future beckoning, though Sahara continued to administer her expanding salon empire.

All until...

All until Gordon collapsed with a heart attack following a sell-out show in Leeds. Two upcoming gigs were cancelled while the other dates were postponed, as his mates waited for their chubby guitarist to recover. But the interruption was enough to break the spell and they were never to play live again, having exhausted their final hyperprismic breath. At least on the live circuit. There was still public demand for their work and organiser Phil made sure that this time there would be evidence of their achievements, recording their first (and last) CD – *Prism* – which sold well on the European Prog market. Gordon's parts were dubbed later when he came out of hospital.

Phil expanded his home studio and began working with a number of international companies to provide original music for radio, film and television. He even recorded Sahara's much-vaunted solo album, *Darkest Phoenix*, where she employed her former band mates to provide the instrumentation – excluding Don this time, who had finally completed his much-delayed book and was out promoting it (but in a Christian way). Sahara's line-up included the rehabilitated and much leaner Gordon, the one-time chunky Guitar God who was having a new lease of creative life. For Gordon was now an enthusiastic devotee of both his local gymnasium, BigSlim Universe, and (more especially) a fashionable beauty salon run by a wonderful, dark-haired Rock Goddess of his acquaintance...

A Tune in June

"I like the way Reader Four borrowed a secondary character from Two to finish off his story arc," Dara told me. "Giving 'Axe' Bell's lieutenant 'Chancer' a fitting send-off. Tied up a loose end."

"Do they do that often?" I asked, though I wasn't really interested. I was still digesting the saga of *Kleptomania Hyperprism.*

"Occasionally," Dara replied. "I look upon my readers as a single organism, sharing ideas, making casual or causal links. That's why almost none of them ever say who they are. They prefer to remain anonymous. It's a very special, singular kind of club."

I wasn't listening. There was a brief silence and then Dara burst out with: "See! A heroic woman! In the pizza shop. You must have known there was one in there somewhere. They do exist, Will."

He didn't get the reaction he expected. But at least I nodded, still distracted

"I was in a band once, briefly," I told Dara. "Very briefly…"

He nodded, as if to concur. "You said…"

"So was my dad. Jazz trumpeter."

"Yes…"

"Of course, for me it was around the time when almost everyone I knew was either in a band, knew a band or one of its players, acted as a roadie for a band, or drove the guys around to rehearsals and gigs because he was the only one who owned a van.

"I only did one gig at first, in a pub. It was horrible, full of rowdy and disinterested drunks. A bit later I was talked into giving it a go again. We even wrote our own songs – me and a mate – and the band was getting a bit of local popularity until our guitarist fell off the Old Man of Hoy. He was on a rock scaling weekend in the Orkneys and broke both his legs. He was only about twenty five feet up the four hundred and fifty foot stack when he lost his footing, but he was still lucky he wasn't killed. He'd been warned not to free-climb the thing, but he had more bravado than brains. Just an enthusiastic amateur. He offered to carry on, playing from a wheelchair, but my mate said it didn't look too rock'n'rolly so the band folded.

"We got together a few years later, like the kleptomania boys, aiming to try and re-ignite the whole thing. I was even up for it, despite the previous disasters, to give myself a chance to write some lyrics again, and maybe get out there with people. But it all fell through – less spectacularly than in the pizza story, mind you. We all agreed to meet again and finalise things and… well, everyone just forgot. Don't know where they all are now."

It was through that first band, the one playing covers of chart numbers, that I met June. She'd been part of the small and rowdy audience and had seen how nervous I was trying to hold all the tunes together, clutching a little notebook with the lyrics scribbled inside just in case I forgot any of the words, which I did, often. She came over at the bar and just started talking, which was odd because women rarely talked to me as, well, I suppose I don't come over as the strapping, confident type who'll press them to my chest and protect them from other manly predators. Maybe I seemed harmless and easily manipulated. Anyway, we hit it off: we had similar tastes in music and she was apparently writing a book: a historical romance set in Regency times. A right little Georgette Heyer clone, though I didn't tell her that as I didn't want to discourage her the way I had always been put off my literary expectations by the purposefully indifferent.

She had this explosion of curly black hair which might have been dyed, a string of freckles across her nose and cheeks, pale almost translucent skin, dark penetrating eyes with heavy mascara accents, a pouty blue-tinted mouth and a gorgeous, shapely body squeezed into a knee-length black dress and tights. I was smitten, I have to admit. She was a typist for a firm of solicitors, but she seemed much sharper than that, more like a legal secretary, and undaunted by criticism, which was good for me!

We had what they call "a whirlwind romance," though at a distance physically. I mean we were happy together but we weren't streaming up any car windows along the way. Not sure whose fault that was. Still, things looked brighter when she told me she'd been forced to leave her flat and I offered her the spare room – the one sister Brenda vacated when she did the aisle thing. We got on okay and my two-storey-terraced was closer to her office, so she agreed. I was even more smitten with her by then and thought the new arrangement would lead to, you know, something a bit more intimate. Well, it didn't.

After a couple of weeks of friendly interaction but no signs of any naked wrestling she announced that her boyfriend – boyfriend? First I'd heard of him – needed a place to crash and could he move into her room – air quote – "*just for a few days?*" After three weeks I suggested they leave and they did, without any real complaints, I think they'd found a flat to exercise in, and I never saw her again. He was a cocky sod, handsome, slim, physically fit and superfluously healthy; cycled everywhere, always in those fluorescent body suits that make your ribs, and everything else, stand out provocatively. What was it with bloody cyclists? Brenda had fallen for one as well and he'd turned *her* inside out too.

At the time I thought it was odd that I should remember those details at that precise moment in *Dara's Bar*...

Spokes

There is a striking moment as you unexpectedly lose control when you realise *I'm not going to get out of this...* Or, depending on the swiftness of an event, *I'm dead...*

Especially when the steering wheel whips out of your hand, when the world around you revolves frantically, where you hear the squeal of friction and smell the scent of burning rubber, when you want to vomit or to leap out of the way, to safety.

Then you hit a grassy edge, the whirling stops and the plunge begins; when you see the rocks below racing towards you and you realise the noise that you can hear over the crash of tearing metal, soil and rock is the sound of your own scream echoing behind you.

Finally there is the hit, the crunch of steel and glass, the hard stab of a fatal injury and the darkness; the moment when the world slips away from the lingering image of a sunny day, its gentle breeze and the narrow cliff-side road; when you feel a faint reflection of an approaching cyclist, right in the middle of the carriageway, head down and struggling up the gradient overburdened with two packed panniers, of slamming on the brakes and the car going into a spin. Then nothing...

Seconds earlier, architect David Conrad had just spotted the granite two-mile marker for the tiny Cornish village of Penhaven, but had seen neither the *Sharp Bend* sign nor the three red and black distance posts pinned along the cliff drop with decreasing white lines of three, two and one. He was too busy chewing over the past and the reason for his abrupt journey to explore secret West Country hideaways. As the cyclist appeared, he braked his sports car hard and everything else became a blur.

Night fell. Or, at least, it seemed like it. He had no sense of time passing.

And then he was sitting in the driver's seat, as usual, his heart pounding, his hands glued to the steering wheel at ten-to-two in a white knuckled grasp, staring wildly at the descending road unfolding on the passenger side of his slewed vehicle, the sun warming his neck.

The cyclist he had just missed annihilating – or who had just missed annihilating *him* – had apparently continued up the hill without a backward glance. He had disappeared so completely that he just might not have been there in the first place. So David reckoned he had been unconscious for some time. Regaining his fractured composure, David undertook several minutes of heavy breathing accompanied by some unrestrained swearing before re-starting the stalled engine. It purred into life as if nothing had happened. He carried on down to the bottom of the hill at a much slower pace and stopped just before the bend at the bottom of the gradient where a sharp left turn led towards the village he was seeking.

When he saw the colour of the country lane snaking away to that hidden place he instantly thought of his wife Dorothy, the yellow brick road and the Land of Oz. It had the same magical quality.

But instead of yellow, the route shimmered salmon pink in the June sunshine. It was pink from hedge-to-hedge as far as he could see along the tree-lined straight, disappearing into a dip and around another left hand bend. It reminded him of a community crèche he designed a year earlier.

David was tired and hungry and Penhaven – that's what the sign said, atop a load of other clutter he couldn't be bothered to read – looked perfect for a rest break on his last-minute house-hunting holiday escape. Even the name was inviting: a haven for the pen. Idyllic. In the pink, quite literally. Almost a fantasy island of calm.

And at least he wasn't dead!

Sick of city life, David wanted to move to the country, to slow the pace and spend time with people who had time to spend with you: real people, not pass-you-by folk with a brisk little wave of the hand and a hollow, preoccupied greeting. At forty, looking twenty-five, he had no plans to retire. His modest architectural business was successful and his reputation for quality, accuracy, flair and precise deadlines assured him a string of eager clients wherever he was based. Penhaven was a possibility and would be added to the relocation list. If you set up your stall they will come wherever you are, as his greengrocer grandfather used to say.

"Follow the Fibredeck road," he sang, in fine if damaged spirits, indicating the turn with a casual flick of the hand and turning his cherished MG on to the pink pathway, canvas roof tucked down at the back, a faint offshore breeze fluttering the pages of an open road atlas on the empty passenger seat. The blushing bitmap rumbled contentedly under his tyres and his empty stomach joined in.

Dorothy – his wife, not the fictional pigtailed schoolgirl with her yapping fleabag Toto – would not be part of his new future. She loved the constant scuffle of city life, thrived on challenge, found rural backwaters insufferable and saw no reason why she should have them inflicted on her smoothly running life, thank you. Much younger than her husband, she worked out at the deluxe gym near their home – a big three-storey cul-de-sac property at 22 Orchid Gardens – and liked the nightlife.

She said she still loved David, of course, but some arrangements had their limitations and their four-year marriage had just exceeded its sell-by date. Naturally, she'd cried when he told her that their relationship was over but he had more important things to do and she was grown up enough to understand. Times changed, and a future in the solo lane was beckoning nicely.

He was finally settling down and the sweat that had so recently drenched his forehead and the small of his back was now dry, his heart less percussive. He had been pounding down the cliff road approach a little too swiftly, angrily chewing over how he had discovered the faithless Dorothy and her gym-based lover Brad had been hiding their liaison from him; this was when he had spotted the pair of them, togged out in fluorescent Lycra, peddling along together on a country lane near a spot where he was working with a client.

Bikes again! he had growled then, angrier at the lovers' mode of transport than their amorous association. For his father had been killed on a bike, in a fatal race with a bumptious colleague, when David was only ten; his mother had run off with a pedal-powered postman only weeks before the crash; and his aunt, who took him in, was more interested in her cycle repair business than looking after an orphan.

He was just spitting "*Fucking Dorothy! Fucking cycl...*" when his car and his life went out of control...

Now the precipitous hill was well behind him he was back to his relaxed state, the swearing had stopped and he no longer wanted to kill the next bike rider that came into view. He had managed to push the imaginary crash onto the rocks to the back of his mind, frightening though it was. But he still couldn't get the all-pervading Dorothy to flutter off in tandem. Nevertheless, he had managed to guide the black sports car off the main road towards the village of Penhaven, now about half a mile away from that cluttered road sign; something about twinning with some more unimportant civic bumf underneath.

He was travelling between empty fields, grass yellowed by the continuing hot spell, the sighting of an occasional cow, a blue wedge of sea filling a dip in the now-distant cliff line on the passenger side, framing the battered chimney of an obsolete engine house poking up from the bleached slope. In a moment the fields gave way to two strings of matching cottages, clean and bright with their whitewashed walls and slate roofs, and a simple sandstone chapel surrounded by a small courtyard of granite headstones.

David thought Penhaven looked brand new, as if the place had sprung up overnight, and it was also idyllically quiet. His engine purred unobtrusively, a vehicle that was well serviced. There were no cars in the driveways – no driveways, even – and no people in sight. It was almost the community of his dreams. Dorothy would hate it, he told himself. No gymnasium for a start, where she could tone herself to perfection with weights or the multi-gym; in the pool, at the step aerobics, on the cycles... *Bah!*

Without warning he struck a small, unseen pothole, bit his tongue and swore at both the sudden pain and the taste of blood in his parched mouth. His fears returned, briefly. A little shiver; a sigh at a disaster avoided. *Stop thinking about Dorothy! Every time you think of her something horrible happens!* he told himself.

No, whilst Penhaven would be too ordinary, too pedestrian for Dorothy it would be fine for David, seeking the comfort and anonymity of some pastoral obscurity where he could lose himself and drop off the intrusive social radar for a while. On the negative side, however, there seemed to be no pub – a situation unheard of in an English village – and his heart sank into the even louder complaining rumbles of his empty gut.

He was slowing down, resolved to return to the main road to find somewhere with better catering, when he saw a large wooden CAFE sign staked into the top of a turfed stone wall, its hand-painted arrow pointing towards a large whitewashed bungalow. David's mood improved and he turned the car towards a paved area behind the wall adjacent to the café; but his mood sank again as he pulled to a swift halt at the entrance, momentarily surprised by the sight ahead. He gave a groan.

The space was crowded with brightly coloured bicycles, springing up everywhere like a casually sown crop. Reluctantly easing forward, David had to weave among the bikes with great care to avoid a domino effect. Multi-coloured microshell helmets dangled from handlebars like drooping flower heads pregnant with seeds and several machines had panniers, water bottles and child seats attached. *Very Tour de France*, David thought bitterly and inaccurately as he carried on in and pulled into a wide space facing the roadside wall.

He shook off an unaccountable shiver in the base of his spine as he could still smell phantom traces of burning rubber from his tyres; then he killed the engine, stowed his road atlas in the glove compartment and peeled off his black leather driving gloves. He stepped out, pocketed his keys, looked around him and smiled faintly. Leave your kit on your bike in the city, he thought, and it would be nicked in seconds – bike as well. In the countryside you could leave your front door open and nobody would walk in and help themselves, which was refreshing. He took a breath of the ozone-scented air, puffed it out with satisfaction and strode briskly into the road.

The front of the impromptu cafe, set forward from the parking area, had a plank porch surrounded by white fencing, giving it the appearance of a Victorian cricket pavilion. There were net curtains on the windows and a scattering of kids' mountain bikes outside, some flat on the porch, others propped against the fence. A large upright sign above the guttering advertised *Spokes Restaurant* in bold blue letters. Appropriate name, David thought, giving the parking area and its despicable pushbike crop a brief sideways glance; then he marched up the three front steps, strode over the creaking boards and stepped inside, triggering a gold bell suspended over the door. It tinkled loudly.

The cafe was packed with diners and there was a smell of boiled vegetables and a light hum of conversation. Around thirty adults and children were tucking into their meals at a dozen tables. Each table was set with four chairs, a white tablecloth with a central posy of tiny flowers in a recycled pepper pot and each diner was dressed for cycling. A few were in the casual shorts and tee shirts of summer, but most were togged out in body hugging fluorescent cycle suits. A handful turned to stare at the newcomer, their faces glowing with health, their eyes bright and inquiring. David became instantly aware that his open-neck designer shirt, cream Chinos and German leather sandals were inappropriate strip for parochial Penhaven.

Even so, he offered a bright and general "Good morning!" and the adult company returned the greeting like a touring coach party, some without looking up.

"Lovely day." Murmur of agreement. "Good for a ride." Further affirmative murmur. "Pretty village."

"We think so," a lady in green nodded, smiling warmly.

David was feeling comfortable again. If he tried holding a conversation with a room full of strangers at home the warmest response would be a surly grunt. It was different in the countryside. So warm, so friendly. He would fit in well. Only subtly conspicuous. Even in a room full of bloody bike fanatics. The only downside.

There was a cough from behind and he turned to face a Formica counter and a large woman in an orange tabard who stared at him quizzically from between two tiers of chock-a-block cake displays under glass domes.

"Hello," he said. "Twenty Rothmans and a menu, please."

"We don't sell cigarettes," came the reply. It was cool, reserved, though not entirely frosty. The woman was middle-aged and tanned, with black hair and sharp black eyes. She wore a plaid dress under the fluorescent orange tabard, a white blouse and matching frilled cap and swayed slightly from foot to foot, as if she was at sea. "No-one smokes around here," she added and cleared her throat, seemingly making an ecological point.

"Really," David replied. Did she mean no one smoked in the cafe or the whole village? The cafe, surely. Nothing surprising about a non-smoking food premises nowadays. Even so... "Do you have any pasties?"

"Vegetarian menu."

That meant no. Pity. He fancied beef and Stilton. His gut gave another insistent gurgle.

"What about a beer?"

"Fruit juice."

No ciggies, no meat, no ale. Was this a Cornish/Amish backwater? Were they strict Methodists, all plain clothing and temperance? Or was the place too remote for regular deliveries and they'd just run out of popular lines?

Rather than paddle his city-based canoe any further upstream in a resolute current, David picked up the proffered menu, ordered a veggie burger and an orange juice and took a vacant table near the door. He slipped a brown leather wallet from the back pocket of his Chinos and it fell open to reveal a wad of notes and plastic cards on one side and the colour photograph of a pretty brunette on the other. Dorothy. He felt another small shiver, quickly flipped the wallet shut and placed it deliberately next to him on an oval table mat. He stared out through the gauze-draped windows at the cottages, the chapel and the empty playing fields on the far side of the winding pink roadway and stroked his chin thoughtfully, absorbed for a moment with other matters.

David Conrad was clean-shaven with a tidy mop of dark brown hair and electric blue eyes, a characteristic he had inherited from his Swedish mother, along with her driving ambition and unshakable confidence. The hair colour and occasional lapses of sound judgement came from his late father, the former custodian of a sea bird rescue centre and posthumous cyclist. As for Dorothy (the one without the tin, straw and carnivorous companions), she had fallen into his heart and his bed through a mutual client. Now that she was out of the way and he was effectively single again, somewhere like Penhaven could be the answer to his future. Out of the way; remote, *hidden*.

He became aware of his close inspection by a small boy with red hair, freckles and a gooey green blob dangling from one nostril. The child was turned fully in his chair, his legs dangling either side of the seat, his food-stained chin resting on one arm stretched across the back. The other arm hung limply at his side.

"You don't live here, mister," he said solemnly, his voice cracked and shrill as if he had a throat complaint.

"That's right, I don't," David replied. The boy's parents, each side-on to him, ignored the conversation and continued mutilating their meals with oversized silver knives and forks that seemed better suited to weeding a border than addressing a dinner plate. He told the boy where he lived. The boy ignored it, seemingly unimpressed.

"What you doing here?"

"Holiday. Maybe looking for a place to live."

"You've got a place to live."

"An alternative. Somewhere nicer," he clarified. "Like Penhaven."

At this the boy's father turned to look at David, the ascending fork stalled at his lips, a plump radish speared on the tines. He returned his food to his plate and cleared his throat.

"Why do you want to come here?" he asked, in a broad local accent.

"It seems so nice."

"It is. We keep it that way."

"I can see that."

"We're very strict."

David frowned. What did he mean by that?

"Strict?"

"About who we let in."

"Oh. You like to screen your newcomers, eh?" David smiled.

"We've got a committee."

David's smile waned. The man's wife was looking at him now. She had high cheekbones and thin lips and shared both the red hair and the identical yellow polo shirts and striped satellite trousers of her husband and son.

111

"They're very particular," she added and returned to her food, as if the issue was closed.

David was still considering a suitable response some minutes later when the woman from behind the counter arrived with the veggie burger, the orange juice and the bill. He thanked her, took a sip and a bite. She did not move. He looked up, in mid-chew. Several patrons were looking in his direction now, including two black-haired and thick-set juveniles slouched in the far corner and each dressed in matching track suits fashioned to resemble blue overalls. They looked like trainee car mechanics or the product of an ill-advised breeding experiment between cousins; each wore a hand-stitched name tag on the left breast, unsettlingly proclaiming them to be Bill and Ben. David felt uncomfortable again.

"Sorry, do you want me to pay now?" he asked the waitress.

"No."

"Fine."

She continued to hover at the table looking at him, her green eyes assessing him closely.

"Yes?" he asked. "Is there something else?"

She shook her head, turned tail and as she walked away he was certain he heard her mutter: "He's a rum one."

He didn't challenge her this time and instead sat there chewing over his food and his testing times with Dorothy. But when she got back to her station he waved in her direction.

"Ketchup?"

She glared briefly, as if she was about to demand a "please," then she reached under the counter and strolled over with the red bottle. She put it down with a light thud.

"Anything else?"

"No, thank you, Miss."

"Mrs... Mrs Tinman."

Though keen to finish his meal and leave, David tried to lighten the mood. "All the bikes outside – are you having a cycle convention?" he asked, waving his fork in the general direction of the rest of the room.

"No," the woman replied, once more swaying slightly from foot to foot, a mannerism David found unsettling. "Just friends."

"Have they come a long way?"

"All my customers live in the village."

"They must be pretty keen – and fit."

"It's how we get about, around here."

112

"Sorry?"

"It's how we get from A to B. On two wheels. Some of the best machines in the country, too." She paused and gave David a deeply inquisitive glare. "You're not familiar with the saddle are you?" she asked, wiping her hands on her pinny.

"Sorry?" He wasn't.

"You don't ride."

"Never could," David admitted, taking a large bite of the burger. After a vigorous chew he added indistinctly: "I tried, but I used to wobble and fall off." He chomped seriously for a moment, then added: "My MG's parked outside. The only car in your car park, actually."

He caught a glimpse of the two stooges in fake dungarees. They were looking at him with wide, toothy grins as if anticipating some unforeseen revelation. Then they glanced at each other and guffawed like a pair of animated bears, classified on the retard side of bright. For the first time that day since the near-accident David felt truly threatened, but could not understand why.

"You *drove* into Penhaven?" the woman asked coldly.

"Yes. How else do you think I got here? Your village is pretty isolated."

There was a mass grumble from the tables, sounding dark and low as a swamp. It hit David squarely, like the chill breath of an open freezer door. Then a low male growl, like a dog: "Polluter!" He ignored the remark. But the next comment, from a woman, chilled him. "Gassing our children's lungs."

"I'm sorry?" He turned, bewildered by their sudden venom, affronted and a little scared.

"So you should be. Bastard!" Another woman, thirties, bright red lipstick.

"Go back home to your stinky city!" Child, about ten, short blond hair, gender indeterminate behind the maroon Lycra.

"Yes. We live here, you don't. This is a clean village." Old woman, someone's granny.

"No vehicles. No fumes. No accidents." Prim young woman, possible postmistress. (*So, how did the mail get here?* David wondered).

"Didn't you see the sign?" the cafe proprietor asked coldly. "The colour of the road?"

David dropped the remains of his burger back onto its plate and reached for his wallet to pay the bill. He had not expected such a vicious reaction. What had he done? Christ, everyone had a car now. Okay, there were cycleways here and there, but...

A sudden thought. He glanced anxiously towards the table in the far corner as he fumbled with his money and then sighed with relief: the two big lads had disappeared. He hadn't seen them go. Maybe they used a back door. He didn't care. They could have been real trouble.

But, as Springsteen put it, when we're born into the world trouble is never far behind. Especially when umbrage is on the prowl, David thought.

There was a loud bang as the café door flew open and the two twenty-somethings in their matching overalls marched back in; they were each scowling with fists clenched, blocking the exit. At their arrival, conversation died.

Regardless, David placed a tenner on the table, pocketed his wallet and moved towards the door, determined to walk out with as much dignity as he could muster – and without being pummelled to death on the way. The Neanderthal duo continued to block his path. Close up, his previous assessment seemed accurate: they looked like trainee car mechanics or the product of an ill-advised breeding experiment between cousins; he even sensed the sinister plucking of duelling banjos as he gestured to them to move. Each wore a hand-stitched name tag on the left breast, those unsettlingly proclaiming them to be Bill and Ben, though they were clearly not Flowerpot Men; the matching breast pocket on the other side of each outfit was marked *JAX BYX* within a cycle wheel, which David assumed was a clumsy contraction of *Jack's Bikes*, presumably a cycle sales and repair shop run by an apparently absent Jack. Each of them had a bizarre swearing vocabulary, as if standard cursing has been banned from the village along with booze and smokes, though *bastard* had seemed acceptable a moment earlier.

The shorter and stockier of the two barked: "He's right. There's a *spoking* car parked outside!"

The general silence continued, though David detected two kinds of concern in the faces around him, one of them for the diners' own safety and one for his – but he knew which took precedence. He reiterated what he had already said, but tried not to show any concern in his voice.

"I told you, it's mine," he said calmly. There were a few sharp intakes of breath around him, as if the rest of the café clientelle hadn't really believed him the first time round.

"*Be afraid*," said the taller of the greasy duo, echoing an old horror movie. "*Be very…*"

"Can't you read the *spoking* signs?" shortarse interrupted, scratching his stubbled chin. "No *spoking* vehicles. This is a car-free zone, mister. Are

114

you stupid?"

David considered this a rhetorical question and instead posed one of his own. "Then how do your shops get serviced?" he asked.

"Horse and *spoking* cart," said shortarse, possibly facetiously. "We don't want your kind around here."

"Don't worry, I was just leaving," David sighed, looked back into the café and added bitterly: "I won't thank you for your hospitality, though."

He stared down Bill and Ben as if challenging a rampant two-headed bull. "If you'd like to move, gentlemen, I'll be on my way."

There was a low call from behind of "about time, too" and the twin mechanics parted, reluctantly, one opening the door for David. He didn't try to trip him up as he passed. As he left the teashop, quickly and now quite shaken, several of the young male cyclists, each dressed in reptilian green, began spitting at him, which drew a health-and-safety rebuke from the waitress. Some threw uneaten food from their plates – the ginger-haired kid lobbed a banana skin – and half a jacket potato hit him in the neck.

When he got to his car he found a nail had been scraped along the driver's side, ripping the paint and denting the bodywork. He didn't stop to complain. He jumped in, started the engine, put his foot down and squealed out of the car park, making as much noise as possible, scarring the tarmac with burnt rubber and tipping three of the bikes off their prop stands in his haste, though it might have been deliberate. He heard an angry shout and saw one of the two morons in blue shaking his fist, the other picking up one of the fallen bikes. David smiled. Good. He bet it was those two oafs Bill and Ben who had taken the nail to his bodywork. And *scobalob* to you, he thought, taking the turn sharply, adding a further layer of black rubber to the ragged skid lines left (presumably) by previous victims.

He drove back to the edge of the village and pulled up. No one was following him. He wiped the sweat from his forehead then glanced back at the blue Penhaven village sign. He had not spotted the cycle crest underneath the name on the way in, distracted by thoughts of his ex, nor the detailed message in white letters under that.

Penhaven
Twinned with St-Chely-d'Apcher

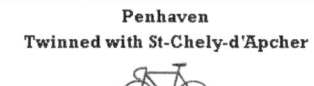

Department of Social Resources
New Community CycleZone
An experiment in environmental management
No vehicular access
Thank you for your co-operation

David gave an angry shout and aimed his car towards the main road, butter trickling under his collar, planning to leave the great, exclusive pink cycle way behind him. He heard that damn song again, jollier than before. *Follow the yellow brick road...*

Fuck Dorothy, he thought and a force like a steel girder hit him hard in the back of the head.

This was definitely not a potato, though something else wet and warm was running down his neck into his collar. Then the pain kicked in. It was excruciating. He gripped the steering wheel hard, let out a cry, squeezed his eyes shut (he may even have blacked out). When he opened them again he saw the cafe waitress standing at the junction with her arms crossed on her chest and a bike resting in the hedge behind her. She no longer looked severe, but seemed concerned as she unhooked her muscular arms and began walking towards the car.

David flinched. "Leave me alone." He reached for the keys in the ignition: to start the engine, to get the hell out of there.

"There's no need to worry," the woman replied, still approaching.

"Like hell. Your people attacked me. I was chased out of your cafe."

"Not at all."

"Look at my bodywork!" He ran his hand along the side of the door. The damage felt even worse than he remembered.

"I'd better take care of that," the woman said, advancing to the car and pointing to his head.

"Wh-what?" David reached back, touched his neck and drew back a palm covered in blood. "What the hell?" He scowled. "I think I've had enough abuse for today. Just let me go."

"It's all right," the woman comforted. "We didn't know."

"Know? Know what?"

"About Dorothy."

David froze. Dorothy? What could they know about Dorothy? Then he looked at his bloody hand.

"You did this to me," he croaked. "Those damn kids."

"No," the woman assured him. "That wasn't us." She pointed upwards. "Damaged tree branch on the oak there. Detached from the trunk as you roared by. We've been meaning to lop it ever since that storm the other night. Just as well it wasn't a bigger squall. Not so bad, considering. It'll heal quickly enough."

She brushed the leafy detritus of the branch off the boot of the car and asked: "Can I join you?"

Without waiting for approval she opened the passenger door and got in.

"It's all about Dorothy, your wife," she explained.

"You know my wife?" David asked, feeling colder by the moment. Perhaps he was going into shock.

"Only by reputation," the woman replied. "My name is Tinman, Mrs Tinman."

"Yes, and this is Oz," David replied, frivolously.

"Depends on how you look at it. The key to your situation is your wife."

"I've left her," David blurted out. Then added the qualification: "At home."

"I know."

"How?"

"Never mind. Start driving. There's something you must see."

"I'm hurt."

"You'll manage."

David started the engine and the waitress directed him to turn at the junction and go back the way he had come, up the dangerous hill and away from Penhaven.

"Where are we going?"

Mrs Tinman ignored this. "The truth is," she told him, her eyes on the road ahead, "you didn't leave Dorothy. Dorothy left you."

David sighed. She was right, of course. It was something he'd wanted to keep from his friends and associates, even from himself. Men did not like being abandoned. It cracked their ego, made them vulnerable, put them at fault; made them the butt of bad jokes. No, men did not like the Dear John scenario at all.

"So?" he demanded. It was none of her business.

"So, you've been fooling yourself – telling yourself that you walked out on her. But she just couldn't stand your arrogance any longer, David."

She knew his name. David felt colder, his hands seemed freeze-dried to the wheel. She was right again. He had not left Dorothy weeping and begging at the doorstep. In fact, she had packed a bag, to move in with another man, 'a kind man' – *Brad* – someone who didn't treat her like a convenient possession. She'd met him at the gym, training – what with him being a professional...

"Cyclist," his passenger said.

"Yes, he is."

"No. Mind the cyclist!"

David swerved, narrowly missing the wide panniers of the startled man with the Polyurethane skull protection.

117

"Where are we going?"

"We're nearly there." There was a pause, then: "Did you have to do it?"

"Do what?"

"Kill her."

David braked, though not as sharply as earlier. He was shaking with the cold now. Reality hit him hard and dozens of unconnected thoughts were pinballing wildly around his mind. He had been trying to bury what he had done – along with the corpse of his wife, rotting under the greenhouse in plastic sheeting at 22 Orchid Gardens, the tyre iron that had brought her down from behind tucked by her side. No one walked out on David Conrad, he told her as he finished her off. No one...

"I don't know what you mean..."

"What have you told yourself? You're on holiday? You're house hunting, planning a new future? You're on the run, David!"

"Get out!"

Mrs Tinman looked at her watch, nodded and did as she was directed. "It's time, anyway," she said, stepping on to the thin passenger side verge.

"Time for what?"

"You were racing down the cliff road," she replied. "You were composing a little fantasy on how Dorothy left you. Something you could tell your friends, your work associates, the police, yourself. You felt certain they would believe you. Perhaps you'd even suggest something sinister with the cyclist, her innocent lover, when you got back from your holiday."

She paused and stared directly into David's face. "But you don't get back," she said. "You misjudged the bend."

David opened his mouth to speak and a sharp stab of pain hit him. He caught a brief glimpse of a cycle wheel lying on its side spinning slowly, the sun's rays glinting on the silver spokes. There was the brief blur of rocks and grass tufts flashing by and the sea rushing towards him. He may have screamed. Just before the CRASH.

Mrs Tinman pulled the mobile phone from her pinny and dialled. There was a short delay, and then she heard a voice. She spoke. "Is that Bill? Oh, Ben. Can you get the tow-truck out? There's been an accident up the hill from the junction. Right. You'll need ropes. And call Derek at the police house. Thanks."

She rang off, and turned to the cyclist, gawping back at her from ten yards away. "You had a narrow escape there," she said.

The man looked white and sweaty. "He was going so fast – came out of nowhere, round that bend," he replied, his bike at his ankles like fallen knickers, his gloved hands trembling.

"Underestimated the curve," Mrs Tinman said.

"But did you see his face? Staring straight at me. He looked like he wanted to hit me. Why me? I don't know him. I'm just a cyclist."

Mrs Tinman glanced to the side of the narrow road where the descending tyre streaks disappeared into two muddy ruts. Then she looked down the scrubby cliff face to the brown rocks below and the black metallic shape that had once been a sports car.

She turned back to the cyclist. "Come down to the cafe. I'll make you a cuppa," she offered. "You're pretty shaken up."

"Why do drivers always need to go so fast?" the cyclist snapped, anger replacing fear. He picked up his bike, pulled some grass from the spokes, and then began tottering towards Penhaven.

Mrs Tinman sighed. "He was certainly rushing," she said, eventually retrieving her bike from the hedge and tucking in behind.

"They all rush when they come down here. Think it's like bloody London."

"He was rushing to meet his wife," Mrs Tinman added. "They've got a lot to iron out, under the circumstances."

They reached the junction and began walking towards the peaceful little village of Penhaven, their footsteps echoing from the grey tarmac. They left the village sign board behind them, a sign board that simply read

> **Penhaven**
> **Twinned with**
> **St-Chely-d'Apcher**
> **Please drive carefully**

119

June Bugs

The weird thing about Storyteller Five was how much he resembled June's bloody boyfriend, Chad. It wasn't him, of course. Couldn't be, under the circumstances. But I felt a chill anyway. In fact, I was sweating and shaking. How could he know? I asked myself. How could he *possibly* know? Chad, Brad, it was all the same, hounding me, exposing me, tarnishing my future. But five was not Chad, of that I was certain. At least, I think I was.

I doubt that Chad was able to string together sufficient sentences to tell a convincing story, but he could certainly strut like an over-egged Olympic athlete. No, reader five was slim and lithe, not a dark hair out of place, confident and, I guess, much like the titular David Conrad. I disliked him immediately and scowled to myself when I clapped his oration.

I tried to follow him into the crowd – well, gathering, it wasn't like a football stadium in Dara's Bar! Just with my eyes; I didn't want to stir from the stool. Couldn't, anyway. But Five sank into the misty brown fug, a merging of low light and tobacco smoke at the back of the room, like a boat slipping into a North Sea haar.

As I said, it all started when June moved in and I discovered that while she might be pretty and sexy she had little sympathy for my creative – and sexual – frustrations. Her father was a renowned chef who had served various cafes, pubs and small restaurants before taking on his own large, expensive eatery known for a few exquisite signature dishes. However, she wouldn't cook for me.

"Not my thing – that's daddy's court," she would say, spreading peanut butter on a floppy slice of off-white toast.

"I love you," I would say, usually late of an evening.

"Uh-huh," she would reply, without looking up from her book, usually a murder-mystery. I don't know what happened to the Regency romance she was supposed to be writing; I'd never heard her typing.

We had never slept together, meaning the previous Xmas was crap, especially as she had been helping out her father in his kitchens. She said she had an unspecified but non-venereal condition that prevented our conjoining. But I suspected it was not something like vaginismus (I looked it up), and all the awkwardness and alarm that constraint implied.

On the contrary, it was probably a condition called Kenny, a strapping pâtissier who worked in the artisan bakery next door to the restaurant who she'd been seen with in more-than-friendly mode on several social occasions when she told me she'd been working. Looked like it wasn't hard work. And then Chad-the-Room-Share turned up.

A couple of days before the interloper arrived I told her how important she was to me.

She stared me in the face and replied: "You're more interested in your scribblings than me."

"That's not true!"

"Well, you spend more time upstairs at your desk, locked in your fantasy world, than you ever do with me, down in the lounge, in the real world."

"What, the real world of game show twaddle?"

It wasn't the most tactful response as June was frosty but she wasn't stupid. Not intellectually, anyway. Her choice of TV shows was just an undemanding way of relaxing after a tough day fending off solicitors' demands.

I remember her reading one of my fledgling stories, back when I still had the courage to show her one.

"That doesn't work," she said dismissively, tossing the pages aside.

"How do you know?" I snorted in reply. "You're not a writer."

"But I am a *reader* – and without readers, writers have nowhere to go – beyond their own egos, that is."

"Sounds like you're jealous."

"No, just bored. The story didn't hold my interest. And it was a bit juvenile too."

Bitch!

Dara interrupted my rambling train of thought.

"You were disturbed by that Conrad story, weren't you?" he said.

"What, the bike thing? No, no. Not at all," I replied, a tad too quickly, as if I was hiding something. Well, I was. Big time.

"Yes, you were. Your eyes were all over the place and your hands were twitching."

Against my better judgement, I found myself blabbing about the flat, the spare room, Brenda, June, Kenny the bagel banger, and the residential Chad. I remembered Chad arriving one morning, before he finally moved in, dressed in lime shorts and a second-skin tee shirt and boldly showing off his fitness while I was bemoaning putting on a pound or two chained to a desk all day in an office.

Chad-the-cycle said I should have joined the staff tennis squad, to put a spring in my step, and began rattling on about how my breathing would be less laboured if I took a bit of exercise and how, if I let the fat ascent continue, I would end up in the crematorium quicker than I was probably due. And I thought how pleasurable it would be to take a shovel to the posing little prick, bury him next to the potting shed in the communal allotment and plant a sapling on top.

Dara raised an eyebrow, and then a second. "And did you?"

"Of course not! Why on earth would you think that? I could never kill someone. Not even a prat like Chad."

"What happened to June?"

"I told you, she left."

Dara leaned in closely, conspiratorially and whispered: "Do you have access to a greenhouse?"

There was a pause as the inference sank in.

"Wh... what do you mean?" I asked, shaken.

"Like the architect David Conrad, lost in the Cornish lanes?"

I was trembling: the rise of anger, or maybe a touch of fear?

"This is ridiculous!" I snapped and drained the final dregs of a pint in front of me. "I told you, I'm not a killer."

It didn't sound convincing and I changed the subject. "There's an awful lot of predatory women in these stories."

Dara smiled, as if some obscure penny had dropped, some untold event had been revealed. "How do you mean?"

"Well, the backing singer in the rabbit suit, the charity shop manageress, the wife in that cycling story..."

"Dorothy."

"Yes."

"Dorothy was the victim. She was the one who ended up dead. So was Ellie, Booth's replacement daughter – a victim, that is, not dead."

I acknowledged my oversight with a dubious turn of the head, and then added: "But the singer in the bunny tale; she was going to kill him."

"Well, she was a victim too. Delf had treated her despicably, even though he was just a small part of an industry that sucks them in and spits them out again – and look what eventually happened to *him*. Popular music can be a very short career, Will – as you know! There can be lots of initial media glitter but it can soon be followed by obscurity or seedy nightclubs. Perhaps that doesn't justify Avril trying to kill Bunny, but... You know what they say about crossing a woman! Like Sara in the pizza shop, and she was the hero... Heroine."

"That just leaves you with tottering Alice in the charity shop. She was just angry that some non-local was taking away her responsibilities in a job she'd been doing for decades, though I admit she took a rather ill-advised opportunity to nobble her nemesis."

"I never understood women," I said. "One of my songs for that second band – well, the words, anyway – was *She Doesn't Feel the Same Way (As Me)*, with the last two words in brackets. That was me asking why all the girls I ever fancied, from olive-eyed Melba to dusky-haired June, never felt the same way as I did. Why was I seen as such a dodo? Why did I appear extinct to them? Why did they flock to arrogant assholes so much? I only wanted to treat them right and not smack them about – and that was considered a weakness."

"It's probably not as black-and-white as all that – if one can still say that in these sensitive times," Dara replied, looking over at his clients who might have overheard his comment for any signs of protestation. None came. "A woman needs to be confident in a man, and to know that he's confident in himself. Maybe you just seemed nice but..." He paused to seek the right word, and probably didn't find it. "...*woolly*."

"Ineffective."

"Well, I didn't mean like a mammoth."

"I wasn't. Woolly, that is."

"Maybe. Doesn't matter. It appears to be what they thought, which is all that counts. No blame, Will. It was just the way you were, with your family background and all that emotional baggage – an ultra-competent father with no faith in your abilities and an estranged mother who apparently only stayed in the marriage because of the holidays." He paused to shuffle some beer mats. He didn't attempt to play Patience.

"Anyway, maybe you just expected too much of them: the women you wanted to be close to. Putting them on an elevated plane way above you, so when something went wrong you blamed them, not your own faulty judgement. Everyone's human, you know, and the darkest of us have a softer side. Even Adolf Hitler loved his dog."

There was another pause, and then he added: "You have very old memories for someone who appears so young."

I stopped scooping peanuts from a glass bowl on the bar and stared at Dara.

"What do you mean?" I asked.

"Your recollections of primary school and of secondary school, now a long-departed educational system. They seem so out of time."

"Out of...?"

"They don't fit the time frame."

"They're my memories." I stressed. Though I was feeling less confident under the barman's piercing gaze. Why couldn't I remember why he looked so familiar?

"Not your parents', your father's? Perhaps a close friend? Their memories?"

"No, no, I was there. I remember those things clearly."

"Well, perhaps they're from another life," Dara said, and he didn't seem to be joking. "You know, something you lived in another time, or another dimension."

I laughed, though there was a nervous edge to my humour. Was the man mad? I knew what I knew; rather, know what I know. I knew who I was and where I was. I was Will Buckwater, I was in my late twenties/early thirties and I was in Dara's Bar, the place set to the right of a narrow and shadowy alleyway accessed by a flight of a dozen granite steps, raised high above the sloping side street of a busy rural market town. I had come there by accident and had met all these spirited storytellers and their pluck and verve in telling their tales was inspiring me to move forward. I was no longer feeling like a dispossessed soul; I was feeling that I might be able go home refreshed at some point, sit down at the desk and write some tales of my own.

The only thing holding me back was what I had done.

"You just seemed older than... Never mind. Some of us just have elderly minds."

This seemed like a point too far, and I was about to reject his hasty assessment when I found myself distracted by an unexpectedly pretty face and a whiff of floral perfume as a beautiful young woman stepped forward. I was surprised that I hadn't spotted her before now, though she might have been sitting in the far far back. She had intense green eyes, pale skin and black black black hair plunging down her back like an onyx waterfall. She was wearing a cerulean roll neck jumper and white slacks and stood out amongst the male storytellers like a beautiful bluebird about to sing. And sing she did, though not literally; not like in *Oklahoma!* And I forgot about ageism as the scene turned from rabbits to bears.

Was this *Animal Farm* night?

The Bear

When Mrs Bluefinch's stuffed bear was elected chairman of the parish council it caused quite a stir in the otherwise drowsy rural backwater of Madeleine.

Some quite liked the eccentric gesture, but others with a perceived stronger sense of public duty pooh-poohed the whole thing. Still, the decision had been made, ratified and the residents and officials of Madeleine seemed stuck with it for at least a year.

The parish magazine, *Madelanes and Byways*, took it all in good part printing a picture of the new village ambassador on its front page with a brief page three biography of the "former prizewinning bear" that had "lived in the community all its life."

Mr Placebo was the largest member of the Brenda Bluefinch bear collection that ran to thirty eight specimens of all size, maturity, hue and species. The valuable stuffed toy was a metre tall with ginger fir, piercing black button eyes, soft padded paws and a mouth sewn into an enigmatic Mona Lisa smile with black twine. Each limb moved independently, but Placebo had been frozen in a seated position for as long as anyone could remember, suggesting a quiet Buddha-like statesmanship.

Mrs Bluefinch had recently died, leaving the parish council her bears and ten thousand pounds, to be spent in the community. She had been deputy chairman of the council at the time, a post endowed a year earlier by her fellow members in deference to her extreme age and long service – though they had no intention of allowing the potty old duck to take the chair at the next election, fearing her eccentric ways would lead to major gaffs and reflect badly on the council. The deputy's post usually involved no decisions, official duties or endorsements, so Mrs B could bathe in the honour with none of the responsibilities and perceived calamities. And the titular mayor, the chairman, made sure he never missed an appointment, which might bring Brenda out of hibernation as a last-minute replacement.

The meeting that made the momentous decision to install Placebo was a private affair. The council had co-opted a retired steeplejack to fill the Bluefinch vacancy and councillors had gathered informally at the home of the parish clerk, a diminutive chain-smoking piano tuner, to decide who would lead them for another year.

It was the usual bickering between Party members and independents with the outgoing chairman, the vicar, reminding everyone that "parish pumping" was "predominantly people-powered, precluding politics," an alliterative minefield of a mouthful that nearly dislodged his dentures.

The deputy post was decided quickly, bestowed on another long-server. But the chairman's role was more contentious and tactical voting by one group of Party members to prevent another group from gaining sway, coupled with the even number of twelve councillors, prevented the emergence of a clear winner. With the vicar refusing to use his casting vote, jostling for position went on for two hours until an exasperated village postmistress facetiously suggested that Mrs B's bear be elected, as a tribute to its cash-injecting former owner, and to "get this ghastly business over with." A fellow independent, also relief postmistress, seconded the proposal. The clerk advised there was nothing in standing orders to prevent them electing a stuffed toy as their chairman, though there was an obscure and peculiar sub-section banning livestock from the post. Each of the parties felt they could vote for a neutral candidate, did so in the flush of wild late-night enthusiasm and several glasses of homemade wine, and the imprudent move was passed by eleven to one, the vicar abstaining. Then they all sat back with a sigh and a plate of shortbreads and gaped at what they had done.

The meeting took place two days before the annual parish meeting when members met their electors to set out what they had accomplished in the last twelve months. They would have a lot to tell them: about the cash windfall – how it would transform the network of parish footpaths, improve the children's play area and fund an extension to the village hall. And, of course, about their latest member, Councillor Bruin.

Only six members of the public turned out for the meeting, on a rainy night in a draughty parish hall. But this was a thirty per cent increase on last year's attendance and as one of the sextet was the local gossip word of the decision spread quickly. Some felt the village would be better served by replacing the entire council with stuffed bears, but no-one seemed to think its members were really acting any more foolishly than usual.

The district council elections officer investigated, but could also find no reason to quash the decision. The statutory number of Madeleine representatives had technically been increased to thirteen, but as the unlucky addition was not human the rules did not apply and a constitutional crisis was avoided.

There was a question that the "bear-faced" act might bring the authority into disrepute, but the parishioners seemed happy enough (whimsically amused, he thought, but not opposed) and as long as the new furry chairman was not invited to attend district council meetings as a formal delegate (he could sit in the visitors' balcony as an observer, accompanied by a responsible adult) there seemed no question that the serious business of local government was being ridiculed.

Two months later the authority decided to feature the story prominently in its summer holiday brochure with one outspoken member wittily suggesting that if Madelaine had been a town council the new furry chairman could have been its mayor, bestowed with a proper civic chain and Winnie the Pooh insignia.

Village WI members responded quickly to this suggestion. Two of their number took instruction from a local metalworker and both designed and created a proper civic brooch – though in aluminium rather than precious metals – with a chain, decorated with rectangular badges along its length leading to a crest in the shape of a shield with MADELAINE LORD MAYOR inscribed on its face around an archetypal castle gate and twin lions, reflecting several larger national conurbations. They also designed a less flamboyant insignia, a single capital M on a simple shield, for more intimate community occasions. This was stuck on his chest with patches of Velcro.

Even the local paper had been positive, feeling the appointment was an improvement. The Nationals were incredulous and produced the usual round of puns and clichés, including *HERE COMES THE MAYOR BEAR* and *DON'T POOH-POOH THIS PARISH!* But after a short period of ridicule they became bored with the subject, moved on and Madeleine faded into obscurity once more.

Placebo was officially presented with his badge of office, allowed to sit at the head of the council table – on it, in fact – during debates and even opened the village fete (in the arms of the deputy chairman). The bear was welcomed enthusiastically at twinning celebrations, carnival events and the annual beating of the village bounds (where it was traditionally "bumped" on each mile stone by a careful handler).

Meetings went well. No-one fell out with anyone else and the life-sucking element of Party Politics was placed on hold. For the chairman was no longer perceived as a threat, either politically or as a "headmaster" figure, by keeping them in line. Instead of becoming unruly pupils without a leader, the councillors became diligent and attentive. They were not even intimidated by the chairman's sexual identity, for Placebo was clearly neither male nor female so could offend no-one on gender grounds. The chairman did not interrupt or direct; it merely listened, and that meditational response brought a pleasant concord to the meetings.

Placebo was unanimously re-elected chairman the following year after a term of office that had seen greater co-operation, good humour and graciousness than ever before in the village of Madeleine. There were more visitors, attracted by both the bear story and the better facilities provided by Mrs B's fiscal bequest. And Placebo never once had to use the civic gavel to hammer away dissent at meetings: firstly, Councillor Bruen's colleagues had shown a restraint and responsibility previously absent from their deliberations, which were now based solely on the needs of the community; secondly, as a stuffed bear there was no way its stubby paws could get a grip on the handle anyway.

Carvery

There was a roar of appreciative laughter from the other readers, Placebo having been a true panacea. There's always at least one fluffy little story that ends up being a "filler," I thought, deeply unsatisfied, sounding like my Uncle Donald who never read any books written by women – even the most famous ones – because of their perceived inability to write about men. Or perhaps he resented the fact that they were generally spot on in their assessments, especially in his idle case.

"*You no likey?*" Dara asked in a weird accent.

"It was amusing, but hardly Raymond Carver," I said, being over-critical, rude even. But the reader looked so much like the pretty black-haired albatross of my receding life, June. Annoyingly so, and I think I still fancied her.

Though he was much revered by readers, I wasn't that familiar with Carver. I'd read one or two pieces, enough to get by, but I'd only used the name because I'd heard that it was a good one to drop into conversation when talking about writing – especially short stories, his forte – to make you sound appropriately cultured.

Storyteller Six seemed not to agree, overhearing my comment, and stepped forward.

"Carver's stories are nicely written. He has a great sense of place and character," she said. "But many of them are just *incidents*, short and pithy with no before or after; no set-up or consequences; no real plots – often frustratingly so."

"The ones I've read have a beginning, middle and end. He's a great inspiration."

"So, what was *your* last piece about?" Six responded bluntly, apparently in character with my dreadful ex.

I briefly corpsed. "I'm working on something," I lied, weakly defending the indefensible.

"Of course you are," she replied with a smirk. "So what didn't you like about *The Bear*?"

"The satire was a bit wet; not enough bite."

"Not enough Carver?"

I blushed, but said nothing. Her interaction with me was proving unhelpful and a tad unnerving.

Number Six shrugged. "Okay, try this one."

She turned to Dara for approval, and then to the audience. "Do you mind another?"

Dara nodded and there were cries of "Not at all," "Yes, please!" and the rather patronising "Go for it, girl!" while Six turned to the next page in her binder.

"Unless you can do better," she said to me, raising a quizzical eyebrow, and as she began to read I shrank away like Brenda's tortoise face.

J. Returns

And when Jesus returned he presented himself at the White House.

"There's another of these messianic head cases outside," a Gate Guard informed the Aide by phone from the entrance. "Says he wants to see the President."

"He's the fifth this week," the Aide replied. "Get rid of him."

"He's attracted a big crowd."

"Lot of them do. Give him a signed ten by eight of the Chief and let the City PD deal with him."

"He's apparently fed them. The crowd."

"So? He took some of them to a diner. Does that make him a celebrity all-a-sudden?"

"He fed all of them with a burger and fries."

"So, he's a cheapskate as well as a maniac. Stop bothering me."

"No. He made one burger and fries go around two hundred people. Several said they couldn't eat it all."

"Oh, Christ. He's probably some guy doing a promotional shtick for Ronald McDonald."

"The crowd's getting insistent."

"All right," the Aide sighed, overworked, over-stressed and over a barrel. "Show him in. I'll get someone to meet him downstairs."

Ten minutes later Jesus was shown into a white-panelled room with red velvet drapes, mahogany desk, three leather chairs, a bookcase and a cocktail cabinet where the Aide awaited him. A gold-cased carriage clock flanked by a pair of matching blue vases ticked loudly from the shelf over a white, imitation fireplace and the space smelled like the counterfeit Spring fashioned by excessive furniture polish. It was clearly too sumptuous to be an Aide's office.

The unwanted visitor wore a simple grey gown and sandals and his long flowing golden hair, light brown skin, short beard and luminescent blue eyes matched the description the Gate Guard had given.

The Aide shook his hand. He had short black hair and black eyes and was dressed in black leather shoes, a grey three-piece suit, lime green shirt and orange tie. He was white-faced, clean-shaven and also smelled chemically fragrant.

"I'm sorry," he began. "The President can't see you now. He's a very busy man and today he's wall-to-wall with world leaders, business advisors and economists."

"He'll want to see me, I'm Jesus," said Jesus simply.

"I'm sure you are," the Aide replied patronisingly. "But I put in a call to our top Evangelist, Billy Boy Billykins III, while you were on your way to my office and he says you can't be the original Jesus because he, Billy-Boy, would've been told. He would've been advised of your coming – sorry, His coming – and we'd've been able to plan ahead."

"This Billy-Three is the President's spokesman?"

"Well, he sure is on anything Religious. I mean, you're in the most Christian country on God's green earth, and the finest. Want to know anything about The Lord, Reverend Billykins is the man to ask. He's executive chairman of the Evangelical Administrative Advisory Board and Sabbath raffle league, so he knows what's what and more besides."

"He has more power than the President?"

"Well, there's always gotta be a Power behind the Throne, sir. And here we've got Big J at the summit top: that's the *real* Jesus so to speak, the wondrous wispy one, none finer. Billy's a rung below with the First Lady next in line – she's a lawyer and a priest, amazingly graceful – and then (and I'm not boasting), you've kind-of got *me*, his political advisor."

"I'd still like to see the President. What I have to say is for his ears only."

"Sorry, no can do. But you can tap out a brief message to him on my laptop here and I'll be sure to give it to him someday soon."

"You don't believe that I'm – how do you Americans put it? The *real deal*."

"Not really, no."

"I can turn water into wine if you need convincing."

134

"I saw Lance Burton do that one on television once, along with that tired old bottle/glass thing. Neat. Magicians! Hey, what's that all about? Believe me it won't open doors."

"I can walk on water."

"Yea, yea, yea. So can the President when he needs to."

"No, I can really do it."

"Look, buddy. I don't need you splashing around in the fountain on the lawn just to make an exhibition. Just write your message and I'll have you escorted back out."

"I understand the Dalai Lama was here last year."

"Yep. Nice guy. Always smiling. Reminds me of Jay Leno – without the mullet."

"So how can he get to see the President, and I can't? He's a spiritual leader too, not a social politician or a monetarist."

"Yea, but he's a real man. Doesn't claim to be a God."

"Neither do I. There is only one God."

"Sure, sure. Try telling that to the damn Muslims."

"They would agree. They just don't accept me as the Son of God, that's all. More of a prophet, like Muhammad or Gautama Siddhartha, or a teacher. I don't take offence. Believing is the important issue."

The Aide shook his head. "We could do with a few more of those in Washington. Teachers, that is. Make the kids more obedient, more respectful to the flag and traditional values. You any good at teaching English?"

"It's not my first language."

"Pity. All my kids ever learn is stuff off *The Simpsons* and death metal singers. Try and peel 'em off their tablets and into reading some seminal American literature like – uh – Chandler or Spillane and it's like torture to them."

"That's probably because they have no concept of real torture."

"Hey, shit, you don't want 'em scared out their minds, do you? There's enough bad things on the streets out there without it coming into the home."

"But you see all that horror every day on your 24-hour television news."

"Yea, but that's like entertainment to my kids."

There was a brief pause.

"I think I ought to be speaking to your President now," Jesus said.

"Look, it's not possible. And, frankly, if you were really who you say you are you would've bypassed me entirely and gone straight to the top.

Walked right through the wall or something. No-one could have stopped you."

"That would have been impolite."

"But you could have done it. Poof! Gone from here, reappear in the Oval Office."

"I'm not a magician. I don't click my fingers and produce pigeons from my sleeves."

"I'm glad to hear it. We like to keep the office clean. Don't want it full of bird plop."

"I like to be invited in."

"Like a vampire?"

"No, not like a vampire. They're a human myth. They don't exist."

"You ain't been Downtown."

"The President..."

"The answer's still No. You could write him a letter."

"I'm sure this Billy Boy person has no trouble getting in to see him."

"That's different. He's got a track record."

"He's an athlete?"

"No. He's a proven advisor. And he's converted thousands to The Faith."

"I think I may have played a small part in that as well."

"That was a long time ago. You died. Well, Jesus did. Billy Boy spreads your – His – words, though."

"Who is this Billy Boy person?"

"Well, he's someone who knows how to give a sermon, that's for sure. Likes preaching on subjects that all start with the same letter. Like C for chastity, and so on. Real tidy and concise."

"Sounds more like your *Sesame Street*. Instructions for children."

"He gave a five-pointer last Sunday on topics all beginning with P – purity, patriotism, profits..."

"Which of the Prophets? Isaiah? Moses? John the Bap–"

"The dollars his Ministry was bringing in," the Aide interrupted. "The congregation's contributions had dropped off a mite during the previous fiscal year. Said God wouldn't be pleased. Mentioned tithing again – you know, giving ten percent of your wages to the church. Boy, he sure gets that one in regularly. But he's got his own helicopter, and I guess that costs a lot to upkeep doing the Lord's work."

Jesus frowned. "I never promoted tithing. Or gaining personal wealth from spreading the word of God. It sounds like Mr Billykins could do with the overturning of some tables..."

The Aide laughed. "Hey! C for Crash."

"More like A for Armageddon."

The Aide frowned. He had other things to do than talk semantics with a kook.

"Yea, yea. Well, it's been fabulous meeting you. I'll get that nice man in the corridor in the uniform with the service revolver to show you out."

"There will be death."

The Aide reached for an inside pocket. Perhaps he was reaching for a gun. Perhaps he was freeing his shirt, sticking uncomfortably to an arm pit.

"If you're armed you won't get past Security," he said. "There's no way any assassination attempt's going to succeed."

"I'm here to prevent it."

The Aide narrowed his eyes. "You know something about a death threat?"

"We're all going to die, even your leader. You may recall that I had a pretty significant brush with death once."

"Hey, POTUS has protection! No-one's gonna get to The Chief."

"People have in the past, with previous incumbents."

"Yea, well our boss is shielded by his core voters. They won't let anything happen to their hero. They're well armed."

"Do you mean your National Rifle Association?"

"Hey, the NRA don't fool around."

The visitor's brow furrowed in thought.

"I was always puzzled why a *rifle* association should embrace members who possess automatic weapons that can fire up to 1,500 rounds a minute. It seems a little excessive for a deer hunt. And some everyday people – you might call them 'ordinary Joes' – have arsenals large enough to take on a small country. Or a neighbourhood junior school..."

"The big guns are regulated," the Aide snapped, a nerve clearly tweeked. "Anyway, you're splitting hairs over the rifle thing. If it's got a barrel it's a rifle in my book."

"I must remember to pass that on to the next tank commander I meet."

The Aide scowled. "You mentioned a life threat to the President."

"No immediate danger," Jesus replied, with a benevolent smile of reassurance. "It's just that I may be the only one who can talk the President out of his current plans, which could have a catastrophic consequence – not just for himself."

"You've been watching the news."

"I don't have to. I know everything."

The guest made no aggressive moves and the Aide relaxed slightly. "Yea, yea. Put you on a quiz and you'd win a Buick! Look: these are tough times. The President has made a decision, Congress is backing it and the people have been told they're behind it. Nothing more to be said. Especially from you. I mean, if you're who you say you are, well, you're not even an American."

"I am Everyman."

"But aren't you an Arab, or something?"

"Jewish."

"That's not Christian."

"I am the very heart of Christianity!"

"Well, you don't sound like Billy Boy to me. You're a bit too calm for my liking. People want a bit of tub-thumping these days. Louder is stronger! Gets 'em on their feet. Gets 'em behind you. Gets 'em behind The Chief, anyway – and that's all that matters."

"Only if your Chief says and does the right things. What he's doing at the moment could destroy him – and this country. Perhaps the world itself. Do you think he really wants to carry the burden of that?"

"You ask an awful lot of questions for someone who claims he already knows the answers."

"There are many answers to each question. Except for one: Does God exist?"

The Aide laughed. "Well, I guess you'd go for the Yes button on that one. As for the President, he chose to run for office, bagged the popular vote and gets paid a lot of *spondulicks* to do the job. He's got top advisers and he knows what he's doing."

"Does he, really?"

"Better than you, I reckon."

He looked his visitor up and down and frowned.

"Oh, and hey, the robes: they don't work. Too 'old school.' This isn't Christmas pageant time; this is the real world in the two-oh century. I mean, I'm no lifestyle guru here, but *sandals*? No, no, what you need if you're going to hook up with the whole Evangelical thing is some nice high-end trainers, let you move about effortlessly, like you're walking on air, or water, no pun intended; and a white suit. The white suit's a given. And a haircut, unless you just want the hippie vote. Gotta look the part, gotta look smart, as they say. You're in need of a serious make-over if you wanna get the ratings. Trust me. Anyway…"

The impromptu dress code advice was ignored, though Jesus gently but firmly tightened the rough cord around his waist that secured his grey robes.

"Can you telephone him?" he asked.

"Well, I could do that. But, as I said, he's a busy man."

"I have information for him that could be crucial. Tell him who I am. He'll want to hear my words." Jesus paused, and then added: "Can you afford *not* to tell him?"

The Aide thought this over while the clock ticked away musically in the empty silence. Then he picked up the red phone on his desk, punched in some numbers, waited a moment and spoke.

"Sorry to bother you, sir. There's a man here to see you. Says it's important. Claims he's Jesus and he's got a message for the Commander-in-Chief. No, that's *you*, sir. Yes. Correct. Jesus. Right, sir. I know time's getting on. Yes, sir. Sorry again, sir."

He put the phone down. "He won't see you."

"Why not?"

"Thinks you're crazy. Sorry. But, you understand..."

"Only too well."

The clock over the imitation fireplace pinged the quarter-hour and the Aide took the visitor by the arm, firmly. "Time to leave."

"I understand. When you next see the President you'll tell him that he needs to think again, to change his decision, to accept that you are all the same people on one very small planet; that you should not throw away your global brotherhood quite so recklessly?"

"Sure. I'll tell him."

"It's important. Vital."

"Yea, yea."

"Otherwise, the experiment fails and We have to decide whether to begin again."

"What experiment?"

"The world." He gave the Aide a piercing stare.

"I'll tell him!"

"Will you?"

The Aide scratched his head. "I guess not. He's got more important things to do. Like revitalising the country; like saving the planet from nut jobs. Without your help. Let's go."

He relinquished Jesus's arm, turned his back, adjusted his jacket, opened the door and called to the Corridor Guard outside. "Escort our guest out," he ordered.

"What guest?" asked the Corridor Guard, peering into the room.

The office was empty. The Aide's mouth fell open; the Corridor Guard just stared. Outside the sky was growing dark.

Being You

This time I took the coward's way out and said nothing. Six had surprised me with her second story and I had even laughed – quite a lot, too, and it was equally well-received by the other patrons. She was definitely not June then, as June had neither the capacity for satire – though she was pretty good at biting sarcasm – nor the ability to impart or even understand the simplest of jokes. Not only that, but Six performed the voices of the two protagonists to perfection, without a blink, from the quiet and compassionate Christ to the radically uptight Washington political aide. This time I nodded my respect for the reader as she returned to her seat in a corner looking well vindicated.

"So, you write like Carver?" Dara said to me suddenly, breaking the spell.

"Not really," I replied. "I'd like to, but…" I paused.

"Don't have the *feel*?" he asked.

"Definitely not!"

"So how would you describe your stories?"

I thought for a moment, then said: "They're a bit off-beat. A bit, I don't know, *silly*?"

"A bit like *The Bear*?"

"Maybe," I reluctantly conceded. "Maybe not quite so…" I searched for the word.

"Sweet?"

I didn't reply.

"A bit too much about real people?"

"*The Bear* isn't real."

"But it has a version of real people in an unconventional situation. Like the other stories tonight."

"Carver would never have written anything like that. Like those."

"But he did write about real people in an unusual hitches," Dara persisted. "And *J Returns*? What if he wrote that?"

"It's harder-edged, but I don't think Carver was party political. Not overtly, anyway." I hadn't the foggiest.

"And you are?"

"Sometimes. There are things in this world that need addressing..."

"But mostly you write silly stories?"

"I didn't say that! Well... People have said..."

"What people?"

I sighed. It was one anecdote I didn't want to tell. Yet another.

"I took a story to a local evening newspaper a little while back. I was really chuffed with it and I thought it suited a regular fiction section they ran in one of their Saturday pull-outs. I got to see this deputy editor or some such and he took a quick look at it, started smiling and then tossed it across the desk at me. 'Not for us,' he said. 'It would be better elsewhere.' 'Where do you suggest?' I asked and he pointed and said 'There's a waste bin in the corner.'"

Dara smiled too, seemed to be restraining a full-blown chortle, and then looked me closely in the eye and said: "That's just the sort of thing you want to incorporate into your writing. Daft anecdotes from real folk. People can be very odd and quite entertaining, you know. Take a notebook with you: write down what they say."

"I started doing that. In cafes and shops and so on. Not long back there was this woman who walked into my local supermarket carrying this huge inflatable birthday letter, about five feet long. She went up to customer services and said 'I want to change this for a C.' When she was asked why she said: 'I didn't realise you don't spell Celia with an S.'"

This time Dara did laugh. "Just the sort of thing," he said. "Take that gem and expand on it. There's a whole story in there waiting to be crafted. Anymore?"

My Uncle Donald used to pepper my childhood with those delightful epithets that never made life warmer or clearer and certainly shed no light on, well, anything. I'd ask him an important question and he'd mull it over for a short while, chewing quietly on a sliver of flesh on the inside of his mouth and tugging on a protruding nose hair; and then he'd nod sagely and say something like 'I always say *Never push your granny while she's shaving*;' and then he'd wander off chuckling like an old man who'd just discovered a crumpled copy of *Playboy* in a corner of the woodshed. Another strategic inanity cloaked as perception rattled along the lines of

'Walk under a stepladder, expect to be handed a paint brush.'

"When I was very young, the family – mum, dad, me, baby Brenda and Uncle bloody Donald – used to go for long drives in the countryside and now and then we would stop for fish and chips on the way home," I told Dara. "It was never routine, however much I wished it could be. But sometimes, quite often in fact, I would drop heavy hints that *chish and fipps* was what I wanted for my tea.

"There were these trees – I can't remember what species they were and probably didn't know at the time. But whenever a line of them swept into view on the fringes of some farmland field I would cry out 'Oh, look, it's the fish and chip trees!' which my family would steadfastly ignore – except for my mum, who would often say 'That's nice, William,' in that distracted voice she always used when she didn't want to engage with a topic. There would be no fish and chips that night…"

Dara nodded. Though he didn't appear especially impressed with my gastronomic revelations, he still pressed on with his astute advice.

"Never let other people tell you what to write, no matter how erudite they appear to be. Don't be put off by someone who doesn't get it. Sometimes it's like offering a Mickey Spillane thriller to an old Etonian who only reads Virgil, or recommending fifteen-year-old single malt to a teetotaller. Just let what's inside your head come out on to the page. If you like what you see, others will too, eventually, though they might need some encouragement, maybe from someone else who likes it."

"It's just that nobody ever saw it – my potential," I said. "Not my parents, my girlfriend, my bosses, my friends… Even at school. You know, just before I left, about a week before what happened – or didn't happen – to Melanie, we had a visit from a careers information officer who interviewed everyone ending their final year. He asked me what subjects interested me most, what grabbed my attention, what inspired my enthusiasm, what I was good at. I said: 'English, literature, art (though not Zash Cavern and his mutilated mice), music...' I said I hoped to be a writer one day, maybe a journalist. And the jobs bloke paused for a tiny second, no more, looked at a list on a clip board and asked me in a bored voice: 'Have you ever thought about being a plumber?' It was pretty insulting and unhelpful. Looking back on it now, I'd have probably been much better off financially if I'd been a plumber – more independent, able to afford my own holidays in the sun a couple of times a year, and so on."

"You think life is all about stretching out on some gritty sand somewhere for two weeks and ending up looking like a lobster on the evening of the first day?"

143

"No, but… Well, I never achieved what I wanted anyway."

"And whose fault is that?" Dara asked. "We all have the potential to do anything we want, anything we are physically or mentally able to tackle. Were you waiting for somebody else to make it happen for you? Because I've been round the block a few times, Will, and I can assure you they won't."

He folded his arms and frowned. "You should stop whining and start shining," he said.

I was really fired up now, flushed with anger and preparing to squawk defensively when it finally struck me that Six was indeed the first storyteller I had actually spoken to, had actually engaged with, and who had in turn spoken back to me. Before I could determine if there was any significance to this, Storyteller Seven stood, moved into the reading light, cleared his throat and opened his folder.

He came up with a great character name…

Out of Season

For Bradley Parnsip it had been a disastrous summer season at Clapperton-on-Sea.

As he walked along the windswept concrete pathway that ran the length of Clapperton sea front, the agitated grey sea sploshing about around the tidal defences below on a cold and dreary October morning, stuffed into his parka, hood up, hands in pockets, nose bright red and dribbling, he muttered hopelessly to himself about disaster piled upon disaster – much of it entirely his own fault for not listening to his conscience. He kicked out angrily at an oval pebble cast up by the previous night's storm and it flicked away to the right, cracking a glass panel in a council-funded information board. That was just another example of how his luck had finally run out that year.

He was on his way to meet the full Clapperton-on-Sea town council at a private session where he was either to be sacked as resort manager or expected to figuratively fall on his invisible sword and resign. Either way, he was on his way out, without another post in sight. At least, he hoped the sword was figurative, considering the almost homicidal way the Mayor had castigated him two weeks earlier. He could hear the man's words now, echoing around his brain, cushioned from the cold in the fluffy parka hood.

"Perhaps the truly high point of your appalling selection of summer delights for the tourists was your pornographic puppet show."

"It wasn't mine," Parsnip had tried to explain. "Just the person I hired –

145

was supplied with. And it wasn't really pornographic."

But he'd known he was on a losing wicket. Town mayor Evan Hartpress was loud, outspoken, bull-headed and, unfortunately, dead right.

"It was certainly graphic," he barked at the council's quivering employee. "The puppets were naked."

"They were anatomically correct."

"They were anatomically fucking generous!"

"You've got to have some exaggerated features with puppets," Parsnip had replied. "Look at Mr Punch's nose..."

"I don't think anybody was looking at Mr Punch's *nose*," Hartpress bawled, going red. "Anyway, you can't put on a puppet show for children and on the day put a sign up saying *Dr Paunch's Precocious Puppets*."

"I didn't know he was going to do that..."

"Written in chalk on a board, so that some resurrected Mary Whitehouse was able to change *precocious* to *porno*!"

"I took it down as soon as I saw it. And, to be fair to the man, he never said the performance was for children."

"It was a *puppet* show, Parsnip! It was on the pier, next to the crocodile ride. Heaven's to hopscotch! And what about your so-called illusionist, Doctor Scream?" Hartpress had now gone puce. "Sawing a woman in half next to the ice cream stand. You never said he was going to try to *actually* saw a woman in half."

"Be fair, we caught him."

"We only just got that poor woman out of the box in time: a school cleaner from Nottingham on a weekend break. She didn't stop screaming for an hour. You can bless your lucky stars that she isn't going to sue us – even after we paid for her entire holiday as compensation. You can also be thankful that the chap in charge of the donkey rides was a carpenter in the off season and spotted the real saw, in his lunch break, or you'd be in custody as well."

"I didn't know Dr Scream was fresh out of a psychiatric hospital. The agency told me he'd done cabaret."

"From the way he was dressed in that black tux and top hat the closest he ever got to *Cabaret* was a seat for a fleapit screening in the one-and-nines!"

No, the whole thing had gone badly, Parsnip mused. If only he hadn't gone to the Hadley Brimblecombe Talent Agency to book the acts. It wasn't the most salubrious of agencies, but at least it was cheap. Even so, alarm bells should have rung when he was offered a whole tranche of

146

seaside entertainment acts for a third of the cost of the previous year's selection, at that time acquired via the select and reliable but prohibitively expensive Parker-Brelle Agency.

To be fair, the town council had been over the moon about the Brimblecombe deal. They'd told Parsnip he had to cut his entertainment budget by half and he'd served their requirements even more effectively than expected. In fact, they had congratulated him on a job very well done. Now *he* was about to be very well done.

He picked up speed as he didn't want to be late. This was not courtesy: the council didn't deserve that civility. It was a desire to get the inevitable dressing-down over as quickly as possible and maybe go home and start packing. As he drew near to the council's 19th-century headquarters, visions of some of the other prime acts from his appalling season drifted across his fevered consciousness.

Mr Chummy's Ukulele Band, forinstance: a dozen-strong group with more grinning false teeth than seemed possible performing a set of songs so repetitive that by the fourth number much of the crowd had drifted away. Those that remained in their uncomfortable wooden chairs in the modest music marquee next to the bowling green were treated to an ill-judged comedy turn by Mr Chummy himself, a red-faced and pun-obsessed Mancunian, who both looked like an aged and especially dyspeptic Gallagher brother and was completely unaware of his crashingly unfunny and dated material.

The Mighty Miller Tones, a Glenn Miller tribute ensemble, was as instantly forgettable as a bland breakfast porridge, due to the fact that there were only eight of them, including just one saxophone player and no signature clarinettist. And he tried his best to forget the ten overweight and geriatric hoofers that made up Binky's Eleven O'Clock Tea Dancers...

Consequenty, Parsnip arrived at the town hall feeling thoroughly dejected. He wasn't a bad resort manager, he'd just been dealt a dreadful hand of cards thanks to a stingy bunch of employers. If anyone was truly to blame for the summer season shambles it was Clapperton's witless and parsimonious councillors who balked at spending a reasonable sum to entertain its summer visitors but were quick enough to raise their own out-of-pocket expenses whenever budget time approached.

He scuffed his way up the granite steps of the imposing building, past its twin concrete pillars and through the glass paned double doors. With a resigned sigh he trotted up the carpeted staircase to a small landing, housing a bronze bust of a former grand alderman whose inept handling of several bloody campaigns as an Army general in WW1 had led to the death of thousands of British troops and thus earned himself a clutch of medals and a formal citation as a great war tactician from none other than the cold-hearted Field Marsh Haig himself.

He took the left hand steps to the first floor at a bound and pushed open the doors to the council chamber without knocking. The gathering was fewer than he expected: the mayor, a bristling bull of a man, sat at the head of a clutch of small oak and leather tables arranged in a horseshoe, accompanied by seven other councillors, four men and three women, all members of the town's entertainments sub-committee. At least this might suggest a less general whip-lashing. He was wrong.

The mayor repeated much of what he had told Parsnip two weeks earlier, while several of his nodding municipal colleagues joined in with their own variations of outrage and disbelief. What he had not expected was the olive branch, the astonishing get-out that he was to be given "one more chance" to redeem himself. "At least until Christmas," the mayor added.

Stunned, Parsnip asked: "How can I do that? The season is over. And we don't have the money, do we?"

No-one reacted to the gibe.

"There's Christmas," planning sub-committee chairman Belinda Bakersfield replied, peering over her owl-like spectacles and pointing a bony finger in his direction. "A chance to make up for the financial losses – not to mention the losses in public confidence that we've incurred. Well, *you* have."

"But how can we do that?" Parsnip reiterated. "It's too late in the year to mount anything substantial, and the audience – well, it just won't be there."

"Ah, but it *will* be there if we can pull off something spectacular that will draw in the crowds from all over," deputy finance chairman Wilfred Brace said, spreading his stumpy little arms wide as if to show off a freshly-netted prizewinning haddock.

"Okay," Parsnip replied. "Then how are we going to achieve that, and what with?" He was becoming irked. He was the expert and these were amateurs who wouldn't let him do his job without interference, which was why they were in their present pickle.

"A truly *big* show," said Cllr Bakersfield, fanning herself with her agenda papers as if the room had suddenly become warm with anticipatory tension.

There was a dramatic pause, as if his employers were waiting for a grand revelation. It came from the mayor himself and comprised two words.

"*Billy Shoehorn.*"

Parsnip's mouth dropped open, but all he could articulate was a weak

148

"Billy…?"

"One of the best music hall artists I've ever seen," Hartpress said, looking like a lottery winner who had just discovered that his anticipated £25 prize was actually £25,000.

"In the day he could pack out houses night after night with his mix of songs, comic monologues, magic tricks," he enthused. "And his juggling, well, that routine with the poles and the plates was staggering; never missed a plate. The fire breathing, like a little human dragon. Amazing. He's as loved now by the public as he was when he was in his prime."

Hartpress beamed the beam of one well satisfied with an exceptional four course meal, cheese board, cigars, brandy and the favours of an accommodating waitress. He even stroked his ample belly absently, lightly polishing the ornate crest on his gold civic chain as a bonus, proud as a fully-clothed Punch at his top-notch inspiration.

"He came here once, in 1955, and brought the house down," he added.

I'll bet he did, Parsnip thought.

Parsnip knew a lot about Billy Shoehorn – and it was a lot that he had a fair bet Evan Hartpress knew nothing about.

He tried his best to steer the mayor away from his obvious obsession.

"He retired," he began. "Hasn't worked for, what, twenty years?"

"Exactly!" Hartpress replied, his eyes brightening even further and bulging with delight. "That makes him a valuable commodity. Someone people would like to see, fall over backwards to see, possibly for the very last time."

"I doubt that he'll do it… I doubt that he *can* do it."

Hartpress held up a hand for silence. "Listen, Parsnip. I telephoned Billy personally two days ago and persuaded him to come down. Just for a one-off commemorative swan-song show in December. A way to say a proper goodbye to all his fans and go out on a high note.

"He was reluctant at first, of course. Sounded like he had a cold and was a bit under the weather. But by the end of the call he sounded positively *glowing* and offered to do three straight nights, 21st to 23rd, and at no extra cost to the borough – three nights for the price of two. Now, that's a good man for you. He's going to get us out of the financial doldrums by his generosity. What a trooper! Every inch a performer!"

"He might be…" *How can I put this?* Parsnip thought. "…a little past his prime now. I mean, he's in his eighties."

"What of it?" Hartpress bristled. "I'm eighty-one. Are you saying I'm too ancient to run a town council, Parsnip?"

His employee gave an uncomfortable splutter. "But that's not the same as giving a two hour show on three consecutive nights, singing and dancing, producing pigeons…"

"Come on. You know how long some of our planning committees last. They can be a song and dance too – and I've many times had to pull something out of the hat to calm things down."

Several of his colleagues chuckled knowingly at the mayor's feeble puns.

Not with a flock of pigeons stuffed up your jacket, Parsnip thought. "But his age…" he insisted.

"Never heard the like of it!" the mayor's momentary good-humoured wit evaporating. "Are you saying anyone over forty – that's about your age isn't it? – is too old and in the way; a dribbling half-witted incompetent who should be pensioned off?"

"I didn't say that, sir…" *Though in your case it's pretty accurate*, Parsnip considered.

"I should think not. Well, in any case, it's all settled. Billy will be here on the 18th and you'll book him into the Grand from the 18th to the 24th so that he has a couple of days in hand to settle in, rehearse and get used to the venue again in time for our special, our *magnificent* seasonal three-night extravaganza, leaving an overnight for him to rest up before travelling back to Bolton on the Christmas Eve service."

Parsnip scribbled the dates in a notebook.

"The shows won't only fill the local coffers that your dreadful summer events have emptied – or, at least, *not filled* – but they'll bring punters in from all over the county – all over the *country*, as we're going to advertise it nationally: all to see a big big draw like Billy and put Clapperton well and truly back on the map!"

Parsnip sighed, but well under his breath. If he knew Billy Shoehorn, and he certainly did know a thing or three about the vintage performer, he would certainly put their little seaside resort back on the map. But not in a way Mr Mayor was anticipating, and he left the room with an even more disheartened tread than when he arrived.

By the time he got back to his flat, Parsnip was feeling a little better about the whole situation.

If the town mayor had given the Shoehorn show the green light, set it up personally and was enthused to a high degree never before seen in the former blacksmith, this could be a way of getting Clapperton's resorts manager off the hook. If he could encourage Hartpress to personally endorse the show – perhaps with the promotional strap line *Evan Hartpress*

Proudly Presents… – then there was no way Parsnip could be blamed for any potential *irregularities* that followed. And he knew Mr Mayor had the kind of rampaging ego that led to him promoting himself in any and every way possible. Especially with a *photo opportunity*.

For the first time in fourteen days, Bradley Parsnip began to whistle.

Clapperton-on-Sea had been a major bucket-and-spade destination in the 1950s when trainloads of beach-loving holidaymakers descended on the small coastal community with its two industries, fisheries and tourism, arriving from all points north armed with all sorts of plastic paraphernalia for a happy sunbathe or a vigorous splish-splash in the surf.

Out of season it was usually empty, its sea front theatre closed and its nearby cinema open only at weekends screening the kind of up-to-date people-pleasers that would have attracted a crowd even if the venue had been isolated in the middle of one of the inland moors. Clapperton's summer activities included regular fairs, the occasional travelling circus, eight-hole greens golf, crazy golf, a wacky train that made its eccentric circles around the lawn that divided the sea from a parade of fancy hotels, the largest and most luxurious being the Grand, and a selection of arcades and beach kiosks offering everything from slot machine slots to winkle huts.

The Eagleton Theatre was gifted to the town in the late 1800s by Alderman Frederick Eagleton, born in the town and a former music hall entertainer himself who took his trade to all corners of the country all year round. At first it had even offered luxury first floor opera boxes for the more important and moneyed members of the community, though an opera was never performed there, but these had been removed during a stark late sixties renovation including the installation of second hand cinema seating. This was when the scale of visitors to the town was diminishing and its stage shows tended to be more oriented to periodic pop gigs and productions by local amateur dramatic groups with classic movies screened by a private film club during the rest of the week, to the annoyance of the management of the main cinema.

The town was fortunate to retain its rail link for a fading holiday clientele and this was only possible because it lay on the direct West Country route between London and Penzance, though the frequency of stops shrank over the years. Now trains stopped maybe five or six times a day when they used to pull up and disgorge every hour or so back when seaside holidays were paramount and stay-at-home television was still in its infancy. Few trains disgorged at Clapperton any more, their passengers few and far between and the most persistent travellers being term time clutches of

151

children on their morning and late afternoon journeys to and from out-of-town schools and universities.

Where most towns in the area were winding down for the festive season, with the last of their Christmas shows ending before Christmas week, Clapperton was abuzz with excitement at the prospect of the forthcoming three nights of music hall mayhem promised by the resort's voluble and irrepressible mayor that would climax the night before Christmas Eve.

This was the very last chance to see legendary performer Billy Shoehorn on stage, in person, in a little local seaside resort; it was unprecedented and tickets began flying off the shelf. Of course, many of them went to older patrons, some of whom hadn't been inside a theatre in decades, but who had known Shoehorn in his prime and seen him on several of those weekend TV variety shows popular in the sixties and seventies. He'd featured on a dozen Palladium nights, slotting in seamlessly with both British and American guests, and even made a couple of well-received appearances with comic staples Morecambe and Wise and Mike and Bernie Winters. But a number of younger patrons were keen to see him too, after a late nineties re-release of his mischievous sixties comic song *Grandma's Apples* was endorsed by ageing punk supremo and present-day darts pundit Tank Glumley.

Parsnip got a string of calls from former theatre owners who had been blighted by what became known in the industry as The Shoehorn Curse, but he thanked them for their concern and assured them that any knotty problems in the star's past had long since been ironed out: the mayor had guaranteed this – even though, in his ignorance, he had done nothing of the sort. Parsnip expected a spectacular but stress-free farewell performance from a one-time firebrand now in his respectable dotage. At least, that was what he hoped, and certainly promoted. They all wished him well and several even expressed disappointment that they weren't hosting the potentially lucrative shows themselves.

Came December 18, the day that Shoehorn was due to arrive, Parsnip got up early, put on his best suit (he only had two) and trotted down to the rail station to meet the performer from the noon train. The aged and rather overweight Shoehorn tumbled from the carriage dressed in a roll neck sweater, brown jacket and plaid trousers. He was carrying a leather brief case containing his sheet music and was closely followed by a harassed-looking assistant dressed in tweeds and Doc Martins. The assistant wore little round spectacles, had closed-cropped brown hair and was tugging a large travelling trunk on wheels secured with three leather belts; a small suitcase, presumably his own, was strapped to the side.

"Bradley Parsnip, I assume?" the impresario said, holding out a sweaty palm, a phlegmy purr in his voice. "Billy. But, of course, you knew that."

He had a very round face, like a football in shape, peppered with several blotches, warts, peduncles and liver spots. His thinning locks were swept back in a swathe of hair tonic and his blue eyes sparkled in the unseasonal sunshine. He had a stubby nose and slim moustache. They shook hands and Shoehorn flicked his head in the direction of his luggage supervisor. "This is Manfred. He looks after me and plays the piano onstage."

The two men exchanged wordless nods. Parsnip smiled. Manfred didn't and instead gave the resorts manager a dead-eyed stare, as if his mind was elsewhere. For a moment Parsnip thought the assistant looked familiar, and then he dismissed the idea: he'd never seen this intense-looking individual before.

"Now, Bradley, or is it Brad? I'll need to get settled into this hotel of yours and then I'll want to see the theatre," Shoehorn continued.

"Of course," Parsnip acceded. "I've set up a Press call for one o'clock with the mayor. He's a big fan, as you know. Quick photo session with the two of you shaking hands, a small interview with the local rag, nothing too taxing, and then I'll take you to the Eagleton."

"The what?"

"The theatre."

"Oh, yes. Played it years ago, when I was a jot younger and a little slimmer." He illustratively rubbed his belly with his spare hand and chuckled. "Well covered now, with many years of mirthful maturity."

Parsnip was impressed. So far Billy Shoehorn seemed amiable, co-operative and quite a model client. The three of them popped into a taxi and arrived at the hotel in less than five minutes where the sullen Manfred dragged the trunk from the boot and bumped it up the short staircase on its fragile wheels and into the lobby. At this point, Shoehorn asked a question that sent a brief chill up Parsnip's spine.

"Now, dear boy. Where's the bar?"

The photographer from the evening paper arrived just before one, accompanied by a trainee reporter who looked like she had been born long after Shoehorn had retired – a stunning if slightly scatty little blonde called Rhoda or Rhonda; Parnip couldn't remember which as he spent too long gazing into her beautiful blue eyes. Fortunately she had mugged up on her interviewee's career using pieces carried by the paper after the mayor had announced the seasonal shows back in early November. One of these articles had comprised a full page feature with neat archive snaps of the performer in his glory days, one showing him with his arm around entertainer Roy Hudd and another, curiously, accompanying one-time prime minister Edward Heath who had apparently played the piano for Shoehorn at a Downing Street social event. She asked a few on-script questions and the gruff photographer, who seemed more interested in the sausage rolls on hand for the occasion, took several shots of the mayor hand-shaking with his prize act.

Shoehorn, who appeared just a little flushed, was dressed in his own signature costume – a yellow chequered Zoot suit, hiked up to just below his latterly-developed man boobs that were fortuitously hidden under a matching waistcoat and red silk shirt. There was a green cravat at his throat and he wore a jauntily-placed cream fedora – all as he would on stage for his three performance nights.

With his thin grey moustache, heavy eyebrows, flashy garb and liver spots he looked a little like forties American jazz singer and bandleader Cab Calloway in his latter days. But there the resemblance ended personality-wise. Onstage Shoehorn was the consummate performer, talented, likeable, a crowd pleaser. Offstage he was anything but. Or, at least, he *had been* when on tour decades earlier. For the moment he seemed genial and jovial if a little short of breath and Parsnip wondered how the man was going to get through three consecutive two-hour shows at his age. Then he thought perhaps he'd rather not know.

The performer seemed especially entranced by the reporter and he quickly dismissed her photographer, Parsnip and – to his distress – the mayor, to whisk Rhoda or Rhonda into the bar for a "quiet, one-on-one tete a tete." They were there for more than three hours and Shoehorn emerged looking like a cat that had scored more than a simple bowl of cream. Rhoda or Rhonda followed, a tad flushed, and gradually tottered back to the office clutching her handbag and notebook close to her ample chest after several giggling mentions of champagne.

Much to Parsnip's surprise – and relieved delight – the first two appearances went by without incident. Shoehorn was his old, brilliant self, his songs were on pitch, the piano loaned by the local Women's Institute was in tune, his dances were pretty fluid for a man in his eighties, his magic tricks all went as planned and no pigeons were lost in the rafters. Backstage Shoehorn was remarkably affable and only took the occasional sip from a bottle of Jack Daniels that the taciturn Manfred kept in a former violin case with a padlock on the clasp. Parsnip could not believe his luck – and the luck of the mayor who was staking his reputation on the shows.

Hartpress – basking in the colourful snap of town mayor in full regalia and his celebrated hero, well-zooted, blazing from the front page of the Thursday edition of the evening paper, presaging opening night – was in his theatrical element. At each show he echoed his promotional posters' endorsement of his idol and on the final, climax performance he formally gave the dazzling music hall legend the symbolic keys to Clapperton-on-Sea.

"This is, and always will be, *your* town," he boasted, handing an especially crimson-faced Shoehorn a huge cardboard replica skeleton key, painted silver and adorned with the town crest, to a ripple of applause, the pop of a Press flashgun and the twinkle of several mobile phone cameras. "You may have been born north of the border, but you will always find a warm heart for you here, in the rural West Country, right by the ocean," he added.

Let's hope you don't *die* here, thought Parsnip, still plagued by doubts even though two nights of virtually flawless behaviour from Shoehorn had begun to relax him. Perhaps it would all go smoothly on the final night and both he and Clapperton would be saved from another great entertainments disaster. The problem was Parsnip still couldn't get Cleethorpes out of his mind: the place that had hastened Shoehorn's early retirement and given final fuel to the curse rumour. It wouldn't happen again, he decided. It couldn't. And if it did, or something like it, at least Mayor Hartpress and not Parsnip would be carrying the can.

Shoehorn's problem was drink, which was probably why his assistant Manfred kept the booze locked in an old violin case. In truth, alcohol abuse wasn't the main problem, or the most serious: that horror, sadly, was the pyromania.

The condition had only appeared in his latter performance days. Shoehorn could drink maybe three quarters of a bottle of any strong liquor and he would be fine; a little wavy on his legs and crimson-cheeked, but fine – a mature performer, ripe but effective. Anything over that amount and he became possessed with a need to set fire to anything that offended his gaze. This had mostly involved dressing rooms and other backstage areas out of sight of the general public – incidents that theatre managements and landlords tended to keep quiet due to the high profile and popularity of their act. There were standard "electrical fault" excuses bandied about for any local Press that got a whiff of black smoke from behind the curtains. Nevertheless the word got around the right circles and fire retardant dressing rooms began appearing in any venues due to host an appearance by Billy Shoehorn. This had all ended in Cleethorpes. And

Parsnip, on a weekend break, had been there to see it.

There had been little to disrupt Shoehorn's acclaimed one-man show that Saturday in the popular Cleethorpes Winter Gardens at around the turn of the century and the Humber estuary fishing port and tourist resort's theatre-goers were delighted by the entertainer's wide-ranging act. He was even poised to have a glowing review in the local paper, but that never happened.

No-one quite knew what triggered the incident that followed the show, excepting the booze which no doubt acted as an impetus if not a trigger. But very early on the Sunday morning, just after dawn and a mere handful of hours after the final curtain, Shoehorn went berserk.

Armed with portable containers of wood alcohol and lighter fuel, he began his rampage by setting fire to his room in an otherwise comfortable digs, almost exclusively frequented by theatrical folk appearing at various local venues. He left there and headed for the deserted leisure centre which he entered by breaking a back window and set light to a reception area.

Within minutes of this he broke into the pier and lit up an ice cream stall and several slot machines, eventually (though only incidentally) burning a hole in the side of the building. As if his burglary skills weren't enough, he next attempted to raze the mock castle ruin on the highest part of the surrounding cliffs that had been closed for renovation. He was only apprehended from his mad spree when he was accosted by two park keepers whilst attempting to detach the four foot bronzed statue *Boy With the Leaking Boot* from a water feature with a jemmy. He did not, however, try to set fire to it.

Because of his national popularity and the town's aim to keep the incident quiet, Shoehorn escaped prosecution and was hustled back to Bolton with the minimum of fuss, sans any payment for his services and with a hefty additional reparations bill to be honoured within six months. The cost of his off-stage activities had left him nearly destitute, but his reputation – and that of Cleethorpes – was maintained. He got himself back on his feet by auctioning off much of his cherished memorabilia. Meanwhile Cleethorpes' Winter Gardens, a long-standing venue for a variety of events, was swiftly demolished and replaced by flats. Parsnip hoped Shoehorn's spectacular outburst hadn't had anything to do with the decision.

December 23rd rolled around and Clapperton-on-Sea was bedecked with a blaze of seasonal lights and brightly-coloured bunting. Even the front entrance of the Eagleton Theatre had been highlighted with a large, illuminated plaster model of Santa and his reindeers, the tableaux

156

generously donated for the occasion by a local greengrocer. The place was packed, not a seat unclaimed, and the audience – many of whom had also attended either one or both of the previous night's shows – was buzzing with festive delight. It promised to be a very special occasion. And it was...

The first half went incredibly well, even better than before, packed with different musical hall songs and jokes, Shoehorn's own career reminiscences, and an occasional dance routine, especially remarkable as the man hadn't performed publicly for two decades. At the interval, while Parsnip was congratulating Shoehorn in his dressing room, the resorts manager noticed the violin case had been tossed into a corner, its clasp unclipped, padlock missing, with no signs of its volatile cargo. A shiver of concern should have registered at this point, but Parsnip was by then so beguiled by Shoehorn's infectious blarney that the matter passed him by.

The second half began with several long and rambling 'shaggy dog' monologues, Shoehorn dressed in a generous black tux in readiness for his magic act. They were received with great enthusiasm. Towards the end, Parsnip, who had been watching the act backstage, became aware that Manfred had disappeared. The piano stool was conspicuously unmanned and a large and mysterious black canvas bag by the stage door had also vanished. He crossed to the exit, hidden by the upstage foots, and turned the handle. It was locked. This was unexpected and Parsnip rattled the handle. Fortunately, he had his own set of keys to the theatre and slipped one into the lock. It turned and the door gave.

It was dark outside, but the theatre was colourfully illuminated by the Christmas lights strung along the sea front. There was no sign of Manfred, but the missing black canvas bag was tossed into a nearby flowerbed. It was then that Parsnip noticed that all the exit doors on this side of the building had been chained and padlocked. *WHAT?* he asked himself and began walking along the outside of the hall. All the doors were similarly secured. As he examined each exit and tested the unyielding chains, he could hear the amplified Shoehorn going through his paces.

"Now, you all know what time it is now. It's time to – what is it? – splice the...?"

As one the audience replied in strong voice: "*SPLICE THE MAIN BRACE!*" His catch phrase.

Inside the hall, Shoehorn began toasting the audience from a whiskey glass on a small table.

"It's only water, as usual," he told them. "Don't worry, I'm not doing a Dave Allen!" Laughter.

After several sips he whipped the missing Jack Daniels bottle from a magic cloth and tipped a generous amount into his glass.

"I lied!" he shouted. "It's a special occasion. My last ever show. Now I'll toast YOU, my loyal fans, in the proper manner. Splice the main brace!"

There was a delighted response, plus much cheering and hand clapping. Shoehorn took several swigs, accompanied by the toast and its boisterous echo.

Even then, Parsnip wasn't worried about the booze. Billy could handle it. He was in top form. By then Parsnip was distracted by the antics of Manfred, who was still missing. Only that oddball assistant could have locked up the entire theatre. But why? There were a good three hundred people trapped inside the Eagleton and Shoehorn was launching into his magic act. Parsnip went cold, and it was not from the bracing winter sea air. A magic act that included real fire! *Jesus!*

A now panicked Parsnip began racing around a circuit of the building to get back to the now-open stage door. But he lost his footing as he neared the stage area, tripped over an unseen, abandoned supermarket trolley and crashed into a concrete post head-on, losing consciousness.

Inside, Shoehorn had launched into his 'funny drunk' act. But this time, whilst he was unarguably funny, he was also *really* drunk. As he began wobbling about ineptly spinning plates from a series of flexible poles, causing them to crash on to the stage around him, the audience went into delighted hysterics. And when several pigeons burst from his tux during one spectacular crescendo of shattering crockery and fanned up into the rafters, his fans began rocking in their seats.

Their uncontained mirth hit fever pitch when one of spooked pigeons wheeled away from its colleagues and into the main concourse in a spontaneous bombing run where it splattered the mayor with a generous helping of incontinence only possible from a large and nervous bird escaping the confines of a fat magician's oversized but claustrophobic dinner jacket in a turmoil of shattering dinner plates, after which it fluttered off to perch unconcerned on a spot lamp bracket, cooing proudly and peering under a raised wing.

Kicking aside the broken plates and giggling, Shoehorn produced his unlit brands which he was planning to ignite and juggle.

"And now, be prepared for my most spectacular trick ever!" he announced.

As he wrestled with the brands, he suddenly turned to the audience and

158

said: "Here's a great joke I heard the other day. There was this talent agent who was looking for family acts. One morning a bunch of folk came to see him saying they had the best family act in the world. There was mum and dad, three kids in their early teens, even a toddler in a pretty little bonnet, grandma and grandpa, and they looked like real apple-pie folk, as our American friends would say. So the agent says 'Show me what you've got...'

With increasing horror, Mayor Hartpress, still wiping pigeon guano from his jacket with a crumpled handkerchief, realised that Shoehorn was embarking on the longest, most obscene joke in showbiz history – a notorious tale he had heard in several men's clubs over the years, in which the family perform gross and perverted sexual acts with one another after which the traumatized agent asks: 'What do you call yourselves?' and the father replies...

"*The Aristocrats!*" Hartpress breathed, seeing his valuable career suddenly evaporating. "Oh, no, no, no. Please, no! Not in sleepy little Clapperton-on..."

But the audience was already ahead of him.

To cries of shock, a disorganized scrambling from seats and the placing of hands over the ears of the young, a third of the audience, those not already sitting open-mouthed, rushed and tumbled towards the fire exits – only to find the doors wouldn't open. A loud rattling of the customarily compliant handles began. Seeing the reaction, Shoehorn swiftly brought the joke to its inevitable conclusion in the middle of an exceptionally graphic perversion and, anxious to bring his patrons back on side, began lighting the brands with a sturdy "And NOW!"

It was the last thing he said before turning away, taking a swig of accelerant and swinging back to spray a ribbon of flame through one of the brands and into the air. Unfortunately, in his unsteady state he failed to complete the ninety-degree turn and instead of projecting relatively safely towards the open auditorium he hit one of the side curtains. Curtains, being what they are, and especially in a town as parsimonious as Clapperton, tended to be overlooked by local managers – as in this case. They were old, dusty and hadn't been cleaned in a decade. Naturally, the touch of a naked flame caused the Clapperton drape to ignite like a firecracker.

Apparently delighted with this, Shoehorn deliberately lit the other curtain on the opposite side of the stage. He was now framed by burning swathes of polyester, his face gleaming in the glow, his eyes glassed and popping. The remaining pigeons from his jacket began escaping and flapping around the room, spooked and shitting on the audience who were now screaming and trying desperately to get out of the blocked doorways. It was then that

159

Shoehorn drenched the now-vacated front seats with a mouthful of burning fluid.

Again through budgetary issues, Clapperton's councillors had never replaced the covering of its old flip-up cinema seating with fire-retardant material. Consequently, hit by a wave of accelerant and a naked flame, the front row ignited with the enthusiasm of a line of duck down duvets on a Guy Fawkes bonfire.

It was at this point that the dazed and bloody resorts manager staggered through the open stage door, hidden by the blazing stage left curtain and the already smoking flats at the back. He tumbled into view, keeping clear of the enthusiastic drapery firestorm and its sparks, and scampered down the short flight of wooden steps, stage left. He was gripping a fire axe found backstage and heading for the mayor, who had made his way towards the stage, pushing panicked patrons aside and looking for a way out. Parsnip grabbed the wild-eyed councillor by the sleeve.

"Come with me!" he barked. A stricken Hartpress tried to pull away. But Parsnip increased his grip on the man and growled in his ear: "Now! Or I'll punch you in the face."

Hartpress did as he was told, and allowed himself to be dragged up the wooden stairs, now independently beginning to smoke, around the now-roaring curtain and out of the stage door. Parsnip released Hartpress and swung the fire axe so that it shattered the obstruction securing the nearest exit door. Lock and chain cascaded to the ground and the door burst open. A crowd of desperate theatregoers tumbled into the night, accompanied by a flight of relieved pigeons.

"Now go round the building and get the rest of those doors open!" Parsnip ordered the wild-eyed mayor, looking increasingly like a rabbit caught in the headlights; then he dashed back to the stage door. He brushed against a stern-looking Rhoda or Rhonda who had followed them outside. Hartpress turned to run but the reporter, who had heard the conversation and had also phoned her photographer and the fire brigade (in that order), warned him: "If you run away I'll crucify you in Monday's paper!" After which the mayor laid into the bolted doors with the axe and some renewed vigour.

Inside, the venue was well ablaze, but the patrons managed to escape the conflagration as one by one the exit doors swung open and a sooty-faced mayor moved on to the next egress waving his fire axe around like a majorette's baton. As Parsnip cantered on to the stage, the ferocity of its flames now amplified by the sudden intake of air from the opening exit doors, he saw Shoehorn was now staggering about, seriously inebriated, unsteady on his feet and belching flares of wayward fire in all directions.

He was blindly sucking more and more accelerant into his mouth as if his life depended on it. And it did.

For in one unfortunate moment, Shoehorn's level of intoxication coupled with his continuing intake of noxious fluids caused him to produce a massive hiccough. Parsnip could not believe what happened next – something he thought was contrary to the laws of physics: the performer exploded. Bits of flesh and tuxedo burst outwards from Shoehorn's now-deceased body, its remains pirouetting towards the boards, and splattered Parsnip as he reached too late for a fire extinguisher. Parsnip had been concerned at the fire aspects of the act, rightly so considering... But the mayor had approved the magic act in its entirety so responsibility for that had also shifted away from the resorts manager. Even so, it was a sad end for a man who had given so much pleasure to his followers. Until that final night in Clapperton. Talk about going out with a bang...

The story should end there, but for those who want to know what happened afterwards, well...

Reporter Rhoda or Rhonda (actually Rula) wrote a glowing book about Shoehorn, extensively glamorising his final performance as a "cry from the heart" – his explosive condition allegedly triggered by a disreputable uncle who used to lock the juvenile Billy in a cupboard when he was ten for slurping soup – glamorising and enhancing his reputation well beyond what was probably appropriate.

The man had no family but had agreed that Rula could write his life story, a deal hatched on that first magic tete-a-tete in Clapperton's Grand Hotel bar. He met up with her each afternoon to continue their animated chatter, which some locals viewed as a little unhealthy: a man in his eighties cosying up to a pretty young thing in her twenties, and with alcohol involved. Subsequently, Shoehorn phoned his agent after lunch on the 22nd to set up the lucrative book contract, among other things. His agent, who had not heard from his rather scary client for a good ten years, was surprised to learn that he was still working – and even more surprised on Christmas Eve when he heard he was dead.

Rula's book, *That Final Flame: The Life and Death of Billy Shoehorn*, turned out to be a best-seller.

Its poignant subject had left his entire estate to his pretty biographer, whom he described to his agent as "the daughter I never had." It comprised a substantial and valuable career archive which he had managed to reclaim after the Cleethorpes incident decimated his finances through the support of a huge international network of devoted fans. The bulk of his twenty years of restored wealth also went to Rula, with a generous percentage

161

allotted to various high-profile substance abuse charities.

And it was one hell of a story.

For Rula had also discovered that Manfred was not so much complicit in the Yuletide inferno, but was its architect.

She tracked the maverick down and unmasked him as the former homicidal magician from the Hadley Brimblecombe Talent Agency, Dr Scream, who had nearly sawed a woman in half the previous season on Clapperton pier. Manfred had read about Shoehorn's impending Christmas shows, radically changed his appearance and latched himself on to the incorrigible showman as his assistant/accompanist whilst quietly vowing vengeance on the town that had both sacked him and caused him to be detained in a secure unit for, apparently, not long enough, returning to the resort on a mission.

He could see that Shoehorn had turned over a new leaf and that his days of arson were far behind. But he also knew old '*splice the main brace*' was a largely-reformed alcoholic who could take a few sips of Jack to get him through a show, but was vulnerable to any further intoxication. So Manfred – real name, ironically, Bert Tipsy – had kept the booze under wraps for two nights and unleashed it from its secure case for the third night finale, even encouraging Shoehorn to celebrate his swan song in legendary style by going out "in a blaze of glory." It turned out to be quite a blaze, though its orchestrator missed the conflagration itself by hightailing it away on the last train out of town.

Manfred had also replaced the mild accelerant Shoehorn used for his occasional fire acts, rectified spirit, with the volatile and highly flammable chemical ethanol and the part-time magician had been too drunk by that stage of his act to detect its distinguishing odour. Almost undetectable to the eye, the colourless liquid had rampaged into his bloodstream and made him even drunker. Anticipating the explosive result Manfred had, unknown to his employer, chained and bolted the theatre doors to forever damn the man's reputation and stake his own personal revenge on Clapperton and its pernickety fish-and-chips community by, as he later put it from his prison cell, "frying tonight."

Mayor Hartpress was initially dubbed a hero for helping free the trapped audience. But the mood soon changed when the truth emerged and he was successfully prosecuted and then sacked by his own council for allowing a live fire act to be staged in an enclosed (and now devastated) public space. Council members never liked the vain and bull-headed tyrant anyway and Hartpress gradually disappeared from community life, taking up solitary angling from an isolated stretch of rocks a mile down the coast, his justification of "he'll be okay; he's done the fire thing many times without

162

a problem" ringing pitilessly in his ears.

His fellow councillors had used the mayor's notoriously dominating personality to distance themselves from the booking and its fiery finale. Planning sub-committee stalwart Belinda Bakersfield, hooting sternly through her owl-like spectacles, assured residents, "We never wanted the man in the first place," and deputy finance chairman Wilfred Brace concurred compellingly, adding more pathetically, "We thought he would lower the tone of our beautiful town." Instead it had razed it...

But this pitiful shifting of blame fell apart when reporter Rula published council minutes revealing that at both the crucial October Parsnip-roast, and in the subsequent full council session that ratified the decision to welcome Shoehorn and his uncensored act, members had voted unanimously in favour of the booking. Despite their protestations, all of them lost their seats during local elections the following May. It was uncertain how many thereafter resorted to remote angling to fill their days.

As for Parsnip, he was completely exonerated for his part in booking Shoehorn. In fact, he became especially vaunted for helping save the lives of all of the third night patrons of the Eagleton, which itself had been totally gutted by the unexpected inferno and would later be rebuilt as an amusement arcade. His valiant status seriously enhanced his career prospects and Parsnip was touted nationally by a competing swarm of local councils to become their celebrated and, more importantly, *well-funded* resorts manager – and he never again had to use the cut-price services of the Hadley Brimblecombe Talent Agency.

I think he ended up in Cleethorpes...

A Flickering Log Fire

"Do you know what the most interesting element of that story is?" Dara asked me.

"What?" I asked him, sounding disinterested.

"Point of view," Dara said. "That story could have been written from one of several points of view: the reporter, the music hall performer, the vengeful Manfred, even the bully-boy mayor – and they all would have told the same tale but with a different emphasis. But the writer chose the resort manager. Probably the most satisfying in the end, right?"

"Right," I mumbled.

I was distracted because it struck me how much storyteller number seven had reminded me of my short-lived song writing chum from that long-gone pop band, and the strange irony of the observation. That now distant friend – *what was he called again?* – had an irrepressible sense of humour and was always cracking jokes, even in the most serious of moments; which was okay, but a bit tiresome at more fractious times. He had the high red cheeks of an apple scrumper, a bit like Billy Shoehorn and, had we been closer, he would probably have led me into all sorts of juvenile scrapes and May games. The odd point, however, was this: during the summer season he used to work at the seaside, sometimes monitoring the donkey rides, often manning one of the holiday gift kiosks. He even ran the Punch and Judy stall once when the puppeteer got a disabling bout of curry back draft.

I looked up, prepared to pass on this coincidental info to my friendly barman when I caught a glimpse of storyteller eight from the corner of an eye, standing stock still under the readers' spotlight. The changeover had been so quick I hadn't heard him step up. He was waiting to begin and just staring at me, a tad unnervingly. It turned out that he was actually looking past me and waiting for a cue from Dara. There was a pause and Dara

165

suddenly said: "Why don't we take a short break?"

Eight nodded and retreated back into the shadows. Everyone else began shuffling in their seats, as if preparing to stretch out or to rise for another libation. It occurred to me that until then I had appeared to be the only one drinking.

Surely not…

"You look tired," Dara said, with concern.

It was true, my eyes were drooping.

"I'm not bored," I explained.

"Of course not," he sympathised. "It's just a whole bunch of stories all told together like this, and out of the blue, can be pretty demanding; rather exhausting. Why not get your head down for a few snores? We always take a break about half way through, anyway; a chance to clear the narrator muscles and the mind. Like those four hour Biblical epics they used to show at the local flea pit with an Intermission after the first hundred minutes for patrons to stretch their legs and grab another bag of popcorn and some Kia-ora. Why not take one of the comfy chairs?"

Dara insisted by taking my elbow and leading me away from the bar towards the flickering log fire and an especially snug-looking brown leather recliner. I sank into its interior with a sigh, flipped up the foot rest and the world drifted away.

Intermission

"Where *is* my brother?"

Dr Shana Coleman could see that Brenda Waite was concerned; deeply concerned. She was sitting in a fashionable steel and leather chair opposite the doctor's desk, handbag on her lap, twisting its handle between her fingers like she was kneading bread dough. A slightly built, smartly dressed woman with blue eyes and a pale complexion, she was staring past Shana as she spoke, as if she was focussed on some distant object in the gardens outside the triple glazed windows. In fact, she was looking at the reflection of her own anxious expression.

"Dara's Bar," Shana replied. She smoothed some wrinkles from her striking black dress; her dark hair swept around her shoulders as she made the gentle gesture and her green eyes sparkled, as if her nervous system was charged with an alluring challenge.

Brenda already knew the answer, of course. She had agreed to this option several weeks earlier; she knew the risks and potential benefits of putting her brother Will out into the big big world and had been prepared to take them. He couldn't go on like this: like he had been, shuffling to and from a dreary, life-sapping job. And, anyway, she had her own baggage, sorting out her own life, what with her marriage to Roy collapsing that Christmas and the subsequent sticky divorce, so she had little time to concentrate on the eccentricities of her older brother.

"But it's been a long time," Brenda insisted, flicking a chestnut curl from the corner of an eye. "Will should be back with us by now."

"Not yet," Shana said, trying to calm her. "Big steps to begin with; baby steps at the end. Dara will be kind to him, and hopefully bring an end to all this nonsense."

"It's not nonsense, Shana. It's a need that he has. He has to fulfil it, or..."

167

She let the sentence hang, but both women knew the implications of that dangling conjunction. Worse still, the man was almost too old to start afresh, no matter how youthful his spirit. He was in danger of completely losing it.

Brenda clarified: "It's because he reads newspapers, books and watches films when he gets home – and he drinks too much beer when he's flopped out in that arm chair. Instead of writing his own words he lives vicariously through other people's stories. How is this bar thing going to help, especially with the drinking?"

"Don't worry about the drinking. That will solve itself…"

"I've heard that one before. And then he *cracks another cold one*, as he puts it."

"He just needs to stay there a while longer, uninterrupted," Shana explained. "He's getting so *involved*, and I'm certain there's a breakthrough on the way. He's really responding to Dara – as I thought he would. That barman is a very persuasive mentor and, to be honest, Will seems totally in his element."

"That's the booze."

"Something far deeper is happening."

"I wish I could believe that. It's been so long…"

"Not quite long enough."

"Just a little while longer, then?"

"Yes. Just a little while. You'll see. It won't do any *harm*, you know."

"It's not the harm that bothers me," Brenda said, contradicting herself in her concern. "It's the *good* that I want to see."

"It will be all right, I promise."

"I hope so…"

Renewal

I, Will Buckwater, had the most satisfying sleep in years. At least, I think I did, because it also seemed only a matter of minutes before Dara was waking me with some nonsense about those sixties puppet shows I loved when I was a kid and moments later I was back on a bar stool with a pint in front of me and the expectation of another storyteller in the wings.

"Feeling better?" he asked.

"Much," I said. And I was. Renewed.

"Ready to go again?"

"Ready."

Number Eight stood once more, cleared his throat noisily and began.

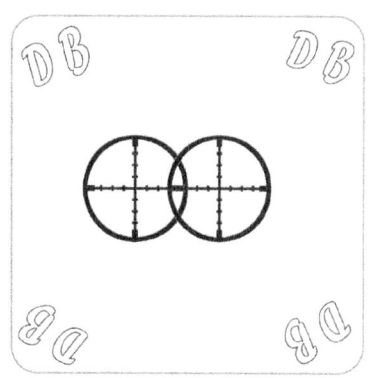

One For the Price of Two

I was pulling up the last of the season's potatoes when I heard the latch on the gate of the allotment snap back. I looked up and saw an elderly man with white hair and a determined expression striding up the grass path between two rows of lettuces. He was well-dressed in a check shirt and beige pants and held a plaid jacket over his right shoulder, relaxing in the late summer sunshine. He came to a halt about six feet away from me and as I straightened up to meet his gaze he said: "I hear you're going to kill me, Mr Black."

I knew who he was instantly. What surprised me was that he knew who I was, what I was planning and how he had found me in one of my most obscure hidey-holes: a First in my fifteen years as an assassin. He was Sir Walden Sparks, owner and CEO of Hoove-Laytton Pharmaceuticals, custodians of the BrightSun range of medicines and one of the largest drugs companies in the world. A man you couldn't get to see in his office, let alone wandering around unprotected, sans chaperone, in a tiny public allotment in a small, out-of-the-way village in West Cornwall.

I dropped the spuds in a basket. "You must have me confused…" I began. My head was briefly twirling a roundabout of confused thoughts.

But he immediately interrupted. "Let's be straight with each other, Mr Black, if that really is your name. We are adults and, at our age, more suited to straight talking. You were hired by my two lieutenants at Hoove-Laytton, Mr Parsons and Mr Clarke. Very smart and ambitious young men who failed to impress you so much that I understand you refer privately to them as Mutt and Jeff. A lot of talk and no listening."

It was the first time in my professional life that my mouth had dropped open. You only read about that happening in books, but it really happened to me, including an accompanying dribble of drool. And I've seen some pretty terrible things in my time...

My guest didn't seem to notice and continued: "Believe me, Mr Black, if those two corporate morons could find you on the dark dark web, why would you think I couldn't track you down as well, with the extensive communications network I have access to?"

"You'd better come in," I said, indicating the large wooden shed I had built for myself just after I signed up for this big corner plot of the village allotment. The shed had a wide window at the front, a high roof to take into account my five foot eleven, toe to dome, and a secret space below ground where I kept my rifles, files and a top-of-the-range military drone and its controls. There was a park bench outside, just below the windows.

"I prefer to stay out here, under the circumstances," Sparks replied, and I noticed he was standing a little to one side of me. Just enough for a skilled marksman on the far side of the football field spreading out either side of the two-acre growing space to get in an unimpeded shot. Not so unchaperoned, then. I nodded and waved him towards the seat. He obviously had something important to say to me, so there was little chance of his bodyguard shooting me in full view of the lads playing a lame but spirited five-a-side match twenty yards away on the grass – and, contract or no contract, I was going to listen to what that was. We sat, my future target on my left, each crossing our legs away from each other but without disdain. He cleared his throat.

"You remember what Parsons and Clarke told you?" he asked.

I nodded. I remembered it well. I didn't like either of them; too self-assured, to the point of narcissism. But they gave a good case and an exceptional fee and it was just another job – perhaps a retirement gift.

They'd called it a "double-header."

That was their kind of joke, they said.

I said I never joked when a man's life was at stake. But they still laughed – again – and said it was a good joke. A double-header: shooting the head of the company in the head. And they laughed a third time.

I allowed myself a dark smile. They were paying me well enough for the assignment (and could afford it, being sharpshooters within their own province in an industry where hundreds of billions sloshed around): half a Mill up front and another half Mill on completion. That's twice what I would normally charge for a medium-profile shoot; kind of one-for-the-price-of-two territory, and that's OK with me.

172

But shooting someone in cold blood from a distance with a high-powered rifle isn't something you turn into a stand-up routine, even in these days when pretty much anything goes. It's a serious business: it takes time, a lot of planning and, yes, even some thought for the victim, such as how he will look at the end of it. Also, do you want it to appear vindictive or just unfortunate? Though I guess any shot to the head is going to look pretty vindictive ultimately, and pretty messy. Like penetrating a water melon with a small rock launched at 2,500 feet per second.

It's simple, they told me: we set him up for you, you take him down, we sort out the fallout, pretend to grieve, mollify the family and the business reverts to our control. Just needs to be done in public, so both of us are clearly off the hook, and leave the rest of the alibi to us.

I'll give them this: they were nothing short of confident. And prepared. I'd have to watch my back with these two.

Most times I like to meet the victim beforehand, socially if possible, and without too many witnesses. It's nice to know if there are any character traits that might come in handy when setting up the target, such as beneficial idiosyncrasies, location and so on. Some are indoor birds, which can be a little restrictive as my speciality is long-range assassinations, so the outdoor freaks are the easiest to dispatch.

I had met these prominent paymasters in a squalid little pre-fabricated hut in a remote rural quarry. They had contacted me through the usual dark channels, made their proposal and arranged the secluded meet-up to present their case. I carried out the standard security checks to protect my back, armed myself, used a sophisticated facial modification make-up to disguise my real appearance and arrived at the location in an unpretentious, untraceable saloon.

We nodded at the doorway but did not shake hands. The unit had a main office, where I sat in one plastic chair near the entrance and the party of two behind a serviceable desk, one in a comfortable seat and the other shoehorned into a plastic replica, like me. It was pretty Spartan with a separate relaxation space at one end, where workmen ate their meals and listened to the radio, and a lavatory and washroom at the other. Set amongst a forest of mature pines, the hut looked like it was used by a logging company but there were few signs, short of deep tyre ruts in the ground and the scent of potpourri and petrol chainsaws. The whole area was deserted.

One of the two men handed me a computer disk and a colour snap of their boss, Sir Walden Sparks, the former, which I watched briefly on my tablet, showing him talking at some medical conference in Geneva. This guy seemed a nice enough soul, calm and cultured voice, around sixty, carrying his grey hair with distinction, fit and athletic for his age but bearing the rheumy eyes of someone who had been doing too much reading or screen work. CEO of Hoove-Laytton Pharmaceuticals he was concerned about a new drug that the company was developing and his stance – that Mutt and Jeff said was far outside any drugs company's remit and highly dangerous to both procedures and profits – was threatening not only Hoove-Laytton but the entire pharmaceutical industry. Okay, I said, unconvinced, and listened.

They announced themselves as Mr Parsons and Mr Clarke which, remarkably, turned out to be their real names, unlike mine. They were respectively second-in-command and third string in the Sparks empire. They were well-appointed and of singular purpose.

Parsons did most of the talking. He was tall with black hair, dark eyes under heavy eyebrows, a thin moustache and a small pink mole on the left of his chin that he fingered occasionally while he spoke as if caressing a nipple. He was self-assured to the point of arrogance, his harsh and strident voice filling the room as he perpetually rocked from side to side in his snug black leather swivel chair, obviously belonging to the site foreman. He wore a blue pin stripe suit, suggesting a perilous slyness of purpose; his black shoes were highly polished with no hint of the mud outside, as if he'd landed from a helicopter, and his socks were red and grey Argyle.

Clarke interjected the odd technical detail here and there and did a lot of urgent nodding. He was clearly the passive side of the relationship, but probably the man who could accurately spout both the scientific and financial elements of any given subject at the drop of a hat. He had a round, almost moon-like face, pale and non-descript, with a distracting twitch in one eye partly hidden by small, oval glasses with steel frames. Shorter than Parsons, he walked with a rolling gait, as if rotating around invisible objects, perhaps the result of a spinal injury, and when seated he kept his legs firmly crossed, as if protecting his manhood. His shoes were brown, as were his socks, and along with his Tweed suit gave him a professorial air, suggesting he should have been scratching formulae on a blackboard with chalk rather than playing second fiddle to his dominant and fragrant colleague.

Parsons dived straight into it. He said that Terradone – the new drug referred to on the disk – would heal the planet as it offered lifelong immunity from all diseases. It was a touchstone cure of great excellence, huge importance: a universal panacea.

"A *panpharmacon*," Clarke interrupted. Parsons glared at him and Clarke mouthed an apology.

"And your CEO is threatening that somehow?" I asked.

"He's had a brainstorm. Down to his age, we think. He's not the man he was twenty years ago when he led the pharmaceuticals industry with his bold and ambitious vision for the future."

Parsons fleetingly sounded like a promotional pamphlet.

"He's had a complete U-turn. He's recently been consorting with anti-jab protesters and is about to change the whole way vaccines are administered. If he has his way, the entire system will be put in jeopardy, no-one will want to be vaccinated and these unvaccinated people – erroneously dubbed 'healthy' with a working immune system, *hah!* – will become a severe threat to happily vaccinated people, who are protected by a unique and unparalleled chemical umbrella of herd immunity."

He leaned forward and glared at me. "Do you want your children and beloved elderly relatives to die because of this unacceptably hazardous unleashing of whole communities of untreated idiots?

"And there's the loss of income to take into account," I said.

"*Precisely!*" Parsons sat back and gave his mole a tweek. "It would cripple Hoove-Laytton for a start, and the impact on the industry in general would be catastrophic. We're talking tens of billions..."

"Perhaps *hundreds* of billions," Clarke added.

"Easily," Parsons said. "Imagine it! A universal panacea for all diseases. Everything from the common cold to, say, ebola; terrorist tools like anthrax. Extraordinary. The pressure is on to achieve it and the public are screaming out for it."

"If it works," I suggested.

Parsons gave me a dark look. "Oh, it will work!" he said.

"Work..." Clarke appended quietly in echolalia.

The man behind the development of Terradone was billionaire Rayland Muscat, Parsons revealed.

"If you ever meet him, it's *Rayland*. Don't call him Ray," Clarke interjected, looking pleased with himself. Parsons ignored him. "Only the President can call him Ray," Clarke added.

Parsons sighed and continued: "Until recently he was in partnership with Sir Walden. Muscat runs Exosphere.

"The internet giant..."

Parsons knew this, I knew this, and Parsons asked Clarke to "go get some coffee." Clarke grunted, rose and scuttled across the room in his rotating manner, as if caught in a strong headwind, returning in moments with a pathetic "Can't find the kettle." He resumed his seat and, avoiding Parsons' cold glances, pretended to be distractedly interested in a wayward strand of cotton on one of his socks.

"We carried out human trials in a village in Angola," Parsons said.

"Bandari," Clarke resumed, unwisely.

"They proved phenomenally successful…"

"Bandari. It means *haven* in Swahili. Rather ironic, considering what…"

"*Coffee!*" Parsons barked sharply, cutting his colleague off and shooting him the kind of daggers that had the psychological impact of a brace of my ballistic knives, launched in anger. "Find a kettle!"

Clarke dropped his head remorsefully. I shook mine and wondered why Clarke was even here as Parsons was clearly in complete control. My view of the proverbial playing field was clear enough without caffeine. Nowadays, it just made me want to piss more frequently and, anyway, I just wanted to get my business done and out of this constrictive atmosphere ASAP.

I looked back at the photograph of their target. And I just thought: In three days' time I'm going to kill you.

Now I was looking at the man himself, in the face, waiting to examine his side of the coin, knowing that no matter how convincing his story I was still being paid a lot of money to bring its telling to an abrupt end. That's if Sparks' own shooter didn't remove me from the board first. I looked around for the telltale glint of sunlight on a strategically-placed gun sight – I'd have chosen that hilly spinney about a mile to the east – but could see nothing suspicious. Perhaps Sparks was confident enough about his safety in this little lost West Country haven to have truly come alone. I couldn't see the village car park from here so there was no sign of a black SUV bristling with antenna. It was unlikely that he was on his own, but not unprecedented. With great power and money comes great conceit.

"As you know, or perhaps you don't, there were trials of Terradone. They took place in Africa. We've done that many times, as have other drugs conglomerates. We went back to Angola. It's a pretty volatile country, the crime rate is high and most of the rural population are illiterate, very poor and comprised mainly of subsistence farmers. The cost of living is astronomical. This is despite its lively trade in diamonds and its lucrative oil industry – it's described as 'the Kuwait of Africa.' None of that income trickles down to the people, mostly due to corrupt government officials – though a government, for our purposes, eager to take the substantial inducement we offered to commandeer one of their villages."

"Bandari."

"They mentioned it."

"Briefly."

"They would. *For medical research*, we said. And, oh, did we research them! There were up to a hundred men, women and children in that village, all fairly isolated from the main population – and we kept it that way.

"No-one in the surrounding area had a clue about what we were doing, nor did the folk at FAPLA – that's the People's Armed Forces for the Liberation of Angola, its national militia. But you'd know that; you've probably been there. They took the money and left us alone. There was the occasional jeep patrol of gun-toting riff-raff, but they were even more easily bribed to keep on going.

"We applied the product and monitored the results. Within days there were several deaths and, as our team continued to scrutinize developments over the next year or so we began detecting other health anomalies, particularly in the infant sector – signs of autism, bone and skin mutations, flu-like symptoms. It was exasperating. In the end it got so bad that Parsons and Clarke ordered a tidy-up and the quiet extraction of the scientists. They brought in a militia group from Luanda who basically massacred the remaining villagers, burned their homes to the ground and bulldozed the charred remains into the soil.

"To ensure none of this got back to the authorities – who, despite their own shady activities, might have taken some action against the company – Parsons engaged a group of US-based mercenaries we occasionally use for clean-up jobs to take care of our resourceful Luandans. They were offered a large bounty for a fictitious job, plus a safe haven following the Bandari affair; then they were lured to an isolated spot and liquidated in a similar manner to stop any of them talking if captured by FAPLA. As I said, we knew that even FAPLA with its deep and eager pockets might have objected to the wholesale slaughter of an encampment of their citizens by an outside Western corporation."

"But why?" I asked. "Apart from the money, why would Muscat want to force a potentially fatal drug on the global human population?"

"Have you heard about the sixth extinction?" Sparks asked.

I wondered if he was talking about one of my hits, so I kept mum.

"It's what's driving Muscat," I was told. "The fear of it."

"Fear?"

"There have been five extinctions in the life of this planet," Sparks continued, assuming I was ignorant of the facts, which, it turned out, I was. "As far as we know, the first was 440 million years ago, and the most recent 65 million years ago."

"Not much to worry about, then," I said, with a faint smile. Sparks remained grim-faced.

177

"Scientists across the globe are currently seriously alarmed that the sixth such extermination of life is imminent and they're saying it will be more devastating than the one that wiped out the dinosaurs. That event, though dramatic, clearly left some forms of life behind. This won't. We've caused it – the human race – and will be eliminating ourselves thanks to sickness, over-population, and some of our unwise technological and scientific choices."

He crossed his legs in my direction this time, so we looked like two mannequins on the bench, about to leap to the right in harmonious synchronisation.

"We're losing species – some of them important *buffer* species – at a rate of up to 2,000 a year, worst case scenario and, as they blink out, infectious diseases increase throughout the animal kingdom, directly impacting humanity's chance of survival."

Annoyingly, he proffered air speech marks with the index and middle fingers of both hands. "This 'biological annihilation' comes from massive anthropogenic erosion of biodiversity – and of the ecosystem essential to keep civilization on course. In other words, we're going to be dead, with no reprieve."

It was a sobering thought, if true. But I was wondering where all this was leading. I was about to find out.

"Rayland Muscat wants to prevent this sixth event."

"With Terradone?"

"With Terradone, yes. Terradone does not work, as I told you. Not in the way they're promoting it, at least. It's not a universal panacea, a magic potion. It's not even a placebo. It has genetic markers aimed at reducing the present population by at least half, mainly the old and those with existing conditions but mostly missing the young, to give our race a fighting chance of survival. So not only is it *not* a cure-all for global health, it's both a population reduction tool and a tracking system as each shot includes an RFID microchip, that's a radio frequency identity chip, so that scientists can track the recipients – and log how many die and how quickly. It will also allow those chipped to check the vaccination status of everyone they meet through a special phone application, so they can report anyone un-chipped as a danger to the herd. This story was dismissed as a hoax by Muscat, and that was generally accepted as the public are pretty gullible if handled with enough authority. But it was a double bluff as Muscat has been stockpiling RFIDs for months.

"Muscat is aware that our annual flu jab is only, at best, 13% effective and its most outstanding and unreported features are that firstly it does not prevent the current season's breed of influenza as its content is based on an earlier version before the strain mutated; secondly, it actually makes its mostly elderly recipients more ill than if they just caught the annual bug naturally and used their own immunity to fight it; and three, that it has caused numerous fatalities."

Sparks finished counting off the bullet points on his fingers.

"Terradone's like the Theory of Everything, much vaunted by scientists a few years ago, that was also a myth. You can't combine quantum mechanics and classical physics into a unified approach to explain the laws of the universe. It's impossible to achieve. Like oil and water, the two don't coalesce. But for Terradone, it's a perfect framework to surreptitiously cull the population."

"But that's…"

"Immoral, criminal, despicable: all those adjectives. Fortunately for Muscat, he has most of the world governments and their leaders on his side. They're crying out for something that will effectively remove all disease, and cut back on the numbers of a potentially volatile and threatening general public. And they like his financial incentives. Not only will it make them very very rich, but it will bolster their positions in the polls and lead to long and happy political lives."

"Won't any mass deaths show that something is wrong?"

"No. Because by then the public will be so desperate to be sickness-free that any old story about recipients dying from their own underlying conditions, instead of the direct effects of Terradone, will be seized on with relief by the average Joe. Most doctors will be more than happy to record any Terradone deaths as something else, given the generous kick-backs their surgeries will receive for rolling out the new miracle cure. By then it's likely to be made compulsory by the majority of those grateful heads of state, to 'protect the public as a whole and our invaluable health services.'

"Making it illegal to avoid the jab would be easy for a company with their money, influence and the fact that the drug would be deemed 'medically safe,' through trials at the company's own labs, and its true condition obscured under secrecy legislation initially designed to prevent industrial espionage. Immunity from prosecution would also be achieved, should anyone have a provable adverse reaction to the drug. So all the self-protective boxes are ticked.

"And anyway," he added. "You won't see any adverse comments about Terradone on the net as Muscat runs Exosphere and can censor its content and similarly influence other social media platforms whose operators are only too keen to fall into line with one of the world's richest men."

I just stared. It was a lot to process, I realised – if any of it was true.

There seemed to be an awful lot of conspiracy stuff in there, and one thing I'd learned in life was that there were more cock-ups and intentional obfuscations and deceptions than genuine conspiracies. Were there alien bases on the moon? Had we even landed there? Were those aircraft chem-trails carcinogenic and deliberately unleashed? Was a cabal of world leaders involved in an international paedophile ring? Were those same rulers also part of a New World Order bent on crushing the populace and introducing their own self-perpetuating fascist federation? Was Armageddon real and about to be unleashed on a warped culture?

That said, there was a quagmire of corruption and deceit out there as well, at all levels of what we call Society, so anything was possible. My own unique line of work was constantly dredging up the guilty secrets of politicians, the military, businessmen, science, medicine, religion; that was why my services were constantly required and I had to make morally ambiguous decisions – all for the right price. I could live with that: we all have secrets we'd rather the world didn't know.

Also, one person's conspiracy was another's empirical truth. All you had to do was decide which side you came down on.

After that, Sparks left the way he had come. There was no plea to save his life and no bullet to the head for me from any well-hidden security goons. But he did leave a parting shot of his own.

"I've got extensive bowel cancer, Mr Black. I don't have long and nothing my company can synthesize will cure me, so do what you will," he told me. "When you have carried out your assignment – long overdue in my case, I feel – then you will find a further large sum in your offshore account: my incentive for one more job before you hang up your weapons. To kill Rayland Muscat before he kills us all."

The day came.

In the intervening weeks I had tightened up my security. You don't need to know the details, other than that I went deeper and darker into the deep dark well. I clandestinely left the village and its allotment for another well-protected location and deleted any pathways through the cyber maze that might have led the ageing CEO of a major drugs company to discover me in one of my prime hideaways. My long-past military days had left me pretty adept at avoiding detection from pretty much anyone and anywhere, so this inconceivable breach was unforgivable. Maybe I was losing it, getting too old. Looking like it really was time to retire.

I had found a spot about half a mile from the steps of a science museum where Parker and Clarke had set up the hit. Sparks was joining them for a professional visit to open a special exhibition devoted to contemporary chemical medication. I had a clear view of the area, but was well out of view on the top floor of a nondescript and dilapidated old Regency-styled cinema building in a direct line of sight. I had brought Rover with me and a high-tech control mechanism that fitted snugly into two carrying cases. These stored neatly in the back of my black 4x4, neatly hidden away under a canopy of angling gear.

Rover was my favourite drone as it had the attack ethic of a ruthless canine and the remorselessness of the giant white ball from that old TV show *The Prisoner*, after which I had named it. Some of my previous drones had been disastrous, though thankfully during test runs and not on an actual assignment: most of them couldn't fly in bad weather and couldn't tell the difference between an armed insurgent and a wind-blown bush. Rover is virtually silent, can fly in any weather including a blizzard, can't be intercepted, and can take out more than one target in close proximity at the same time – the main reason for his presence in the abandoned cinema.

The best thing about flying him from my now-deserted shed on the village allotment was that the area was just above a flood plain, I had undisturbed access at night and could navigate Rover down the valley where it flew below any radar installations and couldn't be seen from any nearby properties. My new bolt-hole was even better, however!

Most people – if they ever think of them – consider drones to be those clumpy commercial things that buzz around taking shots of market towns, yacht-packed estuaries, rolling green hills and topless sunbathers: the kind that often get in the way of commercial air space. Or they remember those similarly hefty military machines in movies that can spot and dispatch a terrorist surgically in a crowd of thousands without parting the hair of an innocent child two feet away. All bullshit. Most drones couldn't hit a barn door accurately from a mile away, let alone from a site in Langley. I can hit a barn door from a considerable distance, with the right weapon and scope, and from much further out than a measly mile. I say most drones here. Not the ones I use. Nor the ones some branches of the military and black ops security folk use: they're a different barn door game. Some drones are way more sophisticated, and these are the ones I favour. Rover is a very classy and expensive military drone, around two million apiece for the model; he was recovered clandestinely from a Bosnian field and acquired through deep, dark and reliable weapons contacts.

It's interesting how fast technology can develop when it's used to kill or intimidate others. It's reckoned that by 2050 the US military will have technologically redesigned its soldiers through what they call *a convergence of biology, engineering and artificial intelligence* so that these Joes will be able to control various weapons systems with their minds, including drones.

This apparently involves neural implants for a *seamless mental interface with computers*, employing physical modifications to a war-fighter's brain, ears, eyes and muscles. That's not me shooting the breeze; it's set out in a publicly-available and trumpet-blowing study on *cyborg soldiers* by the Department of Defence.

By then people like me will probably be obsolete, redundant, extinct. Up to now, I've made a successful second career out of deleting troublesome objectives. Some of it I'm not proud of but, as I said, the kind of people who use my services have no conscience and plenty of capital, so why not grab some of that blood money while it's out there?

And, to be honest for a moment, it's the kind of work that's never going to go away. Not in this world. Not until 2050, at least.

The two men guided their boss out on to the steps, nervously looking left and right but not in my direction, of course, which (as I said) was straight ahead and about half a mile away. They were lightly cupping his arms on either side, but from a step behind him so they were only effectively protecting his back while leaving his face and flanks exposed. Clever.

They looked like two secret service agents screening a one-time President, even down to the branded shades; heads flicking, eyes flashing (I could see that pretty clearly through the yellow-green shade of the scope). They paused to present a target even a novice couldn't miss. Parsons looked confident, arrogant; Clarke just looked scared.

It was suddenly time and the drone, riding the air currents at around 300ft, did its duty. Simultanous bursts each aimed at a different target just feet apart; accurate to within a centimetre.

CRACK CRACK.

Sparks looked appropriately startled as his two CEOs parted, wavered a moment and then hit the ground either side of him, their heads like those proverbial blown melons.

Well, I had seen what he'd deposited in my special account, better than his hapless lieutenants had managed, more than enough for my retirement assignment. So down went Mutt and Jeff, as renegotiated.

Now, that's what I call a double header, I thought.

182

I dealt with Sparks at his Hollywood hide-away a week later, with a rifle this time.

I tried to make it quick and clean. He deserved that, at least for his recent change of heart, and with respect for his terminal condition. Then, while I was in the neighbourhood, I scouted the mansion complex of Rayland Muscat. This was much more difficult to penetrate than Sparks' low-security home – though perhaps Sparks had guessed I was coming and had made things easy for me.

No point in detailing the way I penetrated the Muscat security zone. It wasn't straightforward and took a few days, but I got there. Same principal: suitable distance, weapon, lie in wait. Rifle this time. I left Rover back in the UK. A bit tough to get him through customs since 9/11, even with my murky channels. The rifle I'd acquired locally. I was surprised it had been, relatively, so easy to get close to Muscat. But then, past experience and surprise were on my side.

I'd been skulking in the dusk bushes in a prime spot, sights set, finger on the trigger, when I heard a noise behind me. By instinct, I rolled noiselessly to one side. Unbelievably I found myself looking up at the very man I expected to be half a mile away on an open patio. Rayland Muscat. He was smiling one of those smiles reserved for those with an excellent dental plan. Unfortunately, he was also armed and his Glock 45 was pointed straight at me.

"Mr Black, I presume," he said.

There was a crippling pain in my head and the world went a deep, deep dark.

Sad song

Reader Eight left his file dangling from one hand as he accepted the applause. His head gently rolled from side to side and he smiled, first faintly and then broadly, drinking in the heartfelt approbation. But instead of sitting down, he posed a question.

It was "Any questions?"

This was unexpected and for a moment his audience didn't know how to respond. It seemed like they had never been asked to comment on a story before. Surely not! The applause was replaced by polite if embarrassed murmuring, like the *rhubarb-rhubarb* noise background actors used to make in movie crowd scenes, and then Reader Six put her hand up.

"How can Mr Black narrate the story when he's dead?" *The Bear*'s writer asked, pertinently rather than the *imp-* version (I mean impertinently).

Her deep green eyes glinted cheekily as she flicked her long black hair back from her striking face. Reader Eight smiled an even wider smile, as if delighted at her perceptive observation.

"Because there's a sequel," he said. "Would you like to hear it?"

There was a further murmur, partly of anticipation and partly of exhaustion, and Dara intervened.

"I'm sorry, but there's only one story per reader," he said. "We've had so many tonight and we've maybe got a couple more to go before you all drift off into the night." He looked at his watch. "The rather *late* night," he added. "And, before you say it, I made an exception for our lady author, both out of politeness as our only lady reading here this evening – and also because her bear opus was very short, more of an anecdote."

Reader Eight nodded gracefully, accepting the ruling. "Perhaps next time," he said.

I began my bar side rambling again, sounding sadder than I thought I felt,

185

if that makes sense.

"I tend to get bogged down in the whole grammatical thing when I write. I mean, I'm okay with my grammar, but it's all those *don't* rules that get me: don't start a sentence with *and*, don't use adverbs, don't split your infinitives, watch that apostrophe…"

"Like the missing squiggle in my bar sign?" Dara asked, recalling my insensitive entrance much earlier. I blushed, though it might have been the ale flushing my cheeks.

"Don't get bogged down letting yourself get bogged down," he continued, without waiting for a response. "Especially over grammar! Yes, get your basic grammar right – your *I*s and *E*s, and so on. You don't want to look a fool. But remember that rules are often pedantic and made to be broken, or at least bent. Look at the crazy style of classics like Selby's *Last Exit to Brooklyn* or *Finnegan's Wake* from Joyce – '*river-run past Eve and Adam's*' and all that. What a start! Go with what feels right for you, the creator, and don't make your sentences awkward and stilted just to appease some grammar guru.

"You know, the great Raymond Chandler stuck it to the split infinitive lawyers when an editor had the gall to say he'd spotted such an egregious error in one of Chandler's stories. Chandler – a well-educated and top-selling thriller genius, mind you – bristled and replied: 'When I split an infinitive, God damn it, I split it so it will stay split!' How's that for socking it to 'em?"

Again I was distracted, though I loved the thorny anecdote.

I was aware that things were taking a darker tone, bringing death into the picture a bit too prominently and I wasn't sure if I could handle it. I hated the thought that I might leave Planet Earth without ever making the tiniest mark on its surface. Even so, we should live for the Now, for we know not what tomorrow may bring. I read that somewhere. Maybe Eckhart Tolle.

"It's just the death stuff that's making me maudlin," I said.

"And there's likely more of that to come, Will. Our new teller of tales is on the oche and pointing his story darts at the board."

He was indeed, and I didn't even have time to take in the face of reader nine, buried behind a blue folder, before he began one of the strangest tales of the night. And that's saying something!

@ded-n-gon.com

There was one thing my old chum George used to say to me whenever he carried out one of his reckless escapades or when he drank or smoked far too much weed on one of his 'pleasure benders,' and that indifferent remark was: "We've all got to go sometime, son." Trouble was that, for him, 'sometime' had been way before what I would have called his rightful time, when he literally drank himself to death after an especially taxing legal tussle with an avaricious ex-girlfriend.

I heard about it in a phone call some weeks after the event from a farming neighbour who lived across the field from the isolated rural property George had acquired to "get away from everything." The farmer had been due to meet up with George for a merry bevy on that fateful night and went into the house to find his drinking buddy stiff as a board on the sofa accompanied by a dozen empty scotch bottles, the sleeve of an AC/DC long-player, now silent on the record deck, draped across his chest and a half-eaten can of tuna on an adjacent pillow.

I was away in France on business at the time, so I missed the news, the funeral and the ensuing chaos when someone dies without leaving a will, and by the time I got back to England the proverbial dust had settled and there was nothing for me to do but consider my memories. Oh, and delight at a set of Edwardian chamber pots he had left me that belonged to a great grandmother – a benefaction that I never actually saw as they somehow disappeared at an auction house during the final settlement of his estate.

Still, I typed his name, George Tallow Robbinson, into my search engine for old time's sake but there were few entries – most of the variants not him – and there wasn't even a Wiki mention. The one GTW reference that tallied was a report of his death from his local newspaper. Reading through the brief account I saw mention of his old home Tallowfield. I did a search and found an estate agent's report on the sale of the property to George back in the sixties; and then a further entry popped up mentioning the Tallowfield Trust, something that George seemed to have set up not long after buying the place. It wasn't entirely clear but the Trust seemed to be all about protecting a colony of horseshoe bats in a cave in an extensive nearby spinney – a venture quickly abandoned when the colony was removed by health officials due to the creatures' association with corona virus and the 2002-2004 SARS outbreak.

Somewhere in that estate agent's report I found a small section on the administration of the apparently defunct Trust and that seemed like a good place to start. I typed in the reference Admin12@Tallowfield.com. There was a pause and a black screen flashed up bearing the slate

WELCOME. For further information contact:
georgetallowrobbinson-tallowfield@ded-n-gon.com.

@ded-n-gon? I asked myself. Is someone taking the piss? I typed the phrase into a search engine. Nothing. Odd. So I went to my email server, typed in the full email address and the subject info, and then sat back and considered what to say.

Finally I wrote:

Hi,

I'm an old colleague of George Tallow Robbinson and I'm looking for some further information on George so that I can write a short account of his life and work for the next issue of *Business Bonus*.
Can you help?
Many thanks,
PJ Habbert.

I half expected an error message to appear. But, no, my email was recorded as sent and no contradiction followed.

Nothing happened for a few days. Occasionally I would glance at my in box but there was nothing more than the usual promotional messages from various sales outlets, supermarkets and finance houses and one or two fleeting contacts from friends, of the kind *In Portugal for a few weeks, weather spectacular (see photo), will call when back.* Alternatively, *Sorry we haven't been in touch, very busy, will contact soon.* There was even an end-of-message *Love to George TW* from someone unapprised of the Tallowfield tragedy.

Then one drizzly Wednesday afternoon I spotted the reply I had been seeking but not expecting and opened the message with a mixture of anticipation and perplexity. It read:

<georgetallowrobbinson-tallowfield@ded-n-gon.com>
To: PJ HABBERT
16 Oct at 14.33

Hi PJ
Sorry about the delay. Busy here. Long time no chat.

Who the hell was this over-familiar idiot? I asked myself, looked down at the name at the bottom of the email and froze. I moved back to the main text, fingers icy, mouth gaping like a harassed duck but without the raucous quacking. The rest of the message read

Being dead doesn't help, does it? Many thanks for the kind offer – a piece on my life would be nice. The old rag did a competent job on the obit, but – how do you say? – it barely scratched the surface. Tell me what you need – ask me questions – and I'll give you the low-down and fill in the blanks. Be hearing from you
George.

I sat and thought about this for days after signing off. It had to be a nasty hoax. Dead people just didn't use the internet. Why would they? They were dead. And how would they use the keyboard if they're *all ethereal*? If one knows anything about death, there are two outstanding things: one, you're supposed to go to a better place where you have no need for your former, earthly life, and two, you're not coming back. Well, at least *mostly*. Maybe George fitted into the exceptional category. Whatever, he was hardly in the Haunting Historic Monuments faction. But who would want to perpetrate such a fraudulent prank – and what would they stand to gain from it? After all, I had searched out George; no-one had come to me claiming to be my departed friend. And they weren't asking for money – at least, not yet. No, it didn't make sense.

189

I had planned to do some investigation into the matter, in my Sherlock hat (not that I have a real deerstalker, I always wear a tweed cap). But, in the end, I thought I'd tackle the matter head-on. With George – or whoever it was wearing his clothes. So I emailed

Sorry, but who are you?
PJ Habbert

It took a few hours, but the answer came that evening. I wasn't sure if I was reassured. I mean, how could I be? Talking to the Otherworld? Even I'm not that gullible.

Hey, PJ. It's me! George. I know it's hard to believe. I mean, why would you? But it really is George Tallow Robbinson. Or what's left of him. If you can't wrap your head around that, ask me some questions and let's – how you say? – see where we go from there. You wanted some stuff for an article. Ask me about my career.

So I did.

He rattled off an extensive CV starting with his school and University education, and his vaunted achievements in team building and customer management. A Bachelor of Business Administration, he published several indispensable papers on leadership, communication and monetary prudence, including the essential *Lashing Down the Tiles: How to Keep a Fiscal Roof on Your Business*. He was widely praised (within a small circle) as a highly skilled, deadline-driven and technically savvy operative in "demanding, ever-changing and fast-paced corporate environments." Yet he sounded like he was rather bored with it all, or he was reading from a crib sheet. None of it really explained how such an "exceptional leader" had ended up a useless, unemployed and impoverished drunk after crashing out of his full-on affair with a stunning redhead commodities trader in her mid-thirties. Or maybe it did. It was all about sex, really – everything. Still, while the info was useful for the article it didn't prove that the George that claimed to be George was, in fact, the real George. The real dead George...

There was one British Prime Minister who wrote me an effusive letter of praise after I consulted on a pressing economic issue a few years back, and I resolved it at a stroke. I was asked to keep the contents of the letter undisclosed. It would be in my correspondence papers, if the solicitor still has them.

Now I didn't know that. But then, as only George could know that, how was I to know that something only he knew about was the real deal? I only had his word for it. Mind you, if it was a counterfeit George, how did the imposter know about the letter – if one existed, of course – and he wasn't just taking a punt into the blue. I needed something I could check. My eccentric correspondent was quick to respond.

OK. Here's one. Do you remember Helen, Helen Awford, that girl from the LuckyDays Ballroom back in the early seventies? The one you said was unobtainable? Well, I obtained her, two weeks before she married that twerp from her accounting firm. She got a bit tipsy on the night the Seeds of Mystery did a gig there, at the venue. She was potty about them. Well, I knew the lead singer, went to school with him, and introduced Helen after the show and she swooned with gratitude. She was dressed in this skin-tight red dress and the whole band took to her like a gratis bag of cocaine. She really purred. So after I'd taken her backstage and she'd bathed in some celebrity sunlight I took her back to my flat and banged her even more senseless for a couple of hours before dropping her back to her mum's. I'd never known her so grateful. Not for the sex especially, though it was great, but for the fifteen minutes of fame-bathing I'd endowed her with her musical heartthrobs.

Now, *that* I could check. I still knew Helen, now Helen McDonald, because she worked in my local building society. She also lived just across town on a newly-built estate and had been pictured in the local paper after she and her husband Donald (yes, Donald McDonald! *Where's your troosers?*) won a competition for a luxury kitchen installation organised as a publicity stunt by a locally-based firm of house builders.

So I tootled into town and, as luck would have it, ran into Helen just as she left work for a mid-day break. We greeted each other cheerily enough, as we'd known each other off and on from school days, and I wondered how best to broach the ticklish subject at hand. As usual, I went in with a broadside.

"Hi, Helen," I said, acting flabbergasted at seeing her. "Do you remember George, George Robbinson?"

She looked surprised, but welcoming enough. She was a lot older now with greying hair, a bunch of tramlines on her face and a body that had moved determinedly south over the intervening years; sadly no longer the appealing teenage temptress who used to shoehorn herself into body-hugging crimson dresses: no longer the Belle of the Ballroom, but still stylish in her dark blue business suit.

She nodded. "George. Yes. I haven't heard that name in a while."

"He asked to be remembered to you. Wanted to know if you remember that night with the Seeds of Mystery at the LuckyDays."

Helen did a double-take. "When did you see George?" she asked.

"Yester-," I choked. "Yesterday it came to mind. He emailed me recently."

"I thought George died."

"Er, the email wasn't that recent. I've been away. First time I've seen you since, well, before the funeral at any rate. I missed it, unfortunately."

"Me too. I saw the obit in the local paper."

"Right. So, do you remember that night? He was really keen to know. Don't know why. Maybe..." I tailed off, lost for a specific excuse.

She stared at me, and though I'm hopeless with people's facial expressions, I sensed her smoothly-running day had suddenly garnered an unexpected crease. Maybe I was looking too much like I already knew the answer to the question because a delicate coolness descended, as if a small rain cloud had suddenly materialised through a meteorological incongruity and she didn't want to pursue matters any further in case she got really soaked.

"That's so long ago," she replied. "What a nice band they were – the Seeds... I really liked them. Well, I must be getting along. I'm meeting my husband for lunch."

Not *Donald*, but specifically *my husband*. That had to say it all. A question of possession – and the rights thereof. The only problem was that it did and didn't say anything about the matter in hand, and both at the same time. She might have been saying *Don't rake up the past*, she might have genuinely forgotten about that night and its explosive conclusion, or George had been fibbing and she was as innocent of a pre-marital transgression as a new-born lamb. (No, she was never *that* innocent). Still, it didn't prove anything and I was back to square one, possibly with one less friendly acquaintance in my address book.

She walked off stiffly to a "toodle-oo." But she only got a couple of yards before turning on her heel, caught by an afterthought. She walked back.

"Donald thinks he's his," she said calmly. "A beautiful boy. He's a man now, a bio-chemist in Luton. Now George will never know. All for the best."

192

She turned away again with a tiny smile in the corner of her mouth and even flicked her derriere at me impishly as she headed for a Costa. Some people never change, I thought. But should I tell George? In the end I did, and he responded:

Of course I knew about Kevin. Only after I came here, though, which is a long time coming. I remember thinking at the time that Donald was a bit of a dark horse, impregnating his bride so quickly; must've been desperate, I thought. I also wondered whether... Never mind. I'm glad the lad has done so well for himself. My lad. Oh, well – how do you say? – all in the past, PJ. But you know what they say? We move on. Jo hops a dingo!

And then I *knew* it had to be George! He had used the expression over and over, even into adulthood. He'd been using it since he was, oh, about ten, when he first read that obscure childrens' book written and illustrated by an Australian author – can't remember her name, but it was great fun. His folks picked it up on a surfing holiday over there and it was never published in the UK, as far as I know.

So, the story, actually called *Jo Hops a Dingo* and told in simple verse, featured a little girl unsurprisingly called Jo who lived in an isolated community inland from Brisbane. Her parents always told their outdoors-exploring daughter never to venture far into the bush alone, to places so far afield that she could no longer hear the cry of the kookaburra. This was erroneous information, as you can hear a kookaburra pretty much anywhere in eastern Australia as its tones echo stridently across the landscape. Still, never mind, it *was* a tale for kids.

In the story Jo goes off into the bush and, of course, she gets lost. She's suddenly approached by a scraggy-looking wild dingo that growls at her hungrily. Jo backs up to a tree and when the animal makes a lunge for her, the athletic little girl jumps in the air, over the animal's head and sprints away. The dingo smacks into the tree and stuns itself. Well, I said it was for kids.

"Jo hops a dingo," she says to herself proudly as she escapes and eventually finds her way home, unscathed but to a parental scolding.

As the book goes on (and on), she uses her memory of this successful little jump to get herself out of a host of bad situations – a brown snake slithering from a wood pile, a school bully slithering from an alleyway, a pushy cyclist swerving out from a supermarket car park – and each time she avoids catastrophe she tells herself proudly, *Jo hops a dingo*. Before the end of the book, Jo has learned she doesn't have to physically leap into the air to protect her skin and starts using clever words and phrases to psychologically extract herself from sticky situations, overcoming all obstacles. And the phrase *Jo hops a dingo!* becomes her touchstone. On the last page she tells herself:

I used my legs
Now use my head
I'm happy now
When tucked in bed
Tomorrow's choices
So sublime
I'll hop a dingo
I'll be fine!

Mind you, this still didn't conclusively prove that I was communicating with a dead man. This could just be someone from his solicitor's office coming across the book among George's belongings – like the dubious PM letter – and using it to play a stupid game with me, their client's old friend. Even so, for what purpose?

I told George this and his email reply came back immediately.

Look, PJ, I don't give a floating, farting fuck if you believe it's me. Do you want to carry on with this or not?

194

And from that moment, I *really* knew it was George! I didn't know *how* it was George – I mean, he was clearly dead as they'd publicly buried him and I wasn't about to ask them to exhume the bugger so I could check – but there was no doubting it now. He'd always been a widely discourteous prick in real life – and apparently in real death as well.

I wrote:

> Got it, sorry. It's you! This is extraordinary. I've got so many questions. How does it feel to be where you are? What did you feel when you arrived? What's it like there?

There was an immediate response:

> The old life goes black, then the new one lights up. It's very attractive. You know what those NDI people say about tunnels and lights and all that? (Sorry, *Near Death Experience*.) Sort of like that in a way. How does it feel? What's it like? Can't tell you too much, not because there's anything preventing me, it's just that it's – how you say? – on a need-to-know basis. Some things the old world knows about already, and we can communicate with those people who do have some inkling; the rest is up to them – to you.
>
> Still, I'll to try to answer: You know how sometimes you wake suddenly from a dream and that dream may involve someone you know, but don't know that well, and you wonder why you've dreamt about him or her? Well, that's some kind of crossover you're getting from – how best can I phrase It? – from the ether. It may be some strange, coded message from beyond or it may just be a jumble of insignificant thoughts tumbling about in the back of your mind because you ate too much cheese before bed-time.
>
> But you know when you wake up and when you go for your shower or your breakfast, whatever, and you're still more in the dream than in your customary reality? You may be soaping your back, but you're also still in that last scene in the dream? Well, that's a bit like it feels here, except the dream state is where you used to be – where *you* are now, PJ – rather than your new location. It kind of switches around like that. But you can still hold on to the other place if you choose, or even summon it up. Eventually it fades. It's not like being constantly on a telephone or computer connection. You don't really feel the need to keep continuous contact with the old place – just visit it occasionally, for old time's sake; maybe to help out a former buddy or loved one. It's not mandatory.

At least you've only touched on one of the four most annoying questions that can be asked by the living: proof of identity. Are you really you, dead person? Sometimes we, over here, wonder why we bother. The other three most irksome queries? One of the most popular is How is Uncle Bertie or Aunt Winnie? [*Insert name of recently deceased relative.*] I mean, do you have any idea how many billions of folk of all race, colour and creed have bitten the bullet since the Dawn of Man? Also, why do you think we can all communicate effortlessly with each other, no matter the difference in language and social background? I mean, try explaining something simple like an electric toaster to a 12th-century Cumbrian hill farmer.

I didn't believe a word of this.

The next most popular enquiry is *Can you make my Euro Millions numbers come up on Saturday?* Honestly, when you get here, you realise your financial situation before you pegged it is of SO little consequence. I mean, what are you going to spend it on? Wing wax?

I sensed the acerbic George was re-emerging; he was certainly no angel. I thought all that angst was supposed to change once you passed through the proverbial veil. Still, he was on a roll.

And the last one? The classic: *Tell me about God.* Do you know how many times we hear that? Almost as many times as the total tally of dead since the Dawn of. It's so *boring*! And there's never an answer to it – except to say that God is whatever your God is to you. And that doesn't play well in the provinces, as they say.

It was the longest message I had so far received from my new (old) confidant. But I think it cleared some blocked psychological pipes as he became more affable thereafter and we began communicating daily.

He told me about my elderly mum's next-door neighbour who always collected her parcels for her when she was either out or suffering one of her many bouts of convenient doorbell deafness.

Under the Royal Mail's 'leave it with a neighbour' scheme he would accept her deliveries and pop them round when she got home or when she appeared suddenly at a window looking puzzled (as she did most of the time). I used to post her a package of chocolates on a weekly basis, if

I couldn't get over, and sometimes they didn't arrive. I queried this with the local Post Office who confirmed they had been left with Mr Potter (the neighbour). I asked him about it, and he said he'd passed them on to my mum, who was "a bit forgetful. You'll probably find them in a cupboard somewhere," he said. But this happened once too often so, at George's suggestion, I set a trap.

The next time I got a box of Lately's Luxury Chocolates – a favourite of mum's since she was a girl, and they hadn't changed much since the 1930s – I took them to the kitchen, carefully opened the box, impregnated each chocolate with some Grim Reaper 'Extra-Scorching' Chilli Sauce using a 2ml needle and syringe and sealed the product up again. I posted it and warned my mum not to open it but to let me know when it arrived. And arrive it did, after about a week, showing some signs of being tampered with. At least two of its contents had been replaced. I used this close examination as an excuse to visit Mr Potter on some friendly pretext. He looked pale and haunted.

"I've been so ILL," he told me. "Must have been something I ate."

He stared pointedly at me, but I gave nothing away.

"Yes, mum has been hit with a bit of a bug too," I lied. "I told her to lay off the chocolates for a while. *You never know what's in them these days.*"

Message delivered, I wished him well and returned to mum's.

Her chocolates were never intercepted again. *Thanks for that*, I told George. *Are you really allowed to do things like that – to interfere with the still-living?* George gave me the *What the eye doesn't see* routine and we continued corresponding. He seemed to have a particular grievance with bad neighbours, for the next person in his sights was *my* next-door annoyance Ian Wilkins.

I was driving around in a tatty maroon Fiat Tipo at the time which latterly developed a form of paint cancer, where sections of the bonnet gloss began peeling off in ugly patches. One of my work colleagues said it was probably caused by seagull shit as there were quite a few of these noisy seabirds in my village due to several disillusioned biddies putting out bread and cat food for their culinary enjoyment – plus their guano was full of nasty chemicals (the birds, not the biddies). My view was it was the sun's blistering – we'd had a really hot summer. That, coupled with a bad spraying job when the car was born in the late eighties.

One morning I found scratch marks on my bonnet, right next to a big circular back-to-the-metal peel wound, like a child had been running a toy car round and round the spot, its wheels digging into the original steel. Now, I knew Wilkins had a ten-year-old son who was – how would I express it? – *troubled.* I don't think he was actually mentally retarded or anything; he was just a self-absorbed, stroppy little kid, just like his devil-may-care dad, a tall, gangly motor mechanic who kept singing *If I ruled the world* loudly when spraying a door panel in his domestic garage on the other side of the fence.

I asked him if he'd seen anyone damaging my bonnet, being that I parked my car next to the pavement a few feet down from the Wilkins driveway.

Wilkins shook his head. "Nope. I'm in the garage, out of view, for most of the time," he told me.

"Looks like someone was running a toy car around there in circles," I said pointedly, as Wilkins' son Altan (!) and six-year-old daughter Mollie were the only kids in that part of the Close.

"We got rid of Altan's Dinky toys weeks ago," Wilkins responded, with suspicious haste. "He's getting too old for those sorts of juvenile distractions now. We're hoping he'll study to become a doctor or a lawyer, you know."

No pressure on the kid, then. I guessed dad had visions of his belligerent offspring becoming an outstanding professional, in the historic footsteps of TV's Dr Kildare or Perry Mason. His name meant Red Dawn, Turkish in origin, and probably not intended as a shepherd's warning. Even so, it should have alerted all of us that Altan (unlike Paul Simon, you *can't* call me Al) was a storm waiting to unburden itself on the unprepared.

I thought the brat was more likely to become a drug dealer, considering what a bully he was, truly appalling. He would wait until his parents were distracted and punch his younger sister in the arm, or push her into a hedge – and he would time it so that her cry would make his parents turn around and all they would see was Mollie punching Altan in retaliation, from their perspective an unprovoked piece of sisterly spite. Then father would bark: "Don't hit your brother, Mollie. You know he's special!" And she would look so hurt, knowing that her blond-haired, blue-eyed brother would always be better than her because he was her parents' first-born, their golden child, their chosen one, their burgundy daybreak – expections weedy Altan probably already knew he could never live up to – and that she, little Mollie, was just a bit of delayed afterbirth.

I know these assaults happened because I saw them take place all too regularly. One time Altan did it right in front of me when I was outside polishing my Tipo (this is not a euphemism). The family had just tumbled out of their four-by-four and were heading down the drive, father in the lead carrying the front door key, his wife Jessica, a thin and unusually pale redhead with a haunted look, hurrying behind weighed down with two heavy bags of supermarket shopping. Mollie was behind her, moving slowly, and Altan was at the rear, looking menacing. Suddenly he kicked

198

his sister in the back of the legs and she toppled; she kept her balance, squealed, spun round and clocked her brother a corker on the chin. Now *he* squealed – and that was the only thing that father saw. Having successfully negotiated the front door lock he spun round and laid into Mollie, calling her a "wicked, violent and spoiled little madam" and to go to her room as there would be no tea for her.

Mollie ran indoors crying and her father hurried up to Altan and hugged him, tousling his fluffy hair as if his son had just been rescued unharmed from the grip of a malevolent paedophile. He made soothing noises, then quickly disengaged, said "come on" and headed for the door, the trauma instantly forgotten. Altan made to follow. Then, remembering that I had seen it all, he looked straight at me, his pale blues boring into my twin browns and gave me what I can only describe as an evil, twisted smirk. Then his face changed and he skipped away lightly like a normal, carefree ten-year-old on an Easter egg hunt. I felt an unseasonal shiver and thought about Stephen King stories.

Not long afterwards I found a nail embedded in one of my tyres. My car dealer removed it and plugged the hole. A few days later I found another nail in a different tyre. Over the next two weeks I found two more, both of which led to expensive replacements. I began to detect a message. I might have been wrong; I might just have been driving along bad sections of back roads and picking up industrial detritus. But this seemed to smack of a juvenile warning: "*Don't tell or worse will happen.*" Whenever I saw Altan – the child most likely to end up in a secure unit – that was the sort of look he gave me.

Then one Saturday morning I came out to find a pint milk bottle smashed behind a rear tyre. This time I complained to world-ruling Ian who happened to be in his driveway brushing up some wood shavings from a branch sawing session. I pointed at the glass and told him about the nails and that I thought it was more than a coincidence. He didn't comment, but he did nod occasionally as if in sympathy. Then he took his brush and swept the glass shards into a nearby drain; the pieces clattered down through the grating and plopped into the dark water below. Finally, unbelievably, once the shards had been removed from sight, he claimed they had been chunks of ice. Ice? In August?! Fortunately, the family moved house soon afterwards and I have never missed a bunch of neighbours less.

On reflection, maybe Altan was finally able to escape his father's obsession that his first born was a kind of new Messiah rather than just a very naughty boy who deserved a containing slap now and then. I heard he became a drummer in a death metal band which would have worked off some of his aggression in a positive way. I just hoped his sister found her own feet away from the bullying and made a success of her adult life.

Anyway, back to my life with the otherworldly George.

We kept the emailing going for the rest of the year, with the celebrated business executive giving me little titbits about issues in my life – though nothing vital, controversial or financially rewarding, just being a superlative and congenial correspondent. I probably talked more with him as a corpse from the heavens than I ever did as a friend across the bar stools.

Just before Christmas the messages became less frequent, long gaps began forming before I received replies to queries, and all communication finally ceased the following February. The very last message from the Tallowfield Enigma popped up on Shrove Tuesday, a few minutes after the arrival of an unexpected pre-paid mail delivery from a local bakery, the white box festooned with red ribbons. The note inside, along with the sweetmeats, just said

Enjoy the pancakes. George.

It seemed so final somehow, as if George had found – how would I have said it? – other fish to fry. Perhaps he had moved on to Helen, the unpredicted mother of his only child. That would blow her mind! Whatever and wherever, it was sad to lose this strangely uplifting to-and-fro that held more depth and wonder than anything we ever discussed on an earthly plain.

I rarely take much interest in emails nowadays. They seem less appealing somehow, less nourishing, as there was something about George Tallow Robbinson that transcended the everyday and, whoever or whatever he was – wispy apparition, prankster, hacker or the real George from another dimension – he brought new meaning to my life. The only downside was I had been counting on his netting a massive Euro Millions win for me…

This hole in my life lasted for years, my hair became grey and my walk became less athletic, and I'd almost forgotten about the extraordinary man, his Trust and its undesirable bats – until one autumn afternoon when I ran into Helen in a bus queue. She looked pale and distracted, yet apparently anxious to talk to an old friend. She had retired from the building society and was working part-time for a volunteer group, friends of a local hospital. It turned out that her son Kevin had gone on one of those expensive African safaris and was currently missing. He'd just wandered away from a party of eager elephant snappers and not returned. There was talk of a wild animal attack, though no indications of that bloody event had been found.

I told her what she wanted to hear: that that was a good sign, that everything was sure to work out fine and Kevin would soon be home telling tales of his great adventures in the underbrush. She seemed a little comforted by this and thanked me profusely.

"Don't worry, someone will find him," I told her. "There's always someone looking out for you."

How true that is, I thought. The one who finds him may not actually be *living*, but it will lead to quite a reunion. That's if the kid had a working tablet or laptop with him. I wondered if George could help – if he was even there, the voice in the machine. It was worth a try. So I hurried home, powered up the desktop and tapped out the familiar address. Nothing. I tried typing a message. Again nothing. Not even a *Not Known*. Maybe our allotted time had passed. I was stumped. Finally – I don't know why – I put my own name into @ded-n-gon and found this.

Site reserved for Paul James Habbert, Ref No PCF 7239003/C. See you soon, subscriber!

I'm not sure if that terrified or reassured me. But at least I now know there really is somewhere else, whatever it turns out to be like, when I'm dead and gone. The old seventies pop song played momentarily in my head and I sang along to the cheery chorus. Accent on *when*, I thought. But there was no need to panic just yet, to tidy up all those irritating loose ends, as there was nothing to indicate exactly when I would cease to be a life form to become resident of an obscure IP address.

Still, as an old friend once told me: "We've all got to go sometime, son."

Now I guess that at least I know *where*. Sort of.

And that I can always send someone pancakes.

Don't be late. Locate, land, liberate and love
LATELY'S LUXURY CHOCOLATES
Available from all good stores near you

(See page 197)

One Big Car Crash

It was the first time I had considered the order of the tales I was hearing. This excursion into the afterworld ether was the ninth reader in sequence – and I knew something about the number nine: I'd read a book about it. It was supposed to have peculiar properties, wasn't it? Something to do with spiritual enlightenment, destiny, karma… Before I could satisfactorily chew on this sudden insight, Dara broke my concentration.

"You might want to get on with your story writing before you find the opportunity has gone forever and you're resident in Tallowfield," he told me.

I shook my head, though not in disagreement. "They say everything is revealed in death," I replied, more gloomily than intended.

My closest friend used to say something like that, though he never intended to leave the planet as suddenly as he did – at just fifty-one, with so many precious years to go – crashing his car on one bleak, foggy night in an especially dank October. An unrepentant drinker, he'd had a few too many bevies after work and taken a familiar back road to avoid any unwanted main road encounters with the breathalyzer. There was a sharp right hand band on one stretch of this high-hedged route that he normally took and was familiar with, way out in the countryside, and he usually slowed down to accommodate the ninety degree nightmare. Whether it was primarily the dark, the fog, the booze, or all of them, that night he blazed on without even braking and drove straight into a farmer's field, the entrance to which was right on the bend. Fortunately, the farmer had left the heavy, slatted oak gate open; less fortunately, he had left a large combine harvester parked about ten yards inside it and my friend blithely smashed into that obstruction with no signs of even attempting to brake, leaving a large dent in its steel panels and both driver and his modest saloon as write-offs.

It was tragic because he left three nice kids – well, young adults with their own lives – and a complicated estate that probably hasn't been properly resolved even now, eighteen months later. And he looked so peaceful, at last, on the coroner's table at the hospital afterwards, his silver hair neatly parted, a sense of sober relief in his pallid face. The accident was especially upsetting for me because not only had we been pretty close for a time, with identical tastes in music and humour, but we had recently had a big blow-up and neither of us had found time to apologise, so he'd left for that long trip of no return without the air being cleared.

We had been planning to put together a collection of poems, some of his and some of mine, for some self-publishing project. We knew this guy with a backstreet bookshop that did a lot of little books and leaflets like that. Not vanity publishing as such, but letterpress printmaking: cheap but cheerful and an effective and inexpensive way of getting our stuff out there. But our writing had drifted apart in recent years, 'like rootless icebergs is an ocean of uncertainty,' he told me rather floridly. My verses had taken an optimistic air, despite my feeling of being adrift, where his recent batch had become dark and disturbing, with hysterical lyrics about terrorism, abortive romances and frosty stanzas about starving children, climate change and fascist rulers. I foolishly asked him to consider shelving those poems, just in the short term, as we would get a more receptive audience with cheerier pieces, like mine. I should never have opened my mouth, especially as I had not intended to *dis* his compositions, or to suggest that I was a superior being.

"You always thought your lines were better than mine," he barked back, unexpectedly. "Always thought you were a better writer; thought I was crap. You ought to get a life and learn how to make a success of your scribblings. It's no good stuffing them in a drawer and only showing them to me!"

"I didn't say..." I began. Then the phone was slammed down. He sounded like he had been drinking. As usual. It was the pressures of work, I suppose, and his own demons.

It's always horrible when you don't get a chance to say goodbye, to say how much you miss someone and how you wish they were still around, making the world a brighter place (except when they're in their cups or producing poems about dystopian futures). And friends always seem to die so unexpectedly.

"I thought you said you didn't have any friends," Dara announced suddenly, as if overhearing my reflections and breaking my train of thought. Had I said all that crash stuff out loud? Probably.

"Here was someone you knew well enough to write poems with, to be creative with, even if it didn't end quite like you wanted," Dara continued.

"Nothing ever does," I said gloomily. "It was short-lived, but it was intense." My past was one big swamp and I'd been dragging my heels through it for a long time.

"I guess we all want to be remembered after popping our clogs," Dara said, leaning on the bar. "The desire is so strong to put down something to justify your time on this planet, to make those you leave behind say 'Well, that was pretty amazing;' maybe something like a novel or a symphony, a great pop song, a painting, a piece of architecture – or perhaps just being seen as a decent person. What are you planning to leave behind?"

"I don't know."

"Chad?"

The question seemed undemanding and was delivered completely flat. I wasn't sure if it was sympathetic or loaded. Either way, it was somewhere I didn't want to go. I couldn't go, more to the point.

"Who?" (I knew who well enough).

"June's cycle-crazy boyfriend. The one who took up residence with her in your sister's old room."

"What do you mean? What does Chad have to do with anything?"

"To move forward you have to leave all that baggage about Chad behind you. I saw how you reacted to storyteller five."

I felt a constricting in the chest. "Wh-what do you mean?"

"The whole thing with Chad and June. It's tearing you apart and you can't write, can't think of anything else, can you? It's not just the loss of a girl you cared for. It's something more. You have to let it go…"

"Now?"

"Now."

And I did.

I leaned forward and in an agitated undertone, speaking low enough so that the other patrons couldn't hear, told Dara how Chad had come round one evening just before he and June left the spare room for pastures new. He began reasonably enough by telling me how much he appreciated what I had done for June and offered to pay me two month's rent to make up for my loss of income. I wasn't in the mood for him to be reasonable. He'd never been reasonable before. So I said I didn't want his money; I wanted June. And I'd never charged her a penny to use the spare room, anyway. I was angry that he thought that his money would make up for seducing

205

away the only girl I'd ever really cared for.

We got into an argument that went on for quite a bit before Chad turned his back and strutted off, back to his racing bike that he'd left outside leaning against a downpipe. I followed him and he called back over his shoulders that I should grow up and get a life, one that didn't involve pretending to be a writer, one that might cure my obvious impotence. *Impotence?!* I lost it then. I picked up a spade that I'd been using earlier to unearth some potatoes and I hit him in the back of the head. It was quite hard and he went down like the bones in his legs had given out, which I guess they had.

When I touched his neck there was no pulse. He was quite dead and I panicked. I'd only intended to hurt him, to say "Don't talk to me like some school bully," not to kill him. But I couldn't take it back now. I wasn't even thinking straight, but one thing I did know: I wouldn't survive the recriminations that would follow when the news got out. So I found some plastic sheeting and, like you see on those TV cop shows about serial killers, I rolled Chad into it, sealed it with duct tape, emptied the garden shed, shoved it out of the way, dug a big hole under it, about six feet, bloody hard work, pushed the Chad bundle into it, and then dismantled his bike in the kitchen and tossed it in on top of him. I filled the hole, flattened the surface, tipped some old grit and dust from the garage over the surface to make it look undisturbed and dragged the shed back into place.

It was so like the scenario delivered by reader five, the David Conrad/Chad Smart clone Brad tale that had thrown me off key, almost haunted me, and led to my final unburdening. At least, as I gave the tale flight, as I babbled away to Dara, I didn't know there was more to come: something even more unexpected.

"It was a couple of days before June rang me at the office to ask if I'd seen her peddle-pushing pimp. It was a last resort. He'd clearly not told her he was coming to see me, which was fortunate, and none of my neighbours had seen or heard anything anyway – they're quite elderly and a couple of them are a bit deaf and there's high fences screening the back garden. So no-one came to see me about the disappearance and Chad was listed as missing. Do I regret it? Yes, I do now – and no. He was a horrible, self-possessed snobbish rat."

My mouth was dry and my heart was thumping. Why had I spouted all this, let alone to someone I had never met before tonight? Dara pulled another pint and pushed it across the bar towards me. His face was expressionless.

"So, shall we get on with the next story?" he asked.

I was too stunned to reply. Had this taciturn barman not heard what I had just said? What I had admitted. I asked myself what I should say next, but storyteller Number Ten was already on his feet and ready to give us his tale. He was going to be the last to tell that night.

This time, I could have sworn the reader looked like me, though he seemed to be in his eighties and was certainly more confident than yours truly as he prepared to address the small but objective crowd, none of them more unprejudiced than me (or so I thought). Except that once he stepped into the spotlight I could see he was black, a cultural characteristic I do not possess. And, it transpired, he was the custodian of a deep chocolate-resonant voice, sparkling eyes, a quiet, but authoritative manner and a very deliberate, thoughtful way of telling his story. He was the kind of person to put you at ease – which was what I needed at this moment, panicky and sweating around my collar. So, a man unlike me in so many ways! I had no idea why I had been so mistaken. Maybe it was because I watched too much TV as the man reminded me of Tennessee-born actor Morgan Freeman, but with no sign of the fibromyalgia he contracted after a car crash in 2008. In fact, Number Ten was pretty animated in a lugubrious way, if it's possible to be both at the same time.

He stepped into the ubiquitous spotlight and opened his file with a noticeable tremble in his hands as if from a slight neurological condition. He slowly turned his head to address the audience and, apparently in character, said:

"My name is Luther Croel and I was a cop way back-along in a major American city. Don't matter which one – just one with an El. That'll do. It's the story that matters here rather than where it lies. And some story. I was there when it all went down, but I didn't learn the extraordinary truth of what *really* happened for more than forty years. And it blew my socks off. So, let's get into it."

He read the title of his tale and then he got into it.

The Moon and a Park Bench

1: Now

There's a shiny gold plaque on a large but otherwise nondescript wooden bench in a leafy park downtown from the commercial district of The City, a green lung between the poorer districts in the east and the expensive apartments of the middle-rich business folk on the west side. The plaque reads

IN MEMORY OF "WOODY"
THANK YOU
FOR BEING IN THE RIGHT PLACE
AT THE RIGHT TIME
LOVE FOREVER – LITTLE AMY

The rectangular brass plate around the size of two Marlboro packs end-to-end can be seen from right across the park, especially when it glitters brightly in the winter sunshine and its fading rays hit at just the right angle before those glistening beams scatter behind the surrounding skyscrapers. The notice was paid for by its signatory, Amy, and is pretty old now, more than four decades, but has retained its pristine lustre as if someone takes a cloth to it every morning with just a dab of polish – maybe lemon and baking soda.

I first came across it while researching a story that, in the end, I was never able to complete. An aspiring journalist for, oh, fifty-odd years, what I'd really wanted to be before joining the Precinct, I tried to submit that story for publication more than once, but I could never bring myself to write the conclusion. I guessed people would never have believed it, even though it was a strange and beautiful story of the bond between a homeless old man and a ten-year-old girl; a girl who grew up to become a major player in the state legislature. It was that little girl Amy, now in her sixties, who told me the tale – the whole tale, and its ending – a few years after her retirement. I was the first person she had ever told, for the same reason I was unable to pass it on: that's believability and retaining public esteem. Recognised me from the park, when she was tiny. She asked me: "Weren't you that cop? The nice one? The one who treated Woody right?"

I said yes I was.

I was pretty well educated, thanks to my folks who were both lawyers, and instead of heading for a newspaper I became a cop. For the same reason: because I wanted to do some good in the world, like them. I learned the job from the street upwards, which was just as well considering the racist attitudes of some of the white cops at the time who saw an "ed'cated nigga" as an affront. Fortunately, our precinct Captain was a wiser man and without him I'd've never been allowed to join the 21st, let alone write pieces for the local paper.

These pieces, they were nothing like *On Patrol With Officer Croel*, of course. The top brass would never have sanctioned that, and nor would the Captain. Had nothing to do with the fact that he was a friend of my dad. A cop's main requirement, at least in the US, is to carry out his duties impartially, so I couldn't comment in any way publicly about the work of the Blues or the folk they encountered. I wrote about remarkable or historic city figures, getting the info from off-duty sessions in the city library. This appealed to the Captain and the precinct hierarchy, though initially I had to write under a pen name.

I got to interview Judge Amy Carlson much later, after both of us retired. As I said, she knew me from the park days when she was a kiddie because I was the only cop who didn't hassle her friend Woody. She recognised me in court as one of those complainants who lost money to a finance company that was being prosecuted; this was after I'd left the precinct with the rank of sergeant and my pension pot had gone down the Swanee due to the scam. I'd been writing freelance articles for a long time, for the main metropolitan newspaper and a couple of suitable magazines. That's how I got to write her life story. As for the city, well, it was a place with – trust me, this is relevant – an elevated railway, as I said before.

There were only a handful of places left in the US with an El, as they're referred to, back when all this happened, and just a single one now. But they were a brilliant way to get across town without having to face a tussle of cars, vans, buses, trucks and yellow cabs that clog the routes in, out and through. When you can travel with ease past first and second floor windows, click-clacking your way to your destination, relaxing and maybe reading a newspaper rather than, these days, squinting and glaring angrily at a sat-nav and dodging around twitchy pedestrians – well, why do it any other way?

So, who's this Woody guy? Well, I'll get to that.

It started when I was a rookie, around 20 or so, when I was sent to patrol a place called Prayse Park. That's the place I mentioned earlier that has the bench and the plaque. It was created in the 1920s by a guy called Charles Lester Prayse. That's Prayse with a Y, and nothing to do with the Methodist activity centre in Indiana. At the time Prayse built it – its twelve acres of trees and grass, a duck pond, kids' play equipment and padding pools – it was a bright, fresh and rather grand breathing space between tall blocks of apartments and offices, several of which Prayse had built himself – or his company had. By the time me and Woody came along the park had become less popular, especially at night, and was looking a bit tired and run down.

I was one of two cops who used to patrol the place, switching between day and night shifts, and we both discovered Woody in that time. Woody was a dispossessed old man who hung around the less salubrious southern end of the park. There was a narrow backstreet away from a piece of derelict land near a paper factory and he'd often sleep at night in a dumpster, one filled with old packing materials, cardboard and paper from that paper factory just across the roadway that ringed the green. There were times when he slept in trash, sometimes damp from old food and whatnot which often smelled so bad he had to keep the lid ajar, which made the interior cold and draughty.

For want of a better word, Woody was a hobo. At least that's what my beat partner Officer Lairy used to call him. But Woody was no wandering worker or useless vagrant. He stayed in one place, and that place was this distant strip of Prayse Park. He wasn't entirely a bum either, as he used to work little jobs when he could get them – so he wasn't a tramp either, the sort who only turns his hand to tasks if he's forced to. He would tell me: I'm not a tramp or a bum, or even a hobo. I'm just a traveller in a different carriage. And he'd look over wistfully at a passing El as if he knew only too well what it meant to be a passenger on the route, stroking his long, grey beard and shuffling in his ankle length tan greatcoat.

Oh, I meant to say: part of the El's tracks passed over this piece of derelict land, tracks about two storeys up, just south of the paper place. Its

211

carriages rattled by once an hour in the daytime and on until about midnight. The train didn't stop anywhere around there, it just passed by, going from someplace to someplace, uptown to downtown and back.

Anyway, this scrubby bit of redundant land underneath the rails was where people would dump all their garbage – anything from broken electrical appliances to battered furniture and cracked toilet bowls. Woody would pick through the piles during the day and any pieces of bric-a-brac worth selling he'd take to Manny's Market to get enough coin to eat at Harvey's Delicatessen on the corner of 5th and 11th or bag a few provisions from the drug store on 9th, neither of them too far away from his part of the park.

When the supply of free merchandise dried up and he couldn't pay for his food anymore he started using a soup kitchen, optimistically called *The Friendship Café*.

It was run by some young Christians and you could always get a bowl of homemade hot soup and a bagel for the simple price of joining in with a sing-song of a few hymns. Woody didn't mind; he used to quite like Jesus back in the day when he had a job, a proper working life and an optimistic future.

Woody wasn't his real name. Not sure how he got that. I only heard what his real name was much later, when it didn't really matter anymore.

But enough stage-setting. You've got the picture by now: big city, beat-up little park, nearby El, ancient vagrant. Now it's time to bring in the little girl. And this is what that little girl Amy told me, all those decades later as she prepared for a long retirement.

2: 1969

"Hello. My name is Amy. What's yours?"

The old man looked up from the park bench where he was sitting, preoccupied with feeding a flutter of small birds with some scraps of stale bread, flicked from a pair of mittened hands. Some of the crumbs speckled his long, grey beard as if he had been sampling the stale fare along with its winged recipients. His watery brown eyes alighted on a little girl standing two feet away from the bench and maybe around chest high if he'd been standing.

She had a pale white face, determinedly peeping out though bright blue eyes and a neatly trimmed blonde fringe topped by a pink and white striped bobble hat; she was wearing a red scarf, an expensive pink ankle-length

212

coat with fluffy white collar and cuffs, white gloves, white stockings and bright red shoes. With her two long plaits roaming down the front of her buttoned coat, each tipped with a miniature red bow, she looked a little like Dorothy, sans rainbow, Oz and yippy terrier. Her feet were planted apart as if she had no intention of moving on without an answer. The birds fluttered aside a little but made no attempts to fly away from her as they pecked at the spring ground with distracted intensity.

A cracked voice replied: "Good morning, little Amy. My name is Woody."

"My full name is Amy Mary Carlson," the girl said, somewhat formally, as she had been taught to address someone in that way when meeting them for the first time.

"I'm just Woody," the man replied. "My original name got lost over the years."

"How did it get lost?"

"Oh, things happened." The man changed tack swiftly, as if wanting to forget a past that had led him to the wooden slats of a lonely park bench on a draughty March morning and he wrapped his long tan greatcoat closer around his broad shoulders. "Are *you* lost?" he asked her.

Amy shook her head vigorously and explained she was out for a morning walk with her grandfather. She was staying with her grandparents because her real parents had been killed in a plane crash and she was all alone. They were kind grandparents, but she did like to sneak away from them now and then "to get a bit of time for me."

"To grieve."

"I've done that. Now I just know my mummy and daddy are always with me, even though I can't see them anymore," Amy said sensibly. "I can still feel them and I think they understand. I saw you from across the park, when we were over by the pond where gramps was talking to that big policeman."

She pointed.

"Oh, *Officer Lairy*," Woody grumbled with a slightly sour air. "He'll be over here in a moment, enlivening my day."

"I thought you looked lonely, like me. But you were feeding the birds so you also looked okay."

Woody smiled and tossed the last of his bread to the path.

"Do you live here?" Amy asked, moving to sit next to her new companion. The birds moved aside for her and several flew up into a nearby tree with irritated squawks as they gave up on the last of their feed.

"Around here," Woody said, spreading his arms in a vague sweep of the big, green park.

"What, all the time?" Amy said, looking up at him from the other end of the bench with astonishment.

"All the time…" With a hint of regret.

There was a long pause and then Woody gathered himself, unused to conversations, especially with children. His days of being a people person were long gone.

"I wasn't always like this," he said, indicating his shabby state with a sweep of his bread crumbed mittens. "Once I had a career plan, a life insurance plan, a plan for family and kids, a retirement plan…"

"So why are you here in the park, on this bench?"

Woody thought for a moment and replied: "I guess it's God's plan."

And Amy wondered why God could be so cruel.

A dark Irish voice broke into the conversation and a thick-necked cop strode into view with Amy's concerned-looking grandfather in tow.

"Officer Lairy," Woody said, a note of resignation in his voice.

"Mr Woody," came the sardonic response. "And what are we up to now? Not only blocking up this fine park bench but filling a young lassie's head with your old nonsense, I see. Off you go, little girl. Your grandpappa was worried about you. You don't want to spend your time associating with unwelcome strays like these."

"Come along, Amy," her grandfather said, though not unkindly. Even so, he gave Woody a concerned glance as his pretty orphaned granddaughter stood up and walked over to him and took his hand.

"Goodbye, Woody," she said, turning back. "I hope we meet again." And she followed her grandfather back down the path towards the duck pond.

The cop watched them go, his hands on his well-armed hips. He was around fifty, hated his beat and his inglorious career and especially hated the tramp in the greatcoat.

"And *you*," Officer Lairy said loudly, returning his attention to Woody. "Move on. Get your sorry backside out of here. This park has gone downhill enough over the years without scroungers like you hanging around and messing up the place."

Woody stood, arthritic knees cracking, and moved on, knowing that when Officer Lairy had finished his shift he would be back at the bench again, awaiting the night and the kinder stop-overs of young Officer Croel.

As spring turned to summer, little Amy spent more and more time with her new friend Woody. She even brought slices of stale bread with her so that

214

the two of them could feed the birds together, her legs swinging happily beneath the busy bench. She had acquainted her grandfather with Woody and she now had his permission to seek out the vagrant in the long coat, who seemed both kind and harmless. Her grandfather had also spoken to the acerbic Officer Lairy and told him his granddaughter was perfectly safe with this dishevelled vagabond and to leave them alone when they were together – though he still watched the two of them from a discreet distance, from a seat by the duck pond, pretending to read a book.

One time, Woody reached into an inside pocket and pulled out a neatly-carved wooden bird whistle. It was shaped like a hummingbird, though the tip of its long curved beak was broken. It was painted in red and green paint and when he turned it over Amy saw there was a big W carved in the base. He put the tail feather end to his lips and when he blew it, it made a sweet chirping sound.

"Did you make that?" she asked, amazed at the attention to detail.

Woody nodded. "Before Officer Lairy took my penknife away."

"He can't do that!" Amy said angrily, her little cheeks turning pink.

"Don't worry, I got another one," Woody said and smiled.

As the months passed, Amy began to learn more about Woody's nomadic life. He was polite, genial and warm from the start, but it took a while for him to move on from the trivial and to truly open up to her gentle persistence. It started with their love of the El.

One morning around June time, Woody put down his bread slices and leaned back in the bench, a wistful look in his tired eyes as the 11am service clattered by behind him, its unique sound echoing over the rubbish dump below.

"My father used this line all the time, from a boy going to school right up to retirement age when he took it to work at his insurance office downtown," he said. "You know, in those days, back in the 1950s, you could get a subway ride *and* a pizza slice for 15 cents. Don't get anything much for 15 cents now.

"It was built in the late 1800s, the line. My dad was born not long after. They upgraded it from single to triple tracks over the next forty years and now it's one of the last survivors. Sad. All the rest are being demolished and replaced with bus services. "

His eyes grew misty.

"It was like being in another world on the El: flying over the streets and peering into second and third storey windows; trundling past brick

215

buildings with fire escapes, store signs, washing lines with their clothes whisking to and fro like dancers; wooden platforms and turnstiles with their hissy gas lamps, all electric now. Then governors – like brakes – were placed on the wheels of all the trains to control their speed. That took some of the excitement away. Five car trains with doors in the centre of each carriage; smelled of wood polish and cigarette smoke. Noisy, clattery, romantic; commuters lost in the news of the day.

"Sometimes the carriages were packed, sometimes almost empty and a bit spooky. An old workmate said he could reach out of the window of his apartment and almost touch the rim of the catwalk. He'd call it 'the edge of ElWorld,' as if it was another planet."

A couple days later, he greeted Amy with: "Just blew my little tweety whistle for Officer Croel. Said he thought it was cute and asked me to make him one. But I said I'd lost my best knife."

There was a long silence as Amy joined him on the bench and they flicked flakes of bread on to the path in front of them to delight the eager beaks. Finally Woody spoke.

"My father had me when he was 17. He worked like hell to get me through college and I still ended up in an office."

"What did you do? Insurance, like your dad?"

"Like dad, I was good at math. I worked for a finance company."

"How did you end up here?"

Woody's eyes misted over and he stared into the middle distance. "Too painful," he said. "I was done wrong, very wrong. I'll tell you one day." But he never did.

One day Amy saw Woody in the distance on the west side of the park, a place she hadn't seen him hanging out before. She hurried over, her right foot propelling the bright red scooter her grandparents had bought her back on her tenth birthday, and found him staring up at a smart apartment block. The lower floors of the condominium were hidden behind the brownstones and overflow offices of the Prayse Park outer zone and Woody seemed to be concentrating on one specific area of the tall, grey, multi-paned building, shading his eyes from the summer sunshine.

"What you doin?" she asked.

All Woody said was "Twenty-third floor." He was distracted and a little gloomy, bitterly looking skyward and adding threateningly towards the building: "Comin to get you, one day!"

It would be forty years before Amy discovered what he meant.

216

"You like this bench. You're always here." Amy said one morning as June slipped into July.

"It's my bench!" Woody responded. "Though Officer Lairy has other ideas about that."

"Oh, he's just a pig. The other cop, the black one, he's nice."

"He's a good kid, Croel. Bright, sympathetic. He'll go a long way."

"The bench," Amy insisted, as she tended to do when a subject interested her.

"Well, this bench is far enough from those hectic avenues and the popular centre of the park to give me some privacy, some peace. I don't ask for much anymore. It also means I don't get hassled by any of the gangs that roam the park at night. They don't usually bother to come this far south; it's too dilapidated and there's no easy pickings. And it's also lit by that big globe over near the paper place that looks like a full moon shining through the trees. It's the heart of that huge power company advertisement on that corner brownstone. Odd place for it, but the park was a busier place when it was put up."

He pointed. Amy could just see it. It *was* huge.

"Looks best at night," Woody said. "Especially around 2am when the world around pretty much stops. Sort of sets off the street lights, but a lot of those go out overnight."

Amy said she liked the street lamps around the edge of the park with the big white globes, as they looked like "little moons."

"They're about to be replaced," Woody said. "Been there for decades. It's a shame, as they look so *right*. But I suppose it's moving with the times. Guess you've never seen them at night when they light up. They make a *whishing* kind of noise in the dark, when it's quieter, when most of the traffic's died away and I'm ready to get my head down. They sometimes sound like they're offering you to *Wish a wishhhh a wish...*" My wish is always to have this bench. It's a pretty simple ambition." And the word came out as amb-*ishhh*-ion.

Come August, Amy was spending more and more time chattering away with her new-found friend on his familiar park bench. He was still feeding the resident birds, but they had become less numerous with the increase in seasonal bugs to charm their palates and the smaller varieties had been replaced by bickering pigeons. They had been talking about the way the park had deteriorated in just the few years that Woody had been resident. Even the dump had given up all the benefits it might have afforded him.

217

"How do you eat?" Amy asked, noting that he never touched the slices of stale bread she brought him for his feathered friends. It was hard to tell under that greatcoat but he seemed fleshy enough, like he got at least basic sustenance.

Woody smiled and pointed at his chin. "Hole under the nose."

Amy snorted, though it came out as a giggle. "No, *really*."

"At the beginning I used to root around the dumpsters for any old sandwiches or burgers. They're OK if you pick the bits off them, lumps of packing materials, metal filings, fluff and so on."

Amy grimaced.

"I used to cruise the park benches too as there were often piles of nuts left behind by lunchtime eaters from the paper factory, or from one of the nearby bail bonds or lawyers' offices. I always managed to grab a handful before the pigeons and squirrels got to them.

"When the tip was still new I used to forage half-decent items to sell at Manny's so I could grab a cheap bite at Harvey's corner deli, or Denny's diner in an old railway carriage on the other side of the park. When I ran out of stuff decent enough to sell I found this soup kitchen run by some Jesus folk and that keeps me going these days with a once-a-day bowl and a roll. I try to make the evening servings as the warmth of the food helps me sleep."

Amy looked back at the dump, noting the old bed frames and car tyres building up on its far side.

"What's that tree?" she asked. "Right in the middle, sticking up between the old fridges and broken cabinets."

Woody turned and followed her gaze.

"Oh, that's the *Chakanaka* tree," he said. "What I call it, anyway. That's after the noise made by the wheels as the El clatters over the tracks and rattles all the boards and girders: those vibrations make the tree shiver, like it's cold, and the lights from the carriage windows flicker through its leaves and branches making quite a light show after dark. A bit like those infernal flashing light devices..."

"A stroboscope."

"Right. Officer Croel told me it's a deciduous tree – shedding leaves in winter. I don't really think too much about trees, their names, their species, except that they're nice and cool to sit under on hot days and they make the park green and airy. They're also safe perches for the birds. And they keep the rain off.

"Someone told me my *Chakanaka* was a beech and was more than a

218

century old, but I didn't think that stunted little runt was big enough – and, anyway, someone else said urban trees didn't outlast half that timescale and those planted next to city streets lasted less than a decade.

"It drops these little seeds like helicopter blades, so it was more likely to be a sickly adolescent sycamore. Mind you, sycamores can hit 130ft, so maybe that info was wrong too. It gets its flowers and leaves each May."

"So you do know a lot about trees."

"There was this gardener chap used to stop by. Harbour, something…"

"Arboriculturalist."

"That right? See, you know a lot about trees too."

He was looking smarter than usual one August afternoon. Amy had brought him a pair of hairdressing scissors two days earlier so that he could trim his beard and his hair after an unseasonal downpour had left him looking extra straggly – like a scarecrow, she said. He had acquiesced, and taken off several inches of matted pelt with the blades before Officer Lairy confiscated them, calling it "possession of a dangerous weapon."

Lairy said: "You don't want to be one of the heads brought in for processing tonight, do you laddie? I'd cuff you and take you in right now, but my shift's nearly over and I can't be arsed. Just don't let me see you armed like that again."

He moved off, and then turned back as he slipped the scissors into his belt.

"You know, if you'd stabbed someone I'd have made sure it was a heater case – you know, put on the *front burner*, laddie – to get you off the streets so fast your feet wouldn't touch the sidewalk. Don't think your new, smart look is going to win you any favours. You're still a tramp."

He rubbed the back of his thick neck.

"I can't figure you, Woody. You're a real almond joy case, aren't you? Sometimes you look like a nut and sometimes you don't. Course, mostly you do. And we can do without nuts in this park, even if it is going to the dogs."

And he ambled off, whistling cockily and waving his nightstick around in one hand like a noiseless corrugaphone.

Amy's grandfather later lodged a complaint with the precinct Captain and the scissors were returned to the family. Everyone knew Officer Lairy was close to retirement after a stunningly ordinary career and was livid that he'd spent some thirty years with the force, made little or no impact and had never once looked like climbing the promotion ladder. This gave him his bilious attitude. The precinct would be glad to see the back of him and

219

a couple of years later he retired to take a post as head security officer for a downtown drugs company. This lasted precisely six months before he was invalided out after getting on the wrong side of one of the company's defence Dobermans and being savaged in the shoulder.

Come September Woody had attracted a cough. It was not severe, but Amy was worried about the unwelcome development as winter was not far off and the days, and especially the nights, were getting noticeably cooler. He brushed off Amy's concerns with "I get something like this each winter. No big deal. Don't concern yourself."

The condition seemed to improve as the last two weeks of the month welcomed some glorious, spring-like sun-kissed days with adults sunbathing on the grass of the park, kids dabbling in the paddling pool and a parade of late summer clothes, ice creams, ball games, book readers and picnics.

Woody seemed lifted by the bright colours and the joyous cries of contented fun. Prayse Park appeared to have reverted to its heyday, when it was the focal part of downtown social life. Couples strolled hand-in-hand, music played from small radios and a great peace descended. Richard Nixon became the 37th President and though there had been violent student unrest in the country troops were finally coming home from Vietnam and we'd even landed a man on the moon.

But the weather turned, and eventually the cold snap came, turning bitter as wind chill brought temperatures plunging. Amy had seen less of Woody through the autumn, partly due to schooling and partly due to a new group of friends her own age. But she still made the occasional trip to the park to check up on him and found him in good spirits each time. His hair and beard had grown longer again and his cough had returned, but he seemed well enough and was visiting the Christian soup kitchen twice a day come late October.

Officer Lairy had been re-assigned from his Prayse Park beat, so Woody saw more of me, Officer Croel, and I always tried to keep him on the straight and narrow. Approaching winter had pushed him away from the bench at night and back to the dumpsters, where he could at least get out of the wind and wrap himself in cardboard and newspapers. He'd done it before and been okay come the return of the warmer months.

Despite his size, I guess he looked like a small furry animal curled up in his steel-sided crib in amongst the refuse. His battered shoes were thin, but the Christians had promised to get him a replacement pair. One dumpster he used was down an alleyway at the back of a block of brownstones, washing lines hanging overhead from some seedy apartments and looking like coloured flags with their dangling pants, shirts and dresses. But he preferred the dumpster alongside the paper works that had less domestic waste, like old leftovers and empty beer bottles. Whichever one he chose, he had to take care he was out of them in the early morning before the garbage truck arrived, hooked and shook it.

Woody finally got back to his cherished park bench one cold December night. There was no competition from any other homeless takers, perhaps due to the first snowfall of the month which had brought the overall temperature up a notch or two but still hung in the air prohibitively. I'd caught him sleeping there several times, all greatcoat and packaging insulation, so I guess I'm the only person left to talk about that joyous night, using some poetic licence.

The bench is lit with the faint glow of that silver globe on that big power company advert three hundred yards away. Woody smiles with satisfaction and then he lies down and covers himself with some cardboard from the dumpster. There are newspapers under his clothes, several of those thick broadsheets. He is coughing badly and bringing up spots of blood. Just then, the clouds part and the real moon emerges and illuminates him and his bench. It's like the light at the end of a tunnel people see when they're having near-death experiences, only this one's got grey spots and craters. He closes his eyes again, at last feeling truly happy, at one with the Universe. As he settles down, he smiles and thinks no-one will move him on tonight... His last thought before the folds of a peaceful sleep took hold could have been: Here I am, the El-ephant man.

3: 2010

It was an unseasonably warm autumn day when Judge Amy Carlson discovered the real name of the vagrant Woody, the kindly old man she had befriended forty years earlier and who had long since passed on to more comfortable surroundings in the Hereafter.

Shafts of bright sunshine illuminated the courtroom through its high multi-paned windows on that glorious September morning and Judge Amy was overseeing the climax of an embezzlement case lodged against downtown investment company Oakwood Finance, a business that had been based in a luxurious building just a couple of blocks east of Praise Park. Oakwood had escaped legal scrutiny for some time, but in the end the case had sprung from the reports of an insider who claimed all was not well and that millions of dollars of investors' money was being siphoned off to a selection of overseas accounts operated by three of the company's eight directors. A subsequent FBI investigation discovered that all the post-retirement directors were, in fact, culpable but two had fled the country and were being vigorously sought. Three were now before the court, their nefarious activities having apparently been underway since the mid-sixties.

The case had taken ages to come before the court. But the shifty trio had now run out of arguments, stalling tactics and several attempts to abscond. The three remaining directors were still in the wind, and possibly in Mexico.

Oakwood and its representatives were definitely in breach of fiduciary duty – acting irresponsibly for its clients. But its elderly directors were also on the line for negligence, misrepresentation, failure to supervise and bare-faced fraud. Millions went missing, investments belonging to hundreds of loyal but otherwise impoverished customers who had found their nest eggs cooked on retirement. Many of the older clients had died and their relatives were seeking justice, and a payout. It was unlikely that those on trial would ever be able to make up the vast sums owed, Oakwood having become insolvent some while before the trial. But it was a start. And the whole sorry business was at least getting a public hearing, having spent weeks in the headlines even before the court appearances.

To cut a lengthy trial short, as well as cut to the chase: one of the worst Oakwood monsters had been the young Perry Jackson, now 66. It was Jackson who had started the whole embezzlement business at the firm, together with his two co-defendants, siphoning away the very money that the company was charged with investing responsibly. When the first sniff of wrong-doing hit the air in 1964, Jackson and his two colleagues set up a false paper trail that implicated an innocent fellow employee, one Roland James Bark. Bark was dismissed immediately, with no further investigation; all further salaries and benefits were suspended and he was evicted from the company's luxury apartment building on fourth and eleven, the one with the fine views over the city and the greenery of Prayse Park that a 23rd floor location afforded. Instead, Jackson moved in to that apartment as a reward for identifying the culprit.

"And what became of Mr Bark?" Judge Amy asked, interrupting the proceedings.

Jackson shrugged smugly. "Who knows? Living on the streets probably. He was collateral damage."

After that any sympathy the Judge held for the now-aged Jackson took a nose dive.

In a recess, Judge Amy asked the prosecuting attorney for a copy of the company's annual reports for the 1960s and found a photo of Bark among the staff pictures: a bright looking older man with a clear complexion, an innocent expression and a thin moustache. Even without the beard she recognised him as her Woody, better dressed and quite a dashing figure, but still a lot like she remembered him from when he trimmed his locks with her scissors back in 1969.

Needless to say, Jackson and his buddies got a real hammering during the trial and were all three jailed. But that's not the point. Amy had found her Woody, and she finally understood why he was "coming to get" the devious usurper of his former home and job.

4: 2015/1969

Five years after the trial Judge Amy Carlson retired, at the early age of 55.

It was then that I approached her to write her life story. She had turned down a stack of offers from newspapers and magazines, some pretty lucrative. But she told me: "I don't need or want their money. If I'm going to tell all, I want someone I can trust; someone who can write the truth and not exaggerate for the sake of selling a few more copies; someone who will *understand*."

She had previously promised to give me an interview after she retired, partly due to my kindness to her and Woody when she was ten and partly due to my other pieces, which she had been monitoring ever since she donned her lawmaker's hat. She called my work exemplary. Guess I'd done a good job in her eyes, which was a very special compliment, considering her glowing reputation on the bench. She mulled it over a while and then said yes – as long as she could read it before publication and have a say in how it was edited and where it was published. I knew a good place to publish it and agreed to her terms.

I won't go into the fine details of her stellar career now, but it was pretty stunning, a judge who was much-admired for her even-handedness. Her favourite film was *Twelve Angry Men*. She'd never tried anything of real historical significance – no high-profile Mafia bosses or serial killers. But she'd seen her fair share of murderers, con men, extortionists, thieves, thugs and liars to recognise a defendant's true soul as soon as he or she took the stand and opened their mouth. Latterly she specialised in financial irregularities trials, hence the Oakwood business – and its revelations.

The interview took place on a frosty October morning at her beautiful home in the city suburbs where she lived with two cats and a friendly German shepherd (security-wise, Bonzo would've probably licked a burglar to the ground accompanied by a full tail wag). The judge looked relaxed and happy, dressed casually in brown slacks and a grey knitted cardigan and spoke in a quiet but precise voice, eager to please, but not too eager. She never married or had offspring but the house was still full of pictures of other people's kids, mainly from her charity work with the homeless.

Anyway, come the end of it all, I was packing away my notebook and little pocket tape recorder when she looked me in the eye with one of those unreadable expressions, like she was going to tell me something out of place, out of court; something she'd been bristling to tell ever since whenever.

"One more thing…" she said, and then added "Another coffee?" as if we were going to be there for a while.

I welcomed the coffee, but I sensed that wasn't the other thing she was referring to.

And while I supped that fine, warm drink, she told me this.

"I remember that last time with Woody. It was you who found him."

I nodded. It had been brutally cold that December night – an unexpected chill that not even the TV weather people had forecast – and it swept over the bay and across Prayse Park like a fatal gust from the Arctic. It must've hit its peak at around 3am but by the time I began patrolling at about 8.30 the temperature had risen by quite a few degrees and the sun was starting to melt the smattering of snow and the ice on the paddling pool and duck pond.

Woody had finally secured his park bench overnight and I found him stretched out across the boards, snug in his greatcoat and newspapers, a thick wool hat on his head, better shoes on his feet and a pile of cardboard blankets from head to toe. He had this lovely, almost angelic smile on his face, like he'd been granted his long-sought greatest wish. He looked so calm and peaceful that I expected him to leap up and sing at any moment. But that would never happen, as he was frozen solid.

The coroner reckoned Woody died at around 3.30am and by the time Amy said she arrived at the park it was way past eleven, the sun was quite warm and, unknown to her, Woody had been stretchered off to the morgue. She was wearing her pink coat, gloves, muffler, woolly hat and snow boots and carrying her ice skates. He grandpa trailed behind. He'd been waylaid by the guy on the hot dog stand near where they always entered the park, chattering about the latest global worry, and he called out for his granddaughter to be careful. For a moment he lost sight of her as she hurried towards the duck pond. She looked towards Woody's bench in the distance, but it was empty. Then she pulled on her skates and dived onto the ice.

Ten minutes later her grandfather found her by the side of the pond pulling off her skates. She was sitting in a dark puddle, soaking wet, shaking, muddy and both laughing and crying at the same time.

And this is what Amy told me in the front room of her house as I sat and supped her coffee forty six years later.

"My grandpapa looked horrified as he saw the state I was in. He asked me what had happened and I said I'd gone skating on the duck pond, just like I was planning to do when we left home. Everything was wonderful, not too cold, and I was doing my turns, edges, spirals and steps and just as I went into a toe loop I heard this cracking sound. It was too late to pull aside and make for the bank and I felt the ice give under me and I just went plunging through.

"It was so cold and most of my breath was knocked out of me. I was being dragged down to the mud, even though the pond wasn't that deep, and I could see the ice looming over my head but I couldn't see the hole I'd fallen through. I didn't have much air left and I was panicking. I managed to get away from the mud by flapping my arms and legs. My clothes weighed me down, but I still managed to rise a little towards the icy ceiling. Even so, I knew my air wasn't going to hold out. Then I saw a shadow cross the ice, it suddenly broke apart and a long arm snaked down towards me; a hand grabbed my coat and the next thing I knew I was on the bank shivering and gasping for air.

"Then I recognised the big grey coat and the beard and such a gentle smile and I gave my lovely rescuer a big big hug."

"Your grandfather saw what happened and…"

"It wasn't my grandfather."

"A timely passer-by."

"It was Woody! He dragged me out on to the ground and dabbed some old newspapers over my clothes to soak up some of the water. He didn't say anything, but he kind-of wheezed when I hugged him. I sat down to get my skates off and when I turned around to thank him again he was gone. My grandpa appeared in a terrible state, pulled off his overcoat and wrapped it round me and I began to feel warm again. I told him that Woody had saved me, had pulled me out and hadn't even waited for a proper thank-you and we needed to find him and thank him correctly because he'd saved my life.

"My grandpapa looked at me strangely. Then he said it couldn't have been Woody; that he'd been meaning to tell me what the hot dog guy had told him moments earlier: that Woody had died in the early hours of the morning and his body had been taken away.

"I didn't believe it – wouldn't believe it. Woody was my friend, and friends don't just die on you like that. I was inconsolable. But when you, Officer Croel, confirmed to grandpa the next day that Woody, that dear, kind soul – who I now know to have been that wickedly treated accountant Roland Bark – was indeed no more... Well, I broke down and me and grandpa never ever spoke about what had really happened, what he thought was my imagination, being saved by a dead person. But it was him, Luther, it was Woody."

I looked at the judge long and hard. And then I said: "I can't tell this story, Amy. People will think you're..." I made a circular motion with my free hand against the side of my temple. "You know, crazy."

She smiled and nodded, understanding.

"And just in case you think I'm half a packet short of cookies," she added. "I know it was Woody, whatever world he was in at the time, because he whispered *Don't forget to feed the birds* and gave me this..."

She reached into a cardigan pocket and pulled out a neatly-carved wooden bird whistle, shaped like a hummingbird but with a broken beak and painted in now-faded red and green with a big W on the base. And when she blew the tail feather end, it made such a sweet chirping sound.

Assessment

Reader Ten and his denouement were received with great enthusiasm. No-one had seen that ending coming – well, at least I hadn't – and it seemed like a perfect tale to conclude a grand night of fantastic chronicles. But just before he closed his file and resumed his seat reader ten added: "By the way, my name *really is* Luther Croel and the story I just told you... Well, it's true."

As if anxious to prove the point, he produced a small wooden bird whistle from his pocket and blew a sweet, hypnotic note.

"A gift from Amy," he said. Then he moved out of the spotlight into the gloom of the room and disappeared into a sofa.

There was a stunned silence, no more stunned than from me, the Buckwater writer-in-waiting. It was a truly eerie end to a truly bizarre evening – even taking into account Nine's incredible internet excursion, though he never claimed that was any more than a story. Was Croel telling the truth? Was he even Croel? Either Ten was seriously deluded or there are more things in heaven and earth... And if the last story was true, as Ten claimed, what did that tell me about my life and its consequences? Did it mean that anything was possible? Could a character as hopeless as me make a difference in the end – particularly to myself?

Or did it really matter? I'd been transfixed by Croel's story. So had everyone in the shadowy room, and there was suddenly nowhere else to go. There were certainly no more storytellers wanting to tell their tales – on this particular occasion, at least. Talk about an irrevocable ending, a full-stop, everlasting period, a brick wall, the final destination of the very last El...

With some cheery but muted farewells, a quiet rustling of coats and hats and a vigorous shuffle of belongings, the ten readers left the place without further prompting from the barman, forming a ragged crocodile of satisfied souls. I nodded at them all as a respectful parting, except for reader five, the cycle story man: I shrank away from him. Did he really know what I had done? He looked puzzled, but he smiled his farewells anyway. It didn't help. The heavy entrance door bumped shut after the last of them as they vanished into a night that had since become transformed into the fragile dawn of a new day.

The bar was empty now, save for Dara and me, and the fire had turned to dark ashes. I was still sitting on the now rather uncomfortable bar-side stool and Dara was again placidly polishing a sleever with a paisley cloth and smiling benignly. I thought he must have had the cleanest glasses in the whole catering industry – unless, of course, it was always the same cloth. And the same glass…

"Have you ever been to America?" Dara asked.

I was briefly sidetracked. I thought he would want to talk about my earlier scandalous admissions about June and Chad, now that we were alone. He seemed to be in no hurry to eject his final customer, so I went along with him, taking the less severe option, and began babbling once more, just like when I arrived unannounced in this strange establishment all those hours ago.

"Me? No. I always wanted to," I said. "I wanted to see New York, but it always terrified me and I hated all the hassle of tickets and airports and flying, and I was certain I'd get lost or killed by some ruffian in broad daylight in some terrifying American city, so I never went. A friend went to New York once, lost his girlfriend and ran frantically around this big hotel looking for her and was on the verge of calling the NYPD when she turned up saying she'd gone to the wrong floor because the place was so big. Unfamiliar vastness, she said. They don't have an El in New York, do they? They do in Chicago, but I was more scared of that place, what with the Mafia and all that."

Dara sighed the sigh of a man recognising delusions of inadequacy.

"What about San Francisco? Hippie central, summer of love, and all that. That should appeal to the song writing part of you, at least…"

"God, no! I've seen *Dirty Harry*…"

Dara raised an eyebrow gently, put a hand over his mouth as if stifling a titter, and shook his head as if to say "silly boy." But I ploughed on anyway.

"Never been anywhere much, really. I went to Portugal on a firm's weekend once and someone unscrewed the legs of my bed on the first night and the thing collapsed when I got in, showering me with cocoa – my nightcap mug. We had to share accommodation and I wondered why my room-mate had offered me the double instead of the box room single as he wasn't known to be especially charitable. There was a lot of smirking next morning at breakfast."

Dara nodded, though he seemed preoccupied, anxious to get on, perhaps to close the bar, tidy up, throw me out and get to bed. It had been a long night, after all.

"So, what about your story?" he asked. "It's down to you now."

"I don't have anything that matches those," I said.

Dara looked closely at me, raising the other eyebrow so that he looked rather like a shocked monkey.

"Do you actually like your own writing?" he asked.

"Yes, of course I do. When I can get any done. Most of it's in my head."

"But you seem to be more concerned about what people think about *you*, rather than whether a bit of writing works or not."

"There was this girl at work, a long time back," I said, the incident suddenly dropping into my memory in-box. "It somehow came up that I wrote stories and I promised to bring one into work for her to read. She brought it back next day and I said 'Did you like it?' She pointed to a page of the manuscript and said 'What does that word mean?' I told her and she just grunted and walked away."

Dara smiled. "Some people just don't like it when they find someone can do something that they can't. They seem to find it somehow offensive or threatening and reject it – doesn't matter if it's good or bad or indifferent. To them it only matters that it might be an attack on their own status; that you might be trying to peg yourself above them in the universal pecking order. So, naturally, they don't like it.

"On the other hand, some people will always think your writing is worthless unless you're already famous. Then they'll shout its virtues publicly, even if it's not up to scratch, thinking it's got to be brilliant because it's *published* – by a pukka publisher. And that they know you personally, of course.

"On the bright side, others will just accept you for who you are. Seek their company if you want genuine personal praise. As I said, just get out your computer, typewriter or note pad and start writing – and to hell with all those pointless distractions."

He paused. "In fact, that's what your stories are: distractions; distractions for you, *from* you, even. You try to hide the real you; the inventiveness, your skewed view of the world, your sense of the ridiculous. It's as if you think that your – how can I say? – *eccentricities*, your different view of

229

things; different from the norm, from the established outlook – are somehow going to make you look peculiar, so you won't be accepted, maybe shunned, somehow socially unacceptable. You should think about that old Zen command: *Original face, now!* Find the You that's real – not the you that you have cultivated to hide behind."

"I told you my problem."

"Yes, writer's block. I don't accept that! Anything can be overcome, and everyone has a story of some sort inside them, as you've already seen. Tell me yours."

"I can tell you about the block," I said, reluctantly. I normally hated talking about myself, but somehow with Dara I couldn't help myself.

"That would be perfect, especially after that – how should I say? – *torrent* of disparate tales tonight. You've nothing to lose, and I may be able to offer some advice, as a curator of those fanciful fables."

So I put down my empty glass, looked briefly at the exit door, a way out, thought better of it, and began.

I told him everything: about the dead parents, the failed relationships, briefly revisited girlfriend June and her supplementary live-in boyfriend, Chad; how the writing had dried up and how I'd sought the help of a therapist, through my sister Brenda, as a last and hopeless resort. Even though I knew I'd told him most of this before.

"And now it's time to face some truths," Dara said. He put down the glass and cloth and leaned towards the beer pumps, taking two of the curved shafts in his hands. "Let's start with June and her cyclist lover."

I'd known we were going to go back to this sooner or later and I felt my chest constrict. This was one story too many – the one that would finally consign me to the nut house, if you can use that phrase these days... Never mind. That's where I was bound.

"It never happened, you know," Dara said.

I stared. *What?!*

"Oh, your past life is pretty much the way you painted it, the abusive father, the unhappy school days, the stultifying workspace, the failed romances, your perceived impotence..."

"I don't remember telling you that."

Dara shook his head. "Well, you do ramble quite a lot between stories."

He let go of the pump handles, reached down below the bar and produced a thick, buff folder. It had my name on the front, **WILL BUCKWATER**, printed in bold black capital letters in a rectangular white label with a long strand of combined reference numbers and letters below the name. The cardboard wallet was secured with a mauve toggle strangled by a length of coloured string to contain its contents and seemed quite bulky.

"How did you get that?" I gasped. "That's my case file. It belongs to Doctor Shana."

"Now, where do you think I got it from?"

"But that's protected information, personal, private. Shana can't just pass it around to anyone – it's unethical – and, respectfully, especially to a barman in a drinking den full of people I don't know from Adam..."

"But better clothed," Dara said, under his breath.

I made a noise that sounded like the snort of an adolescent hippo.

"Trust me. I know what I'm doing, and so does Dr Shana," Dara replied and began slowly unwinding the string binding. That achieved, he spread the folder open on the bar, flipped over the opening portrait photograph of a wide-eyed Will looking as if he'd been disturbed during a midnight burglary by some meddlesome security guard. He flattened out the first of many documents, clamped to the spine with a small metal bar, and looked up.

"Let me tell you a story," he said.

My mouth was dry, despite all the pints I reckoned I'd downed over eleven long readings in probably as many hours.

"You didn't dispatch live-in girlfriend June's cyclist boyfriend."

"What?!"

"You didn't bury him under your greenhouse and dismantle his bike to keep him company."

"But I..."

"In fact, June didn't even live with you, did she, Will? You offered; she turned you down. It's all in Dr Shana's notes. And your sister Brenda saw them together – June and, what was he called? *Chad*! – just the day after you told her you'd murdered June's lover. Just as well she ran into them in the high street shopping for cycle clips, as she was going to have you committed. It was just another one of your hidden stories."

I sighed both with anger and relief. It was time to come clean, for once.

"Pretty much everything about June was a lie," I admitted.

Dara said nothing and just listened. He didn't even pause to polish a sleever; he returned to leaning on the pumps and nodding as my shoulders slumped. I was starting to feel very old. Perhaps I was. Certainly older than I felt when I entered Dara's bar several lifetimes ago.

"Yes, we did meet at a pub gig and we did get together loads of times afterwards. Neither of us had lovers, so we filled some sort of emotional gap for ourselves. We would talk about our plans, our mutual interests in music and writing; we'd tell ourselves all the highs and lows of our lives, we'd laugh and cry together – mostly laugh – and had a real understanding of each other. At least, I thought so. I felt the urge to write again, though I still didn't dare show her any of my stuff.

"We never had a physical relationship; not even a romantic one. It was slightly flirtatious – the way relationships are when two people get on well – especially for the bloke, when he's with a beautiful, curvy twenty-something like June. She never shared my house and I don't even remember us having a row or any bad words between us. She was never cold, cruel or sarcastic – just gracious and supportive. I only invented that discord for myself later on, to protect myself from the hurt I was feeling. We were even gigglers and I missed that most when she went. We took country walks and talked and talked. We had a lot of fun.

"Then Brad came along. Sorry, *Chad*. Chad Smart. And not very smart, either! Chad was so much like that home-wrecker Brad in the bike story. What was it called? *Spokes*! Even the storyteller looked like him. Chad, that is. Chad was real, everything that the fictional Brad was like only worse, except for the room sharing thing and the incident with the spade, neither of which happened. Sorry about that. And June fell in love with him. Suddenly *he* filled that emotional gap in her life, not me, and provided the missing sexual activity as a bonus. So, that was the end of our association, June and me. It probably didn't need to end even though Chad's attitude would probably have made that innocent friendship difficult. But I couldn't stomach sharing those little confidences we'd shared before with that arrogant cycle buff hovering in the background making nasty jibes.

"I invented all that bad stuff about June being a heartless bitch, like I said, because I missed her friendship so much, to put a wall around what I was feeling, to put a mask on my face; I never intended to blab it to others. But when I was low and drinking it kind of slipped out, with a couple of the band members, with Brenda… The worst thing is, June could have still been my friend, especially when her liaison with Chad fell apart after a couple of years. She would have been the one great muse to get me writing again – properly this time. But she was gone – and it was my fault that that connection, that special bond we had, came to an end."

Dara nodded. "But you were still disturbed by the *Spokes* tale: all that stuff about Brad and David's wife Dorothy; the murder. There was something bothering you all the time."

I shook my head. "I was ashamed."

232

"That you belittled June in such a callous way? That you invented that ridiculous Chad murder?"

"No. Well, yes. But it wasn't that." I drew a deep breath before realising it was foolish to feel so discomfited over something so insignificant, at least on a global scale. After all, I hadn't killed anyone. Again, it was all about another bloke, another outsider...

"The one thing I didn't tell you that's been hounding me for years: I didn't go to my sister's wedding," I said. And Dara smiled, though kindly, as if he had been expecting me to come up with something much less sinister than murder, and more pitiable.

Brenda has always supported me, in her own frightened way, but I didn't support her when she needed it most. She even told my parents that they should encourage me with my writing and not take every chance to poke holes in what I was doing. It was making me reclusive, emotionally and physically. Of course, my folks had already made her withdrawn, which was why she fell hook, line and s(t)inker for future husband Roy when he came along. Roy Waite. A fireman. Someone who showed her some real attention and made her feel good inside, saying she was bright, beautiful, talented, sexy and all that smarm charm.

That all changed once they were legally shackled together and he became overpowering, manipulative, malicious and distanced, just like dad, and often never *there* for her – off somewhere, never saying where. Not attending a fire, that was clear.

And I couldn't even be bothered to at least show up for her wedding and show her some real heart; that there was someone in her real family that truly cared about her, about her well-being, her sanity even. But I selfishly stayed away on some feeble excuse because I didn't want anything to do with rotten Roy, his family or his loathsome friends. She must have felt so isolated, unsupported.

"He would come to the house before they were married and when Brenda was out of earshot he'd say things like *Oh, you're the writer who doesn't write. That's about as useful as a doctor who can't diagnose measles.* Or *What's the latest masterpiece from the Buckwater writing club?* Or *Your sister will be well away from this barren scribbling shop.* Or *Why don't you grow up and start living in the real world?* Or *You're going to get even fatter sitting around watching TV like a slob.* And so on.

"Did I say he was a cyclist too? I can't remember. He had all the gear, the biceps and the snippy, egocentric attitude. Wore a helmet camera and screamed at any car drivers who came a bit too close to him, even if they were several feet away, telling them he'd filmed them and he'd be getting on to his solicitor. He nearly got thumped more than once for his paranoid claims. The only time he got injured on his bike was when he ran into a bollard while he was shouting at a lorry driver in the opposite carriageway! So I guess you can say I hate cyclists.

"Anyway, I couldn't believe my luck when I heard Roy had dumped Brenda for a 17-year-old fitness student, a pretty but apparently witless new member of his cycle club. Of course, Brenda was devastated, even though Roy had been getting more like my father every day, but thankfully without the mutilated rodent cartoons. Bren came round to see me, but it didn't end well with a lot of recriminations being thrown around by both sides and we didn't see each other again for ages. By then she'd dumped Roy, found a quiet flat, a new job and a pet parakeet. We eventually started talking and she began supporting me again too, always telling me I needed the right opportunity to let my writing shine through.

"She's probably behind my having the courage to come in here, into Dara's Bar, where the *storytellers tell*. A few years ago I'd have just kept walking past."

"And has it helped?"

I didn't know. But it felt okay. Apart from my little altercation with Storyteller Six over her bear tale it had been a pleasant and encouraging experience and I hadn't felt any real animosity, any criticism or disparagement over my writer's block, if that's what it was.

"Yeah…" I breathed tentatively. "I guess so."

He made to tap my forehead, but I eased back out of reach, as if I thought he was about to poke me in the eye.

"You'd be surprised about what's in there," he said, index finger poised in mid air between the pumps and a couple of inches from my face. "Deep inside."

"Maybe."

"You know, some people find it hard to put The End on a story. You find it hard to put The Beginning."

I shrugged.

"You didn't feel… *inspired* by tonight?"

Oddly enough, I had – especially after *The Moon and a Park Bench*. It had set me tingling. I'd even felt a tear coming on.

"I think I need to get to the keyboard," was all I could say.

Dara's face lit up with a big, beaming, welcoming smile. "Then my job is done," he said, leaning back from the beer pumps and picking up a new sleever with intent to polish.

234

"Not before time, either," he said. "Your documents say you were born in…" I didn't prompt him, so he put the glass down and worked through some sums on his fingers. "You're sixty-nine, Will. Time is getting shorter. You didn't look that old when you came in here, ten tellers ago."

"I didn't feel it," I said, astonished that the age revelation hadn't surprised me. My ass was really aching now on that bar stool.

"Well, age has never prevented anyone from getting down to it on the keyboard. Not even arthritis in the fingers, but I see you don't have that condition. So, let's get to it before you do!"

He flipped the file – my file – shut with his elbow and took cloth to glass again. And then he said a peculiar thing. Not for the first time.

So," he said. "You know how *Thunderbirds* begins? Five–four–three–two–one… AS YOU WERE!"

And he clicked his fingers.

I was staring directly into the pale green eyes of a beautiful woman.

"Let me tell you a story," she said.

Afterbar

I was staring directly into Dr Shana Coleman's eyes. It was unnerving.

"Are you alright, Will?" she asked.

I blinked, eased my head back, stared around.

The room was sparsely decorated with a handful of small pictures and several framed certificates; there were miscellaneous plants bulging from a cluster of hand-painted pots and a dominating picture window overlooking luxurious gardens a floor below. I was sitting in a fashionable steel and leather chair, not an uncomfortable bar stool, right across from a wide and fastidiously tidy oak desk. Shana sat behind this desk, leaning back slightly, her fingers steepled on her chest, the garden view at her back. There was no sign of a bar, or storytellers, or a barman called...

"Dara?" I said, brow furrowed with confusion.

"Dara's gone," Shana replied. She unlocked her fingers, leaned forward, picked up a worn pencil and began tapping it on a notebook as if setting up the rhythm for a song. "Or was it Darras? At the beginning."

"On the sign outside the bar."

"Yes. You know that *darras* means a *doorway* in Cornish? A doorway to your soul, perhaps. To your inner creativity. Just a suggestion."

I looked around, still confused, my head flicking to and fro like a distracted golfer looking for his ball in some scrub.

"You've been here all the time, Will, in my workspace," Shana explained. "I just sent you to Dara so that you had the chance to talk to someone else about your problem. To help you confront it."

My eyes returned to my therapist. Confused? You're damn right!

"Are you saying hypnosis?"

She nodded. "One of my skills."

"I always said it wouldn't work on me," I challenged.

"Well, Will, it *did*. I used your favourite sixties TV puppet show introduction to put you under and to bring you back."

I was adamant. "No, no, no. Can't happen." But Shana remained placid. "So you just hypnotised me into talking over a pint or two to some mythical barman in the hope that it would bring back my mojo?"

"Yes. The belief in the alcohol you were apparently consuming helped loosen you up."

"And then you just read me a whole bunch of other people's stories to get me writing again?" I slapped my knees in annoyance. "Pretending to be this Dara bloke? I don't believe it. And even if I did… Well, it's not going to work."

"You think not?" Shana was the one smiling now, just like Dara had done for most of the evening in… his pub?

"I *know* it's not," I replied. "I've tried everything. You're aware of that. I told you. Even forcing myself to sit at the computer until something creative came out, and the only thing that did emerge from my consciousness was an email to an underwear supplier asking when my overdue boxers were going to arrive."

"Oh, for God's sake, Will, stop being such a self-obsessed WIMP!"

My mouth dropped open. Not for the first time. *Wimp?!* I was paying this woman, and probably a tidy sum, so she could at least be civil. Well, I think I was paying her, unless Brenda…

It was my sister who recommended Dr Shana Coleman to me after the therapist had steered Brenda through her divorce from rancid Roy Waite and brought her out of her funk on the right side of crackers. My sister told me she first met Shana at a small literary festival when she was 17 and Shana was 25. The latter was finishing her last term teaching history at a private school in Herefordshire, based in the beautiful Wye Valley and a vigorous stone's throw from the ancient market town that eventually became a great literary Mecca from the late 1980s. Brenda was on a school trip that day.

Shana was introduced to Brenda by Shana's first boyfriend, one of the lecturers at the festival, who was a caring enough soul but, sadly, possessing the charisma of a walnut so he was now long gone from her life. Shana found that Brenda, even though bogged down with household horrors, was bright, funny, daring and rather pretty – away from her claustrophobic parents – in a sweetly terrified sort of way, and the two women hit it off immediately. They were pen pals for years while Shana went into the travel business, journeying to places like Nepal and India where she began her private studies into alternative cultures, beliefs and practices; she married briefly and had a son, currently a doctor/homeopath in Kathmandu, and studied medicine, psychology and hypnosis on her return to the UK.

"Sorry," Shana said, though she didn't sound it. "That was rude. But *honestly*, Will. Get yourself together! You're only letting yourself down. You should be more settled at your age!"

She leaned forward and reached out to a cassette deck on the corner of her desk where a tape had been quietly rewinding for several minutes. There was a click as it switched off automatically and Shana pressed the PLAY button.

"This is part of our sessions," she said.

There was a pause and a slight hiss as the tape spooled forward from the leader to meet the heads, and then there was a voice. It was Shana's.

She announced: "*Please commence your tale.*"

The next voice I heard began: "*If there was one thing Dan Shutter hated most it was chasing the damn rabbits…*"

I sat up. "What's this?" I asked. "Wait, that's that bloody bunny story."

Shana nodded.

And then the truth sank in. I stared vacantly at the doctor and finally said: "That's *my* voice."

She nodded again, with more emphasis and muted the recording.

"It's you speaking while you were in session, under the influence of a technique you said couldn't influence you," she said. "You performed all of that, Will – from the rabbit-chasing photographer to the city park tramp. Either on the spur of the moment, or raiding your memories of stories you created at home and stored away. Didn't you spot some of the repetition? So many sets of green eyes – the colour of your hypnotist's!" She gestured upwards to show them off. They were sparkling like gemstones.

"The number of biffs on the head, the similarity of names such as Chad and Brad, the number of bicycle incidents, the reappearance of Chancer, lots of mouths dropping, the fact that most of the protagonists are a similar age to you. It's like you don't want these stories to die before you do! Then there's how pizza-lobbing Sara-Zara-Sahara looks like a fantasy version of

239

your old girlfriend, June. How all the story tellers look like people from your own life. It was all your own work, brought out by – I must say so myself – a skilfully-created scenario involving a backstreet bar, its literary customers and some pertinent visual stimulus."

She reached into a drawer.

"I showed you these during the first stage of putting you into a trance. Told you that's where you were going and to venture up the steps and push open that big purple door."

Shana handed me three photographs. One showed a narrow and shadowy alleyway, a dozen granite steps, a metal handrail and two stone walls (one sun-washed and the other in shade); there was an empty courtyard with blank windows and an apparently photo-shopped sign saying DARRAS BAR. *Cornish for doorway...* The place was easy to miss, hidden away up those uninviting steps – if it had ever existed, that is.

The second snap showed a TV personality that was the spitting image of Dara – and I still couldn't remember his name.

The final image was of a dimly-lit tavern with spotlights illuminating the optics and loads of cosy furniture to one side disappearing into the shadows, the relaxed legs of indistinct clients caught in a weak reading beam; numerous bookshelves packed with multi-coloured hardbacks filled the background.

"You did the rest," she said. "Put it all together, and off you went. I couldn't believe it, it was so quick. It was a last ditch attempt to put you right. It was like a dam suddenly bursting or a fence falling away to reveal a different landscape. You even began talking freely about your personal life, your parents, your house, your sister, your schools, even the band you were in; about June, the lies you told yourself... Much more than you ever told me in our open sessions."

"I wrote those stories?" I responded, a little breathless. "That's not possible. I can't..."

"Just listen to the tape."

I did, for a while longer. Bits of it. Shana fast-forwarded and I found myself with CI Booth, mad charity shop manager Alice and the fated David Conrad, my own voice clear and unwavering, each chronicler seeming so familiar as my brain pieced together images of faces from my past: my father, Uncle Donald, pop band colleagues, even Number Six who looked like June, who looked like Shana... And Dara: a professional performance from the doc, worthy of a BAFTA.

"Are you saying they're *all* on there?" I asked. "Every story I heard? I told... To myself..."

Shana nodded. "All of them, yes – in what appear to be abridged forms, but the gist of them all. We took a break after reader six as you were becoming visibly tired and about to guess too soon what was actually going on, especially with your reaction to reader five and the Brad/Chad business. That intermission is when I told your sister Brenda how you were doing. You were just feet away, asleep next door to my consulting room at the time."

"I actually *wrote* those stories!" I repeated, aghast, this time with astonished acceptance.

There was a pause as I locked eyes, perhaps unwisely given the circumstances, with my mesmerist.

"Oh, shit, not *The Bear*! Don't tell me I came up with *that*."

"No," Shana reassured me. "That was mine. I don't know what your problem is with that one. I thought it was a lot of fun; pretty good – for a *woman*, eh, *Uncle Donald*!"

I grimaced. Had I become so much like my most unpleasant influences? Uncle Donald wasn't me, nor was my psycho father and his *thin mice*...

"Also I wanted a female storyteller on the scene, one that would attract – or, rather, *dis*tract your attention. All of the other readers were male – obviously, like you, written from your genetic perspective."

I started to apologise, then thought better of it. My sex was my sex: I couldn't help it – had no say in it, in fact. My therapist seemed not to notice the half-formed excuse.

"*J Returns*. That was my story too," Shana continued. "And I liked the way you tried to counter it with a riotous story of your own about mayhem at a seaside resort. But *J* and *The Bear* were the only exceptions. I wanted to throw a different flavour into the mix. And it really worked, considering the stuff you came up with after the break!"

"You do a good Jesus voice," I offered.

"As long as it's not considered sacrreligeous."

I looked more closely at Shana. She had the intense green eyes of so many of the characters that appeared during my bar stool journey. She also had pale skin and black black black hair plunging down her back like an onyx waterfall and was wearing a cerulean roll neck jumper and white slacks – just like reader six – with a long strand of pearls around her neck. Indeed, she looked like an older version of June in her twenties. A startling coincidence that she had used to her advantage.

This was confirmed when Shana said: "I suggested to you that the lady reader look like the very real June, too, just to aid the cause. Oh, and the storyteller was reader number six."

I shook my head dumbly, not comprehending.

"Number Six. To subtly remind you, Will, that you were acting like *The Prisoner*. Remember the TV show? But you weren't just a captive; you were also the jailer, so you had no motive to escape. You'd imprisoned yourself in your delusions: not that you can't write, not that people hate what you do write, but that you'd convinced yourself that you *couldn't* write when you clearly could, and you locked yourself into that particular cell and threw away the key. Together we had to find that lost key. And I think we did.

"It was me, as Six, who asked Reader Eight about the assassin story, when he said there was a sequel. Well, is there, Will? Are there more stories hiding away?"

I didn't know. That was then, under the spell, and this was… now. Maybe…

Shana sat back in her beige padded reclining chair, warming sunlight suddenly bursting into the room on cue from a break in the clouds, cascading through the large picture window behind her. It was like a moment of revelation, when the imaginary halogen lamp appears over your head and you go *Oh! Of course!*

"Then I guess I have a future after all," I said feebly.

She nodded, and with a pedantic edge to her voice added: "Let us hope that this time you don't go confessing to a murder you didn't commit just to make yourself look significant."

I briefly slumped in shame, though this time I was wearing a faint smile of relief.

Finally she told me: "The session's over and it's probably the last one. Now go home, Will, and *write*. Take the tape with you. Remember, you *can*! You *have*."

And I suddenly thought: She's right! *I can, I have*. It was all an illusion, but it was also real. I had finally found myself, picked myself up from the debris, dusted myself off and my future would be so different from now on. It would have to be. That was a promise from myself to myself!

"Brenda…" I breathed as I left Dr Shana's office. Gratefully this time. I had a lot to thank my lovely sister for.

And Shana, of course.

And, especially, that amazing barman, that marvellous tankard-polishing mentor and whispy phantom called Dara… And his bar.

The Transforming Man

I went home right away and started writing up these stories; these unheralded stories from that hidden place that always seems to stay buried until the purple door opens to let something – or someone – in. Clearly the Dara's Bar patrons wouldn't mind me poaching their work, under the circumstances!

I found some significant papers in a drawer, but not all. Some adventures had been created on the fly, in that mythical drinking place for those facially familiar clients and that inexplicably recognizable barman, whose real-life persona still escapes me. It took me several months to complete the project and the content is pretty much exactly what my other selves told me over that long night at Dara's Bar. Shana even gave me a waiver for her twin contributions. The result is what you're holding in your hands now, dear reader (as maestro Stephen King would say), for good or bad.

OK, the stories are somewhat long-winded. My bad. That's because they're little novelettes, dinky versions of weightier novels and literary breezeblocks. Well, except for that damn (*honestly, I'm really just a teddy*) bear. (*What do they say? If it's black, fight back, if it's brown lay down, and if it's white goodnight. Now I just say, it was really okay; I can bear the bear*).

Maybe I've stuffed each tale too full with anecdotes and sidetracks, but that's what my head has been like over these past decades with too much to say, but little commitment. I'm happy now to let it all go. Shana told me: "Re-write these tales and give them some more spice, flesh them out, give them presence. But don't overdo it. Don't put too many toppings on the proverbial pizza." But I like toppings.

Also, I left in a lot of deeply private things that I would previously – pre-bar, that is – never have dared sharing. But, hey, if I'm chucking stuff out on to my sleeve – well, on to the page, anyway – it ought to be all of it, right?

Still, you have a choice as reader. You can consume each of the stories, fully topped, and forget about my tired and twisted personal narrative, or you can read my embarrassing life story and skip the intervening stories. I just hope you read the whole thing, just as it happened to me, trapped on that bum-numbing bar stool. Then you get the why as well as the how – and maybe realise how easy it is to be completely reckless – stupid, even – and damage your own life and its possibilities through needless fear.

I'd like to report that my bar-side revelations produced the kind of happy ending most readers prefer – one that offers love, a lifelong partnership even, maybe kids and a secure and successful future. But I can't. Not yet. At least, not until I've taken my former muse June to dinner this weekend to properly welcome her back into my life and present her with a freshly-minted copy of my epic adventure *Dara's Bar*. Written under a pseudonym, of course. I'm not *that* confident yet. And I've changed a lot of names to protect personal privacy, including my own!

I met June again, by chance, at a new art gallery of all things, some weeks back and we've kept in touch. Still single and as beautiful in her sixties as she was in her twenties, she told me she'd long ago ditched bikes and bikers (hooray), was single, working part-time in a charity shop (though not homicidally), was still attending gigs. She had finally written that historical novel she'd been planning all those years ago and was wondering what to do with the manuscript...

We laughed quite a lot.

So maybe this unforeseen reunion will kick-start a real relationship – something enduring for our twilight days; something to fuel the inspiration for more magic moments. Perhaps it will be the romantic, idealistic conclusion we all seek. There might even be lots of little chirping birds at our feet to throw crumbs at.

Maybe I'll let you know what happens – whether the restaurant's flickering candlelight ignites the flames of two floating souls.

Maybe I will.

But probably I won't.

Still, the next time you're in a quiet bar, perhaps one like Dara's with the bookcases, the soft furnishings and the murky corners, you'll raise a glass to – what shall we say? Not me. Let's say Life's endless and unexpected possibilities. To the stories that we have hidden away inside each of us; the tales we have just one short life to make real, or just to *tell*, for others' enjoyment. Just like those still waiting in a sideboard in a back room of my little brain that I'm looking forward to raiding.

And do you know what sets me tapping away, creating imaginary worlds and quaint little adventures, finally free from my own chains? That special something that turns night into day and lazy brain cells into busy factories of carefully selected words and phrases?

Well, it's just the gentle sound from blowing a brightly-painted wooden bird whistle with a broken beak and a mysterious W (for *Will*?) carved on its base.

I found it in a high street charity shop for 50p...

WiLL x

The Real Author's Notes

Dara's Bar. As Alan Bennett observes in his introduction to the paperback edition of *Talking Heads 2*, "...the relationship between life and art is never as straightforward as the reader or the audience tend to imagine." The book *The Never-Ending Tales of Dara's Bar*, its setting and all of its featured characters, is a work of fiction, though some very minor incidents have some basis in fact. That said, Will Buckwater and yours truly are completely different people. Like most folk, I had a rather dysfunctional family when small, but neither my parents nor my schools (in the main) were as bleak as Will's. Also, I am fortunate to have never experienced serious writer's block. Somehow I can never stop the ideas coming, falling over each other and clogging my think box. Of course, that doesn't mean all those ideas are good ones and, in any case, they are constantly impeded by my own lethargy, as it's always much easier to sit down in a comfy chair and enjoy someone else's story than to take the stairs to the office and give life to my own ideas. I guess I'm a little like Will in this, but through sheer laziness rather than dog-eared resignation. Most people have been both kind and encouraging about my writing over the years – and I have never wanted to become an international celebrity author, anyway, even if there was a chance of that, considering the exceptional competition.

This little diversion of a book has what I like to call a "portmanteau" construction, like the diversely packed sections of a traveller's trunk: not just the two halves coined by Lewis Carroll, but many layers. Imagine a trunk with lots of drawers, each filled with something completely different from the next – socks in one, toiletries in another, faded love letters in another (I could go on, and often do) – yet all of them enveloped in that one big unifying box. *The Never-Ending Tales of Dara's Bar* came about through all those books and movies I've enjoyed over the years that merge seemingly unrelated (and rather oddball) short stories with a continuing, vaguely associated narrative; tales of disparate folk painting versions of their own lives but eventually coming together to spread their oils over some wider and potentially unexpected canvas.

Any errors herein are entirely the responsibility of Will Buckwater.

The Long, Long Night of the Bunny Ruse. My friend Andy Rees once had this large framed print of a painting on his lounge wall, *Sunset St Pancras Station* by John O'Connor. There was so much detail to look at, but we didn't know the title or artist at first and spent ages trying to identify the busy cityscape of 19th-century London. Eventually we tracked it down, found the area on a map and, as part of that research, discovered Ilsington Council's Joseph Grimaldi Park where the renowned Georgian clown (1778-1837) is buried – the inspiration for the fictional cemetery encounter by Dan Shutter in his great bunny pursuit. And whilst the Reisenden clown family are fictional, Cairoli and his incident with Hitler and the watch are real; also, whilst the Marsden Hotel doesn't exist, surgeon William Marsden and his philanthropic work did.

Booth's Grand Finale. When I was a reporter I used to make regular police calls at the local cop shop for information on crimes in the area, chatting to uniformed officers, CID and top brass. The relationship between police and press later became more strained, even estranged, but the results for both sides before that came about was generally beneficial, mostly honest, and was on my mind when this story emerged. My late friend Michael Dunn and I began our writing careers on a local newspaper in Cornwall, both of us on separate publications produced by the same company but eleven miles apart. We only met when I moved to Devon and found (a) we were again working on separate papers, this time seven miles apart and (b) he had just left the paper I'd just joined! We were friends for 45 years.

As for the off-colour cartoonists mentioned in the following bar sequence, Zash Cavern is clearly fictional. But I loved the "funnies" in New York's satirical *National Lampoon* magazine back in the eighties, especially the graphic Charles Rodrigues tales including warring Siamese twins the Aesop Brothers. Their array of talented artists always managed to give me a (sometimes guilty) laugh. Shary Flenniken's observant *Trotts and Bonnie*, Gahan Wilson's slightly gloomy *Nuts*, and so on. Some might dub a few of them a little "sick," but they were certainly observational.

And Will's dad in my tale? Well, he was just a sad sadist.

248

Big Slip-Up at the Chattery Shop. I have spent a lot of my free time trawling charity shops for books, DVDs and CDs (again, much like our featured neurotic Will), with some notable successes. I've discovered many authors, films and music I would never have come across without these fertile grazing grounds. The 'Chattery' incident was born as a result of those visits and the kind of conversations overheard, though they were mostly about the ailments of others. It is entirely fictional (I hope), as is the shop featured – and the bird whistle from *Moon*.

The Genesis Pizza. I used to sing with a couple of rock bands in the 1980s that played their own songs, had some modest success locally, and its members did meet up in a local pizza house some years after those glory days as a possible prelude to playing together again, though gigs never materialised. An early set-up involving some of its members did have a young and attractive female singer, though nothing like the theatrical and fictional warbler of this tale. As for some of the groups mentioned: singer Zara's tee shirt venerates Magma, a dramatic French progressive rock band founded in 1969 by drummer/composer Christian Vander; her fantasy doppelganger (according to chubby guitarist Gordon, at any rate) is Floor Jansen, a striking 6ft 1in Dutch singer/songwriter and stunning vocalist with Finnish symphonic metal band Nightwish, an operatic soprano with a vocal range of three octaves who joined her previous band as lead singer aged 16.

Re the story's fictional band name: *Hyperprism* is the title of a wind and percussion piece by French composer Edgard Varèse (American musician Frank Zappa's favourite composer) who referred to his unconventional music as "organised sound." Despite Gordon's insistence, the word has little to do with spectral colours. Oh, and yes, apparently Jean Paul Sartre did perform Donald Duck impersonations. The creator of existentialism also played piano, sang jazz favourites like *Old Man River* and even wrote the lyrics for the song *La rue des Blancs-Manteaux* for renowned French singer Juliette Greco (1927-2020). See the absorbing *At the Existentialist Café* by Sarah Bakewell, p14 and p167 [Chatto and Windus 2016].

Spokes. I'm Cornish, and proud of it. However, the Cornish village of Penhaven doesn't exist, nor does its unique environmental experiment. But its stated twin town is real and twinned with the North Yorkshire market town of Tadcaster. Saint-Chély-d'Apcher is a commune in the Lozère department in southern France and is home to the bizarre tale of the Gévaudan Beast which attacked women and children regularly in a three-year period from 1764-1767 causing terror in the neighbourhood and was recorded as having the appearance of a wolf or a werewolf. This fascinating true story, which has nothing to do with the events in Penhaven apart from the "ghostly" element, is the subject of the thrilling 2001 *Matrix*-style French thriller *Le pacte des loups* (*Brotherhood of the Wolf*).

The Bear. This brief little fantasy is the result of spending too much time as a local reporter nodding through dreary parish council meetings on cold winter nights, often at a rickety card table (once even perched on a piano stool), aching for something interesting to write about other than litter, footpath maintenance and dog fouling. I am sure there may be some constitutional obstruction that would disallow the election process told here. But wouldn't it be fun if a potty but rather sweet decision like this broke through official procedures? Re Raymond Carver: for those interested in this American storyteller but who would rather watch than read, I recommend the 1993 comedy-drama *Short Cuts* from director Robert Altman that covers nine of Carver's tales and a poem. It includes his finest outing *A Small, Good Thing*, from his collection *Cathedral* – the O. Henry Award winning tale of a belated birthday cake and its consequences.

J Returns. This piece was originally written during the George W. Bush Iraq War era and submitted for a short story competition. I heard nothing more of it (surprise, surprise). It seemed to me it was still relevant today, so I revisited the text – several times. It is mainly aimed at the sad disarray of American political, social, medical and religious attitudes rather than at any specific US President – though it does seem to accommodate many of them in some way or another, especially the WASP element.

Out of Season. A last-minute addition: a fragment of this tale was found in a file of unfinished pieces and I'd forgotten all about it. I liked the beginning, where the harassed resorts manager is looking back on his disastrous summer entertainments season. So I started working on it, the character Billy Shoehorn and his problems arrived fully-formed and the rest wrote itself.

One For the Price of Two. This idea came to me after watching a movie about a sharp-shooter assassin and reading about some of the recent reckless "developments" in medical, commercial and military circles. For those interested in learning more about the potential death of humanity, see *The Sixth Extinction: An Unnatural History* by former invertebrate paleobiologist Elizabeth Kolbert or, for a fictionalised version, James Rollins' cracking thriller *The Sixth Extinction* from his tremendous Sigma Force series.

Apparently, the previous five Earth extinctions were: Ordovician-silurian Extinction, 440 million years ago; Devonian Extinction, 365 million years ago; Permian-triassic Extinction, 250 million years ago; Triassic-jurassic Extinction, 210 million years ago; and the Cretaceous-tertiary Extinction, 65 Million Years Ago.

The late writer Lloyd Pye, who had a justified scathing view of the intransigence of the scientific and religious old guard of self-validated "experts," declared that as many as two dozen worldwide extinction events "had left their imprints on the geological/fossil records over the past 550 million years that complex life has existed on the planet." [*Everything You Know is Still Wrong*].

We're apparently due for another mass extinction any time soon, and the fear is that we are bringing this catastrophe upon ourselves through overpopulation. There are those who believe that the global pandemic that kicked off in 2019 and the subsequent world-wide vaccination programmes allegedly aimed at countering that alleged pandemic were engineered to achieve that population cull. As for the Raymond Chandler anecdote, that comes from the excellent *How Not to Write* by Terence Denman (Piatkus 2005), a book "for the grammatically perplexed."

@ded-n-gon.com. Will's bickering with his un-named band mate came from a similarly silly tussle with my late musical collaborator, Pete Gretton. I found a company appropriately called *And Vinyly* which, for a four-figure sum, offers to press your ashes into a vinyl record allowing you to "live on from beyond the groove." You can have a choice of content for the 12-minute-a-side disk, including songs, humour or just the simple sound of "pops and crackles" emanating from the needle. In the process the ash is sprinkled on to a vinyl puck and pressed to create the grooves. The company was founded by music producer John Leach in 2009. When I jokingly suggested to Pete that we could do this with one of the songs we'd written together – once we'd passed on, musically-unheralded – he got into one of his occasional unanticipated rants, not realising that, while I was joking, *And Vinyly* wasn't – at least in a commercial sense. Sadly Pete is no longer with us, ending our 43-year association, and neither his ashes nor his wonderful music have been preserved in vinyl.

The song reference *When I'm Dead and Gone* recalls a chart success for McGuinness Flint in 1970. Anyone interested in numerology will find Cecil Balmond's *Number 9: The Search for the Sigma Code* (Prestel, 1998) an obtuse but entertaining read.

The Moon and a Park Bench. This story expands on and completes the scenario of the eponymous nonsense song from the unreleased CD *Why Not?* by The Bivalve Quickstep, a duo comprising myself and my late friend Pete. The lyrics for that song are below, written by me in an off-the-cuff way and sung in the style of Tom Waits, who always gives true voice to the lives of lost city vagrants. The above story makes sense of some of the poem's references, though admittedly mainly with hindsight, suggesting the tale was always lurking in the back of my consciousness. The last line suggests how humanity constantly works its way through those tiny incidents that bother our lives and bind us like insistent loops of thread – and how we are often complicit in their effects. I guess it's also and obtuse joke.

Homeless is the Chakkanakka tree
Thoughtless by an iron bedstead
Bric-a-brac won't take me back
To Harvey's corner delicatessen.

Homeless me as a homeless bee
Without a home and sleeping on a step
Look out, that light on the 23rd floor:
I'm a'comin' to get you!

Stroll the street with rice paper shoes
Waiting for the moon and a park bench
Happy the wire grabbing yesterday's washing
Unload the trash can - I'll sleep there.

Turn out the whishy street light song
It'll seem better with a cock-crow
Coil like a bandicoot in a heap of garbage
And wind the twine infinitesimal.

By the author of

Guts
A comic novel about a group of co-workers trapped in an isolated hotel with a killer is on the loose.
"Made me laugh out loud."

The Other Side of the Ribbon
An illustrated scrapbook of eccentric real-life adventures in local newspaper offices.
"A rollicking read."

The UFO Armageddon
An illustrated extraterrestrial entertainment and parody: the real untruths about space visitors.
"Brilliantly funny."

When Rabbits Go Bad
A zany collection of comic poems, song lyrics and cartoons.
"A must-have collector's item."

Petals
A collection of serious poems.
"Beautiful… wonderfully expressive."

The Testing of Dottie Oxbridge and Other Grand Adventures
Six tip-top terrific tales based on some original comedy scripts.
(*E-book only*)

These and **The Never-Ending Tales of Dara's Bar**, all are available from Amazon in paperback format.

Out of print

Newton Abbot in the News
The story of a Devon market town in the 1970s, seen through the columns of local weekly tabloid the *Mid-Devon Advertiser*. Obelisk Publications, 1996.

As illustrator:
Reflections
Off-beat tales of Cornish towns Falmouth and Penryn, with cartoons.
Author/publisher Mike Truscott.

Printed in Great Britain
by Amazon